KISSES
book Two

I0601068

moonlit
KISSES

DEBRA ST JAMES

Moonlit Kisses

KISSES — BOOK TWO

DEBRA ST JAMES

Moonlit Kisses | Kisses — Book Two

Website: www.debrastjamesbooks.com

Email: debrastjamesbooks@gmail.com

Published by: Debra St James Author

Edited by: Double AA Author Services

Formatted by: Debra St James Author

ISBN: 978-0-6457395-1-0 [Paperback]

ISBN: 978-0-6457395-2-7 [Discreet Edition Paperback]

ISBN: 978-0-6450483-6-0 [Ebook]

inspiration

This story was inspired by the lyrics ...

—> *I've Fallen in Love with You by Joss Stone* <—

playlist

I've Fallen in Love with You … *Joss Stone*
Push It … *Salt-N-Pepa*
Love Junk … *Diesel*
Don't Cha Wanna Ride … *Joss Stone*
Picture of You … *Diesel*
Put Your Hands on Me … *Joss Stone*
Trouble Sleeping … *Corinne Bailey Rae*
Super Duper Love … *Joss Stone*
When I See You … *Macy Gray*
Sweet Baby … *Macy Gray feat. Erykah Badu*
Someone Like You … *Van Morrison*
I Get to Love You … *Ruelle*
Take My Name … *Parmalee*

You can check it out here:
https://tinyurl.com/moonlitkisses-spotify

CHAPTER 1

—molly—

THE GRAY SKY MATCHES MY CURRENT MOOD AS I STAND OVER the matching coffins being lowered into the icy ground side by side by side, the clay soil a stark contrast to the dirty snow. I can't believe they're all gone—just like that. Wrapping my arms tightly around my middle, I give myself the only comfort I can at this point. I have to be strong. I'm all I have left in this world.

As the service concludes, the few family friends we have—or is it had?—file past me, hugging me, giving me their condolences. It's okay for them, they'll go home, and their life will continue as normal. Sure, they'll miss Mom, Jack, and Ethan at social events, but my loss will affect me every single moment of every single day.

At twenty-six years of age, I'm an orphan.

Mom won't see her forty-fifth birthday. Jack won't ever share the crazy advertisements he finds in the newspaper or online with me, and Ethan will forever be thirteen years old.

I draw in a deep breath and then release a heavy sigh as yet more tears track down my cheeks. I didn't think I'd have any more tears left at this point. All I've done is cry since the police knocked on my door late that night, fourteen days ago. They said my family's car veered into the path of an oncoming truck and the coroner since found that Jack had suffered a heart attack at the wheel. It must have happened on the way home from checking out the Christmas lights. It was the first year I hadn't gone with them because I was volunteering at the shelter. I still don't understand. The guy was a fitness freak. He couldn't afford a gym membership, which meant he would run daily and use stuff around their trailer to keep in shape.

Trudging away from my family's ultimate resting place, I glance over my shoulder one last time. Everyone left as soon as the service was over, leaving me to my solitary grief.

Solitary.

Now there's a word for me, one I guess I'll have to get used to. Peering around the empty graveyard, I shiver. I'm not sure how long I was standing on my own, lost in my head. But it was long enough for a chill to seep through to my bones. I'm going to need to clear out their trailer, but I can't go there today. I'm too raw, too exposed, too shattered.

Pulling up in front of Mom and Jack's trailer I pause, my eyes scanning the outside. Even though they didn't have a lot, they always looked after their trailer. Mom believed you should always have pride in your home, no matter what type of home it was. Hell, she was grateful to have a home, as was I.

I can't believe that when I walk inside, it will be empty. Mom won't be baking chocolate chip muffins in the oven and Jack won't be pouring over the newspaper. Ethan won't have one leg slung over the arm of the couch as he watches cartoons, his bangs falling in his eyes. There'll be no more tight hugs, making me feel as though I'm the most important person in the world to the inhabitants.

I exit my car, full of dread. As I close the door, I catch sight of Ron, the park manager, striding toward me. He waves wildly in my direction as his steps hasten, bringing him right into my personal space. His eyes trail my body from the top of my head to the tips of my toes, pausing on my breasts and legs. Ron's always been a bit … I don't know … weird, I guess. He doesn't seem to understand personal boundaries and can be rather inappropriate. I've always felt uncomfortable whenever he's around.

"Hi, Molly. It's just tragic what happened to Nicole, Jack, and Ethan." The upbeat tone of his voice doesn't match his words and before I can say anything, he continues. "Any idea when you'll have the trailer cleaned out? I've got a waitlist of prospective tenants, and well, they only paid until the end of December and it's January eighth now, sooooo?" He leaves his statement hanging and all I can do is blink at him. "You know, I don't wanna be a dick or anything, but you know …" He shrugs. "It's business. You know."

As he stands looking at me with wide eyes, I realize he's waiting for an answer. "Uh, I'm here to sort through their things today. They don't have all that much. I can possibly have it all done by tomorrow night?" My last sentence comes out more like a question than a statement. I guess I can understand it from his side. The trailer is sitting unoccupied and not earning him any money. But he's speaking about my family as though it doesn't matter that they're no longer here. I hitch my thumb over my shoulder. "I'd better get started then." He nods, obviously happy with my answer, and then heads back the way he came.

It takes a bit of jiggling to get the key to slide into the lock, but I finally get the latch to release. When the door opens, I'm overwhelmed by the musty smell. I haven't been here since the day I had to collect an outfit for each member of my family to be buried in. The place is compact: two bedrooms; one bathroom, complete with a toilet; and the open plan living, dining, and kitchen. It's slightly larger than the one-bedroom apartment I live in not that far from here. I open the curtains and the dull light of winter makes its way into the room, highlighting the disturbed dust motes floating in the air.

With a heavy heart, I start in Ethan's room, making piles to keep, trash, and donate. I'll probably take the donations to the shelter I volunteer at. Often, women have to escape a shitty situation in a hurry and don't have time to pack, leaving with little to nothing but the clothes on her and her children's backs. As I move the last of his clothes out of the drawers, my fingers scrape across a scrapbook. A smile touches my lips unbidden at the memories flooding me. Dropping to my butt, I flip open the cover and run my finger over the lines on the page. Ethan loved to sketch muscle cars. Jack taught us both how to draw and while I'll draw whatever takes my fancy around me, Ethan was one hundred percent dedicated to drawing the great American muscle car. Page after page of sketches, gradually improving in skill and detail as he became more competent. Closing the last page, I hold it to my chest, deciding I'll keep it as a little piece of Ethan. I take it out to my car and place it on the passenger seat, then collect the boxes I brought with me and head back inside.

Throughout the weekend, I work like a Trojan, only stopping to eat the meager supply of snacks I brought with me. Memories trap me as I come across photo albums, scrapbooks, and special treasures that remind me of what I've lost. Mom was never just my mom. She was my best friend. She was only eighteen when she had me, and we spent the first eleven years of my life living in her car and occasionally staying in women's shelters. Our bond was unbreakable and now she's gone. An unbidden loud sob breaks the silence at the thought of never speaking with her again, never hearing her voice, or experiencing her hugs. I tilt my head up toward the ceiling, asking whatever force, *why*? It's not like we had a lot, only each other. Why take that away from me? I'm not sure I'll ever make sense of such a loss.

Darkness infiltrates the trailer, so I check the time. It's only five, but the storm rolling in has made it feel much later in the day. Looking around the space, I'm satisfied with what I've accomplished and decide to load as much as I can into my car to take to the shelter before it starts to rain, making sure I set the items I want to keep in a separate space. I don't want to get them mixed up. I'm not sure what to do with the furniture. There isn't much, only the basics. Mom and Jack never had a lot of money left over after paying all the bills and ensuring Ethan and I had everything we needed. They were never about collecting material stuff. It was more important to give us their time and love, to put nutritious food on the table, and to make sure we were happy and well cared for.

Loading the last bag into the back of my car, I give it a shove so I can close the door. I turn away from my car and Ron's right there, in my space, wearing the same clothes he had on yesterday.

"Just the person I needed to see." He claps his hands together, his smile stretching from ear to ear. "You nearly done? I've got a woman coming through in about ten minutes to look at the place."

Dumbfounded is the only word I can think of to describe how I feel about Ron and his enthusiasm. "Uh … uhm." I wrap my arms around my body to keep myself standing. Once I walk away from here, I won't ever be coming back. It will be final. I turn, my eyes canvassing the trailer, taking in every inch; the cute hanging baskets, the plastic table and chair set, and the neat curtains hanging over each window. "I've just finished, Ron. The only thing left is the furniture, and I'm not sure what to do with it."

He tucks his thumbs in the top of his jeans and rocks back on his heels, his smile returning to his face. "That can stay. No problem. I'll be able to charge more for a furnished trailer." My head spins at his lack of empathy for the situation.

"Uh, hello!" A young woman, maybe eighteen at the most, holding the hand of a little boy, calls out, interrupting our conversation.

Ron steps away from me immediately and heads toward the woman, his hand outstretched in welcome. "Hi. Mia?"

"Yes. Ron?"

"That's me." He turns toward me. "Thanks, Molly. You can go now."

My head flies back as though he slapped me. His dismissal is abrupt, and I don't know why, but it was also unexpected. Speechless, I climb into my car and drive out of the trailer park for what I *know* will be the last time.

CHAPTER 2

—max—

"Maaaax, phone for you!" Emma's voice startles me out from beneath the car I'm working on. Did I forget she was bringing the boys over this morning?

As I stand to my full height, I stretch out my back and stride toward my small office. I barely spend time here, choosing to do most of my paperwork at home. At the end of the day, I usually take whatever paperwork I need to complete home, then bring it back with me in the morning. I even bought a cheap laptop to make things easier to transport. My sister hands the phone to me, studying me from the top of my head to the tips of my steel cap work boots.

"Hello, Stanfield Auto Repairs, Max speaking."

"Hi, Max. I'm having car trouble again. Would I be able to trouble you to look at the old girl for me?"

"No problem, Mr. McNally. Would this afternoon be okay? Around three?"

"Perfect. Thanks, Max. I knew you wouldn't let me down."

"See you then."

"Great. See you at three. Bring your appetite. Jean will

make you a snack." *Oh yeah*, Jean knows how to bake. This is my lucky day.

I laugh. "I definitely will." Ending the call, I glance at my sister, then around the small room. The boys are nowhere in sight. "Where're the boys?"

"Hanging out with Theo. I had to get some supplies for work and was passing by." She hands me a takeaway coffee. "I thought I'd stop in and have a quick coffee with my little brother."

I scoff. "Little brother!" I may be younger than her, but at six-foot-three inches, I tower over her five-foot-seven frame. I take the coffee from her, grateful for the warm beverage. Wrapping my hands around the paper cup, I take a sip and sigh with gratitude. "Thanks, Em." Leaning forward, I kiss her cheek in welcome. "Good to see you. How are the boys, and Kenny and Theo?"

She makes herself comfortable on my lone desk, her smile broadens, and a twinkle lightens her eyes. I've never seen my sister this happy. Theo and Kenny have been a great addition to Emma's family, and to our family. "They're great. They love hanging out with Theo and Kenny. Though, if Austin knew I was here, he'd be mad that I didn't bring him along." She chuckles.

"You should drop him over one afternoon. He can hang out here with me."

"You have enough going on. You don't need to be watching Austin when you have so much work to do. Speaking about how much work you have to do. When are you going to hire someone to help you with the office stuff?" she asks, as she studies the piles of papers on the corner of my desk.

I shrug. My family has been nagging me for ages to employ some staff, and while I could comfortably afford to pay some part-time wages, I don't have the time it would take to teach someone the job. It's a double-edged sword because I could use the help. It would free up my evenings and possibly give me some free time to … I don't know … maybe date. After seeing Emma find her happiness, I've realized how lonely I am and I want some of what she has. I want a family of my own. I take another sip of my coffee to delay my response.

Emma slides off of my desk and steps forward. She rests her hand on my forearm and tilts her head up. "We're worried about you, Max. You work too hard; you need to free up some of your time."

Sighing, I drop my voice. "I know. I just don't have the time to train new staff. Ya know?"

Her eyes soften and she gives me a small smile. "A little time upfront could save you a lot of time down the line. Think about it. Okay?"

I nod. "I have thought about it and I'll think about it some more. Promise." I finish with a smile to let her know I appreciate her concern.

"I'll leave you to your day in peace. See you at Mom and Dad's tomorrow?"

"Definitely. I wouldn't miss seeing my favorite people." I bend down to kiss my sister goodbye, careful to keep my greasy hands and body away from hers. "Thanks for stopping by, Em. Say hi to the family for me."

"I will." I follow her out to her car and watch her drive away. To her family. Something I don't think I'll have any time soon. Heading back inside the workshop, I mentally calculate how much longer I need on the job I'm working on, to ensure I leave on time for my house call this afternoon. I definitely need to consider hiring an office manager.

Aaron's hand lands heavily on my sweaty back as I bend over at the waist, trying to catch my breath. I'm getting too old for this shit. Not that thirty-six is old.

"You okay, old man?" he snickers.

"Fuck off. You're six months older than me. Cut the 'old man' bullshit!" I stand to my full height, pushing him away playfully.

"You coming for a beer?"

"Yep. I'll meet you guys there." He heads off with Lincoln. They share a place, so it makes sense for them to share a ride to our pseudo-soccer matches. Lincoln's covered in tattoos and looks like he belongs in a biker club, but he's a decent guy who does beautiful tattoo work.

Turning around, I spot Gary walking toward me and I raise my chin. "Good game. You coming for a beer tonight?"

"Nah. Layla's sick. I need to get home. Maybe next week."

"Sure, man. Take good care of your girl." She's been sick a lot lately. I hope it's nothing too serious.

"I will. See ya next week." He jogs off toward his car and quickly climbs inside.

I think I'd prefer to be going home to a sick wife—well … not a *sick* wife, but a wife—rather than going to Brady's for beer and pizza. I thought I would be married by now, but I wasted a lot of years with Mona. When I think back now, I don't know what I ever saw in her. Sure, she was beautiful, but she was fucking shallow and superficial, not to mention rude as fuck to my family. I would always bite my tongue in front of my family so I didn't embarrass Mona, but when we got in the car, I would let her know I wasn't happy with her behavior. She'd always pout and start fake crying, apologizing profusely and promising to do better next time. Her behavior never improved. After the way she carried on about me wanting to help Emma during her cancer treatment, I couldn't take it any longer. My family was, *is*, more important to me than getting laid on the regular.

The bar's packed. It's always packed. And loud. When did this place get so fucking popular? We've been coming here for years. Back when the general population considered it a dive. Now every goddamn man and his mate seem to think this is the best place to be. I mean, it *is* a stellar pub. But c'mon, I just want to go back fifteen years to when it was quieter.

Fuck, I'm sounding old.

I spot the guys in our usual booths which Finn always keeps free for us—one benefit of being on his team. I slide in next to Aaron and opposite Finn.

"Is it busier than usual, or am I getting old?" I ask Finn as I glance around.

Aaron slides a pint in front of me. "It's busier than usual." He nods his head toward the opposite corner. "We have a celebrity here tonight."

Looking across the room, I spot Toby Summer. "I restored a car for him a couple of years back. He still brings her in for me to service a few times a year."

"Oh yeah? What is it?" Aaron asks.

"A sixty-seven Chevy Impala soft top. Beautiful car. Looked like brand new when I finished with her." I remember the expression on Toby's face when he came to pick her up. He was so fucking in love with that car.

The guys let out a collective whistle. "Nice."

I nod.

"How's the Sprint coming along? Surely, you're nearly done with her." Aaron asks before taking a long pull of his beer.

"It's slow. I don't get as much time to do the restoration side of the business. Too damn busy doing the auto repair work and office crap. Which is great and all, because that's what pays my bills, but man, I miss working on my cars." I sigh into my beer.

"Perhaps you should consider hiring some staff to take the pressure off. Give you more time for other things." He motions toward the bar. I glance across to see a group of women, who look to be in their early to mid-twenties, standing in their too-short skirts and too-low tops, reminding me of Mona. *Ugh. What the hell was I thinking?*

I dismiss the idea of hooking up with someone so young and return my focus to my table. "You're not telling me anything my family hasn't already suggested. Believe me, I've thought about it, but I don't have the fucking time to dedicate to training someone for the job. I'm too busy … maybe when things slow down." I hedge.

"Are you an idiot? Things never slow down for you. Your business has only grown busier and busier each year since you opened. You're a fucking outstanding mechanic and people know they can rely on you and that you won't rip them off," Aaron shoots back.

The guys around the table agree, nodding their heads like old men. "You guys sound like Em. She stopped in on Saturday and gave me the same lecture."

Lincoln sits up straighter at the mention of Em's name. "Yeah? How's Emma?"

"Married!" I snap. Fucking asshole knows this already.

"Still?"

"Yeah, fucking still. Probably will be for the rest of her life. Can't see Theo ever walking away from her and the boys." I smirk at the forlorn expression on Lincoln's face. He had his chance to make a move while she was single, but never grew the balls to do anything about it. His loss.

We shoot the shit for a couple of hours, eating pizza and drinking beer. I stop drinking early enough to ensure I'm still under the limit to drive home. It wouldn't be prudent for me to lose my driver's license in my line of work—it would cost me my fucking business. A business I've worked hard to build since I was twenty-four. There's no way I want to fuck it up.

I spot the clock on the wall. Eleven. Nearly closing time. "I'm out. See you guys next Monday." I rap my knuckles on the table as I stand.

Everyone waves goodbye around the table, and I make my way to the front door. A few people obviously have the same idea since it's almost closing time and I bump into a body. Turning my head to apologize, I catch the eyes of Toby. His eyes widen in recognition, a smile spreading his lips.

"Max. Great to see you, man." He takes my hand, shaking it with gusto. His bodyguard and friend, Shane, standing right behind him.

I nod to both of them. "Hey, guys. Great to see you. How's the car?"

We step out of the pub, where the cool air smacks me in the face. I pull my jacket around my body, offering a pitiful shield against the icy wind.

"The car's incredible. Absolutely incredible. Drives like a dream."

"Good, that's great."

"Actually, she's due for a service. When can I bring her in?"

I have a lot on my plate at the moment and I'm unsure when I have an available day. "Call me tomorrow when I have my calendar in front of me. You still got my number?"

"Yeah, sure. Talk tomorrow."

"Tomorrow." I tip my head goodbye and turn to walk in the opposite direction, toward my car.

Stepping inside my home, I toe off my shoes and throw my keys in the bowl on the hall table. The house is pitch black and silent. Coming from the noisy pub, the quiet seems overwhelming. I don't bother turning on any lights and make my way to the kitchen for a glass of water before heading to my room. Monday nights are probably the only nights I don't spend working on my books. The reprieve is welcome as I strip off and fall into bed.

CHAPTER 3

—molly—

My alarm blares as it does every workday at five a.m. I haven't been for my morning run since … well, since my life turned upside down. Today's the day I'm gonna get back to it. Running helps my mood and I need all the help I can get at the moment. It was emotionally tough cleaning everything out of the trailer on the weekend; I couldn't drag myself out of bed early enough yesterday morning, so I genuinely need this run to clear my mind.

The family photo from the last Christmas we spent together catches my eye. Picking it up, I trace the faces of my family. Every year, we would take a new photo together at Christmas. We'll never do that again and my family will be forever frozen in time.

No more family photos—*ever!*

The backs of my eyes sting and I work to swallow down my grief or I won't be running today either and I really need to do this. Placing the photo back on my nightstand, I climb out of bed and dress in my running gear, complete with the hot pink running shoes I got for my last birthday. I can't believe the stuff people get rid of. I don't think these shoes had ever been worn.

Grabbing what I need, I head out into the freezing morning. Careful to take smaller steps as I start slower than usual on the sidewalk, searching for patches of ice under the light dusting of snow. It doesn't take long before I find my rhythm and lose myself in my next step, my breaths forming small misty clouds in front of my face. My body heats as my muscles warm, and I unwrap the scarf from around my neck and tie it around my waist. It's quiet, not another runner in sight today. I don't blame them. It's freaking cold. If I didn't need to work through my emotions, I probably would have opted to stay in bed, too.

I shut down everything in my mind. Concentrating on the force of each foot hitting the pavement and keeping my breathing even. Gradually, my thoughts become completely focused on running, which is exactly what I need.

"Morning," a man calls out as he passes me with his teenage daughter. I've seen them before, though not usually until the temperatures warm up a little more.

"Morning," I respond as my heart constricts. Jack was pivotal in getting me into fitness. He trained me and helped me to build the length of time I could run comfortably daily. The emotional pain steals my breath and I falter. Slowing my strides, I rest my hands on my hips. My eyes burn and it's tough to swallow around the painful reminder. Coming to a stop in front of my apartment building, I bend at the waist to catch my breath. Silent tears track down my cheeks and I angrily swipe at them. Seeing that father with his daughter *should* be a happy memory, not one that makes me sad. I can picture Jack running with the widest of smiles. It was always something he loved to do, and he passed that love on to me. Because of that, I don't want to feel sad when I run.

Shaking off my melancholy, I use the climb up four flights of stairs to cool down, pausing at the top of the steps to stretch my calves on the last step. Releasing a heavy breath, I swipe away the sweat from my forehead with my forearm and notice a sheet of blue paper stuck underneath my door.

Unlocking my door, I bend down and swipe up the note. It's a reminder that my rent's past due. *Damn it!* I'll need to stop in to speak with the building manager before work to explain I need an extension.

Dressed for work, I knock on the door of the building manager. I've never paid my rent late. In fact, I always pay one week early to be sure I don't forget to pay.

Don finally answers the door, a cigarette hanging out of his mouth. Interesting that we're not allowed to smoke within the building, but he can do whatever he wants because he's the manager. He squints at me through the thick plume of smoke, scratching his armpit. "Yeah?"

I hold up the note I found under my door this morning. "Uhm, hi, Don." He has always insisted I call him Don. Not Mr. Ricci. Don. "I was hoping I could ask a favor."

He leans his shoulder against his door, crossing his arms in front of his gray-haired chest. "I don't do no favors." His old eyes scan me up and down, dragging like filthy fingers up my legs. "Not even for stunners like you."

I swallow down the bile his dirty perusal has caused. "It's only a small favor. You see, I'm always on time, if not a little early, with my rent. But, uh, I recently lost my entire family and I've had to use all of my savings for their funeral and burial." His face goes soft, and I think he may agree to give me an extension. "I was wondering if it was at all possible to have an extension. I can pay next month on time plus some of this month. Each month, I could pay a little extra until I'm caught up." I hold my breath, hoping for a little compassion.

He's silent and I'm hoping against hope he's seriously considering my proposal. He stands up straight. "Nope. You need to pay by Friday, or you need to find somewhere else to live. I'm not a fucking charity." Stepping back, he slams the door in my face.

Shit!

Now what am I going to do? I resist banging on his door until he opens it and agrees to my request. My shoulders slump and suddenly I feel … *tired*. Exhausted, in fact. Instead of climbing back upstairs and hiding beneath my blankets like I want to, I turn on my heel and head out of the building to scrape the ice from my car so I can get to work. Glancing up at the building, the sun shining behind it; I sigh. The apartment building isn't great. In fact, it's falling down around our ears, but it's home. The only home I have. It's where I've lived since moving out of the trailer park. I remember my excitement when I picked up the keys to move in; I felt like an actual adult. Thankfully, it came furnished because I had nothing to my name. I still don't have a lot, but I would miss this place if I had to leave.

Traffic isn't too heavy on the way to work, which is a godsend because I can barely focus. I'm more focused on running through what I need to say to Mr. Dunsley in the hopes he'll give me an advance. He was reluctant to give me time off work to deal with the funeral arrangements for my family. I think he only agreed because I couldn't stop crying and he wanted me out of the office because it was bad for business.

Unlocking the office door, I turn off the alarm and turn on the lights, then make my way to the small kitchen at the rear of the building. I set up the coffeepot and head back to my desk to switch on my computer. The bell above the door alerts me to someone entering the office. As I lift my head, I put on my best smile. "Good …" My words dry up as my eyes land on Mrs.

Dunsley. For some unknown reason, she's never liked me and it's made it difficult on my end to be friendly, but I'm careful to maintain my professionalism. "Good morning, Mrs. Dunsley."

She struts by me without a word. Shrugging, I make myself a coffee and get to work, replying to emails, booking viewings, and making appointments for rental inspections. Ironically, I work for a real estate agent, and yet I'm on the brink of losing my apartment. Day in, day out, I facilitate people finding their new homes while I'm not sure I'll be able to keep my own.

A pile of papers lands on my keyboard. "These need to be stapled again. The staples aren't exactly straight with the top of the paper. Do it now because I need them by nine." Mrs. Dunsley storms away without a please or thank you, which is usual for her. I pick up the papers that I stapled yesterday, studying the fasteners closely. She must have freaking measured them with a ruler because they all look parallel to the top of the page to me. Because I know how particular she is, I always take care to make sure I work to her exacting standards. Rolling my eyes, I pull out the staple remover and get to work, removing the staples carefully, because heaven forbid, I tear or bend the pages. She'd have me print the pages again and take the money for the additional expense out of my paycheck. She's done that before.

The bell rings above the door, and when I look up, a genuine smile spreads. "Good morning, Peter." I quickly stand as he comes around to me, his arms open wide. He wasn't in yesterday when I came back to work.

Embracing me tightly, he whispers, "How are you, Mols? We missed your smiling face around here. Are you okay?" He gives me a tight squeeze, then releases me and takes my hands in his. "I'm so sorry about everything you've been through. Is there anything you need?"

Tears flood my eyes, forming streams down my cheeks and dripping from my chin. My nose immediately turns into a snot factory, and it's taking everything within me to stay on my feet. With a hiccupping sob, I work to catch my breath and stifle my tears. With a watery smile, I finally respond, "You– You're the first person to hug me and ask me if I'm okay since I lost my family. I'm sor– … sorry I broke down like that." I'm mortified that my emotions overflowed so readily in front of one of the agents. Peter's always been like a second father to me. It shouldn't surprise me he was the first person to show his care and concern. I didn't realize how lonely and alone I've felt since that dreadful night until he hugged me.

He pulls me back into his large body, wrapping one hand around the back of my head and guiding it to his chest. "Oh, you poor girl. You've been through so much. Too much for someone as young as you." He pats my back, holding me close while I work to get myself under control.

"What the hell is going on out here? Is any work getting done?" Mrs. Dunsley's voice cracks like a bolt of lightning through the small front office. I immediately remove myself from Peter's kind embrace, keeping my eyes on the floor.

Peter's deep rumbling voice cuts through the quiet. "I was checking in on Molly. Making sure she's okay."

"Why wouldn't she be? We gave her time off to deal with her situation." She turns her body toward mine, addressing me directly. "You were supposed to deal with all this in your own time." She waves her hand around my face. "I expect you to be more professional when you're at work."

I feel Peter bristling beside me and place my hand gently on his arm to prevent him from speaking on my behalf. "I'm sorry, Mrs. Dunsley. It won't happen again."

She looks between me and Peter and gives a sharp nod before strutting away. I mouth 'thank you' to Peter and make my way to the bathroom to wash my face. I can't greet people at the front desk with snot running down my face and red, swollen eyes. It would be embarrassing, not to mention unprofessional.

I step into the kitchen to grab a glass of water. As I'm filling my glass, someone walks in behind me. I'm about to turn around to say hello when I hear a huff. My shoulders tense and I mentally prepare for her venom.

"My God, Molly. How many times have I told you the handle on the coffeepot needs to be on the left? I'm left-handed," she huffs as her eyes narrow at me. "Do you do it deliberately? Leave the handle on the right, knowing I have to twist the pot around?" I blink several times, unable to answer. "Well?" she snaps.

Shit. I never thought about it, but I guess if I wanted to annoy her, I could have purposely done that. "I'm sorry, Mrs. Dunsley. It won't happen again." I feel like it's all I ever do around here; apologize for being unable to meet the exacting standards she sets.

"Oh, I *know* it won't." She smirks as she pours her coffee and heads out of the kitchen. *What's that supposed to mean?*

I skip my lunch break with the hope I'll catch up on some of the work I've missed over the past week. It's difficult to focus with my thoughts scattered as I wait for Mr. Dunsley to arrive in the office so I can speak to him about an advance. If he doesn't agree, I don't know what I'll do. I'll be like the women I support every week at the shelter. I'll go back to living out of a car like I did when I was a child.

He finally breezes in at four p.m. "Don't disturb me. No phone calls," he barks at me as he hurriedly strides past my desk to his office, slamming his door behind him.

My smile drops and my shoulders slump. How am I going to ask him about my advance? *Shit!*

I power through the rest of the afternoon, working past my usual finish time. At six-thirty, I gather enough courage to knock on my boss's door.

"What?" Hmmm, he still sounds pissed. Maybe I should leave it for today and ask tomorrow? "You may as well come in now that you've disturbed me," he snaps out through the paper-thin barrier between us.

My hand shakes as I turn the knob and perspiration forms beneath my armpits. I'm going to have sweat stains on my good shirt at this rate. I poke my head inside as the space between the door and the jamb widens. "Uhm, sorry to interrupt."

He waves me in as he rolls his eyes. "Don't be timid, girl. You've interrupted me now. Sit down." He gestures to the chair opposite his large glass desk. "I need to speak with you, anyway."

"Do I need my notebook?"

"No. I'll be quick." He folds his hands, one on top of the other, on the glass table, and I can't help but notice his right leg twitching up and down. "The housing market has slowed considerably over the last two months and we're going to have to let go of some staff." I nod. I've noticed the drop in property numbers. I figured they would have to let a couple of agents go; I only hope it's not Peter. He's lovely and he has teenage boys that he's putting through college. He presses forward, leaning heavily on the glass, which I fear is going to crack underneath his weight. "I'm going to have to ask you to clean out your desk today. We're letting you go." He awkwardly spreads his lips in what I guess is supposed to be a reassuring smile and my mind blanks.

Did he just fire me?

I came in here to ask for an advance. I didn't even get the chance to open my mouth, and he's firing me. On the freaking spot with no notice! Is this a joke?

I scan the office, looking for cameras and for someone to shout out that I've been 'punked'. But nothing is hinting at a trick for a stupid television show.

How can this be happening? I've lost my family. Now I've lost my job and because of that, I'm going to lose my apartment!

Dropping my face into my hands, I shake my head, tears falling unbidden. Trying to suck in a full breath, I raise my head to the ceiling, attempting to stem my tears. "I can't believe you're firing me without notice."

He shrugs carelessly. "Sorry. It's nothing personal, you know. We can't keep hemorrhaging money. It's not like you bring in a commission. We're in business to make money, not lose it."

Mrs. Dunsley strolls into the office, taking up her position beside her husband, her head held up high as though she's better than everyone else. The gleam in her eyes tells me how happy she is that they've fired me.

I stand on shaky legs. He doesn't care that he's hammered the final nail in my coffin. "When will I get my paycheck?"

"You'll get paid as usual at the end of the month. I'm not in the business of changing procedures to suit individuals."

I don't remember leaving his office or packing my desk. I don't even remember the walk to my car and the drive home, but I find myself sitting on my small couch in the dark in my tiny one-bedroom apartment that I'm about to lose.

Numb.

Nothing. I feel nothing.

I wake to gray skies and snow flurries, still wearing the clothes from yesterday. Wiping the sleep and dried-up tears from my eyes, I jump up from my couch in alarm. Shit, have I slept in? I grab my phone to check the time, my heart beating double time. Seven-thirty!

Shit, shit, shit!

Running into my bedroom, I quickly grab a change of clothes and head to the bathroom to shower. My feet freeze as yesterday afternoon flashes like a movie clip. My shoulders slump in defeat. I can't believe how my life has turned to shit. I press my lips together to stifle the sob that wants to escape. The backs of my eyes burn from the tears I'm trying to hold at bay. Spinning around, I head back to my bedroom, drop my clothes on the floor, and climb into bed, sliding down deep under the covers. Maybe if I can shut out the world for a while, I can start over again when I come out. Curled up in a ball beneath my covers, I close my eyes tight and try to get my heartbeat and breathing under control. An anxiety attack is the last thing I need right now. I need to clear my head, get my thoughts in order so I can make a plan.

Maybe this is a sign.

Maybe I should use this opportunity to my advantage.

Maybe I could do something I've always wanted to do.

Maybe I could start over somewhere new.

Memories flood one after the other. When it was only Mom and me, she used to tell me all about her life on the west coast. It's where she grew up. I would ask her why she left if she loved it so much. She would always gently slide my bangs out of my eyes and tell me she moved because she loved me so much. Her boyfriend abandoned her when she told him she was pregnant, and her parents weren't happy with her teenage pregnancy. Her dad wanted her to have an abortion, so she ran as far as she could, ending up in Portland, Maine, where I was born. It's the only place I've ever lived. Her stories of life in the west always sounded magical to me as a young girl.

Leaving the safety of my cocoon, I grab my cheap laptop and make myself comfortable on my couch. A hiss leaves my lips as I check my bank account. If I'm super careful and sleep in my car, I may just make it. I'll need to get a job immediately, but I would have to do that here, anyway. I could pawn my television and laptop and possibly get a little more money. But I may need my laptop to apply for jobs and stuff like that—I guess I could always use the computers at the local library. I look around my small apartment, searching out more items I could sell—I have a couple of things.

Collecting them together, I place them near my front door, ready to take them to the pawn shop first thing in the morning. I load up one of my plastic tubs with Ethan's scrapbook, Mom's recipe books, and our family photo albums, plus all of my important papers. Next, I pack my clothes, toiletries, and linens. I debate what to do with the few kitchen items I have. If I don't take them with me, I'll have to buy new ones, anyway. I may as well take them and save myself some money. I have nothing else I can use to pack them into, so I'll have to get a box while I'm out tomorrow. Putting everything I'm taking with me into a neat pile in the middle of my living room, I wander around it a few times. It looks like a lot. I hope it's all gonna fit in my car.

I lay out my clothes for the morning, take a long look around my apartment, and head to bed to get a good night's sleep. I have a big few days ahead of me.

I doze off to images of west coast sunsets and a fresh start.

CHAPTER 4

—max—

PULLING IN BEHIND MY WORKSHOP FIRST THING, THE SUN barely peeking over the horizon, my eyes narrow as a low *'what the fuck'* escapes my mouth. Parked in my fucking spot is a navy two thousand and one Jetta sedan. Nobody ever parks behind here, because the bays are solely for the use of the business owners within this precinct. Each of the businesses here has an apartment above the workspace, so most of the other bays are already in use.

I used to live in mine until I started earning enough from the business to buy my home ten minutes down the road. As much as I love working with cars, I hated the smell of oil and other chemicals invading my home; I needed to have a separate space to live. Parking off to the side, I climb out of my car to inspect the unwelcome car parked in my space.

Looking around the backlot of my workshop, I notice nothing else out of place. I bend down enough to peer through the windows, which are slightly cracked open. My eyes widen as they land on a young woman asleep in the semi-reclined driver's seat. I glance in the back—there's too much stuff packed in the backseat to allow it to recline fully. As I scan the interior, it looks as though everything she owns is packed into the compact car. My eyes drop back to the woman, and I study her closely.

She's fucking beautiful.

She's young, really young, with clear pale skin and even paler hair. She's what I'd imagine an angel looks like. I watch her sleep for a few moments, her almost white hair fanned around her face, her thick lashes resting on the apples of her cheeks—*fucking stunning*. I wonder what color her eyes are. Not that I should care what color her eyes are. If she's *that* beautiful, she's probably a self-absorbed bitch, like my ex. I don't need another one like her in my life. She must be fucking uncomfortable because she looks tall, too tall for the space she's using as a bed.

It doesn't appear the interloper will wake up anytime soon.

"What the fuck?" I whisper.

I'm incredulous that my car pulling into the lot didn't wake her up. I have a mind to move my car, so it blocks this woman in. I don't want her sneaking off before I can have a word with her about her sleeping arrangements and parking where she's not welcome.

In fact, that's what I think I'll do.

Walking back to my car, I climb in and start the engine, which sounds deafening in the quiet of the morning. I move in behind her, meaning she'll have to come to find me when she wakes. Cutting the engine, I lock my car, then check on the sleeping beauty. She must be out of it because she hasn't stirred an inch.

Shrugging, I disarm the alarm in my workshop and slide open the heavy steel double door. Stepping inside, I turn on the overhead lights and unlock the front door on my way to my compact office to start the coffee machine. It was the one luxury I afforded myself when I was setting this place up. Why

MOONLIT KISSES · 37

skimp on coffee if it's the thing that'll get me through my workday?

Toby's bringing his car in for a service today, but I need to finish working on the Lincoln before nine, so I drink my coffee as I turn on my laptop and then head into the workshop to get started. Lost in fitting the new radiator into place, I hit my head on the hood at the feminine voice calling out from the doorway. Glancing across, I find the young woman who was sleeping in her car out back. Stepping away from the car, I grab a nearby rag to wipe my hands as I walk across to her.

"Uh, hello. Is that your car blocking me in?" Her voice is sure, full of confidence, even though she must know that she shouldn't park where she is.

I was right. She is tall. I keep enough space between us to be polite. "Is that your Jetta?" I tip my head toward her car, parked in my space. I know full well it's hers because I watched her sleep like a creeper.

She swallows and turns her head in the direction I gestured as if to check I'm asking about her car, then back to me. "Yeah."

"You know that's a private parking space on private property reserved for the business owner? Right?" I ask, keeping my voice even. I cross my arms and her eyes drop, widening slightly as she watches the action.

"Uh, sorry. I've," she waves her arm out toward her car, "been driving solid for days, only stopping for gas and to nap. It was too late when I arrived last night to … uh … get a room somewhere. I pulled in here because it looked like a safe place to stop and get some sleep. I'm sorry if I've inconvenienced you. As soon as you move your car, I'll be outta your hair." She takes a step back from me.

"Where'd you come from?" Her accent suggests she's not from anywhere close by because I can't quite place it.

She tucks a lock of silky-looking hair behind her ear. *Gray.* Her eyes are gray. "Portland, Maine."

"What?" The word comes out harsher than I mean it to. "You," I point to her, "drove all that way on your own, in that fucking car?" I wave my arm out toward her car. Is she fucking crazy?

Her posture visibly changes.

Straightening.

Stiffening.

With her spine straight as a board, her shoulders drawn back tight pushing out her round tits—*stop noticing her tits, you perv!*—she snaps out, sharp as a whip, "Yeah, I did." Her gray eyes are blazing hot, her cheeks flushing. Fuck, she's gorgeous.

No, she's not. She's too fucking young. Stop looking at her.

I stride over to her car—even with her long legs, she almost has to run to keep up with me—and reach inside to release the hood. Stepping around to the front of the car, I set the hood on the prop and begin checking the connections, fluid levels, and hoses.

"What are you doing?" She follows every move I make with her eyes.

One of my pet peeves is people not treating their car right and expecting it to keep on running. "You barely have any water in your radiator. You could have blown up your engine."

She pushes in beside me, the top of her head coming to my chin, eyes wide. "Really? Thank goodness I made it then." She looks around. "Do you have a hose? I'll fill it up."

I'm shaking my head in disbelief before I can temper my response. "You can't fill a radiator with tap water. It contains minerals that'll damage your radiator over time. It has to be distilled water." I snap. "Did you even check your levels before you left Portland?"

I glance up from the engine bay to her face. Her bottom lip is wobbling, and her eyes are scarily glassy. I recognize a woman trying to hold back her tears. I have two sisters and I would do anything to ensure tears never fell because of something I said or did. But it appears I didn't offer the same courtesy to this stranger. She's wrapped her arms around her willowy body as if to protect herself from my wrath.

I sigh heavily with regret.

I had no right to be snappy with this young girl. She didn't deserve my Saturday morning grumpy ass. But I can't handle the mistreatment of cars. People seem to think they don't require care and maintenance.

She gives me a watery smile. "I'm sorry. I didn't know I was supposed to do that. My stepdad used to take care of my car for me. I honestly didn't know. I definitely don't need my car to blow up or to put myself at risk. But after the last few weeks I've had, it wouldn't surprise me." The defeat in her voice is heavy.

My eyes scan her face, noting the black smudges beneath her gorgeous eyes. She looks exhausted and her posture screams defeat. Her clothes are all creased and the slump to her shoulders is unmistakable. She needs a break. I can give her that. Pulling the rag out of my back pocket, I wipe my hands again. They're perpetually stained from grease and oil. I don't know why I bother anymore.

I soften my voice, regretting my heavy-handedness. "Come through to my office. I have a coffee machine. You can put your feet up while I give your car a quick check over and sort out your radiator. Okay?"

She studies me closely, her eyes cataloging every inch of my face. Wariness oozes from every single pore. "Uh, I don't have any money to pay you to do that. If you could just move your car, I'll be on my way and out of your hair." She glances up at my hair and I feel self-conscious about the few grays that have made a permanent home at the temples. The girl gestures to my car and raises her eyebrows at me.

A tentative smile touches my lips. I don't blame her for being wary. I was an asshole. "Did I say I was going to charge you?" I hold out my hand. "Give me your keys so I can move your car into the workshop." I get her reluctance, but I want to help her. My gut tells me she needs a helping hand. I wriggle my fingers in a 'give me' gesture and add, "Please."

She looks back at her car, deliberating my offer as she fidgets with her bracelet. I can tell the moment she relents as she huffs out a sigh and her shoulders drop from her ears. As she turns toward the driver's side, the sunlight catches a delicate ring I hadn't noticed in her nose. She retrieves her keys and drops them into the palm of my hand before looking up at me. Her stormy eyes, soft and appreciative. "Thank you."

"No problem. Let me show you to my office. You can make yourself a coffee, go to the bathroom, or whatever while I work on your car."

I brush past the young woman to head inside, assuming she'll follow, but she steps back to her car. I stop in my tracks to wait for her. She digs down into her car, giving me a sensational view of her ass. *Shit!* Don't stare at her ass. She's a fucking kid. When she straightens up, she's holding a backpack. As the girl steps closer to me, she looks down at her bright pink running shoes, then back up at me. "Uh, I have a lot of important stuff in my car. It'll be safe? Right?"

"Absolutely. I'm just gonna move it from there," I point to her car, "to there." I gesture inside.

She nods. "Okay. I just needed to be sure."

I guide her into my office. "There's the coffee machine. Do you need me to show you how to use it?" I gesture toward the poor excuse for a kitchenette, which takes up a small space in the corner.

She wanders over. Turning back to me, she smiles, showing off deep dimples. I'm a fucking sucker for dimples. "Nope.

This is the same one my mom and stepdad used to have at home."

Hmmm. Don't think I haven't noticed the regular use of past tense. I don't think she's driven all the way from the other side of the country for a vacation. I wonder if she's a runaway?

"Okay. There's cream and juice in the fridge." I nod toward a door on the other side. "The bathroom's through there. It has a shower and toilet. Though it's pretty small."

Her eyes light up. "Sir, uh …" She cuts off her words and shakes her head, but I can tell that whatever she was about to say was important to her.

"What were you gonna say?" I prod.

"Uh, would I be able to have … I mean, uh, would you mind if I had a quick shower? I've been on the road for days with only a quick wipe down in gas station restrooms." She's looking at me with pleading eyes and all I can picture is her wiping down those gorgeous long legs of hers.

How can I say 'no'?

"Sure thing. Make yourself at home. I'll need about an hour to work on your car, then you can be on your way." Realizing neither of us has introduced ourselves, I wipe my hand on the back of my overalls before holding it out. "Sorry. My name's Max."

The young woman chuckles, her cheeks flushing pink. "Sorry. Hi, Max." She slides her small smooth hand into mine. "I'm Molly."

Molly. I like that name. It suits her.

I nod my head as I squeeze lightly. "Nice to meet you, Molly. Make yourself comfortable." I gesture over my shoulder. "I'll get started on your car." Glancing down at the only available surface for her to sit and enjoy a coffee, I gather my strewn paperwork into a messy pile and situate it on top of my laptop to give her space.

I give Molly an embarrassed smile, then I turn to leave.

An hour later, I step into my office to find Molly on the phone while doing something on my laptop, a cute set of glasses perched on her button nose. "Yes, Mr. Barnes. I can see that your next service is due in two weeks. Would you like me to book you in?"

I glance at my desk, covered in neat piles of paper. I don't think it's ever been this organized.

"Sure thing, Mr. Barnes. That's all booked for you. Max will see you at eight a.m. on the twenty-eighth. Goodbye." She's smiling, creating deep dimples on both cheeks, as she hangs up the phone.

"Uh, what's going on in here?"

Molly's head snaps up, revealing wide eyes at my sudden intrusion. She glances around my desk, then up to me, shrugging. "I'm sorry. I thought I could help you out since you weren't charging me to check over my car. You don't mind, do you?"

"What exactly have you done here?" I ask, folding my arm across my body, using the nail of my thumb to drag across my bottom lip. Her eyes snag on the movement and follow my thumb as I pass back and forth across the pillow.

She looks back down at the desk and gestures across the surface like a TV show host. "I've sorted all of your invoices according to the type of expense and then I've ordered them further according to when the payment is due. Then there's been a couple of phone inquiries. I'm sorry, I didn't know your charges, so I've taken messages and told them you would call them back later today. I've booked a service and one tire change. I also noticed you have Thursdays blocked off, so I kept that day free."

She competently rattles off everything she's accomplished

in the hour. I also notice her hair's wet and she's in different clothes than when I left, meaning she's grabbed a shower, too.

What in the actual fuck?

"Are you looking for a job?" The words fly out of my mouth before I can even think about them. But there's no way I'm taking them back. I need her here. Working with me. If she can do all of that in an hour, imagine what she can get done in a day. I'll never have to take work home again, nor be interrupted by the phone five thousand times a day.

CHAPTER 5

—molly—

DID HE JUST OFFER ME A JOB?

My first day in town and I thought I'd messed up in a major way, but now I already have the offer of a job. I'm certain my eyes are the widest they've ever been.

"Are you serious?" The pitch of my voice is higher than normal. Swallowing, I work to temper my shock and excitement. "I mean, are you really offering me a job?" I fidget with the leather cord of my special bracelet. Mom gave it to me when I turned twenty-one and I've never taken it off. She had a complementary one, which is now packed with all of my special treasures along with everything else I own in my car. I've found I rub the silver heart between my fingers more since I lost her; it makes me feel closer to her somehow.

Max seems to be schooling his own surprise. "Uhm, yeah." He laughs. A deep rich sound that sounds amazing after the way he reamed me out about my car. "I guess I am."

I jump up and down, squealing in delight. Running around to the other side of the desk, I throw myself at Max's tall body, wrapping my arms around him. Beneath the smell of grease and oil hides a masculine scent that's sexy as all hell. "Thank you so much. I can't believe how well today has turned out to be." I squeeze him again before releasing the man who's given me so much but doesn't realize. "It looks like everything's gonna work out!" I chuckle.

Max is frozen in place. He probably thinks I'm crazy. He doesn't know how much this means to me. How can he? I can't believe that on my first day in this new city, I've already landed myself a job. Things are looking up. Perhaps this was the right decision to make, after all.

The door opens and closes, so I step away from Max to greet the customer. My eyes almost pop out of my head when they land on the guy who's stepped through the door. He looks even better in real life than he does in pictures.

Toby Summer.

I can't believe I'm in the same room as a famous person. Not just *any* famous person. The hottest famous person on the planet. The greeting I should have dies on my tongue. He's followed by another equally hot guy. I've often seen him in the background of Toby's social media photos. He's his bodyguard. Finally, I gain my wits. "Good morning, I'm Molly. Welcome to Stanfield Auto Repairs. How may I help you?" *Look at me being all professional.*

He looks at me, smiling, then raises his eyes to Max, who's standing beside me. "Max, you finally got yourself some help around here!" He steps forward with his hand outstretched toward me! I'm worried I may faint as my hand connects with his. "Nice to meet you, Molly. I'm Toby. My car's booked in for a service this morning."

Max glances at me, his eyebrows scrunched together, making an adorable crease between them. "Thanks, Molly. I can take it from here."

I drop my hand and step back, realizing I've probably over-stepped. I mean, he *only* offered me the position two minutes ago.

He turns to Toby. "Hey, Toby. Shane." He nods to the men. "Good to see you again. The girl needs a service, right?"

Toby nods. "Yeah. She's running like a kitten, but I want to make sure I look after her properly."

Max smiles. "That's what I like to hear. If you can give your keys to Molly. I'm running a little behind this morning, but your car should still be ready for collection at two."

"No problem. Shane followed me in his car. He'll take me home and bring me back later." He nods over his shoulder to the man behind him as he steps forward, handing me his car keys.

I'm holding Toby Summer's car keys in my hand. Oh. My. Gosh! I have the broadest smile as I study them as though they're precious gems.

Max points to a board next to the door, which leads out to the workshop. "You can hang them on there. On the booking sheet, you'll notice I give each car a bay number. Hang the client's keys on the corresponding bay hook. Okay? I've allocated bay one for Toby's car."

I nod. "Sure thing." I step over and hang the keys on the hook that says Bay 1.

"Molly will call you when your car's ready to be collected. Did you need me to check anything particular or are you happy with a general service and check?" Max asks Toby as the men walk back out through the front door.

I follow them, staying inside, but watching through the glass window in the door. I whistle quietly to myself as my eyes land on his nineteen sixty-seven Chevy Impala convertible. Wow! That's a nice ride. Ethan and Jack used to always be looking at muscle cars, making it easy for me to identify Toby's car, which is in great condition.

Max walks back into the small office, smiling. "Okay. Your car is ready, so if you want to head off, feel free."

"Oh, you don't need me to stay?" I'm confused. I thought

he offered me a job, but now he's telling me I can go. "Aren't I supposed to phone Mr. Summer when his car is ready at two? Have you changed your mind about the position?" I hope not, I really need something to go right.

"Not at all. But you said you'd arrived in town early this morning. I figure you need to get to wherever you're planning to stay and settle in. You should do that. Come back on Monday. Eight a.m. You can start then."

"Oh, okay. Thank you." I guess he's being considerate. "See you Monday." I smile at him. With no money for a place to stay, I was planning to sleep in my car until I saved enough, but he doesn't know that. I guess I can use this time to familiarize myself with my new city and locate some safe places to sleep at night. Maybe even some public showers or something.

CHAPTER 6

—max—

STEPPING ONTO THE FAMILIAR PORCH, I HEAD INSIDE WITHOUT knocking—there's no need to. The familiar smells of Mom's Sunday roast waft out of the kitchen to greet me, making my stomach grumble in response. This is possibly the best meal I get all week—not possibly, it *is* the best meal I get all week.

Austin and Kenny notice me first and sprint down the hallway, throwing themselves at my body with every faith that I'll catch them. And I will catch them. Every single time they need me.

I quickly drop Em's gift on the entry table to free both arms.

"Uncle Max! You're here!" cheers Austin.

"Uncle Max!" Kenny squeals at the same time.

I catch them both and lift them into my arms, land a kiss on each of their cheeks, and then place them back on their feet. There was a time, not too long ago, when I could throw Austin above my head, but he's getting too big for that. I mess his hair and relish in his little boy giggles before tickling Kenny under her chin, causing her to giggle too. One of the best sounds in the world is the laughter of little kids.

"I'm here. We can get this party started now!"

"Is that for Mommy?" Austin points to the gift I dropped onto the table.

"Yup, where's the birthday girl?"

"In the kitchen with Nana." The kids run to the kitchen, Austin calling out to Emma, "Uncle Max is here."

My long strides have me approaching the kitchen doorway quickly. Even though it's Em's birthday, I head straight to Mom; if I don't hug her first, she gets all offended for some reason. Placing the gift for Emma on the counter, I wrap both arms around Mom and lift her off her feet.

She chuckles, playfully swatting my shoulder. "Oh, Max. Put me down."

"Hey, Mom." I kiss her cheek.

She brings her hand up to my bristly cheek, looking up at me with pure love in her eyes. That's the one thing I've never had to question. The depth of my family's love for me. "How has your week been, Love?"

"It's been great. Busy. Really busy," I respond as I steal a piece of cucumber from the chopping board.

I move over to Emma, who's busy taking the roast out of the oven for Mom. Once she's placed it down, I wrap my arms around her in a bear hug, lifting her off her feet. "Happy birthday, Em!" I rub my bristles across her cheek before landing a sloppy birthday kiss, causing her to giggle.

Her hands press against my shoulders. "Thanks, Max."

"How's your day been so far?"

She looks across to the kitchen table where Lachlan sits with Theo, a smile touching her lips. "It's been perfect." Contentment and happiness radiate from her, and I'm thrilled she's found that. The muscle in my chest tightens; I want that too. I'm not getting any younger and I want a family of my own.

I hand her the gift I brought. "Here you go. It's not huge, but I thought you'd like it."

She pulls the T-shirt out of the bag, holding it up so she can read it and a full-on belly laugh escapes.

"What's funny?" Sarah asks as she steps into the room, wrapping her arms around my waist in greeting. Wrapping my arm around her, I kiss the top of her head.

Emma turns the T-shirt around to show her the front. Sarah reads the text out for everyone, "I'm a proud sister of a freaking awesome brother (and yes, he brought me this shirt)." She promptly bursts out laughing, too.

"It's perfect, right?" I ask the room as Emma twists the shirt around for everyone to see.

Dad claps me on the shoulder and chuckles. "Only you, Max."

Sarah spins around, removing herself from me, pointing her finger. "Don't even think about getting me one of those." Her grin tells me it wouldn't bother her if I got her one, which I already did. I bought them at the same time, so I didn't have to think of another gift. I'm organized like that.

Everyone settles down, and we set the table ready for lunch. Theo serves Kenny and helps Emma with the boys, careful to ensure Lachlan's food isn't touching. I never thought I'd see Lachlan eating our roast dinner, but Theo's gradually been introducing him to new foods. Theo dishes Em's plate before serving himself and I nod my approval internally. It's fantastic to see Em and the boys being looked after so well. The first few moments are silent as we serve ourselves and take our first few bites of food.

The lamb is incredibly tender; falling apart in my mouth. I can't contain the moan that escapes me, and I refuse to try. "This is delicious, Mom."

She smiles at the praise. Mom loves feeding her family and we love to be fed by her. Being on my own and working the long hours that I do, I only ever make myself the basics for dinner and grab whatever I can from the deli over the road from the workshop for lunch. Which means I really look forward to our weekly family dinner. Maybe having Molly working in the office will afford me some more time and I can actually attempt to feed myself proper meals that take more than five minutes to put together.

"You said you've been busy at work. When are you going to employ someone to help?" Mom asks. At Mom's question, everyone's eyes land on me. They've been nagging me for quite some time to get help at the workshop.

I place my knife and fork down and wipe my mouth with my napkin, hiding my smile. "You'll be happy to know that I have an office manager starting at eight a.m. on Monday."

Cheers sound out around the table. "Finally!" Mom raises her voice to be heard above the din as Lachlan covers his ears. When he was younger, he probably would have cried at such a sudden noise, but as he's grown, he's dealing with the stuff we take for granted.

"How did you find this office manager and are you sure they're qualified?" Of course, Sarah would be the one to ask about Molly's qualifications since she's an office manager herself.

The thing is, I don't know if Molly has all the qualifications or even if she has any at all. She showed me how capable she was and after she left; I checked the work she'd done, and it was top-notch. For someone who wasn't familiar with my system, she did a good job. The only thing she hadn't done on the bookings was assign each vehicle to a bay. I can easily show her my specific requirements on Monday, knowing she has a good grasp of the overall system.

I must have taken too long to answer my sister. Her forehead creases as she asks, "She *is* qualified, right? You didn't just hire anyone off the street?"

Leaning my elbow on the table, I rub my thumbnail across my bottom lip in thought. That's exactly what I did. How do I break it to her?

"Oh my gawd! You did. Are you an idiot?" She rolls her eyes at me and Emma snickers.

"I'm not an idiot, Sarah," I snap, but then temper my tone. She's only looking out for my best interests. "She's highly competent or I wouldn't have hired her," I tell them how Molly came to be employed, leaving out the part about her sleeping in her car behind my workshop.

"Has she got somewhere to stay?" Mom asks, fidgeting with her necklace.

I shrug. "I didn't ask. I would assume she does."

Mom's worry increases. "If she's new to the city, she might need some help to get around and learn the area. Oh, my goodness, will she know which areas she should stay away from?"

My stomach drops. Shit, I didn't think about any of that. I assumed she knew where she was heading. What if she ends up renting a place in an unsavory area? I didn't get any contact details for her, so I can't check if she's okay. She'd be okay, right? I mean, she drove across the country on her own, for fuck's sake. Fuck. Now *I'm* worried about her. I check the time —only eighteen hours until I see for myself that she's okay.

"Now, when you leave work for the day, you can leave your work behind. That's great news, Son. It's been a long time coming for you." Dad pats my shoulder, drawing me back into the conversation, as he steps past me to place his dishes on the counter near the sink.

"How are things going at your office, Sarah? Any news on Eric's retirement?" Emma asks.

Sarah blows out a heavy sigh, her shoulders slumping forward. "Something happened and delayed Adam's move to the west coast. I'm not sure when things will change."

Emma gives Sarah a sympathetic smile. "Well, on the positive side of things, it means you get to work with Eric longer."

"That's true, and it's something I'm cherishing." She tucks a loose lock of hair behind her ear. "I love working with Eric and you guys know how I feel about change."

"Eric's grandson might be a lot like him. You never know, it might be a seamless transition." I do my best to put her at ease because I know how much Sarah dislikes change.

She nods as she places her silverware down, her expression serious. "I have something I wanted to talk with you guys about."

We all give Sarah one hundred percent of our attention. "What is it, Love?" Mom asks.

She blows out a breath. "Please don't judge me. I've thought long and hard about this and it's the right decision for me. I'm hoping you'll all be supportive."

Creases form between Dad's eyebrows. "Of course, we'll support you."

"Great." She blows out a long breath. "I've decided I want to have a baby." The silence in the room is loud. "I'm not getting any younger and it's impossible to meet someone decent. Someone I'd want to raise a family with."

Mom's hand rises to fidget with her necklace. "Oh. Well … uh … that's unexpected news. How will you make this happen?"

"There are agencies that help women like me. I complete a whole heap of paperwork, give them a whole wad of money, and they give me sperm from a baby-daddy of my choosing."

"My sister, Anna, did that." Theo looks across at Kenny with eyes full of love and adoration. "That's how we ended up with Kenny."

"Do you know which agency she used?"

Theo thinks for a moment. "I don't, sorry. Dad might know, though. I'll ask him and let you know."

Sarah smiles at him. "Thanks."

"This isn't the way we expected you to be having a baby, but we'll support you in any way we can." Dad reaches across, patting Sarah's hand with love and affection.

We all offer our support to Sarah in any way we can as she finds a baby-daddy and into the future, through her pregnancy, and then into motherhood. We clean up from dinner and then Sarah places a chocolate birthday cake on the table for Emma. I'm incredibly thankful we still have Emma with us to celebrate her birthday. I was worried we were going to lose her this time last year before she got her proper diagnosis, and we didn't quite know what was going to happen. We sing happy birthday in our usual terribly off-key fashion and then enjoy the delicious cake baked by my younger sister. She's been the designated birthday cake maker since she was old enough to bake.

CHAPTER 7

—max—

PULLING AROUND BEHIND MY WORKSHOP SOON AFTER DAWN, I half expect to find the blue Jetta parked in my space again. I'm not sure if I'm relieved or disappointed that it isn't there as I move through my usual morning routine. I try not to have any cars left over the weekend, leaving the workshop empty except for the Sprint.

Time becomes inconsequential as I get lost in the task of connecting the wiring for the rear lights of my restoration project. As I connect the last wire, I glance up to find Molly hovering inside the doorway to the workshop. Sucking in a sharp breath, I allow myself to release the worry I've been holding onto about Molly's safety since Mom brought up her concerns yesterday afternoon. She looks mighty different from the girl I met on Saturday. Dressed in office attire, I almost don't recognize her. A dark checkered skirt hugs her hips, sitting just below her knees and a white silky-looking blouse highlights her bust. Her almost-white hair is up in some sort of sexy knot on top of her head. She looks like a fucking hot secretary who works in a corporate office, not a mechanic's filthy workshop. *And I should not be fucking thinking about how hot she looks.* She's like twelve fucking years old. I run my hand through my hair as I make my way over to where she's standing, fidgeting with the bracelet on her slender wrist.

"Uh … hello, Mr. Stanfield. I'm ready to start work if the job is still available," she stammers; her eyes flitting around the workshop, avoiding me.

I cross my arms and rub my thumbnail across my bottom lip. "Morning. Why so formal today?"

She tilts her head to the side, not understanding my question. I wave my arm up and down her body, my eyes following. She has a sensational body—long legs, slim hips, not too much boobage—just enough. *Fuck, stop looking at her like that, you filthy pervert! You're her fucking boss.*

She looks down at herself as though to check what she's wearing. "Oh, this. This is what I wore for my last job. I wanted to be professional." She cracks those deep, deep dimples at me, her eyes wide. She looks too fucking professional for this place in that getup.

"You can probably wear jeans and a T-shirt here. I'm not sure what type of office you worked in before, but this is a more laid-back environment."

"Sure." She gestures over her shoulder. "I can change. I have my clothes in the car."

Spinning on her heel, I admire the shape of her calves in the black tights she's wearing. Then it registers that she said she had her clothes in the car.

Why the fuck does she have her clothes in the car?

My long strides catch me up to her quickly, and I'm directly behind her as she opens her trunk. It's not my business, but it looks as though she hasn't unpacked her car. I stroll to the side of the car, discreetly looking inside. Sure enough, the blankets she was using to sleep are folded neatly on the back seat, along with several small packing boxes.

"How come you still have all of your stuff in your car?"

Her head snaps up to me. I'm not sure she realized I was close by as she rummages through her bag, digging out a pair of jeans and a long-sleeve T-shirt. "I haven't found a long-term place to live yet. Most places were closed yesterday and by the time I left on Saturday, I'd already missed a couple of opportunities. I decided it was easier to leave my stuff in my car." I study her closely for a long moment. "You know, so I don't have to unpack and pack again." She widens her silver eyes with her explanation.

I guess that logic makes sense. "Fair enough. Is the place you're staying safe?"

She glances away from me. "Oh, yeah!" Nodding her head as if to confirm her answer, she adds, "Totally safe." She holds up an assortment of clothes. "Do you mind if I use your bathroom to change?"

"No problem. Go ahead. Then I'll run you through a couple of things before you get started. You'll need to fill out some employment paperwork, too." I close her trunk and we both make our way inside. "You want a coffee?"

"Yes, please. That'd be great. Cream, no sugar, thanks," she calls back through the closed bathroom door. I hear the shower turn on. *What the fuck?* I thought she was only changing clothes.

I hold back on making her coffee to ensure it's hot when she finally comes out, and deal with a client as they drop off their keys while she's in the bathroom. The door opens, and steam gushes out of the room into the small office space. "I thought you were just changing clothes?"

She glances back at the bathroom as she shrugs. "Sorry 'bout that. The place I showered this morning only had cold water. I couldn't resist. I hope you don't mind." *Too bad if I did.* I hope she doesn't expect to get away with whatever she wants while I'm waiting on her and making her coffee. From my experience, girls that look like her expect to always get their way.

Hmmm. I'm not used to being a boss, but she's on the clock. *My* clock. Should I cut her some slack? It's her first day, after all. Or should I be a hard ass? "Don't make a habit of it, okay? You're supposed to start work at eight. I had to deal with a client because you weren't ready for work." Hard ass it is, then.

Her cheeks flush prettily as she shifts on her feet. "Sorry, Mr. Stanfield. It won't happen again. I'll run these to my car and be ready to start." She holds up her fancy clothes and I nod.

She takes off and I make our coffee, ready to show her the system I have in place, although she had a pretty good grasp of it on Saturday without being shown. I spend the next thirty minutes leaning over Molly to show her the system. Each time I lean forward, I'm hit with her alluring scent; I can't quite place it, but it's a far cry from motor oil and grease. She's a quick study, even suggesting some ways to simplify the invoicing system, which I'm more than happy for her to do.

"Okay, I'm going to head out to work on the brake replacement in bay one. We need to get your employment forms sorted. Can you please fill them in?"

"Sure thing, Mr. Stanfield." She hits me with those fucking dimples as if they punctuate her sentence.

"Call me Max. Okay? Mr. Stanfield is my dad." I huff out a chuckle.

"Oh, okay, Max. I'll try to remember." I take one last glance at her with those cute glasses perched on her nose as she returns her focus to my laptop, then I step into the workshop to get to work.

"Shit, fuck!" My thumb instantly throbs from the impact of the mallet against it. Shoving it in my mouth, I realize my mistake immediately as the taste of grease coats my tongue. It's not the first time I've done it, and it certainly won't be the last.

Footsteps rush across the open space. "Are you okay? What happened?" My new assistant drops to her knees beside me.

I wrap my free hand around my thumb, attempting to reduce the throb. "Hit my thumb with the mallet. I do it at least once a week."

"Shit. That'd hurt." Molly stands and spins on her heel and runs back to the office. I'm guessing she doesn't like to see people injured. Shaking out my hand, I start back up where I left off, being more cautious of my own body parts. "Here. Wrap this around it." Molly grabs my hand and wraps a cold compress around my thumb, holding it in place.

Her concentration on the task is admirable, but I don't need to be this close to her this soon, especially when I can see right down her T-shirt. I quickly avert my eyes, but they snap back of their own accord to the creamy mounds restrained by a simple cotton bra. This morning was hard enough in my office. I was hoping the workshop would be a large enough space to ensure I didn't have to inhale her floral perfume. I'm not sure what type of magic it has, but it's affected me more than I want it to. At least I know she's not as young as I thought she was, but she's still too young for me.

Plus, I'm her fucking boss! I need to remember that.

I pull my hand away abruptly. "I'm okay."

Her delicate eyebrows drop over her steely eyes. "Are you sure? Your thumb is already swelling. I think it'd be a good idea if you iced it for a while."

I take the compress from her and hold it back on my thumb. "Sure. But I can hold it." I nod toward the office. "You have work to do. How did you go with sourcing those parts I wanted?"

"No luck at the first two suppliers, unless you're prepared to wait for four to six weeks. I was about to try the next one on the list." She fidgets with her bracelet, shifting on her feet. "I'm really sorry."

"What in the hell are you apologizing for? Sometimes I have to go through my entire list of suppliers before I find one who has the part I need in stock." I remove the compress from my thumb to inspect the damage. The ice seems to be helping. "Thanks for this." I hold up my thumb. "You'll get to know which suppliers are better for particular parts. If you're not sure, come and ask. No point wasting time." Molly nods, dropping her hands to her sides.

"Uh, do you want a coffee?"

I glance up at the large clock I have on the back wall of the workshop. It's after one already. "Nah, time to stop for lunch. You should take a break. You get thirty minutes for lunch each day."

"Oh, okay. Thanks."

We walk side-by-side back to my office, her floral scent invading my nose. "What is that perfume you're wearing?"

"I don't wear perfume. It's probably my shampoo and body wash you can smell." She smells her hand, then holds it out for me, and I draw in a deep breath. "Is that it?"

It's a subtle fragrance. "Yeah. What is it?"

"Rose. I'm sorry if it bothers you." What is with this girl apologizing for everything?

"No need to apologize. I was only asking. I … uh … I actually like it."

Her cheeks flush. "Thanks. My mom used to use the same products." Her voice has a shake to it and she drops her face toward the ground. Her mom used to use it. Does that mean she's lost her mom? I don't know her well enough to ask questions, but I make a note to get to know her a little better.

I collect my phone so I can grab my lunch from the deli

across the road. Lawrence makes the best sub sandwiches. "I'm gonna head over the road to grab some lunch. Do you want anything?"

Her head snaps around to me, her eyes wide. "Oh. Thanks for the offer, but I'm okay."

I narrow my eyes. "You have lunch, right?"

She tucks a loose strand of silky white hair that's fallen from the top knot behind her ear. "Not today. I completely forgot about it. I'll have a coffee. That'll get me through."

I nod as I head out the door, pulling my jacket around me as I take my first steps. I don't like the cold weather and today's high of sixty-three degrees makes me shiver. The warmth is a welcome reprieve as I step inside *Lawrence's Diner*.

"Max. How's your morning been?" Lawrence calls out from the doorway to the kitchen.

"It was going pretty great until I hit my damn thumb with the mallet."

His face scrunches up with a pained grimace. "Ouch. You want your usual?"

"Yeah. Thanks. Could you make it two, though, please?"

"Sure. You extra hungry today?"

"Nah. I finally got myself an employee. I figured I'd buy her lunch to celebrate her first day." I stuff my hands in my pockets. "Her name's Molly. She might come over now and then to collect my lunch." I shrug.

He nods and goes about making two of my usual sub sandwiches. Turkey, cheddar, thick-cut bacon, and avocado in a ciabatta roll. Mmmm, my mouth's watering already. He wraps them in paper and slides them across the counter to me. "I'll add them to your account."

Grabbing the subs, I hold them up. "Thanks, Lawrence. I'll see you tomorrow." Waving over my shoulder, I head back out into the cold, rushing across the street back to my workshop.

"I got you a sub," I call out to Molly as I open the door to the office. Turning to face the room, I find it empty. I knock on the bathroom door. No answer. Hmph. I step into the workshop and scan the area. My eyes dart back to the woman sitting cross-legged on the floor near the Sprint, a coffee cup on the floor next to her. She reaches out distractedly to grab the cup, almost knocking it over. I wander over as quietly as I can to see what she's doing. She keeps looking down and then up again. Standing behind her like the creeper that I am, what she's doing comes into view.

"Did you sketch that just now?"

She jumps, her hand coming up to her chest. She looks up at me, looming behind her, with red puffy eyes. With her head tilted right back, she gives me a spectacular view of her elongated neck. If she wasn't so young and I weren't her boss, I would lean down, cup her chin, tease her lips with my tongue, and take them in a long, slow kiss to distract her from whatever's made her sad. I shake my head and take half a step to the side, squatting down to get a better look.

She flicks her eyes back down at her book as if to check what I'm talking about. "Yeah. I love to sketch different things. You know. The lines on this car sucked me right in. I couldn't help myself." She looks up at me. "I hope you don't mind. I won't do it while I'm supposed to be working. I'm sorry. I should have asked if it was okay first."

"I have no problem with what you do on your own time. Just be sure you're being safe when you're on the workshop floor." I hold up the sub. "I got you a sandwich for lunch." I hold it out to her, but she doesn't take it.

"Oh, uh, uhm. I'm happy to have a coffee for lunch. Thank you for the kind gesture."

I nudge it forward. "You need more than a coffee for lunch. Here, take it. Come and eat with me in the office."

She looks down at her sketch pad. "I really can't accept it."

"Why not? Are you gluten intolerant or something?"

She shakes her head in the negative. "No, I'm not allergic or intolerant of anything. Well, I don't think I am." She gives a small chuckle and wipes her fingers beneath her eyes.

"Then take it. Eat. C'mon." I stand and begin walking back toward the office, expecting her to follow. When I glance back, she's only just standing. Collecting her things, she slowly makes her way behind me.

Placing the subs on my clean desk, which is miraculous, I pull over an additional chair. I unwrap Molly's sandwich and then mine. Gesturing to the lunch I've laid out, I coax. "C'mon. I always have to eat lunch on my own." I give a false pout. Fuck. I didn't think I'd have to work this hard to feed her. "I was looking forward to eating with someone today."

She fiddles with her bracelet. I've noticed she does that a lot. "I'm on a tight budget. I can't afford to buy expensive lunches at the moment," she explains, without looking at me.

She mentioned money when I offered to look at her car, too. I press my lips together to temper my tone, careful not to respond too harshly. "Did I say you had to pay me for the sandwich?"

Her shoulders are up around her ears. "Uh, no. But …"

I push her chair out with my foot and gesture toward it. "Sit. Eat with me." I grab my sandwich and take a bite. Softening my voice, I add, "Please."

Her shoulders drop and slight dimples form in her cheeks as she takes a seat. "Thank you. I am a little hungry." She takes a small bite. "This is delicious."

"Lawrence makes the best sandwiches around here." I gesture diagonally across the road. "He's over the road. If you ever want anything, head on over. He'll put it on my tab."

"Oh, I couldn't do that." She shakes her head in the negative, then takes another bite.

I finish my sub well before Molly does and as I ball up my

paper, her sketch pad grabs my attention. Pointing with my chin, I ask, "Mind if I take a look?"

She freezes, her eyes widening. "Uh, sure?"

"If it's personal to you, you can say 'no'. You don't have to let me look if it's uncomfortable for you." I reassure her because I get the feeling she doesn't want me to look at her drawings.

"Oh, it's not that. It surprised me you wanted to look at them." She nudges it toward me, nodding toward her work. "Be my guest."

Opening the book, I study each sketch closely. Turning the pages, I'm mesmerized by the detail and variety of images I see. She clearly prefers drawing objects and nature: buildings, park benches, cars, a stained-glass window, bridges, trees, flowers, the river, the forest, and the beach. I raise my eyes to hers, finding her biting her bottom lip, eyes full of worry. "These are fantastic."

Her shoulders drop and a heavy breath leaves her lips. Her dimples make an appearance as her eyes smile at me. "Really? You think so?"

"Fuck yeah. You could sell these and make a fortune."

She laughs and I love the sound. "I don't know about that. It's only something I do for fun."

"You should think about it. My friend, Aaron, owns a café down by the river. He allows artists to display their work to sell. He takes a percentage of each sale, but the artist gets most of the money. I play soccer with him on Monday nights. I can show him this and ask what he thinks." My excitement builds at the prospect of helping Molly sell some of her work. Molly's face drops, a sheen glossing her eyes as they turn to silver. "You don't have to. It was only a suggestion." I close the book and slide it back in front of her.

She gives me a silent nod and a watery smile. "Thanks. I'll think about it."

—molly—

THE SMELL OF SWEET TREATS GREETS ME AS I STEP INTO THE office. "Morning!" I call out. "What's all this?" I eye the white boxes stacked on the minuscule kitchen counter.

Max drops from the last step, carrying some type of bag over his shoulder, making his bicep bulge. "Morning! It's Thursday." As if that explains anything to me.

I open a couple of lids to check the contents inside. Tucked neatly inside are a variety of doughnuts and pastries. I can't remember the last time I could afford to splurge on some sugary goodness. Oblivious to my musings, Max unzips the bag and pulls out some type of contraption. As he works to open it, I discreetly enjoy the show he's unwittingly providing me as his muscles stretch and flex with his movements.

"Uhm, am I supposed to know what's special about Thursday?" There aren't any bookings for today. I assumed he kept the day free to catch up on office work, which he no longer needs to do now I'm here, but clearly, I'm mistaken.

He looks at me over his shoulder as he continues to set up whatever it is he's setting up. "Thursdays are dedicated to single parents. They can bring their vehicles in for a checkup, have me look at any issues they may have, or do a minor service. If I find anything major that needs further attention, I speak with the owner about it and work out a way to help them with the repairs for the lowest possible price. I don't charge them for my time, only the cost price of any parts I need to supply. It works out well for them." He stands upright after pushing the last strut into place.

A playpen. He has a playpen for the kids. Of course, he does. I'm guessing all the pastries are for the moms and dads, too. I rub the center of my chest to contain the flutters that erupt at his thoughtfulness. Not only is he providing a valuable service, but he's also making the experience special for the clients.

"If you don't mind, I'd appreciate it if you could look after the ladies and gents while they're waiting today. Normally, they mostly help themselves to the pastries and coffee, but since you're here, it would be great if they could relax a little while they wait for their car. Don't worry about doing too much office stuff. Just answer the phone when it rings." Creases form across his forehead as he waits for my answer.

"Of course. Anything you want me to do, I'll do. No problem." I gesture to the boxes of pastries. "How busy do you get?"

The tension releases from his face and he runs his fingers through his hair, drawing my eyes to the salt and pepper strands at his temple. "Pretty busy. Not everyone has their kids with them because some of them are at school, but some customers have young babies and/or toddlers, so it can get pretty noisy in here."

"How do I know if they're a single parent and not just a regular customer? Do they have some sort of token or something?"

He folds his arms across his chest and uses his thumbnail to rub back and forth across his bottom lip. I notice he does that often. I have to make a concerted effort to concentrate on his words and not get lost in thinking about what that lip would feel like against my skin. "There's a sign on the front door that says today is single parent day. No bookings required." He motions with his head toward the front door.

"But anyone could walk through the door and pretend they're a hard-up single parent. How do you monitor it?" This world is full of scammers, and I would hate to think someone would take advantage of Max's generosity.

He raises one shoulder in a careless shrug. "I work on honesty and hope my clients do the same. I've had no issues so far, and I've been doing this for a while." If it's worked this long, who am I to question it?

I nod. "Okay. Sure thing. I'll check the bathroom is clean." The cleaner came by Tuesday night, and I think he comes back on Saturday morning, so I don't think it'll hurt to give it a once over.

"Thanks, Molly. Can you please set up the changing table in there? It's upstairs. I'll run up and grab it." He makes his way up the stairs, two at a time, allowing me a superb view of his ass. To say I haven't enjoyed my man candy this past week would be an outright lie. But he's my boss and I can't go there. I desperately need to keep this job and falling for my hot boss would be a disaster. But there's no reason I can't enjoy the view. Right?

I grab the bucket of cleaning supplies and get to work cleaning the toilet, vanity, and basin. I check there are spare rolls of toilet paper close by and that the paper towel dispenser is full. It doesn't take long before it's pristine and I have the changing table set up in the corner, making the space tighter than it normally is.

I unlock the front door and our first client walks in with a toddler in tow. "Good morning, welcome to Stanfield Auto Repairs. How can we help you today?"

"I've been having trouble starting my car. I was hoping Max would have time this morning to take a look?" Max steps out of the bathroom in his overalls and the woman's eyes light up, raking over him in a not-so-subtle sweep. Her lips widen as her eyes sparkle. "Max!"

"Oh hey, Georgia. Car troubles?" He steps closer to her, reaching out for the toddler, who giggles wildly as Max tickles him. "Hey, Ryan."

"Yeah. I'm having trouble getting it started some mornings. I'm hoping it's not the battery."

He holds out his hand. "Let's take a look." She lowers her car keys into Max's hand, and he closes his fingers around them, her touch lingering beyond what would be deemed respectable. I resist, barely, rolling my eyes at her overt flirting. I bet it happens a lot on Thursdays. Max holds out his hand toward me. "Georgia, this is my new office manager, Molly. She'll take care of you while I work on your car."

From that point on, the day is a flurry of men, women, and children coming and going. I spend the day making cups of coffee and tea, handing out pastries, and playing with babies and toddlers of all shapes and sizes. It's crazy, but Max seems to be in his element. He's always happy when he's working on the cars and trucks he repairs, but today he has a pep in his step. Obviously, he likes that he's helping people who need a little extra. He reminds me of myself when I do my volunteer work. Something I want to get back to.

After the last client leaves, I lock the door and peer around the small office. It appears as though a storm has come through the small space. One lone box of pastries is left sitting on the counter. The chairs are all over the place after a game of musical chairs this afternoon; the bin is piled high with used paper cups and napkins, and I'm exhausted. I have no clue how Max must be feeling. He hasn't stopped since this morning, missing lunch altogether. I'm working up the energy to clean up the office when Max steps into the room. His overalls are filthy, and he has grease on his forehead. He looks tired but pleased. Genuinely pleased.

"Today was a great day. Thanks for all of your help. I got through more cars than usual because I didn't need to keep stopping to answer the phone and meet with the clients. That information sheet you made up this morning for each client to fill out helped streamline things."

My chest puffs up with pride. I'm thrilled I could help to make his job easier. "I figured if they quickly jotted down what the issue was, it would save you having to stop working to speak with the client. I'm glad it worked." Once I saw the time he was wasting this morning, I quickly drafted a check-in sheet and asked the clients to complete it. It just had some basic information and space for a brief explanation of the issues they were having with their vehicle. I then attached the sheet to a clipboard and hung it with the keys on the hooks.

Moving toward the bathroom, he undoes the fasteners of his overalls as he speaks with me, exposing his T-shirt. "It worked really well. I'm thinking maybe we can put it in place on our regular days too. What do you think?"

"I can do that. No problem at all. I noticed a couple of changes I'd like to make to it. If you have any suggestions, let me know and I'll add them to the form."

He nods. "Thanks. I'll take a closer look at it tonight." He closes the bathroom door behind him, and I get to work on rearranging the chairs back into position and cleaning up the small kitchen.

When he steps back out, he's wearing his jeans and T-shirt from this morning, his hair's wet and his forehead is now clear of grease. As he steps past me, his clean scent wafts behind him and I discreetly suck in a lungful of the delicious smell.

Shameful, I know!

He works to collapse the playpen I've already sterilized

while I disinfect the changing table and bring it out for him to pack away.

"So, what made you start doing this?"

"What, fixing cars?"

"No, I mean helping single parents the way you do?"

He stops what he's doing to face me. "My sister was a single mom for a long time. I saw her struggle to make ends meet and figured if I could help one person, it would be worth it. In the beginning, people were wary of the offer, but it's grown over time and people in the local community have learned to trust that I'm not trying to rip them off or get them back in for more expensive work."

"Well, I think it's very noble of you. Each person who stepped through that door this morning was stressed." I wave my arm out toward the front door. "When they left, I could see the difference in their features and their posture. They were relieved that they had one less thing to worry about. Thanks to you."

He drops his head down, but not before I notice his cheeks flush, and a smile touch his lips. "Thanks. I like to help where I can."

The sun sits low on the horizon as I slow in front of the old brick building. It has great character and I'd love to sketch it some time. After finding a parking space just down the road, I draw in a deep breath and exit my car. The area doesn't look all that pleasant, so I double-check my locks are engaged. The last thing I need is for my car and all of my belongings to get stolen.

As I step through the large doors, an older lady greets me with a broad smile on her friendly face. She has a warm and welcoming demeanor about her, which instantly puts me at ease. I'm guessing it works well for her in this environment.

Appearances are obviously deceiving because the inside of the building is nothing like the outside. It's clean with simple but modern furnishings. The place has a welcoming vibe, much like the woman who greets me.

"Welcome to *Shelter*. My name is Simone. Come, sit." She gestures toward a couple of comfy chairs off to the side.

"Hi, Simone. I'm Molly."

"How's your day been, Molly?" She asks as she steps toward a counter along the side wall, complete with a coffee machine, kettle, and cups. "Would you like a cup of tea or coffee?"

"I wouldn't mind a coffee, thanks. No sugar, but I'll take cream." She smiles and nods at my preference, then directs her attention to making my drink. "Today's been great. Crazy busy, but awesome."

She turns toward me, her eyebrows raised. "You sound thoroughly pleased." Bringing our drinks over, she places them on the coffee table and then takes a seat in the chair opposite mine. "What brings you to *Shelter* today, Molly?"

I give her my best smile. "Well, I'm new to the area. Back home, I used to volunteer a couple of nights a week at the local women's shelter, and I wanted to do the same here." I take a sip of my drink, hoping there's some way I can help. "If the opportunity is available," I add.

Simone's smile widens, her eyes twinkling. "We can always do with volunteers. How wonderful of you to offer your time. Can I ask where you volunteered previously?"

"Sure. I moved here from Portland, Maine recently. I used to volunteer at *FemCity*. I would help with the sign-in registrations, chatting with the ladies, setting up the beds for the night, cleaning, and putting together the overnight toiletry kits. Oh, and I'd help in the kitchen if needed. Though, to be completely honest, I think I was more a hindrance than help in the kitchen." I chuckle.

"You sound like me. I'm terrible in the kitchen, too. When were you thinking of starting and how many evenings can you help?" Simone asks, leaning forward to collect her coffee.

"I'm happy to help maybe two or three nights a week and I can start anytime you want me."

"Sounds perfect. Would you mind completing some paper-work and then I'll give you the tour?" She takes a sip of her coffee. "I hope you don't mind, but we do need to run a back-ground check. It only takes a few moments."

I nod, eagerly. This sounds promising. "That's not a problem at all. They had to do the same thing at *FemCity*, so I was expecting it."

Simone heads to another room and returns with a clip-board and a couple of pages of forms that I need to complete. "If you wouldn't mind completing these. Then I'll show you around. We'll start getting some ladies coming in soon, I expect."

I set to work filling out the paperwork but come up against a snag. I don't have an address. Shit! "Uhm, I don't have a permanent address yet. I only arrived on Saturday. Is it okay if I give you the address for where I work?"

Her eyes narrow ever so slightly. "Where are you staying?"

"Just couch surfing with some friends at the moment. As soon as I get a permanent spot, I'll let you know." I don't want to tell her I'm sleeping in my car because I have very little money. When I was young, Mom and I would only use the women's shelter on freezing nights. She never wanted to take a bed away from someone who was worse off than us. She always said that while we had our car, we weren't truly home-less. As an adult, I've learned that's not technically true, but I still don't want to take a bed from someone who needs it more than I do. Mom taught me all the tricks of the trade for surviving in a car and I'm managing okay so far.

"Sure. That shouldn't be a problem." She gives me a reassuring smile. "I quickly need to check that we're ready for registrations. Be back in a minute." I nod as Simone pats my arm on the way past me, then I continue to complete the forms.

I hand Simone my completed forms, and we begin the tour. "This is obviously where we meet with women as they come through the door. We like to have a quick chat first to find out how we can help. This facility has space for women who need short-term accommodation as well as overnight facilities to escape a night on the street. Unfortunately, we never seem to have enough beds, but we do our best. We find it best to offer our ladies the opportunity to have a warm drink during our initial chat. Like we just did." She smiles at me, then guides me around the corner. "We have a play area here for the little ones."

The area is well decked out with a playpen, similar to the one we used today at the workshop. There are toys that would suit different ages, from babies up to young children. There's a small table in the corner with a collection of writing and coloring pencils, as well as a pile of coloring and puzzle books. "Wow. This area looks great. I bet it's popular."

"Yeah. These kids have very little, most only have the clothes on their backs. Having this area set up gives them a sense of fun. It allows them to be kids for a little while, at least." I nod in agreement. As a kid, I thought it was the absolute best when Mom bought me a new coloring book. I always made it last as long as possible, only coloring a small amount each day.

We walk down a short hallway to a dining area. "This is the dining room. We have tea and coffee-making facilities that are accessible to our ladies. A microwave, fridge, stove, and toaster. We want the women that stop in here for any length of time to have a sense of independence. Often, they've lost that in their situation."

The tables are arranged as you would find in any restaurant. At the last shelter I volunteered, the dining room looked more like a mess hall. Long stainless steel tables with chairs on either side. It didn't allow for this level of personal interaction.

"Are you available to stay and help tonight?"

"Absolutely. Put me to work."

"Great, I might get you to come back and restock the counter over here with tea and coffee." I nod. "Also, on the nights you volunteer, feel free to grab a meal and join the ladies. We find it a great way to interact with the women in a way that's non-threatening and less invasive. They tend to open up more about their situation when you share a meal with them."

I'm loving the sound of this place. "That sounds like a great approach."

Simone gives me one of her warm smiles. "We do our best to make our ladies feel comfortable and at home." She guides me out of the dining room and into the kitchen. "This is where the meal prep and cooking takes place." A small woman, probably in her fifties, with bright pink hair is checking something in the oven. "This is Rhonda, our cook."

"Hi, Rhonda." I give her a small wave.

"Rhonda. This is Molly. Molly is going to be volunteering with us. She recently moved all the way from Portland, Maine."

Rhonda wipes her hands on the side of her pants and holds out her hand. I shake it. "Wow. That's a long way away. What made you move over here?"

I shrug and swallow down the lump that always forms at

the thought of why I've moved all the way to the opposite side of the country. "Wanted a fresh start, I guess."

"Well, it's great to have you on board. We can always do with more volunteers."

"I'm excited about getting started."

"I'm giving Molly the tour. Then she's going to come through to top up the tea and coffee center. If there's anything you need her to do, let her know."

Rhonda nods and waves us away. "Rhonda's been with us since we opened. She has quite the story to tell and will happily share it with you."

"I would imagine there are a lot of stories within these walls." Some of them may even be similar to Mom's.

"You bet." She waves her arm out as we enter a large dormitory. "This is one of our dormitories. We have three dormitories. Twelve beds in each. This dormitory doesn't have any cribs. It's for women who don't have children."

The room has twelve simple beds, divided by low panels to offer a semblance of privacy. There's a single lockable cabinet and a large drawer beneath each bed. The area is spotless—ready and waiting for tonight's guests. Simone shows me through the other two dorms and then takes me to the back of the building.

"Here we have ten small rooms which have two beds and cribs in each. We can have up to twenty women staying for up to six weeks at a time. It's enough time to help them get on their feet. As you're probably already aware, not all women are ready or at the point where they trust they can make the change toward a life away from the streets."

I nod. "Yeah. Some women don't have that trust in themselves that they're good enough to win and hold on to a job, which makes it difficult to gain the funds to create a home environment."

Simone hums her agreement.

The rooms are compact but offer greater privacy than the dorms we walked through earlier. Simple furniture of drawers and a wardrobe offering the feeling of permanency. We keep moving through the building to a couple of meeting rooms.

"We have Kelly, a counselor, who comes through each morning to eat breakfast with the ladies. She talks with them about their future. Any plans, dreams, and hopes they might have. Then she works with the ladies to help make things happen. We also have Jodie. She comes to us from Women's and Children's Services. She guides the women toward any assistance they're entitled to. Fortunately, we also have access to pro bono lawyers to help disentangle the women from toxic relationships when they're ready to do so."

"This place is amazing and the services you're providing for the women are incredible." I'm impressed by everything they have on offer for the women who come through this facility.

She tips her head, offering me a pleased smile. "We do our best. Our founder was once homeless, so she has a good understanding of what needed to be offered to the women."

That makes this place even more impressive. "Well, it shows. I can't wait to get started."

Simone laughs. "I love your enthusiasm. Let's get you back to the dining room. I know you said you're hopeless in the kitchen, but do you mind helping Rhonda tonight?"

"Of course not. I'm happy to help wherever you need."

We head back to the kitchen and Rhonda shows me where the stock is so that I can ensure the tea and coffee counter is well stocked. Women and children begin to trickle in, and I introduce myself throughout the evening.

Tonight's dinner is roast beef and vegetables, followed by chocolate pudding and custard, served buffet style. I learn

Rhonda keeps the kitchen open until nine p.m. to ensure any late stragglers don't go to bed on an empty stomach. Even if women miss out on a bed for the night, they're encouraged to stay for a meal. The last place I volunteered closed the kitchen at seven-thirty and too bad if you came in late.

After dinner, I help Rhonda with the cleanup. Around ten, things have grown quiet. "We close the doors at ten. So, the women need to get here before then, or they don't get a bed for the night. Often the beds fill by six-thirty, anyway. It would be incredibly rare to still have a space available this late."

"Ah, there she is. I see Rhonda kept you busy for the entire evening." Simone breezes into the dining room a few minutes after ten. "How was your first day on the job?"

I blow out a tired but happy breath. After the busyness of today and then again tonight, I'm dead on my feet, but I feel amazing. "It was great. The women certainly appreciated the nutritious meal and a chance to sit and relax without having to watch over their shoulders."

Simone nods. "Yep. This is a safe place where they can let their guard down." She claps her hands together. "We close the doors at ten. We don't expect you to stay past that time. When do you think you'd like to come back?"

"Oh, uhm, maybe on Tuesday? Would it be okay if I volunteered on Tuesdays and Thursdays to start?" I shuffle on my feet, hopeful they'll be happy to have me.

"Absolutely. That'll be fantastic. You go home and get some rest and we'll see you on Tuesday."

A warm feeling fills my stomach, and I can't stop my smile. I've been in this city for less than a week and I have a job and now I have a place where I can give back to the community. Life's looking pretty great. Stepping toward Simone, I wrap my arms around her. I hope she doesn't mind, but I'm incredibly thankful for this opportunity. I need to hug her.

Simone chuckles. "It's like you're already part of the family. Right, Rhonda?"

My eyes sting and the lump in my throat feels more like a boulder at her use of the word 'family'. I guess I didn't realize how much I loved and needed my family until they were gone. I duck my head to hide the tears I'm fighting to keep at bay. "Thank you." I step over to Rhonda and embrace her too.

"It's been heaps of fun working with you. Thanks for being patient with me and showing me the ropes. Next week, I'll be an expert from the time I walk in the door."

Rhonda chuckles. "It was my pleasure. You're an easy study. I'll see you on Tuesday."

I grab my things, and Simone walks me out. "Where did you park your car?"

"Just across the street." I point in the direction I parked.

"When you come on Tuesday, there's parking around the back. Park out there, okay?" She points to a driveway at the side of the building, and I follow with my eyes.

What a relief to know I have a safer place to park my car in the future. "That's great. I was a little concerned about leaving my car on the street."

She nods. "Yeah. It's not the greatest area, but it's tough to find a building large enough to suit our needs at the right price. So, this is where we ended up."

"Okay. Well, bye. Thanks for everything."

"No. Thank you. It's been a pleasure and we'll see you on Tuesday."

I head down the steps as Simone locks the doors behind me. Even though I'm completely exhausted, I know I have a pep in my step and a smile on my face. It's been a great day. First, helping Max to help the single parents and then tonight, helping all the women who will spend tonight at *Shelter*.

I pause, looking up at the night sky. Tears sting the back of my eyes and I swallow past the lump in my throat. "It's such a great place, Mom. You'd love it here." A breeze blows a lock of hair across my forehead, and it reminds me of the times Mom would gently push my bangs out of my eyes as a child. The tears become too much to contain and fall at the memory. I scurry to my car, locking myself inside so I can have my moment in safety.

—molly—

As I CROUCH DOWN TO COLLECT THE DIRT I'VE SWEPT together in the workshop, I smile to myself. Max was clearly shocked when I pulled out the broom to clean up at closing time. I've thoroughly enjoyed my first week at my new job. Max is a great boss and I think I'm going to be very happy here working with him. He works incredibly hard every single minute of every single day. I'm not sure when he had time to do his office work because he's always fully booked, with a minimum of two cars in the bays at a time. Even on Thursdays, the day he doesn't take any bookings, he's crazy busy if not busier.

I think I fell a little for my new boss last Thursday when I discovered the reason he doesn't take bookings. I mean, I'm pretty sure I developed an instant crush on him based on his looks alone, once I got past his gruff demeanor when we first met, but over the past week, he's been nothing but kind to me. He even bought lunch for me each day, which has helped me make my meager stash of food last longer.

"Are you ready to go home?" Max's deep voice reverberates through the workshop. Tilting my head back, I catch my breath as my eyes land on him in navy shorts and a white T-shirt, a bag slung over his shoulder. A navy logo of a knight's helmet surrounded by the words, *Monday Knights*, sits on his right pec. The T-shirt hugs his torso, showing the ridges of his stomach and the outline of his chest. Glancing down, I notice he has great thighs—powerful. For an older guy, he's in great shape. I wonder if he realizes how good-looking he is because he doesn't come across like he does. "Molly?" I realize I haven't answered him.

"Uh, I need to finish the cleanup for the day. Then I'll be on my way. Sorry if I'm holding you up."

"You don't need to apologize *or* clean. You know I have a cleaner come through to do it."

"I can do it as part of my job. To be honest, you don't have enough office work to keep me busy for the entire week. I'm happy to add this to my duties and save you some money."

He moves closer to me, towering over my crouched body. "I've been getting through a lot more work since you started because I don't have to keep stopping to answer calls or chase up parts. I don't want anything to distract you from doing that work."

I stand. We're only a couple of feet apart and the overhead light is highlighting the green flecks in his eyes. "It won't inter-fere. I'll do all of that and then do the cleaning before the shop opens and after it closes. No problem."

He studies me closely, thinning his lips, then nods slowly. "Okay. But that means I'll pay you what I would normally pay the cleaner. You don't need to clean every day either. I only have the cleaner come through twice a week."

I shuffle my feet, uncomfortable with the idea that he thinks I'm doing it to get more money. "I wasn't offering to do the cleaning for extra money. You're paying me enough to do both jobs already. I was hoping to save *you* some money."

He drops his bag, then turns on his heel to head back to the office. "We'll work it out." He calls over his shoulder as he disappears inside. I notice the number seven on the back of his shirt with STANFIELD in bold print across the top. I crouch back down to sweep up the mess and a couple of minutes later, he returns to me with a set of keys and the code for the alarm. "You may as well have a set of keys in case I'm late or need to leave before you." He shows me how to work the alarm system, which is similar to the one at my last job. "Make sure you lock everything up tight, okay? I have a lot of money tied up in the tools and equipment, not to mention the project car I'm working on." He nods his head to the farthest bay and the car I've been sketching.

"Don't worry. I get how important it is to keep this place secure. You can trust me." He studies me for a long moment and my body heats under his gaze. I'm going to need to shut down my reaction; a crush on my hot boss is not something I can afford. I need to sort myself out before I even think about getting involved with anyone, especially this sexy man.

Once I'm on my own, I turn up the music and dance around as I sweep. I've missed my morning run for a while now and I desperately need to move my body. I freeze in place when I realize I'm happy for the first time in weeks.

Mom would want me to move forward and be happy, but I'm quickly filling up with guilt. Mom never let anything stop her or slow her down, and she shared the importance of moving forward with me. She always said that it was okay to have my time for wallowing when something didn't work out, but then I had to pick myself up, make a plan, and move forward. She wouldn't want me to dwell on my losses, but it's tough when I've lost so much.

Without my family, I feel adrift; they were my anchor, my port that I knew I could always rely on. Now, I only have myself and it's a scary prospect. I think about Mom when she ran away from home: seventeen, pregnant, and completely alone. Living in her car and never knowing where she was going to get her next meal. She must have been terrified for her future, but she made it through. If she can do it with a baby on the way, I can do it too.

I wipe away the tears tracking down my cheeks and finish my task more somberly. Turning everything off, I secure the building, and head to the location I found close by on the weekend. It means I'm not using a lot of gas commuting to and from work, saving me some precious dollars until I get paid on Friday. The sports field comes into view as do the dozens and dozens of cars and trucks filling the parking lot. My lungs deflate in disappointment.

Teenagers are playing multiple games of soccer as grown men run laps around the perimeter of the field. I doubt I'm going to find a park while everyone's here. Driving past, a matte black Dodge Charger catches my eye. At lunchtime, Max said he was playing soccer tonight and he was dressed for sport when he left the workshop. I'm guessing this is where he is. The temptation to stop and watch him play is strong and after a few seconds of internal debate, I decide to do it. I'll stay away from the action, so he won't see me.

I eventually find a park at the far end of the lot and sit on the hood of my car to watch the action. Once everyone leaves, I can move my car to the spot behind the building where I normally park. It's mostly hidden from the road, and nobody's bothered me on the nights I've used it.

Watching the teenage kids playing brings a lump to my throat. Ethan loved playing soccer. He always moved with ease, maneuvering the ball away from their goal toward their strikers and the opposing team's goal. He would dodge left and right between his opponents with a bright smile because he was doing something that he truly loved. I wipe my cheeks as my emotions get the better of me yet again. Shaking my head mildly, I smile at the memory of him receiving a trophy last season for being the fairest and best player on his team. It's stashed away with all of my other treasures.

A group of men run past, laughing and pushing at each other, shirts tucked into the back of their shorts, leaving their torsos sweaty and bare.

Oh, boy!

This really was a good idea. I think this might become my favorite Monday night activity.

Another group follows behind and I notice they're wearing the same-colored shorts and T-shirts Max had on when he left. These guys are equally bare and equally sweaty. My eyes catch on a dark head of hair above everyone else in the group. My heartbeat picks up speed as he smiles at his friend. I duck my head at the last second, hoping he doesn't notice me. As they run past, I raise my eyes to find him staring directly at me over his shoulder. Shit, he's caught me. He raises his eyebrows at me, gifting me a gorgeous smile, then turns forward to continue his run with his teammates. He passes by once more before they stop to do some stretches and run some warm-up drills.

Three whistles blow, indicating the end of the teenage games. The boys leave the field after congratulating the winning team and the men make their way onto the field. I wish I had some snacks to enjoy while I watch Max play his game, but I need to be sparing with the food I have. He already knows I'm here; I may as well move closer to the field so I can enjoy the game properly. I rummage through my car to dig out a blanket to sit on and take up a spot on the sidelines. The guys get into position, and I'm pleased to see that Max takes up the same position Ethan used to play.

For forty-five minutes, I watch the guys run, dribble, and pass the ball from player to player. Max's team is getting hammered by the other team. My voice is becoming hoarse from all the cheering I'm doing, and it feels great to have a genuine smile and enjoy the moment. I'm not thinking about my worries or where I'm going to sleep tonight. I'm having fun, like any other woman my age. The guys move off the field during halftime, grabbing drinks and laughing amongst themselves. I figure, while they're taking a break, I'll use the bathroom facilities before they're locked for the night.

Max is leaning up against the wall as I step out of the building, his arms crossed over his chest, his legs crossed at the ankles. His posture looks casual, but his face is another matter. His eyebrows are drawn down low and his mouth is tight. Glancing across to the field, I see the game has already started. He notices me and stands straight, towering over me. "Are you okay?"

I look down at myself, my eyes scanning all around. "Yeah, why?" It's funny. I thought the first thing he would ask about is why I'm here watching him play soccer.

"You were in the bathroom for a long time. I got ... worried." I'm stunned he noticed. It took me a while, because I brushed my teeth, and wiped myself down in all the important places since I won't get a shower tonight.

"I'm fine, truly. You don't need to miss your game for me." I wave my arm out toward the field. He studies me closely, then nods his head once.

"You sticking around 'til the end?" he asks as he jogs backward away from me.

I have nothing else to do or anywhere else to be, so I shrug. "Yeah, I figured I'd wait so I could congratulate the other team on hammering your ass into the ground." I snicker.

His eyebrows shoot up and a sexy half-smile touches his lips. "We'll see." He turns and jogs straight onto the field and I can't believe he left his teammates a man down while he was checking on me.

The last half of the game is intense. Max's team has upped the ante, scoring three goals in twenty-five minutes and not allowing any past their defense. They need to hold the other team until the end of the game, and they'll have the win.

In the last five minutes, the other team hits the back of the net, leveling the score. The excitement and energy are palpable on the field and off as Max wins the ball from the center pass and expertly dribbles it down the wing before passing it to their striker. I hold my breath as he lines the ball up and strikes the ball with a powerful force. Only seconds are left on the clock as the ball hits the back of the net. Max and the other guy go ballistic, running toward each other and falling over in an all-out hugfest.

The whistle blows three times, and their other teammates join in, piling on top of the pair, and jumping up and down as though they've won the World Cup. I'm cheering and celebrating on the sidelines as though they've won the Cup. It's crazy good!

I'm jumping around like a madwoman when a pair of muscular arms wrap around my body from behind, spinning me around, and lifting me off of my feet. My heart rate spikes until I realize it's only Max. His smile is wide and his eyes are sparkling with sheer elation. Sweat trickles down the side of his face, his hair sticking to his head, and he looks so freaking good. "I guess you won't need to congratulate the other team, hey?" He puts me down and I'm disappointed that I'm no longer trapped against his body.

I fake pout, shaking my head. "Very disappointing to see them come undone like that. They showed such promise."

"Oh yeah? Are you some kind of soccer expert?" My mood drops as I remember all the hours spent watching soccer games on television and attending practices and matches for Ethan. "Are you okay?"

I mustn't have hidden my thoughts well enough. Looking back up at Max, I nod. "Yeah." I clear my throat, putting a fake smile on my face. "You guys played a great second half and that last goal ..." I mime a chef's kiss. "Beautiful teamwork."

"You wanna come celebrate with me and the boys at Brady's Pub? It's close to here."

I brush off his offer with a flick of my wrist. I'm sure he didn't mean to ask. He's just excited about the win. "I didn't play, so there's no need for me to celebrate."

"You helped us win with your cheering and dancing along the sidelines. You had some sensational moves, by the way." *Is he flirting with me? My hot boss.* "You should celebrate with us." He winks.

"Nah. You go have fun with your teammates. I'll see you at work in the morning."

"You coming, Max?" A couple of the guys call out to Max from several feet away, then they tip their heads to me. "Thanks for the entertainment, Blondie!"

I was so caught up in the excitement of the game and cheering the guys on that I didn't stop to think that I might cause a scene. My cheeks heat and I drop my head to look at my shoes. How embarrassing. "I'm sorry if I caused a scene and embarrassed you."

"You didn't cause a scene, and you definitely didn't embarrass me. Maybe yourself though ..." He laughs, leaving the sentence hanging. He waves them off over his shoulder, calling out, "Meet you at Brady's." His friends walk toward the parking lot, leaving him behind, and I shuffle on my feet. How am I going to get out of this? "C'mon. See, the guys honestly appreciated your support. One drink and some pizza. My buy." When I take my time responding, he asks, "Do you have somewhere else you need to be?"

"No, it's ... uh ... I don't want to intrude." I don't want to tell him I have barely any money to get me by until payday, because he seems like the type of guy who would give me money and I don't want him to do that. It's important to me he doesn't know about my situation.

"You're not intruding. You can follow me." He runs back to collect his things, then drops to the grass at my feet to change out of his cleats. Standing, he pulls his T-shirt over his head, exposing his torso to me at close range. It's the first time I've seen him completely bare. My eyes scan the expanse of toned flesh, pausing above his heart where he has a tattoo. I step closer to get a better look at the inked design in the limited light. My fingers lift without permission to trace over the intricately designed mechanical heart which looks to be inside his chest; the skin having been torn open and pulled out of the way. The muscle in his chest flinches at my touch and I realize how inappropriate it is for me to touch him in this way, so I quickly snatch my fingers back.

My eyes snap up to his. "Sorry. I … I didn't realize I had touched you. I was engrossed in the detailed design."

He glances down at the tattoo. "It's okay. I guess I've become accustomed to it, I forget it's there half the time."

"It's beautifully detailed in its design. The artist is very talented." Dropping my eyes away from his, they catch on another tattoo on the opposite side of his body. On his flank, he has an open wound that is bleeding oil instead of blood. I smile as I look back up at his face. "I'm sensing a theme here." I wave my finger around in the general direction of his torso.

"Lincoln," he thumbs over his shoulder toward the parking lot, "did them for me. He owns a tattoo shop." He shrugs. "I've always loved cars. Looking at them, working with them. It's in my blood." He runs his hand over the heart tattoo and then down further across the wound.

I nod. "I can see that."

He pulls a fresh shirt over his head, stealing my view. "C'mon, let's go or there'll be nothing left by the time we get to the pub."

"Do other women join you guys after your game?"

"Hell, no. No women allowed."

My eyebrows jump up. "Then why are you inviting me?" I wave my arm down my body and his eyes track the action. "In case you didn't notice, I'm a woman."

"Believe me, I noticed." His eyes slowly make their way back to mine. There's heat in them if I'm not mistaken. "I'm nominating you as head of our cheer squad, so you're part of the team now." He wraps his arm around my neck and drags me along with him toward the parking lot. "You wanna come with me? I can drop you back here afterward."

I push at him, wiggling from his hold. "Ewww, you smell." Not really, but he was making my stomach flip, and I needed some space to keep myself in check. It looks as though he's not going to take no for an answer and a slice of pizza and a pint of beer sounds awesome right about now. "Sure. That sounds good, but can I trust you not to drink and drive?"

"You have my word. I'll keep you safe. Promise." Even though I don't know him very well, I get the sense he's a man of his word.

CHAPTER 10

—max—

I HAVE TO ADMIT; I WAS COMPLETELY WRONG ABOUT MOLLY. I made assumptions about the girl sleeping in her car that were way off base. Yeah, she's fucking gorgeous, but she doesn't shove it in your face and her looks don't seem to be her priority. She's a hard worker who isn't afraid to get her hands dirty. Over the last three weeks, I've found her to be thoughtful, sweet, and friendly, if not a little guarded. Her capabilities in the office have helped to streamline some aspects that I never knew needed streamlining. And tonight, well, that was the icing on the cake. When I spotted her sitting on the hood of her car while I was warming up, I couldn't stop myself from showing off a little. I'm a decade older than her—not to mention I'm her boss—and have no business trying to attract her attention. But I wanted her to look at me and to like what she saw.

I grab her slender hand as we step over the threshold into Brady's. "The guys are usually in the back booths in the corner. Follow me." Not once on the way here did she worry about what she's wearing or the fact that she had no makeup on or that her hair is a mess. *It's fucking refreshing.*

Those dimples I love so much, make an appearance as she

nods her head. She's still an enigma. She's shared very little about where she's from or what brought her to this city. It's not my business, but I sense she doesn't have many people around her—if any at all—and I wonder why that is. I guess I have to be patient and give her time to get used to me, to trust me enough to share her story. And I think she's going to have quite a story. Sometimes I catch her lost in thought, her eyes glassy and I wonder what's made her sad.

The boys spot us through the crowd, their faces lighting up at the sight of Molly. There was a fair amount of discussion about her during the half-time break until I announced she was my new office manager and told them to cut it out. For some reason, I didn't like them talking about her like she's just a hot body and pretty face. She's so much more than that.

Finn stands, allowing the two of us to slide in, then he takes his position at the end of the booth. He needs to sit on the end in case he needs to see to anything behind the bar. "Pizzas should be out in a minute."

The guys pat their stomachs, showing they're ready to demolish the dozen or so pizzas Finn supplies each week during soccer season. We try to make up for his generosity by buying drinks and eating here at other times during the week.

"Guys, this is Molly, my new office manager. Molly, this is Finn, Gary, Aaron, Lincoln, Brent, Rob, Sean, Matthew, Thomas, and Kevin." I point to each of my friends as I introduce them. "We'll have a quiz at the end of the night to see if you remember their names." Her eyes widen as I laugh. "Only joking."

She waves timidly at the group. "Hi, guys." She chuckles. "I don't think I'll remember all of your names, but I'll do my best."

Everyone says hello and offers her a free pass on remembering everyone's names. Gary stands. "Anyone want a drink while I'm at the bar?"

I pull out my wallet. "I'll take a beer." Turning toward Molly, I ask, "How about you, Dimples? What would you like to drink?"

She chuckles at my nickname but doesn't question it. I'm guessing she's probably been called it more than once. "I'll have the same as you, thanks."

Gary taps the table, takes my money, then heads up to the bar. He has to weave his way through the crowd. I swear it gets busier and busier every Monday night.

Aaron grabs Molly's attention. "So, Molly. What's it like working for this ogre?" He points his half-empty beer toward me.

"Fuck off! I'm a good boss, aren't I, Molly?" I nudge her arm with mine.

"Shut up! She can't answer honestly now that you've said that." Aaron laughs. He gathers his composure, locking eyes with the girl next to me. "Seriously. Is he being good to you?"

She studies me for a few moments, her eyes scanning my face, then she turns her focus to Aaron. "He's been a great boss so far. I have no complaints and I'm not only saying that because he's sitting next to me." She bumps her shoulder against mine and gifts me with her dimples. I think I could grow addicted to her smiles.

The servers bring out the pizzas and Gary returns with our drinks. The talk around the tables dies down as we dig in. It's not until we've demolished almost all the pizzas that we slow down and chatter starts up again.

"How's Layla? Is she feeling any better?" I ask Gary.

He smiles at me, wiping his mouth. "She *is* feeling better. I was going to tell you guys something earlier, but we got sidetracked with our new cheerleader over there." He tips his head toward Molly, then stands. "Guys, if I can have your attention for a moment." Everyone quiets down, even the other patrons close by. "I've been wanting to tell you guys for a few weeks now, but Layla insisted we wait. Layla's pregnant. We're expecting our first baby!" His smile takes up his entire face as we all jump up to congratulate him. Even Molly congratulates him as though she's known him for years. Well, that explains Layla's sickness over the last few months.

Gary pulls out a square piece of paper to pass around. "Here's our first baby photo." He hands it to Molly first, and she studies it closely, then passes it to me. A pang of longing hits me out of the blue. I'm getting up there in age and I'm wondering if I'll ever meet someone and have a family of my own, or am I destined to always be the favorite uncle?

Okay, I'm the only uncle, but I'm still the favorite!

"If you ever need a babysitter, I'd be happy to help. I used to love looking after my baby brother." Molly offers. She never mentions much at all about her family or her life, so I'm surprised by the mention of a brother. I'm not sure she's mentioned him before. I'm dying to ask her about her family, but I sense it's not something she wants to talk about since she never brings them up. As much as I want to ask her more, delve into her history, this is not the time nor the place.

"Thanks. I'll let Layla know. It's been tough trying to get pregnant. I'm not sure she'll ever want to leave Junior behind." He huffs out a short laugh.

I feel like an asshole. I never knew they were even trying to conceive let alone that they were having trouble. "Well, congrats, man. I'm thrilled for you both. You're gonna make great parents," I tell him.

He glances down at the beer in his hands. "Thanks, man."

I spot Molly trying to hide a yawn. "You want me to drop you back to your car?"

She looks around the table. "You guys aren't done here, are you?"

I shrug. "We can leave whenever we're ready. I don't mind."

"If you're sure. Suddenly, I'm exhausted." She gives me an embarrassed smile.

I stand, then help her up. "See ya, guys. We're out."

Everyone says goodbye and I lead Molly out through the crowd, which doesn't seem to have thinned out any.

"I genuinely liked your friends. They seem like a great bunch of guys." She finishes her sentence with another yawn.

"Yeah. We've all known each other for a while now. Been playing as a team since we finished high school."

"I bet Gary and Layla are excited about their new baby."

I turn to glance at her in the limited light inside my car. She's genuinely excited for my friend. A man she's only just met. I hate to compare her to Mona, but she never gave my friends the time of day. She seemed to think she was better than them. Better than everyone.

"I didn't know they had been trying to have a baby. I felt like a real asshole to learn that tonight."

"It's probably not something they wanted people to know. You shouldn't feel bad about it." I pull into the parking lot at the sports field and stop behind Molly's car. "Thanks for tonight. It was heaps of fun. I'll see you at work tomorrow."

"Thanks for joining us. The boys enjoyed having you there." I lift my chin toward her car. "Get in. I'll follow you back to your motel to make sure you're safe."

Her head snaps up to mine. "Oh, you don't have to do that. I'm fine."

"I know I don't have to. I want to make sure you get home safe."

She gives me a tight smile but doesn't argue. Hopefully, she's learned that I don't back down easily on important things and that her safety is important to me. I reverse, giving her space to leave the parking lot, and then follow her fifteen minutes down the road to a dive motel. Slowing, I watch her drive into the central parking lot of the motel, which leads to the rooms. I don't like where she's staying; it looks too rundown.

I wonder if I should stop and walk her to her door. Perhaps that would be too much. I'll see her at work tomorrow. I don't think she'd appreciate my chivalry at this point, since I've already hijacked her evening.

CHAPTER 11

—max—

THE SUN IS ON THE RISE AS I MAKE MY WAY TO WORK. I CAN'T believe Molly's been working with me for a month already. The difference has been incredible. My home life has returned to being my break away from work and I'm able to work on more cars because I don't have to deal with as many interruptions. The Sprint is almost ready to sell because I've had my mornings free to focus on her. That woman has been a godsend. I'm grateful she decided to sleep behind my workshop all those weeks ago when she first arrived in town.

I glance across at the sports field where we lost our game last night. Even though we lost, I still feel energized by the challenge we gave the other team in the second half. It was a damn close game in the end. Turning back to face forward, a blue Jetta parked behind the building catches my eye. Changing lanes, I make my way into the parking lot and pull in behind the car that I'm pretty sure belongs to Molly.

Jumping out, I walk over to check it out.

What in the actual fuck?

She's fucking asleep in the front passenger seat, blankets up at the windows. I'm guessing to give her some semblance of privacy.

I don't want to scare her, so I gently tap the front window where the shade has slipped down to get her attention. She doesn't hear me, so I tap again, slightly louder. Meanwhile, my agitation at seeing her sleeping in a fucking parking lot is growing. I'm pissed that she's put herself at risk like this. What the fuck was wrong with the motel I followed her to last week? I tap louder and she finally stirs. Her eyes open slowly, and she looks around as if trying to locate the source of the noise. Her eyes widen and she bolts upright when her steely eyes finally connect with mine.

I gesture for her to open her door and it seems to take an age for her to do so. Moving around to her door once the lock disengages, I rip it open, surprised it doesn't come off from the hinges.

"Why in the fuck are you sleeping here in your car? What happened to the motel?" I snap.

She tosses her blanket away and climbs out of her car. Her hair's disheveled and her eyes are full of sleep, but she still looks stunning. Straightening her shoulders, her nipples press against the T-shirt she has on as she pulls her hair out of the tie and works her long hair into a fresh ponytail, making her tits jiggle.

"It's not your concern, Max. You're my boss. What I do with my time away from work is not your business," she firmly states, as though it doesn't fucking matter that she's sleeping in her car in a public parking lot.

I work to temper my anger. "Did something happen at the motel that you didn't feel safe there?" As if she would feel safe in a fucking parking lot.

She looks down at her socks, shuffling from foot to foot. "I'd rather not talk about it. I need to get ready for work. I'll see you there soon."

I try to soften further. Perhaps coming at her like a tyrant isn't the way to go. Running my fingers through my hair, I notice her eyes follow the action. "Look, I'm sorry. I was worried about you when I saw you sleeping in your car. I thought you were staying in a motel; that you were safe. I shouldn't have snapped at you like that." Stepping back, I give her space. "I'll, uh, see you at work. Feel free to use the shower in the office, if you need."

She nods, her posture softening. "Thank you." Molly's eyes have a suspicious sheen to them as she turns away from me and I take the hint, leaving her to do whatever she needs to do.

Footsteps sound across the workshop floor as I'm polishing the final panel on the Sprint. I'll be able to put her up for sale this week. It's been a long time coming. Glancing across, I see Molly carrying her things into the office, her head down low. I'm glad she's taken up my offer to use the bathroom. Heading across the road, I grab a breakfast sandwich for each of us. I have a proposition for my employee, and I want to make sure she can make a decision with a clear head, which means she needs food.

The shower turns off, and I set about making two cups of coffee. Her steps stall as she opens the bathroom door, her eyes locked on the office desk. I have two seats set at the desk and two sandwiches. I give her a smile as I carry our coffee to the desk and gesture for her to take a seat opposite me. Looking down at her feet, she slowly makes her way over to me and takes a seat, keeping her spine ramrod straight.

"Thank you," she whispers, eyeing the sandwich in front of her. She takes a sip of her coffee and then her first bite of the breakfast I bought for her. I keep my mouth shut for now, opting to eat in silence.

The atmosphere is stifling and uncomfortable. I've always found her company to be easy and relaxed but this morning is different. It's as though an immense brick wall has been built between us.

I don't fucking like it.

Halfway through my breakfast, I can't take it any longer. "I'm guessing you still haven't found somewhere permanent to live?" I keep my tone neutral, hoping we can have a conversation about her living arrangements.

Her shoulders rise and fall. She shakes her head in the negative, not making eye contact with me. "Uh, no."

"Do you have any family here?" I prod.

"No." Still, her eyes remain downcast.

"What about friends?"

She shakes her head. "No."

The situation is worse than I thought, and I can't believe the asshole that I am and that I didn't push sooner. "Can I ask why you moved here if you had nobody for support?" I know it's a fucking personal question and none of my business, but I can't suppress the questions running rampant in my head.

She shrugs, then slowly brings her silver gaze up to mine. "I don't know. It seemed like as good a place as any to start over. My mom grew up here and I wanted to see the place for myself." She's curled in on herself, trying to make herself as small as possible.

I don't fucking like it.

I want to know why she needed a place to start over, but I need to focus on the matter at hand. Getting her off the street. "If your mom grew up here, maybe you have some family that you've never met." I offer. "Have you thought to look them up?"

"I don't know, to be honest. My mom left when she was

seventeen." She shrugs again like it doesn't matter, but I caught the hurt in her eyes.

"It might be worth a shot to look for your mom's family." I hedge, trying not to be too pushy, but I can't stand the thought that she has nobody. I mean, she has me, but I'm only her boss and maybe we have the early stages of a friendship but that's not enough.

She hums. "Maybe." Standing, she takes her wrapper to the trash and her cup to the sink before coming back to collect mine.

"I have something to show you. Come with me." I take hold of her hand and tug her toward the stairs. The smooth, unblemished skin of her hand is a stark contrast to my stained work-roughened one. The other thing I notice is how well our hands fit together. It makes me wonder how well other parts of us might fit together. My dick decides he likes that idea and I will him back to sleep.

"Oh-kay," she slowly says as we take the first step.

I open the door at the top of the stairs and move to the side to allow Molly space to enter, her rose scent tickling my nose as she passes me. "I was thinking you might like to move in here until you find a better place." I swing my arm out. With wide eyes, Molly steps into the small apartment. "It's not much, but it's better than that motel or your car. I can't believe I didn't think to tell you about this space sooner."

She's quiet for long moments as she walks around the space, bypassing the changing table and portable playpen I use on Thursdays, checking out the bedroom with its double bed and small bathroom-come-laundry. The apartment isn't anything special, but it was good enough for me until I could afford my home.

I move over to the exterior door. "This is another door, so you can come and go as you please without worrying about the alarm in the workshop. It has a separate alarm system from the workshop. You can set it here." I show her the panel near the door, and she steps out, orienting herself with where the stairs lead.

We move back inside. "How much would the rent be?" she asks as she opens and closes the kitchen cabinets, before checking out the small fridge and microwave.

I think this could make or break her accepting my offer. I shrug. "It's sitting here empty, gathering dust. You'd be doing me a favor if you moved in and looked after the place for me until I decide if I want to rent it out."

Her eyes narrow as she looks across at me. "What? You'd let me live here for free?"

"Yeah, sure. Unless you wanted to pay some rent. I honestly don't care." I tuck my hands in my pockets, trying to appear nonchalant as she looks around the space. "Maybe you could clean it up for me and make it presentable or something." She leans her hip against the kitchen cabinet, the sun streaming through the kitchen window creates a halo behind her almost-white hair. She peers around the space, as dust motes caused by our movement float in the air, and I feel I need to sweeten the pot to get her to agree. I sense she doesn't want a free ride. "What about this? How about you clean the workshop and office in exchange for living here, instead of me paying you the extra money? Would that work for you?" Holding my breath, I hope she accepts my offer. I don't want her fucking sleeping in that damn car another night. I'm certain that without her explicitly telling me, that's where she's been sleeping since she arrived in town. That's why she kept all her stuff in her car. It makes me feel like an asshole that I didn't know. "Just until you find your own place." I rush to add.

She looks at me, biting her lip and fidgeting with her bracelet. With a single nod, she says yes, and I take a breath. Stepping forward, I pick her up and spin her around, careful not to knock her into the two-seater couch. Smiles fill both of our faces and I feel the relief of her acceptance of my offer right down to my bones. Setting her back on her feet, I grab her hand. "C'mon, let's go get your stuff. You can move in now." I want to get her settled in before she can change her mind.

She tugs on my hand, and I turn toward her. "Hold on. It's almost time to open the workshop and I need to clean the downstairs bathroom. I can move some of my stuff during my lunch break and after work. There's no rush." She glances around the space again and tucks her hair behind her ear. "I actually wouldn't mind giving it a quick clean before I move my stuff in. Is that okay?"

I consider the space. "Of course. Do whatever you need to do to make this place yours. If you want to paint the walls and stuff, feel free. I'll even help on my day off," I offer.

"Oh, that's okay. It's already nicer than any place I've lived before." Molly slams her mouth shut; her lips closed tight as though she's said too much.

I need to move the moment forward, so she doesn't dwell on the fact she's let something from her previous life slip. "It *is* pretty nice." I lean against the doorjamb. "I lived here for a few years until I could afford to buy my house. The place isn't huge, but it's cozy." I smile and she gifts me those gorgeous dimples of hers. "It's pretty sparse. If you need any other furniture, just shout out. I'm sure we can source whatever you need."

She glances around again, cataloging the main area. "Nope. I think I'm good for now. I can add stuff slowly, but this is enough for me to be comfortable." Molly steps into my body, wrapping her scent and arms around me and pressing her tits against my torso. Her body fits perfectly against mine. "Thank you. Thank you so much for this. You have no idea what it means to me that you've offered me this apartment. I promise I'll look after it. I'll be the best tenant you've ever had."

I laugh. "That won't be hard to do. You're the only tenant I've ever had." She playfully slaps my chest. The agitation I was feeling this morning when I found her in the parking lot has vanished. Something inside me settles, knowing I've been able to help her in some small way and that she'll be safe from now on.

At three, I sent Molly to get herself sorted. During lunch, she said she has somewhere she needs to be after work, so I wanted to give her time to move her stuff in. I'm not sure where she needs to be; I didn't think she knew anyone else in the city, but maybe I was wrong.

Locking up the workshop, I clean up quickly, then head upstairs to check if she needs any help. The door's open, so I step into the apartment, noticing she's brought everything upstairs from her car. I wanted to help her with that. I run my fingers through my hair in frustration. I should have checked on her earlier, but I wanted to detail the inside of the Sprint so I can organize for buyers to look at her.

Music is coming from the bedroom, so I make my way to the doorway. The sight that greets me almost has me swallowing my tongue. She's making the bed, but while she's doing it, she's performing the actions of Salt 'n' Pepper's *Push it*. Her ass, wrapped in skintight jeans, thrusting in time to the music, waking up my cock. Adjusting my jeans to make more space, I try to distract my thoughts to calm myself down. I don't need my employee to turn around and find me with a damn pole in my pants. Once I'm under control, I knock on the doorjamb.

"Hey." She spins around, holding her chest, her eyes wide in alarm. "Sorry. Didn't mean to scare you." I gesture over my shoulder. "The door was open, and I wanted to check if you needed any help."

She catches her breath and giggles. "Sorry. I was in my own world." She waves her arm out around the bedroom. "What do ya think?"

It's pretty sparse, but she's full of pride as she waits for my response. "It looks great. This room's never had a feminine touch."

"I love it so much." She's beaming. "Oh shit! What's the time?" She snatches up her phone. "Shit! Shit! Shit! I need to go." She moves around the room on a mission as though I'm not even standing in the doorway.

She grabs a shirt out of the closet, pulls her T-shirt over her head and my eyes lock on her tits, encased in a simple white T-shirt bra like they're a heat-seeking missile. There's nothing sexy about it, and she's not even aware that she's exposed herself in front of me in her panic. As she pulls the fresh shirt over her head, her tits jiggle and my dick decides it likes the view, working its way to the waistband of my jeans. As her head pops through the top, her eyes connect with mine and widen. "Shit! Sorry." She quickly works the shirt down her body, sadly hiding herself from me. Her cheeks flush prettily as she collects her phone and slides her feet into her shoes.

"I'm not." I raise my eyebrows and lift one side of my lips, tucking my hands in the pockets of my jeans, attempting to disguise my hard-on.

She playfully hits my chest as she passes through the doorway. "Sorry. I need to get moving. I don't want to be late."

"Where are you headed tonight?" I've had this unexpected surge of irrational jealousy every time I thought about where she might be going tonight. Is she seeing someone?

Is it my fucking business?

No.

But did that stop me from ruminating over it all afternoon?

Also no.

She checks the outer door's locked and then makes her way to the internal door, waiting for me to follow. "I, uh, signed up to volunteer a couple of nights a week. Even though it's not paid work, I like to be professional. You know? Which means I don't want to be late." She widens her eyes, raises one eyebrow, and tilts her head toward the door, hinting that she wants to get going. "I really need to get moving."

I finally take the hint and step outside so she can lock up. "Sure. Sorry. Are you going to be okay getting back in tonight? Remember, you need to come in through the outer door." I point to the opposite side of the apartment.

We make our way down the stairs. Molly's almost running. "Yeah, no problem. See you tomorrow!" She waves over her shoulder, and I'm left admiring her ass as she climbs into her car.

CHAPTER 12

—molly—

My legs are burning like crazy. It's been ages since I've run and my muscles are reminding me of my laziness. The streets around here aren't all that flat either, adding to my misery.

I suck in lungfuls of air and remind myself that I love to run. It's the thing I love to do to start my day. It settles my mind and helps me to sleep better at night. I haven't had a decent night's sleep since the night of the accident. More nights than not, I wake with images I never saw stuck in my head and it takes ages to find sleep again.

Finally, the workshop comes into view, and I slow my pace until I'm out front. Walking in circles, my chest burns as my lungs attempt to get enough air. Bending at the waist, allowing my hands to drop to my toes, I slowly grasp my ankles, gently stretching my hamstrings, careful not to go overboard on my first day back. Now that I have a proper place to live, I can get back into my usual routine of running every day. The prospect is exciting—*how sad is that?* I work through my cool-down sequence, then climb the outside steps to my apartment.

A smile touches my lips at having my own space. No neighbors making obscene noises or listening to other people's arguments through the paper-thin walls. Mom would be happy with the way things are working out for me. My smile falls as thoughts of her drift through my head.

I miss her.

I miss my brother, Ethan.

I miss Jack.

Looking at my feet as I breach the last step, I wipe the escaping tears from my cheeks and softly smile at my bright pink runners. My last birthday present from my family. Perhaps I should pack them away for safekeeping?

Mom, Jack, and Ethan were so impatient with me as I slowly and carefully unwrapped the box. The sparkly purple paper was far too pretty to tear, and I wanted to save it to cover my newest sketch pad.

"C'mon, Molly. Just rip it for goodness' sake. It'll be your next birthday by the time you open your present," Mom coaxed.

A chuckle escapes at the memory. Jack was incredibly proud of the research he'd done to find the perfect running shoe for me. They were secondhand, but you'd never have known. They were like brand freaking new! I put them on straight away and went for a run with Jack and E. When we got back to the trailer, Mom had a birthday cake sitting on the table, decorated with twenty-six candles.

Unlocking the door, I step inside and toe off my favorite running shoes. Should I pack them away so I can keep them forever? Or should I use them the way my family intended? I ponder the thought as I strip down and head for the shower.

Turning on the faucet, I wait for the hot water to come through. And wait. And wait some more. I stick my hand beneath the flow and pull it back quickly. The water's still freezing. Damn it. I need to have a shower after my run. It's partly why I didn't run while I was living in my car. I couldn't always guarantee the ability to shower afterward. I remember the shower downstairs and decide to make my way down there.

Grabbing my phone, I check the time. Yep. I think I have time to whip downstairs to have a shower and be back up here before Max arrives. I collect my toiletries and make my way down the internal stairs, rush over to turn off the alarm, and then head for the bathroom. Closing myself in the small space, I turn on the hot water.

Yes!

I'm in luck.

I'll have to remember to tell Max about the situation with the hot water when he comes in later.

I work quickly, lathering up, shaving the essential areas, and scrubbing others. Climbing out of the shower, I grab my towel and dry myself, then use my favorite rose-scented moisturizer all over my body.

The door bursts open, and I freeze.

Max glances up, his eyes locking on me, and he freezes in the doorway.

Oh my God!

Neither of us moves and I don't understand why my body won't snap into action so I can hide behind my towel or something. Anything. I'm not the only one who's failing to act, though. He could close the damn door, but he's too busy trailing his eyes all over me. His Adam's Apple bobs up and down with his swallow, and I notice his eyes are darker than usual. Finally, my sensibilities return, and I grab my towel, trying to cover as much of my body as I can.

"Shit! Sorry." Max drops his eyes to the floor, away from me, but doesn't move to close the door to give me privacy. My body flushes at the thought of the man I'm currently crushing on seeing me completely naked.

Did he like what he saw?

Should I even be wondering if he likes my body?

Probably not.

I should tell him to close the door, but the words won't come. "That's okay. You didn't know I was in here and I didn't lock the door. I thought I had more time before you'd be in. It was my mistake." While his eyes are still averted, I move the towel away from my body to wrap it around myself properly. At that moment, he raises his head, his eyes locking on my nakedness *again*. My breathing picks up speed at the darkness in his eyes, and when I drop my eyes down his body, I can't miss the unmistakable bulge pressing behind his zipper. My tongue slips out without permission to lick my lips and my teeth latch onto the bottom pillow.

Max groans and runs his fingers through his hair, messing it up further. It's crazy hot the way he does that. "Fuck!" It's a harsh whispered word on a breath, but I feel its impact right in my solar plexus.

One side of my mouth tilts up at the knowledge that my hot boss is attracted to me. *Little old me.*

"I should … uh …" He thumbs over his shoulder. "I should close this fucking door before I do something stupid." He steps back and closes the door with a sharp snick.

He thinks it would be stupid to do anything with me. My heart cracks at the thought that I misinterpreted his reaction. *How stupid can I be?* Heavy disappointment floods me as all the air in my lungs escapes.

Shit! This is gonna be awkward now. I have to make the walk upstairs in my towel. My threadbare and too-small towel. Tucking the top of the towel in between my breasts to secure it in place, I collect my toiletries and open the bathroom door. When I poke my head out of the bathroom, he's nowhere to be seen. I hold my head up high and walk with a confidence I don't feel across the office toward the stairs. Closing myself inside my private space, I sag against the door.

I know he's older than me; the age difference doesn't

bother me, but maybe it bothers him. Or is it the fact that he's my boss that's the issue? I swallow down my hurt pride and get myself ready for the day.

I chomp down on an apple; enjoying the crispness as the juice trickles down my chin. It's been great to have fresh fruit on the regular after being paid last month. I had to be careful not to go crazy in the grocery store and buy too much produce, reminding myself that I have money in my bank account now and I can go to the store whenever I need.

I can't delay the inevitable any longer. It's time to head downstairs and start work. Wandering to the far end of the workshop, I find Max working on the Sprint in his regular clothes.

"Hey. Sorry about earlier." I point over my shoulder. "You can get changed in the bathroom now." I know he hates working in his regular clothes. He prefers to keep the grease and oil stains on his overalls.

His head snaps up and his eyes skim my body, making it heat under his perusal. I'm fighting not to rub my thighs together to stem the ache he's creating between my legs. When his eyes finally make it back to my face, his eyebrows snap down, causing a crease to form between them, and I want to step forward to smooth it out with my fingers.

"Stop apologizing for everything. It wasn't your fault. It was an accident. I should have noticed the alarm was turned off and double-checked the bathroom before I entered." He tips his head toward the stairs to the apartment. "What's wrong with the shower upstairs?"

"Oh, uhm. The hot water wasn't working. I let it run for a few minutes and it wasn't even warming up a little. I just checked again, and it's still not working. Same with all the faucets upstairs."

His frown lines deepen, and he climbs out of the car, taking long strides toward the upstairs apartment. I almost have to run to keep up with him and I have freakishly long legs. "Lemme take a look." He walks straight to the bathroom-come-laundry and opens a panel on the outer wall, checking the switches.

I had wondered what that panel was for, and now I know. He flicks a switch and then moves to the basin to check the water. After a minute or so, a smile graces his lips. "There ya go. It used to happen to me sometimes. I'm not sure what causes the switch to turn off, but it's easy to flick it back on." He points to the switch in question, and I move in closer to get a proper look. His arm brushes against my boob as he tries to make space for me. He ignores it, but I can't. That simple touch sends fire scorching through my body.

Surely, I'm not the only one feeling this heat between us.

"I'd better get downstairs and open up. See ya down there whenever you're ready." He contorts himself around my body, careful not to touch me at all. My shoulders drop and I sigh.

I need to work on shutting down my crush. With a new resolve, I close the panel, push my shoulders back, and head downstairs. Moving through my regular morning routine, I quickly give the bathroom a once-over before our first client arrives for the day.

CHAPTER 13

—max—

FUCK! I'M IN TROUBLE.

I couldn't peel my eyes away from my office manager's stunning body. She's fucking perfect in every single way. Even the sanctuary between her legs is groomed exactly the way I like it. I don't think I'll ever be able to close my eyes again without seeing the image of her bent over, massaging that fucking addictive rose scent onto her long, smooth legs. I shake my head, trying to clear the image. I should have fucking closed the door. I don't know what came over me. Standing in the doorway like a letch, my eyes greedily soaking up the magnificence that is Molly.

Molly, my fucking *employee*.

Molly, who is a *full decade younger* than me.

Molly, the girl I can't seem to stop thinking about.

Girl. She's definitely not a girl. She's a fully grown, sexy ass woman. Those pink nipples. I groan as my dick expands in my overalls. At least it's not as obvious when I have a hard-on in these.

I need to shut this shit down. She's my employee. I broke

all sorts of rules and regulations today. If she wanted to take me to task over what I did this morning, she'd fucking ruin me.

And you know what? I would fucking stand in that doorway and look my fill all over again.

How fucking stupid is that?

The woman who's never far from my thoughts steps into my peripheral vision. "I made you a coffee since you didn't get one earlier."

I don't raise my eyes. I can't. I'm embarrassed by my behavior this morning. She has a right to have a shower and get dressed in peace. Her boss should not be fucking ogling her in her place of work *or* residence. I groan internally at myself. "Thanks. Just leave it over on the bench, please."

"Sure. No problem." Her voice lacks its usual confident tone. She steps away and then comes back to stand right beside me, her rose scent playing havoc with my dick. I don't think I'll ever be able to smell it again without associating it with Molly. "What are you working on?"

Turning my head slightly, I look at her. Well, that was a fucking mistake. She's peering right at me. Those silver eyes of hers, bright and inquisitive. I return my focus to the cylinder head cover. "Just taking this off so I can replace the gasket." I drop the bolt I was removing down into the engine bay. "Fuck!" I whisper with a harsh breath.

"Oh, sorry. I'll get outta your way." Her thick eyelashes flutter and her cheeks flush. "What time is the guy coming to look at the car?" She tilts her chin across to the Sprint.

"Four-thirty."

"Okay. I'll leave you to it!" She spins on her heel and walks straight back to the office. Her long white-blond hair swishing behind her. I wonder if it's as soft and silky as it looks.

Stop fucking thinking about her hair!

Molly and I manage to get past the awkwardness of the morning and spend the rest of the day doing our respective work. Me in the workshop. Her in the office. Occasionally she comes out to check a serial number for a part, but we both maintain a professional manner.

It feels forced and I don't fucking like it.

When I glance up, Molly's walking toward me with Martin. He's a long-time client of mine. Martin's been watching me slowly restore the Sprint and, a couple of months back, asked me to keep him in mind when I finished the restoration and was ready to sell. He's studying Molly like a science experiment as she brings him over.

I don't like the way he's looking at her. I'm pretty sure he's married with a couple of kids and he's probably old enough to be her father.

I step between him and my girl, blocking his view. Holding out my hand, we shake in greeting. "Martin. How have you been? How's the family?" *Do you like what I did there? I reminded him he's a married family man.*

"Max. They're great. Holly's in her last year of high school. I can't believe how fast she's grown up." He turns his attention to Molly, holding his hand out to her. "And who do we have here?"

I pull her to my side, wrapping my arm around her waist and landing a kiss on the top of her head. Understandably, Molly stiffens in my hold. She's probably wondering what the hell's going on. "This is Molly. She runs the office for me."

Martin's eyebrows almost hit his hairline in surprise at my public display of affection toward my office manager. Fair enough because this would seem highly inappropriate.

Molly slides her hand into his, gifting him with her dimples. "Hi, Martin. Nice to meet you."

He holds her hand a little longer than what's socially acceptable. His eyes locked on hers.

What in the actual fuck?

I pull Molly back slightly, forcing them to disengage. He shakes his head as though he's waking up from a daze. Directing his attention toward the car, I ask, "What do you think of her?"

He tears his eyes away from Molly and looks at the Sprint. "She's gorgeous. Beautiful color!" He glides his hand over the surface. "Is this the original Rangoon Red?"

"Yeah. I wanted to keep her as original as possible." I follow behind him.

He dips down to peer inside. "Is that real leather on the seats and interior panels?"

"Yep. It's as soft as butter." I open the driver's door and gesture for him to take a seat. May as well put him behind the wheel. He runs his hand across the soft leather before situating himself inside. His eyes are taking in every feature and detail as he gets comfortable behind the wheel.

"This is magnificent. You've done a stellar job, Max." His hands glide over the dash and smooth their way around the steering wheel. He grasps the gearshift, and using the clutch, manipulates it through the gears.

"It has new wiring all the way through. Almost everything under the hood is new." I get out of the passenger side. "Come, take a look."

He peels himself away from his admiration of the interior and steps around to the front of the car. I raise the hood and his eyes light up as he releases a low whistle. "Man, this is incredible." He looks across at me. "You are a master."

"Thanks. Here, I'll raise her and you can see beneath the car." I close the doors and press a button to start the car lift, which raises the Sprint. I'm proud of the work I've done on this car. It was a heap of shit when I brought her in, but the body was in reasonable condition, so I knew I could bring her back to life.

Martin lets out another low whistle. Hands in pockets, he walks the length of the car, head tilted back, studying every single inch. "That exhaust system is beautiful. It's a shame it's hidden beneath the car and nobody can appreciate your work."

I laugh. "C'mon. Let's take her for a drive."

I start her up and the beauty purrs like a fucking kitten. Beautiful. I wave to Molly, and we cruise out of the workshop, making a left onto the street. As we're cruising, I fill Martin in on the specs of the car. It's not until we reach the highway that I can show him what she can do. The deep rumble as I change up through the gears, vibrates through the seats, warming my body. This. This is what it's all about. This is why I love working with cars. This feeling of freedom as you drive a beautiful machine along the highway. Just me, the car, and the road. It's my happy place.

Martin smiles across at me. "Noah's gonna love this. He's really into muscle cars."

"Oh yeah?" I grin back.

He hangs his arm out of the window, catching the wind. "So, how long has Molly been working for you?"

I glance across at him with narrowed eyes. "Just over a month," I answer cautiously.

He must sense my discomfort with the topic because he holds up his hands. "She reminds me of someone. That's all."

My shoulders relax. "She's new to the city. I doubt you know her."

We move away from the topic of Molly, and I run through what the Sprint is capable of. We make it to the coast, and I climb out of the driver's seat to allow Martin the opportunity to drive her back to the workshop.

If his expression is anything to go by, he's smitten. Exactly how I want him.

We make it back to the workshop and Martin carefully parks the car in bay three, where I've been working on her. He slowly turns to me, a smile as wide as anything on his face. "How much?"

I twist in my seat to face him, pulling out my phone. I took photos of the car before I started and then kept taking photos as the restoration progressed as a record.

"Before we talk about the price. Take a look." I hand him my phone. He's engrossed in the images as he flicks through dozens of photos. The first shows the wreck abandoned in a backyard, with grass and weeds growing almost to the top of the roof.

"That's this car?" His eyes are wide, his voice full of wonder.

I nod. "Yep. Looking at her there, though, I knew she would be a beauty."

"She sure is." He twists his body around, handing the phone back to me. "Okay. Hit me. How much?"

"Forty-nine K."

Martin's eyes widen, and his eyebrows shoot up. "Fuck."

I nod slowly. "Worth every penny, though."

"Oh, don't worry. I can see her worth." He glides his hand over the dashboard like any man would caress a woman's body. "Any room for negotiation?"

I tilt my head to the side. "A little."

"Might have to run it past the wife. When would you need an answer?"

"I'm not in any rush. I contacted you first like you asked. If you can't take her off my hands, I'll find another buyer. I'm not worried in the least. Talk to the wife. Bring her and the kids in to take a look, if you like," I suggest.

We climb out of the car and head back toward the office, so I can shut up the workshop behind him. Molly's sweeping the floor as we pass through. Martin's eyes draw to her like a magnet to metal, making my hackles rise again. I guide him straight through, aiming to get him out of the door, but he stops.

"See ya, Molly. It was nice to meet you." Deep divots bracket his mouth as he smiles at her.

She returns his dimples with her own as she responds. "Bye, Martin. Great to meet you, too."

Once I get Martin out of the shop, I lock up and head back to Molly.

"Is he gonna buy the car?" She asks, her eyes wide and hopeful.

"He has to speak with his wife. It's a lot of money to drop on a car that you don't actually need. But if I were a betting man, I'd say he'll buy the Sprint." She claps excitedly. "I need to get changed for soccer. Are you coming with me, or do you want to come later?"

She pauses her sweeping; her face snapping up toward me. "You want me to come with you?"

I shrug. "Makes sense. I can drop you back here after the pub."

She fidgets with the broom for a minute, and I wonder why the decision is so difficult. "Are you sure your friends would be happy if I come to the pub again? I feel like that's possibly time for the boys since you don't normally have women there."

"You're not a woman. You're our cheer squad."

Her shoulders drop, as does her face. With her eyes locked on her shoes, she takes a few moments. "I … uh … I'll meet you at the field if that's okay. I probably won't go to the pub after the game."

I understand she's allowed to make her own choices, and I'd never force her to do anything she didn't want to, but I thought she enjoyed hanging out with the boys. "Have you got something else to do?"

She shakes her head, her delicate eyebrows drawing down low over her eyes. "No. I don't have anything else to do. I'll be there to cheer you guys on the sidelines. Don't worry." She gives me a forced smile and focuses back on the sweeping, basically dismissing me.

The disappointment is strong. I wanted her with me. I've been looking forward to it since last Monday night. I feel like a kid who's been denied a play date with his best friend. I've grown used to her being at our games. Molly and I haven't known each other all that long, but I enjoy her company and was hoping she felt the same.

I collect my bag and move into the bathroom to get changed. When I come out, Molly's waiting at her desk, shifting nervously from foot to foot. "You okay?"

"Yeah, I wanted to ask you something." She's looking everywhere but at me, which is unusual for her.

"Sure. Ask away."

She collects a piece of paper from her desk, holding it close to her body so I can't see what's on it. "I was wondering what you thought about an idea I had." She turns the parchment around, allowing me to see what's on the paper. The air leaves my lungs in a gush, and I step forward to study it more closely. I'm torn between keeping my eyes on the sketch she's showing me and looking at her as she poses the question. "Do you think whoever buys the Sprint would like a framed sketch of it?"

"Are you serious?" She nods. "Fuck yeah! That's an incredible piece of work, Molly." I flick my eyes back up to her face. "Are you sure you want to give it away? You could sell this and earn some extra money."

"Oh no, I could never sell my work. It's not *that* good." She gives a self-deprecating chuckle.

I scoff. "That's bullshit. Your attention to detail and the fine lines are incredible. The shading that you do makes it appear almost like a photograph."

Her cheeks flush and her dimples make a shallow appearance. "You think so?" She sounds uncertain and I'm not sure why. Surely, she can see how good her work is.

"Why don't you bring it with you tonight and show Aaron? He has a pretty good eye for this stuff because he sells it in his café." I check the time. "I've gotta go," I tilt my head toward the paper, "bring it with you. See what he says."

"Oh, uh, I'll think about it." She waves me away. "You'd better get going. I'll see you at the field."

CHAPTER 14

—max—

I'M THINKING MOLLY MAY BE OUR LUCKY CHARM. WE WON again tonight. We've had more wins this season than last.

"We need to make sure Molly comes to every single game. She's like a good luck charm or something." Aaron pats me on the back as he makes his suggestion.

"As if I have any control over her coming to our games or not. I couldn't even get her to come out for a drink tonight."

His head pulls back an inch or two in surprise. "What do you mean, she's not coming out for drinks?" He steps away from me, then calls back over his shoulder. "Don't worry, I'll work my magic."

Oh shit! I don't want her to feel pressured to come to the pub. I only want her to come if she *wants* to be there with us.

"C'mon, Molly. You have to come to Brady's to celebrate with us tonight. We haven't won this many games in a season for a while. You're our lucky charm." He gives her his best smile. The one he uses to pick up when he's feeling like company.

And I don't fucking like it.

I don't like it aimed at my Molly. My gut tightens and I want to push my way between them and punch that smile off his face.

Molly looks down at her shoes, but I can see she's smiling. She tucks her hair behind her ear and then looks back up at him. She's slightly swiveling her body from side to side, like a coy schoolgirl.

Does she fucking like him?

I study my best friend. He can't take his eyes off her. I don't like the way he's fucking looking at her. He's too old for her. He has no business flirting with my Molly.

"Are you sure it's okay?"

"We all want you to come." He turns around to gesture to the guys, noticing I'm right behind him. "Don't we, Max?"

"I already invited her. She didn't want to come," I snap at my teammate while looking at Molly apologetically.

She glances at her shoes and I turn to give Aaron the filthiest look I can muster.

"Okay. I'll come for a little while." She flashes her sexy dimples at my friend.

What the hell just happened? I couldn't get her to join us tonight, but Aaron flashes her his pickup smile and suddenly she has a change of heart.

"Great. See you there." He backs away to collect his gear, tipping his chin to me.

I focus my attention back on Molly, placing my hands on my hips. "I thought you didn't want to come to drinks with us tonight? What's changed?"

"I'm allowed to change my mind if I want." She starts walking toward the parking lot, so I quickly grab my gear and follow behind, watching her ass and ponytail sway with each step. *Fuck! Stop looking at her ass.*

When we arrive at her car, we stop at her driver's door. "I

get that you're allowed to change your mind. I'm glad you're coming." I wrap my arm around her neck, pulling her into my body.

She laughs and pushes at me. "Eww, you're all sweaty." Her hands feel electric on my body.

I release her and grasp my chest over my heart. "You don't like my sweat?"

"Nope." She pops the p like she's popping a bubble gum bubble.

I walk around to the passenger door. "You wanna drive and then drop me back here for my car?"

Her head snaps over to my car. "You're gonna leave your car here?"

"Or … we could take my car and I'll drop you back here to pick up your car. Either, or." I shrug, hoping that she chooses to come with me. She looks between my car and hers "You know how hard it is to find parking. If we take two cars, it's gonna be a problem."

She closes her door and locks her car. "We'll take your car. I'd hate to be responsible for something happening to your beautiful car if we left it here unattended. I doubt anyone will look twice at mine."

I smile inside. "Okay. Sure. Let's go." I pat the roof. "Your car's not that bad." I walk back around to her and guide her across to my car with my hand settled at the small of her back. "Be careful what you say. You don't want to hurt her feelings," I whisper low into her ear as we walk away, making Molly chuckle. I think her laugh is one of my new favorite sounds.

Before I climb into my car; I grasp the back of my T-shirt and pull it off. Searching through my bag, I pull out a clean T-shirt. When I tilt my head up, I catch Molly staring at my chest, and before I can help myself, I flex my pecs. "Did you enjoy the game?"

Her eyes snap up to my face, and I press my lips together to hold back my smile. *Yeah, I caught you checking me out!*

"Huh?"

I change out of my cleats into my running shoes. "Did you enjoy the game tonight?"

She grins at me. "You couldn't tell with all of my cheering and dance moves along the sideline?"

I chuckle. "You're pretty entertaining with your cheer moves."

She curtsies before climbing into the passenger side. "Why, thank you. I'll take that compliment."

We drive out of the parking lot and turn right toward Brady's. "It would have been easier if you'd come with me, instead of bringing two cars," I say as nonchalantly as possible. It's niggling at me that she agreed to come to the pub when Aaron asked, but not when I did.

"I was wondering how long it would take you to bring that up. Maybe, next week, I'll drive with you. Would that make you happy?"

Glancing across, I grin. "Ecstatic."

Brady's is packed as usual. I pull Molly against me to protect her as we work our way through the crowd, toward the guys.

Cheers go up around the tables when they spot us. Aaron, Brent, Gary, and Finn step out to hug Molly in greeting, pulling her away from me. She giggles but accepts each hug. The pit of my stomach sinks as I watch other men embrace her. I know she's not mine, but I don't fucking like the thought of some other asshole having their hands on her, even if I know they're good guys with the best of intentions.

We settle into the booth, and I work to school my features, but Aaron's already smirking at me. He knows me too well, and no matter how hard I try to hide the way I'm feeling, he always seems to read me.

"Pizzas are on their way. You two want a beer?" Finn asks as he glances around the tables.

"Nah, man. You sit. It's my buy." I turn toward Molly. "What can I get for you, Dimples?"

I catch Aaron's smirk out of the corner of my eye but make the conscious choice to ignore him.

"I can get my drink. You don't have to keep paying for me."

"You won't be paying while you're with me. I invited you, which makes you my guest. I'll grab you a beer." Scanning the table, I check the guys' drinks, but they're still looking healthy.

Aaron slides out of the booth. "I'll come with you. I need to speak with a friend of mine."

We make our way to the bar. The usual group of young women checks us out as we approach. They're probably about the same age as Molly, I guess, but the idea of going there with one of them has never appealed to me. Molly, on the other hand …

"What's going on with you and Molly? And don't give me any bullshit. I can read you, man." Aaron slaps me on the back and squeezes my shoulder as he interrupts my musing.

"Nothing. She's my office manager."

He looks back at the table and I follow his line of sight. Molly's looking straight at us as she laughs at something Finn's saying. "You wouldn't mind if I asked her out then?"

"Yeah, I would fucking mind. There're plenty of other options available to you." I tilt my head toward the regular group of younger women close by. "No need to go after my employee."

"Is that the only reason I can't ask her out? Because she's your employee? 'Cause as her boss, you have no say in who she dates, right?" he hedges.

I order our drinks, buying myself some time before I answer my long-time friend, who I'm sure is fishing for information rather than being interested in dating my new employee. "I thought you had a friend you needed to chat with?"

"I *am* chatting with that friend." He chuckles. *Asshole.*

I pay for our drinks, then grab them, ready to head back to our booth, but Aaron stops me. "I can see the way you look at her and the way she looks at you. Are you going to do anything about it?"

My shoulders slump. "I can't. I'll admit, I find her attractive and as I'm getting to know her, I like her. I like her a lot. But I'm her boss, plus she's a decade younger than me."

Aaron sighs. "Sucks to be you."

I take a sip of my beer. "It most certainly fucking does."

We don't need to say anything else. Aaron gets where I'm coming from. That's what years of friendship and support give us.

When we arrive back at the booth, Gary is giving Molly a rundown of the baby's stage of development, and Molly's enthralled. I place the beer in front of her and she glances up to mouth 'thank you' and then returns her full attention to Gary. I can't help but note the difference again between Mona and Molly with my friends. Mona would never have shown any interest in Gary and Layla's pregnancy because Mona was all about Mona.

The pizzas arrive and everyone's quiet as they dig into the deliciously cheesy treat. Molly's oblivious to a piece of stretchy cheese that's landed on her chin as she chats with the guys. Reaching across, I pinch it between my fingers, pull it away and drop it into my mouth. When I glance back across the table, Aaron's studying me with a raised eyebrow, and I shrug in response. It would be different if Molly seemed offended, but she gave me a brief smile, then took another huge bite of her slice of pizza.

I love that she's not shy about eating her food in front of

others. I guess her daily run allows her to eat whatever she wants without worrying about calories, like most women, or maybe she just enjoys food.

Gary makes a move to leave, and I check in with Molly. "Are you happy to stay, or are you ready to head home?"

"I wouldn't mind heading home if you don't mind. I have another late night tomorrow night and I want to get up early enough for my run in the morning." I still don't know where she volunteers. Maybe I'll ask her on the drive back to her car.

We say goodbye to everyone, Molly promising to be at next week's game. I can't stop my smirk, knowing she'll be back again next week. I nudge her shoulder with mine. "See, the guys really like having you around."

Her smile drops and her shoulders slump. "Yeah, I guess so." She turns her face away from me as we climb into my car.

"You okay?" I can't help but notice her mood's changed considerably since we stepped outside.

She shrugs. "Yeah. I'm okay."

I grew up with two sisters. I know for a fact that when a woman says she's okay, in that tone, that she's not fucking okay. It means I've done something wrong. I just don't know what it is.

I open the passenger door for her, then lean down after she situates herself to strap the safety belt on. I suck in a sharp breath as my arm brushes against her tit. That was a fucking mistake because her scent fills my lungs and wakes up my dick, which is becoming a perpetual problem the more time I spend with this woman. I turn my head to check she hasn't noticed, putting my lips close to hers. And that's my second fucking mistake. Her lips are right there. Slightly parted, as though she's waiting for me to kiss her. I glance away from her lips, catching on her molten eyes.

Fucking stunning.

I could lean forward ever so slightly, and my mouth could take hers. I could taste her. Would she taste as sweet as she fucking looks? I pull back slightly, saving myself from a possible lawsuit.

Is that disappointment marring her gorgeous features? Or is that wishful thinking on my part?

Closing her door, I use the opportunity as I make my way around to the driver's side to calm my dick down. She doesn't need her boss making inappropriate advances. I need a distraction. "You never told me where you've been volunteering."

She tucks a lock of hair behind her ear. "Oh, uhm, I volunteer over at *Shelter* on Tuesdays and Thursdays. It's a women's homeless shelter."

Of course, she does, because she isn't sweet enough already. "I know the one. Big red brick building."

She smiles. "Yeah, that's the one. I used to volunteer at a shelter back home." I'm struggling with the irony that she was sleeping in her car the whole time she's been here—well, I'm assuming that's what she was doing—and then she volunteers in her free time at a women's shelter.

"Any reason why you choose to spend your free time helping homeless women?" Her body stiffens and I can see her physically and emotionally shut down. I thought it would be a reasonable question. After all, she asked me a similar question about my Single Parent Thursdays. "Sorry. That was possibly too intrusive. You don't have to answer."

Her hand moves to fidget with the bracelet she wears. "Oh, uh, that's okay." She turns her head toward the passenger window, dropping her voice to barely above a whisper. "My mom and I were, uh … were homeless until I was eleven."

My head snaps toward her. Surely, I heard that wrong. Slowly she turns and our eyes connect, but not for long because I need to keep my eyes on the road. I swallow down the thousands of questions that battle for release. "That must have been tough." *What a fucking understatement.* No wonder she had no problem living in her car.

We pull into the parking lot and I don't want to let her go. I want to know what her life was like as she was growing up. My head can't even go there. It's so far removed from my childhood. The silence in the car sits heavy like Lachlan's weighted blanket. She turns in her seat, so her body is facing me and I want to scoop her up and sit her on my lap.

I want to grasp the back of her head under the fall of her silky hair and pull her into me, so I can kiss those plump lips of hers.

I want to give her a home that will always be hers.

But I can't do any of those things.

I turn forward, staring out of the windscreen, grinding my teeth to stop myself from asking her to stay awhile. To sit and chat. Out of my periphery, I see her lean closer to me and as I turn my head, my lips brush against hers. They're warm and soft and I want to press in deeper, take her mouth with mine.

I don't know where all of this is coming from. It's an impossible situation. I can't go there with her. I don't move, but she swiftly pulls away as though she's been scorched.

"Thanks for the ride." She jumps out of my car. "I'll see you in the morning." She closes the door carefully and jogs over to her car. I watch her climb in and I'm tempted to follow her back to her apartment to make sure she gets inside safely. She has nobody else to watch over her as far as I can tell.

I wait until she pulls out of the lot and then follow behind. I would never forgive myself if something happened to her. I slow to watch her get inside safely and then head home.

Her rose scent is trapped inside my car, playing with my senses and testing my resolve.

I strip off as I walk through my bedroom, my bed calling to me, but I desperately need a shower. Turning on the water as hot as I can bear it, I step under the spray, hoping to release some of the tension that's built in my body during the car ride home.

I think back to Molly's lips skating lightly across mine accidentally and I close my eyes, picturing exactly how I'd like to take those pouty lips. My cock wakes at the thought of pressing my mouth against hers, teasing her lips apart, and taking the first swipe against her tongue with mine. I groan and my dick twitches as I imagine how soft and sweet she would be under my ministrations.

Wrapping my hand around my shaft, I give it a hard squeeze, followed by a quick tug. I picture Molly pressing her tits against my chest, rubbing her pelvis against my cock and my dick grows impossibly harder.

I'm going to have to deal with this.

I lather up some soap and grip myself firmly, using my other hand braced against the cold tile to hold myself up. The soap helps with the slide and pull of my dick, but I know this won't feel half as good as if I were inside what I imagine would be a phenomenally tight pussy. I groan as I picture delicate pink lips separating to reveal her pulsing clit and inviting wet heat.

My hand picks up the pace, sliding up to my crown to finish with a squeeze and a tug, before sliding back to the base with a twist. My breaths come faster and my heart pounds in my chest. Squeezing my butt cheeks together, I thrust forward into my hand, building a rhythm.

Too fast, tingles begin to form at the base of my spine and my balls draw up tight to my body. I throw my head back under the warm stream and shoot my load against the tiled surface, grunting out my release. Cum coats the tile and slides down as I catch my breath. Closing my eyes tight, I shake my head, full of disappointment.

Fuck!

I just came to thoughts of my office assistant.

I'm in so much fucking trouble.

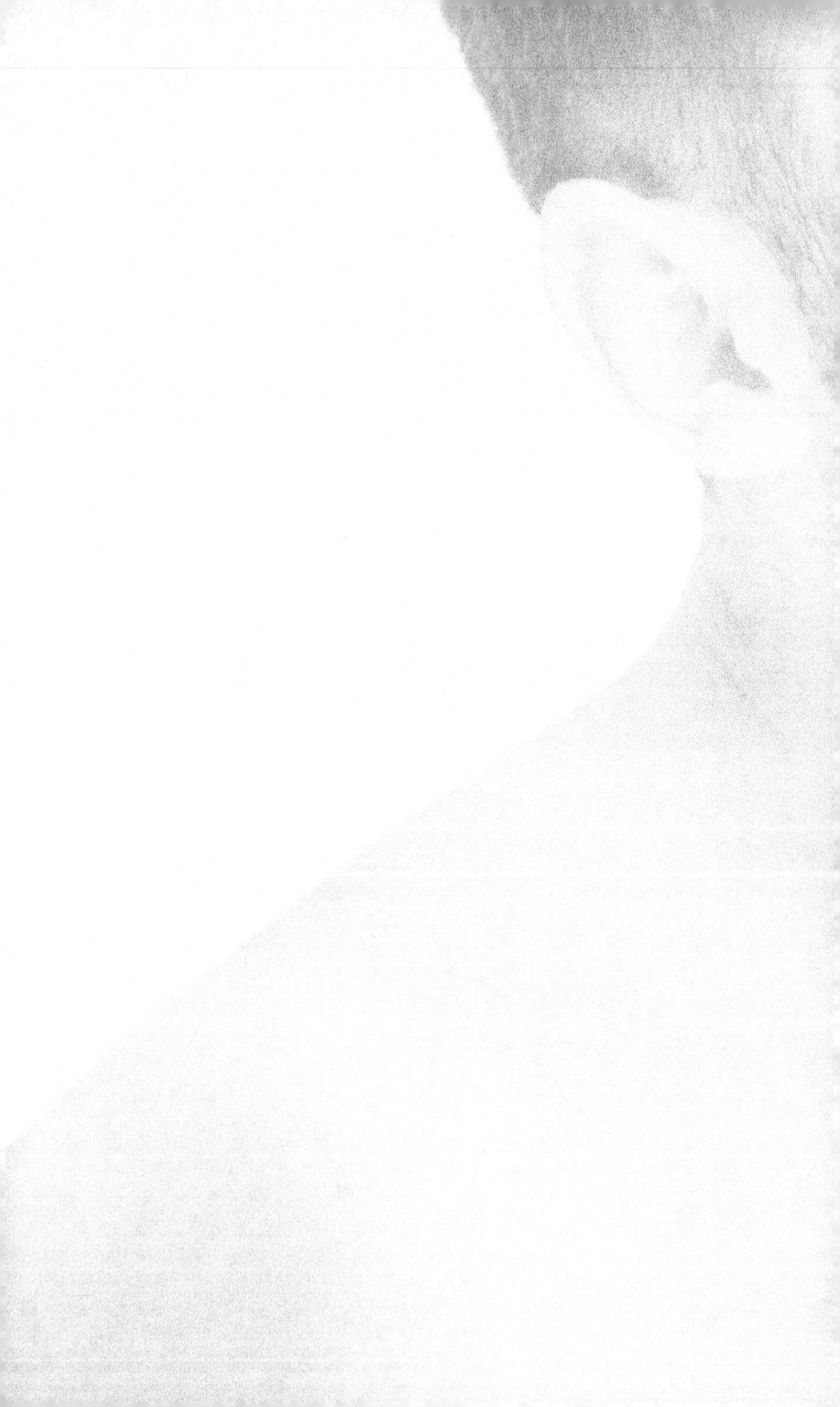

CHAPTER 15

—molly—

S<small>IMONE'S SITTING IN THE WELCOME CHAIRS TO THE SIDE OF THE</small> entry, chatting with a stunning brunette. As she notices me, her eyes light up and that welcoming smile of hers graces her face. She waves me over. "Molly, come and meet Veronica. She's going to be staying with us tonight."

I step toward the two women with a genuine smile. I love coming here. Simone and the ladies have made me feel incredibly welcome from the get-go.

I hold out my hand to Veronica. "Hi, Veronica. It's lovely to meet you. I'm Molly. My friends call me Mols."

She warily slides her hand into mine and without making eye contact, she responds, "Hi. I prefer to be called Ronnie or Ron. If you don't mind?"

"No problem. Ronnie suits you."

She smiles at me and it's beautiful, though it doesn't quite reach her eyes, which catch me by surprise. Her left eye is a gorgeous blue, while her right eye is chocolate brown. I don't think I've ever seen anyone with two different colored eyes.

The door opens, and a woman walks in with a toddler in

tow. She looks completely fried. "If you don't mind, I'll leave you two ladies to get acquainted while I meet our new friend."

We both nod at Simone and then I return my attention to Ronnie, who's busy studying her boots. She's dressed as most homeless women on the street do, as though she's trying to blend in, so she becomes invisible. I'm not sure how successful she'd be with those eyes of hers. They would make her rather memorable.

"I'm quite new to this city and I don't know my way around very well, but I love sitting by the beach and watching the sun go down. I used to live on the east coast and the sunsets were never as good," I say conversationally as I sit next to her.

Ronnie snaps her head up to me. "Really. I never gave much thought to the difference between here and there. Whereabouts did you live?"

"I grew up in Portland, Maine." Her eyebrows almost reach her hairline. "I decided to move here after I lost my family a few days before Christmas because this is where my mom grew up." I swallow down the lump that forms every time my family crosses my mind, but I've always found if I share something personal, the women are more likely to share their story in return.

She swallows and looks back down at her boots. "I'm sorry for your loss. Were they good people?" The fact she even asks that question tells me a lot.

I nod, fighting the sting behind my eyes. "Yeah." It comes out as a whisper, so I clear my throat. "Yeah, they were. The best."

Ronnie offers me a sad smile. "Why is it that the good people leave us too early and the assholes are left here to make our lives miserable?"

I shrug, shaking my head. "I dunno. I wish I knew the answer to that."

We're both quiet for a little while. "Have you always lived here?"

"Yeah." She studies her boots again. "I've never been brave like you to move somewhere new."

"I wouldn't say I was brave. I'd lost my family, my job, and my home in a matter of weeks. I had nothing left there, so I thought I'd quell my curiosity about the place where my mom grew up. Maybe if I were living here, I wouldn't have moved. From what I've seen so far, this is a pretty great city."

Ronnie shrugs, returning her gaze to her boots. She's quiet for long moments and I rack my brain, trying to come up with something else we could talk about, but maybe she's had enough for now.

"Uh, did you want me to show you to your bed and you can have a shower, then grab something to eat?"

She sighs and nods. "That'd be great."

Standing, I gesture for her to follow me, and I show her through to the dorm without cribs. She has a single backpack with her and she's holding it close to her body. If she's anything like me, it contains all of her most important possessions.

"It looks as though the two beds at the end are still vacant. You wanna take one of those?"

"Sure." We make our way between the beds until she arrives at her space for the night.

"There's a locked cupboard here." I show her how to use it. "We have some donated clothes if you want to check them out. They've all been freshly laundered."

Ronnie locks her backpack in the cupboard, and we make our way toward the room with the donated clothes for women and children. In another room, there are a few suits and fancier dresses the women can borrow when they go for job interviews. This place truly is impressive with its attention to detail, which helps women move forward with their lives when they're ready. On the way, I show Ronnie the bathrooms and then leave her with the offer to catch up in the dining room later if she wants to.

When I enter the kitchen, Rhonda greets me with her usual enthusiasm. "Mols, you're finally here! How are you, sweetie?" She wraps me in her tight embrace, almost knocking me over and we both giggle.

"I'm great, Rhonda! What have you been up to since I saw you on Tuesday?"

"Oh, you know, this and that. Catching up with all of my boyfriends." She winks at me and I chuckle. Anyone would assume she plays the field, but she's actually talking about book boyfriends. She talks about them as though they're real people.

"Oh yeah? Who are you dating this week?" I ask as I move toward the sink to wash my hands.

"Jake. Jake Normanton from the Leah Reynolds series." She fans herself. "That man brings everything to the table and I do mean ev-er-y-thing!" She finishes with an exaggerated wink.

Rhonda puts me to work and tells me all about Jake and Leah and their love story, which started back when they were kids. Leah's the daughter of a serial killer and Jake's the son of a drunk. It sounds like a fabulous read.

"Who's the author? I might check it out."

"Uh, hang on. I'll grab my Kindle and check. I'd hate to get her name wrong." She bustles off to the storeroom as I cut the bread rolls. "T. Maree. It's a series of five books. A real slow burn." She gets this smirk on her face. "But oh so worth it!" I chuckle. "How come you were late?"

"I wasn't late. I was chatting with a lady who's staying overnight. Veronica or Ronnie? Do you know her?"

"Oh yeah. Pretty girl with two different colored eyes. She comes in now and then. Haven't seen her for quite some time, though. I was hoping things had improved for her."

"I didn't know she'd been here before. She must think I'm an idiot. I was showing her where everything is."

Rhonda waves me off. "Nah. She's a sweetheart. Doesn't talk much and keeps to herself, but she's super polite. Not sure what her story is because she keeps everyone at arm's length."

The evening passes by in a blur. It's always crazy when I help Rhonda in the kitchen. I didn't even have time to step out and check that Ronnie grabbed something to eat. All the lights are out in the dorms as we close the kitchen down and put everything away. Rhonda's busy soaking a measured amount of chia seeds to add to the oats in the morning when Simone strolls in. She releases a heavy sigh and slouches against the counter.

"This is the first chance I've had to catch a breath. How are you ladies tonight?"

"Exhausted but good," I answer at the same time as Rhonda does.

"I'm ready to head home and soak my feet."

"Me too. Thanks for your help tonight, Molly. Did you manage to chat with Veronica at all?"

I lean back against the opposite counter. "A little. She said I could call her Ronnie or Ron. Told me she's always lived here. Something she said suggested that her family has hurt her." I shrug. "She didn't talk all that much."

Simone raises one eyebrow and one side of her mouth tips up slightly. "Well, you've managed to get more out of her than anyone else has."

I pull my head and shoulders back. "What? Really? I felt like I had failed. And then I got busy in the kitchen and I didn't get the chance to check back in with her after her shower."

Simone steps forward, placing her hand on mine and squeezing it. "You did well. Never feel that you've failed. You're here helping us help them. That's incredible, Molly." She gives my hand another squeeze before letting go. "Now go home. You've earned a good night's rest."

We all say our goodbyes and I promise to return next Tuesday.

I walk through my front door and head straight for the bathroom to take a quick shower, then drop into bed. I'm exhausted. After spending the day looking after the single parents and their kids, then tonight at *Shelter*, I'm dead on my feet. I glance across at the photo of Mom, Jack, and E I keep on my nightstand.

Reaching out, I pull it closer to me. I trace my finger over their faces and whisper, "I think I'm gonna be okay."

Their image becomes blurry, and I let the tears fall. They slide down the side of my face, landing in my hair. "I've met some genuinely good people. I'm pretty sure I made the right choice coming here, Mom. It's such a gorgeous city. You were lucky to grow up here. Thank you for sharing all of your stories with me. After all, they're what led me to my new life."

—molly—

MAX HAS BEEN ACTING STRANGE SINCE TUESDAY MORNING, almost like he's trying to avoid me. Whenever I speak with him, he's polite but short in his responses, then he makes an excuse to get away from me. I'm not sure what I've done to upset him, but I need to speak with him about my hot water. The stupid switch keeps turning off at the most inopportune times and I'm hoping he'll be happy to get an electrician to check it out. This morning it turned off while I was halfway through my shower, my hair lathered in shampoo. The freezing water forced me out of the shower before I had finished washing my hair. It was easy enough to flick the switch back on, but still, I think it needs to be fixed.

The only problem is that I don't want to seem like I'm ungrateful for a safe place to live. The apartment is amazing and I'm thankful that he's allowing me to live here. I don't want to be a pain in the ass and make things difficult. He might decide it's easier to kick me out and leave the place empty like it was before I moved in.

Making my way downstairs, I find the office empty, but the scent of coffee lingers. He must have made himself a coffee a few moments ago. I do the same and then make my way out to the workshop to say good morning, hoping he's returned to his usual friendly self. I don't think I can handle him being aloof toward me any longer. It's been really uncomfortable. I hope he hasn't changed his mind about me working and living here.

Only one way to find out. "Morning." I keep my voice as upbeat as I can.

Without looking up from whatever he's doing in the trunk of the Sprint, he responds. "Morning."

Moving next to him, I try to peer around his body to see what he's doing, but I can't. "I thought you'd finished working on this car. What are you doing?"

He glances up at me. "Martin's bringing his wife in this afternoon to look at her. I'm making sure all the wiring for the rear lights works properly."

"Oh, do you think he'll buy the car today?"

He stands to his full height, picking his coffee up from the floor to take a drink. He shrugs. "Maybe. He was pretty keen, but I guess it's important to him that his wife agrees. It's an expensive car, considering it won't be his everyday drive."

"If he buys it, will you buy another wreck straight away, or will you have a break in between?" I take a sip of my coffee.

"Depends if another car catches my attention straight away. I have my eye on a nineteen thirty-eight Ford pickup truck, so we'll see." He shrugs one shoulder and takes another sip of his coffee.

"Well, I hope Martin takes the Sprint off your hands so you can get the truck. I love the shape of those pickups." The lines are amazing on the vintage trucks, not like the models today. All square and bulky.

Max raises his eyebrows at me. "You know what they look like?"

"Yeah, my stepdad used to always be looking at the older

cars. Muscle cars and pickups were his favorites. He was the one who taught me and my younger brother how to draw."

A smile forms at the memory of us sitting on our front porch in the trailer park and drawing our neighbor's truck. I'm pretty sure it was a late nineteen-thirties pickup, but it was in terrible shape. It always surprised me whenever it started. I chuckle at the memory of the time it backfired while we were drawing it. Ethan nearly pooped his pants.

"What's brought those dimples to life?" Max asks with a small smile of his own.

"Just remembering something funny. Our neighbor had a run-down pickup. One day, we were sitting on our front porch practicing our drawing skills when the old guy came out and climbed in. When he started it up, it backfired and scared my little brother. I think he was about five at the time. I've never seen him bolt inside so fast." Another chuckle escapes.

Max chuckles too. "Sounds like the engine was running too rich." I look at him in confusion. "It happens when there's too much fuel and not enough air."

"Oh, right." I take another sip of my coffee to hide my smile. I don't think he realizes he's actually looking at me as we have a conversation. The first we've had since he turned up at the workshop on Tuesday morning. I relax a little, feeling like we're back on even ground.

Remembering the sketch I've framed of the Sprint, I hold up my finger and take off back to the office to grab it. I haven't had a chance to show Max because he's been so distant. Jogging back, I hold the frame with the sketch facing me, hiding my surprise from him. I can't hold in my excitement. I hope he likes it. I stop next to him and make a big fuss about turning the frame around.

He chuckles until his eyes land on the framed drawing. The car looked great before, but framed with glass over the top, it looks professional. He steps forward, studying it closely and I hold my breath, waiting for him to share his thoughts. I don't need to wait for his words, because his expression shows everything he's thinking. He glances between me and the sketch. "Molly." His eyes drop back to the sketch, before rising to meet mine. "It's incredible." He holds his hand out toward the frame. "Do you mind?"

I hand it to him willingly. The look of awe and wonder on his face allows me to take a deep breath. I think he likes it a lot.

"It's a cheap frame from the discount store, but it makes a world of difference to the simple sketch."

"I wouldn't say this is a simple sketch. It's amazing." He looks back up at me. "As I've said before, you could easily sell this."

I wave off his comment. There's no way my sketches are good enough to sell. "I'm torn about what to do with it. Do you think Martin will want it if he buys the car? Or perhaps you could put it up in the office, like a wall of remembrance of the cars you restore and sell."

His eyes snap back to mine. "You'd let me keep this?"

"Of course." I shrug. "If you want it, you can keep it."

"I like the idea of starting a wall of sketches of the cars I restore. I mean, it's not like I restore that many. It always takes me a while, but I'd love to keep this as a record if you don't mind." He drops his eyes back to the sketch. "I'll pay you for it."

"You will not pay me for it. It's not like it cost me anything to do, besides the ten-dollar frame, and I'm pretty sure that won't break the bank." Well, it won't now that I have a regular job and a roof over my head to boot! I point my thumb over my shoulder toward the office. "It's time I set up for the day. I think you have three bookings this morning. What time are Martin and his wife coming to look at the car?"

"Somewhere around two. I should be finished by then." He

hands the sketch back to me. "Can you put this in a safe place? I'll hang it later today."

"Sure." I take it from him and then get everything organized, and ready for our first client of the day.

It's funny, some people drop their car off and come back to pick it up, while others sit and wait for their car to be ready. Whenever I have someone sitting in the reception area waiting for their car, I feel I need to make conversation, which means I don't get my work done. But the guy waiting on his car this afternoon is giving me the creeps. I'm glad it's nearing two and Max should almost be finished with his car. I'm trying my best to ignore him, but he's not taking the hint. When I get up from my seat to file some paperwork, I catch him giving me yet another once-over. He's not discreet about it either, as his slimy eyes trail up and down my body.

"So, how tall are ya? Your legs seem like they go on forever. Wouldn't mind having them wrapped around my waist. If ya know what I mean." He finishes with a wink and I'm certain my face looks like I've chewed on a lemon.

He steps closer and I try to back away, but I'm blocked by the counter with nowhere to go. I press my body as far away from him as I possibly can, but I'm trapped.

CHAPTER 17

—max—

"WHAT THE FUCK IS GOING ON IN HERE?" I SNAP OUT AT THE same time as Martin slams the outer door closed. His face looks like thunder as he steps forward, his fists clenched tightly by his sides. His wife, standing to the side of the doorway.

Glen steps back from Molly and her body sags in obvious relief. "Just telling your new girl here how great her legs look." He says it like it's no big deal that he was making my employee uncomfortable. *Fucking loser.*

"I don't think I should have to tell you that my employee has a right to feel safe at work." *Yeah, good one.* Let's not mention to the room that you stood in the bathroom door and perved on said employee, while she was fucking naked. "Your car's ready. I'll send you the invoice," I snap. "And you can find yourself another mechanic. You're not welcome back here."

"But, I didn't do anything. You're overreacting, man." He folds his arms across his chest, standing to his full height.

I step forward. I still have a few inches on him and fold my own arms across my chest. "From what I saw, I don't think I'm overreacting at all. Your type isn't welcome in my shop. You can apologize to Molly and then you can get your sleazy ass out of my workshop."

He spits on the floor between us, and Martin takes a step forward, but I motion for him to stay where he is. This isn't his concern.

"I ain't apologizing for nothing. I didn't do anything wrong. It's not my fault if the bitch is an ice queen." He tips his head at Molly with an expression of distaste.

"You disrespectful little punk." Martin steps forward and grabs Glen's shirt, pulling his arm back, ready to lay him out.

Grabbing Martin's arm, I stop him from doing anything stupid. "Martin, take a breath. Don't do anything stupid. He's not worth it."

Glen raises his hand, knocking Martin's grip on his shirt loose. "I'm outta this shithole. There're better mechanics than you around." He looks around the room, knocking into my arm as he passes on the way out.

As the door slams behind him, we all take a collective breath. When I glance across at Molly, she's shaking and tears are filling those stunning orbs, making them appear stormy. I move into her space and wrap her in my arms, cradling the back of her head. Her hands come up to my flanks as she grasps the sides of my overalls. A heavy sob leaves her, and my heart cracks.

"I'm sorry, Dimples. He had no right to speak to you like that. He won't be back." Her sobs rack her body, so I pull her in tighter to me. "Shh, shh, shh. It's okay." I love how her body fits against mine, how she feels in my arms.

Martin steps closer. "Is she gonna be alright?" he whispers.

Molly stiffens in my embrace, attempting to pull her head away from me, but I keep her close. "She'll be okay. She just needs a minute. If you want to show Beth the Sprint, you can head through. I'll be there in a few."

He nods, then guides his wife through to the workshop,

leaving me and Molly alone. It takes a few more moments, but eventually, Molly gets herself under control. I can feel the change in her, so as she tries to pull away, I let her go, but I miss her instantly. Her hands still rest lightly on my sides, and I love having them on me.

I need to remind myself that I'm her boss and she's ten years my junior. It's getting harder and harder to keep myself in check the more I get to know her. I've spent most of this week working my ass off to keep her at a distance after what I did on Monday night in my shower to images of her.

"Are you gonna be okay?" I whisper as I tuck a loose lock of silky hair behind her ear. Her hair *is* as silky as I imagined it to be. Her face is red and blotchy, her eyes puffy, and her nose is red, but she still looks gorgeous.

Her eyes skate past me, and as she bites her bottom lip, she nods her head once. Glancing back up at me, she finally whispers, "Yeah. I'm sorry about that."

Confusion colors my tone. "What are you sorry about?" I thumb over my shoulder toward the door. "That asshole?" She nods. "You have nothing to apologize for. He was the one in the wrong. He shouldn't have been speaking to you like that, and he certainly shouldn't have had you trapped against the counter with nowhere to go."

"Yeah, but now you've lost a client because of me and he probably won't pay the invoice for today's work. I feel like that was my fault."

"Have you seen how fucking busy I am? I won't miss that asshole one bit. Don't give it another thought. Clients come and go all the time." I smile at Molly, hopefully portraying that I'm not bothered. "How about you clean up and meet us in the workshop? You can join us when we take the Sprint out for a test drive. Help us convince Martin's missus that she should let him buy the car." I finish with a wink.

Molly returns my smile and nods. "Thanks, Max."

"No problem."

Martin's gaze switches to something behind me. His eyes turn soft as he takes a step away from me. "Are you okay, Molly?"

Molly forces a smile as an embarrassed flush stains her cheeks. "Yes, thank you. I'm sorry about the drama."

"It was no drama at all. That guy was an asshole who needs to be taught some manners." He guides her toward Beth. "I'd like you to meet my wife, Beth."

Beth sucks in a sharp breath as she gets her first proper look at Molly. Molly glances at me, her frown creating a crease between her eyebrows as she holds out her hand to greet Martin's wife. "Oh, Molly. It's lovely to finally meet you."

Okay, this behavior is fucking weird. Both Martin and his wife have their eyes locked on Molly; it's making me uncomfortable at this point. I can only imagine how it's making Molly feel, especially after what happened in the office with Glen. Molly glances over her shoulder at me with raised brows and I can only shrug. I have no idea what the fuck is going on.

"Alright, shall we take the Sprint out for a spin?" Pulling the keys out of my pocket, I open the front door and release the catch to move the front seat so the ladies can climb into the back. Once we're situated and the workshop is secure, we take off. "Where shall we go?"

"Where would you like to go, Molly?" Beth asks.

"Oh, um. I don't mind."

"Martin said you're new to the city," she says to Molly, then turns toward the front. "Perhaps we should show her the Pier?"

"Please don't go out of your way on my account. I'll slowly find my way around. You guys go wherever you need to get a good feel for the car."

"The Pier's a great idea. That okay with you, Max?" Martin asks.

I catch Molly's eyes in the rear-view mirror. Hers widen in confusion, and I mirror her but turn toward the Pier. It's as good a drive as any to give the Sprint a run and show Beth what the car can do. "Sounds like a plan. Maybe we can stop for a drink or something," I suggest.

Martin and I are quiet in the front, enjoying the drive.

"The interior of the car is like new," Beth comments from the back and I catch her gliding her hand over the interior panels in the rear-view mirror. "And the leather is so soft. It's gorgeous, Martin."

Martin turns to me with a smug smile on his face. "I told you how perfect it was."

A few moments pass before I hear Beth ask Molly, "Martin said you haven't lived here all that long. Where are you from?"

"I moved here from Portland, Maine."

"She drove all the way here by herself," I add from the front seat.

"Oh my gosh. What did your parents think of that?" Beth asks, clearly shocked.

Molly's quiet for long moments and I assume she's not going to answer. I glance up into the mirror because I'd also like to know the answer to that question. She's turned her head toward her window, and I see her throat move. She turns back toward Beth.

"Uh, I lost my family in a car accident before Christmas." *Fuck!*

The car is silent for long moments, nobody knowing what to say to that. If I weren't driving this damn car, I would wrap her up and pull her in tight. I had no fucking idea, and I didn't think it was my place to ask her such a personal question. I could kiss Beth right now for asking, and for providing me with such intimate information.

Once I discovered my first impression of Molly was way off base, and since spending almost every day with her, I've grown to admire her, to like her. I'm man enough to admit I'm attracted to her—who wouldn't be? She's fucking beautiful. But she has so much more to her than her looks. She's incredibly sweet and thoughtful. Kind and down to earth. She could easily be bitter, but I've seen none of that from her, which makes me admire her even more.

"I'm incredibly sorry, Molly." Beth's voice oozes compassion. "That's tragic. Please let us know if there's anything at all we can do to help you. You must be devastated. I can't imagine how much your life's changed."

Martin releases a heavy sigh next to me and stares out his window. The mood in the car is understandably heavy after Molly's confession. I catch the side of Molly's face in my mirror as she stares out her window. There's a sheen to her eyes as she reaches up to wipe her cheek. Turning back toward Beth, she nods. "Thanks, Beth. I'm doing okay."

Silence descends again and I think it would be fair to say that each of us is happy to keep it that way, lost in our thoughts.

I pull into the parking lot at Pier 7, searching for a park. It's reasonably busy since it's a nice day as we move into Spring. I find a spot a fair distance from the Pier, but nobody minds the walk.

I grab Molly's hand as soon as she climbs out of the car and pull her in close. Pressing a kiss on the top of her head, I whisper, "I'm so fucking sorry about your family. If I can help, let me know. Okay?" I catch her eyes and implore her to lean on me.

She gives me a fake smile. I know it's fake because it doesn't quite create her usual dimples. "You've already helped me a lot, Max. Thank you, but I'll be fine."

I squeeze her extra tight, then release her so we can make

our way to the Pier. We stop at *Declan's Diner* and order cool drinks and hot fries to share. While we sit, enjoying the sunshine, I show Beth the same photos I showed Martin, giving her a sense of how much work I've done on the car.

She chuckles and waves off my spiel. "You don't need to impress me. I've already told Martin that if he wants the car, he should buy the car. He works damn hard and gives so much of himself to me and our family. He doesn't drink or smoke and he spends any free time he has with his kids." She looks across at him, her eyes full of love and admiration for her husband. "He deserves to have something special after working hard for as many years as he has to build his electrical company."

Molly gives me a genuine smile. She knows I have the sale. "Even though I haven't worked for Max for very long, I've learned he works incredibly hard on the cars to make sure they're running at their best. You won't be disappointed with the Sprint. He's worked hard on that car to make sure it's perfect."

My heart expands in my chest with her words, which are full of genuine pride in me and my work. My family has always been proud of me. Mona never gave a shit about my work, only ever complaining that it took too much time away from her and that my hands were perpetually stained. This feeling that Molly's given me with a few simple words—that she didn't have to say—makes me puff up with pride in myself. I place my hand on her thigh beneath the table and give it a gentle squeeze in gratitude.

I should move my hand away, but I casually leave it there and Molly seems happy enough for me to do so. The lines between us are becoming more and more blurred by the day.

CHAPTER 18

—max—

"C'MON, I'M TAKING YOU TO DINNER TO CELEBRATE THE SALE of the Sprint!" I clap my hands together in excitement as I step out of the office. She's crouched down low, collecting the dirt she's swept up from the workshop.

Molly stands, brushing her hands on her skin-tight jeans. "Congratulations." Her smile is wide and excited as she leans forward to hug me. "I'm truly happy for you. It was such a magnificent car."

"It certainly was, and I'm happy that she's gone to a suitable home where she'll be appreciated and looked after." Molly chuckles and I pull back to look at her. "What?"

"Nothing. Do you realize you talk about cars like they're people?"

"Well, duh. They *are* like people. They have quirks just like people and we need to look after them, make sure they're cared for, just as we would a loved one."

She bends over with an all-out belly laugh and I feel great that I could make her laugh like that after the heaviness of her confession. I don't suppose she has much to laugh about these days, not that I would have known if Beth hadn't asked about why she moved here. She keeps her private life to herself and generally only shows a bright, cheery demeanor, maintaining a high level of professionalism. There have been times when I've noticed her staring off into space, a distant look on her face as though she's lost in a memory, but she's never let it affect her work.

"Come on. I want to take you to this Mexican hole-in-the-wall place I found. I think you'll like it." She pauses for what feels like an eternity. "C'mon. Celebrate with me." I lift my eyebrows, waiting as patiently as I can for her answer. I never usually celebrate selling one of my project cars, but I wanted an excuse to spend more time with her. After today, I want to check in with her and learn more about her.

Her dimples make an appearance. "I love a good burrito."

"Great. Let's go." I grab her hand to pull her behind me to my car.

"Hang on. I haven't finished here, and I should probably get changed." My eyes skim over her. She looks perfect in her jeans, white T-shirt, and plaid shirt. "Don't worry about finishing up. We can sort it out on Monday morning. It's Saturday. Let's go have some fun."

She shrugs. "Okay, but will this be okay for where we're going?" She fidgets with her shirt.

"Yeah." I shrug. "You look great." I tug her with me and this time she follows.

I find street parking close to *Los Burritos*. Whenever I get the urge to have authentic Mexican, this is the place I come to. The outside isn't appealing in the least and I wait for Molly to arc up about eating here, but she doesn't say anything as I take her hand and guide her inside. It's still early, so it's busy, but not crazy, as we step up to the counter to place our order. The scent of spiced meat sits heavy in the air, reminding me how much I love the food here. Glancing around, I spot a clear booth toward the back that would be perfect for us.

"If you tell me what you want, I can place our order." I tip my head toward the empty booth. "You can take care of our booth."

"Sure." She studies the menu boards with careful consideration. "What do you normally have?"

"Honestly, anything you choose is gonna be amazing. I haven't been disappointed yet. I usually have something different every time I come here."

She nods and returns her attention to the board. "I think I'll have the super burrito with the spinach tortilla and chicken if that's okay?"

"Of course. Go take a seat and I'll be over once I've ordered." The guys working in the open kitchen are calling out order numbers and requests for more ingredients. Orders are taken swiftly and served quickly with fresh and tasty ingredients. I place our order with the friendly staff member and then head to the booth to join Molly as we wait for our number to be called.

"I would have walked right on past this place without a second glance. It doesn't stand out from the street, but judging by how busy it is, the food must be fantastic."

I glance around to see it through her eyes. "It's not even as busy as it usually gets. We're pretty early. By seven, there's a line down the street."

Her eyes widen. "That's crazy."

Our number's called, and I carry our burritos and drinks back to the table. Molly's eyes almost pop out of her head when she sees the size of the burritos. "Oh my gosh, that's huge!" she says with her eyes trained on the food.

"That's what she said," I respond without thinking. Her eyes snap up to my face and she bursts into laughter.

"Maybe you could show me sometime." I freeze and Molly snaps her mouth shut tight, a pretty blush rising from the base of her throat to her face. "Oh shit! I shouldn't have said that. How embarrassing." She covers her mouth with her hand and breaks out into silent giggles. I join in with her, shaking my head because I'm the one who shouldn't have said what I said. *What is it about this girl?*

We get stuck into our meals, enjoying the flavors as they touch our tongues. Molly moans in appreciation and my dick jolts in my jeans. *Calm the fuck down.* This is not the time nor the place. I need a distraction. "You wanna tell me about your family?" I want to swallow the words as soon as they fall out of my mouth. What a way to put a downer on the moment. I wanted a distraction, dickhead, not a fucking morbid reminder of what she's lost. "Sorry. You don't have to talk about them if you don't want to. I'm not sure what I was thinking." I give her an apologetic smile.

She finishes chewing the food in her mouth, and I watch her throat as she swallows it down. My dick bumps against my zipper, imagining what it would feel like if she swallowed around me. *Fuck!*

"That's okay. It'd be nice to talk about them. Uh, I haven't had anyone to talk to since it happened." She gives me a sad smile. "My mom was seventeen when she became pregnant with me and only eighteen when she became a mother. She actually grew up here. I think I already told you that."

I nod and she tells me that her father abandoned her mother, and her parents weren't happy with the situation. Apparently, her grandfather wanted her mom to have an abortion, and that's why she ran to the other side of the country.

"Anyway. Mom met my stepfather, Jack, when I was eleven and we moved into his trailer with him." A smile touches her lips and she looks far away. "We'd been living out of Mom's car before that, so it was incredible to have a bedroom of my own and a shower and kitchen." Jesus, the shit I've taken for granted my whole life is like a magical fairytale to her. "I think because of how things were, Mom and I were super close. She was my best friend." Her voice shakes on the last sentence, so I reach across and take her hand.

"I guess that means you were used to living out of a car, then." I raise my eyebrow. "You never stayed in that motel, did you?"

"No. I'm sorry I lied to you. I didn't want you to know I was homeless and think less of me. All of my money went toward paying for the burials and funerals for my family. Then I lost my job and my apart–"

I cut her off. "What do you mean, you lost your apartment and your job?"

She tells me everything that happened, which led to her deciding to start over here. I'm fucking furious that her boss and landlord didn't cut her any slack knowing what she'd endured. They'd better hope we never fucking cross paths. I take long, deep breaths to get my temper under control. She doesn't need me going off on a rant about the assholes. She carries on speaking about her family like everything that's happened to her isn't a big fucking deal.

"Jack was the best. He was the one who taught me how to draw and trained me to run. He treated me like I was his own daughter. Mom and I were incredibly lucky to have him come into our lives and open his heart and home to both of us." I can't imagine anyone not falling in love with her or her mother if she was anything like Molly. "Then Ethan came along." She chuckles. "He was the chubbiest baby I've ever seen. I fell in love with him the second I laid eyes on him." She pulls her hand from mine with a smile on her face. "Hang on, I have a photo I can show you."

She fiddles with her phone and then passes it across the

table to me. My eyes land on Molly first, then scan the rest of her family. I use my fingers to enlarge the photo, studying Molly next to her mom. "Geez, you and your mom could almost be sisters. It's uncanny how similar you two are."

Molly's smile widens. "Yeah, it's crazy, right? Her eyes are blue, though, whereas mine are gray and she didn't have dimples. She says I got both of those features from my dad."

I move the photo around, allowing me to study Jack and Ethan. "Ethan's like a mini version of his dad."

"Yeah. He would always try to copy Jack in everything he did, too. Jack was such a great dad." Her smile drops and her eyes become glassy. "He would do anything to keep us happy and safe. He would have been beyond devastated that he was the cause of everything." She wipes away the tears tracking down her cheeks and offers me a shaky smile. "Sorry."

I climb out from my side of the booth and move in next to her and tug her body into mine. "Please don't ever apologize to me, Molly. You're allowed to be fucking sad."

"It's just been a lot. Ya know?" I nod. "And I'm trying my best to stay positive and be happy in the moment, but sometimes I slip." She shrugs, tilting her head down toward the table.

"You're allowed to grieve. I get the impression that you haven't had time to do that." I use my finger to tip her face back up. Our lips are so close I can feel her breath on mine, and I'm tempted to close the distance. Her eyes drop to my lips and I lick them instinctively. Just one taste. But that would be an asshole move when she's this vulnerable. I'd be worse than Glen. I pull back and she follows, moving forward, maintaining the hair's breadth distance between us. My eyes dart down to her lips, then back to her liquid silver eyes. "Molly," I whisper roughly.

Her eyes slide up to mine. "Yeah?"

"I don't want to be the asshole here."

"Then don't be."

She moves forward and the instant her soft lips meet mine, everything else ceases. My breath freezes in my lungs and in a split second, I make a decision. I press forward and she sighs, melting against me. My tongue licks out across her lips, and I can taste the barbecue sauce from her burrito.

I should fucking stop.

She parts her lips, and my tongue dips inside to slide against hers.

"Are you guys finished with the table? We're all waiting and you two are over here making out like teenagers," a disembodied voice douses us with its icy tone.

Reluctantly, I pull away and turn toward the stranger who interrupted our moment. I don't like confrontation for the sake of it, so I won't say what's actually on my mind in this situation because, in reality, Molly and I are in the wrong. This is not a fancy restaurant where you linger. It's a hole in the wall where you grab your food, you eat, and then you move on. Molly ducks her head in embarrassment and I decide the best approach is to apologize and move along. Our moment's broken now, anyway.

"Sorry about that. We got carried away."

I wrap Molly's left-over burrito and grab my trash and slide out of the booth. Holding my hand out for Molly, I tug her to her feet and nod our apology to the guy. On the way out, I throw my trash in the can and tuck Molly into my side. I guess we lost track of time because we step out into the darkness. I'm not ready to take Molly home when she's finally opened up to me about her family and the reasons that brought her to me. I want to keep her with me as long as possible tonight.

"Brady's often has a band playing on a Saturday night. You up for checking them out?"

She looks up at me; the stars reflecting in her eyes. "I think I'd like that."

With her tucked into my side and her arm wrapped around my waist, we make our way back to my Dodge. Unlocking the car, I step around to open her door for her, but instead find myself pressed against her, trapping her between my body and the car. My mind flashes back to earlier in the day when Glen did the exact same thing. The only difference is that Molly's eyes heat in response and she doesn't appear to be scared out of her wits. I collect a silky lock of her pale hair between my rough fingers and feel the soft strands, my eyes watching the motion. "You have the most gorgeous hair. I wondered if it would be as silky as it looks." I draw in a deep breath, inhaling the rose scent. "It's better than I could have imagined."

She smiles and reaches up to run her fingers through my short strands, tickling the sides where a few grays have snuck in, reminding me of my age. "I like these." She runs her hands down along my jaw, scratching her short nails through my five o'clock shadow. "I really like this." She presses up slightly and plants a gentle kiss on my cheek, then glides her lips toward my ear. "I'd really like to feel this in other places."

Fuck me.

I think my eyes must be as big as saucers with surprise at her sexy words. My dick wakes up and attempts to break through my zipper. He doesn't need to think twice about her offer, but my brain hasn't stopped functioning just yet.

She's young. Like, really young. And sure, she's been through a ton and she's incredibly mature for her age, but I can't forget that I have a decade on her. Does she realize what she's offering?

I lower my forehead to hers, kissing the tip of her nose. "I'm sorry. I got carried away inside and I shouldn't have kissed you. I'm your boss. I don't know what I was thinking." Her body stiffens as she brings her hands up to my chest and pushes. I step back, giving her the space she's silently request-ing. Her gorgeous smile is nowhere to be seen and her eyes no longer meet mine. "Don't do that, Dimples. Don't look at me like that. I'm trying to do the right thing here."

"The right thing by who? Because I was giving all the signals that I'm okay with taking things further." She wraps her arms around her body, drawing my eyes to her peaked nipples.

It's fucking easy to get caught up in the moment … in my attraction to her, but what sort of guy would I be to pursue something with her when I know it's wrong?

I run through scenarios in my head, trying to find one that makes it okay for a boss to hook up with his employee, and I can't find a single one. Not that I'm looking for a hookup, because obviously, Molly is worth more than that. She's the type of woman you plan forever with, but what if it doesn't work out? I don't want her to be uncomfortable at work and she needs this job and the apartment upstairs. She has too much to lose.

She huffs out a sigh when I take too long to answer. "Look, forget it. Can you please take me home? I don't feel like going out now." Carefully, she maneuvers her body to open the door without touching me. Closing the door, I watch her secure her seatbelt, then face forward to stare out of the windscreen.

I huff out a sigh and link my hands behind my head. I fucked up tonight. I don't know how I'm going to make things right between us, but I'll need to do something.

Pulling my door closed, I turn in my seat to face the woman who has me so damn confused. "I'm sorry. I shouldn't have crossed the line. Please forgive me. I want us to be friends." I sigh when she doesn't respond. "At least don't hate me." Starting the car, I check the road and pull out safely.

"I could never hate you, Max," she whispers into the silence.

I release a heavy breath, my shoulders dropping in relief. Glancing across, she gifts me with a timid smile that doesn't reach her eyes, but it'll do for now. I want to reach across and take her hand, to offer her reassurance that things between us will be okay, but I don't know for sure, and I refuse to make a promise I can't keep.

We pull up to the rear of the workshop and Molly climbs out of the car silently. Perhaps some time apart will be a good thing for both of us.

—molly—

I'M AS SWEATY AS ANYTHING AS I REACH IN TO TURN ON THE shower. I have my fingers crossed that today's the day I can make it through my shower without the water turning freezing. Standing underneath the warm spray, my muscles relax after my run. I tried to outrun my constant thoughts about Max, but it didn't work. He's still in my head and I have to work out a way past them so I'm not awkward when I see him in the next half an hour. I can't believe I came onto my boss like that, but I'm reasonably certain I didn't misread his signals. *How could I get it so wrong?*

Ah shit!

Goosebumps dot along my skin as the water turns to ice. Again. I'm going to have to ask Max to call in an electrician. Which means I'm going to have to pull up my big girl panties and have a conversation with him. I was hoping to keep things strictly professional between us from now on to avoid crossing any more lines. I planned to go for a walk at lunchtime instead of eating with Max. It feels too friendly for a boss and employee to share lunch every day. I'm also planning to make up some excuse to avoid going to his soccer match tonight, which hurts my heart because it's something I love to do. Being at the game reminds me of some of the good times with my family and I'm reluctant to give that up, but what else can I do?

The more time I spend with my hot boss, the harder it is to remember he's my boss, and he's made it crystal clear that he doesn't want to cross that line with his employee. If I were thinking straight, I wouldn't want to cross that line either. I need this job and the apartment that comes with it. It would be crazy to attempt a relationship with Max for it to not work out.

It's not like I've been successful in relationships in the past. What makes me think a relationship with Max would be any different? Then where would I be? Out on the street, starting all over again. I'm only now beginning to feel settled and that my decision to come here was the right one. I don't want to mess it all up on a whim. I have too much to lose.

The smell of coffee entices me as I walk down the stairs, tying my hair into a loose knot on top of my head. I put on my best smile. Fake it 'til you make it, they say, and that's what I plan to do. I'm going to pretend Saturday night didn't happen.

"Morning," I say as brightly as I can when my foot reaches the last step.

Max looks up from his coffee, his eyes scanning my face. Is he looking for my fakery? Does he know me well enough to see through my bullshit? The crease between his brows suggests he's not completely buying my bright greeting this morning. "Hey. How was the rest of your weekend?"

"Not bad. It was such a beautiful day yesterday that I went down to the river to sketch. The location was beautiful. How about you?" *See, I can do this.*

The crease between his eyebrows disappears and a smile forms in its place. "Spent the afternoon with my crazy family. My niece and nephews ..." His smile drops and he grasps the back of his neck, his bicep muscle bulging. "Sorry."

I glance around, confused by his apology. "What are you sorry about?"

"I shouldn't have mentioned my family." He shakes his head. "I can't believe how thoughtless I was."

My shoulders drop. Disappointment takes the place of the hope I felt that we could move past any awkwardness between us. "I lost my family. You didn't. You don't need to apologize for that, Max. It certainly wouldn't be fair or reasonable for me to expect people to never speak about their families while in my company. I can accept that life goes on. My experience isn't yours and I'm happy about that. Enjoy your family and talk about them. It makes me happy to hear about their antics and the fun you have when you're with them."

He nods to acknowledge me, then turns toward the coffee machine. "Do you want a cup of coffee?"

"Yes, thanks. I'd love one." I turn on the laptop, ready for the day, and Max hands me my cup of steaming goodness. "Thanks." I take a sip and close my eyes in appreciation. "I needed to talk with you about the hot water in the apartment. The switch keeps turning off all the time now, even when I'm in the middle of a shower. Would you mind calling an electrician?"

"Sure thing. I'll get someone to come out today. Sorry about that. I should have sorted it out sooner." He pulls his phone out of his pocket.

"I can pay for it. I don't want to cause you any extra expense. If I weren't living up there, the hot water wouldn't matter," I rush to offer.

"I'll pay for it because I'm the landlord and it falls under my responsibility. It's not a problem." He touches the screen on his phone. "Martin's an electrician. I'll see if he can come out today."

I gather my supplies to clean the bathroom while Max is on the phone with Martin. He steps into the room as I'm bending over the toilet, scrubbing it until it shines. "Martin needs to rearrange a couple of things, then he'll be over. He said he won't be too long."

"Oh, I didn't expect him to rearrange his day to fit me in. Now I feel terrible. I can always come down here to shower, but after last time …" I trail off as I remember how my body heated under Max's gaze. Pink stains his cheeks and he shifts on his feet. "Sorry. That was all my fault. I should have locked the door." I turn my back, returning to my task to hide my embarrassment.

"When Martin comes, make sure you come and get me. I don't want him going upstairs with you on your own."

I turn back around. "Why? Don't you trust him?" Why did he ask him to come and fix the fault if he doesn't trust the man?

"It's not that I don't trust him, it's that he acts weird whenever he's around you." He folds his arms across his chest, using his thumbnail to skim his bottom lip. It's freaking sexy when he does that. "In all the years I've known him, I've never seen him act the way he has the last couple of times he's been here. I don't know if you've noticed, but he watches you and it's fucking weird. But he's a great electrician and I trust him with the job. I just don't trust him with you."

"I'm glad it wasn't my imagination. I thought he was weird and when his wife knew that I'd recently moved to the city …" I shiver.

"That's probably my fault. I told him you'd only lived here a few weeks. He said you remind him of someone, and I said it would be impossible because you hadn't lived here for long. He must have spoken with his wife about you."

Another shiver runs down my spine. "Well, that's strange. Don't you think? Why is he talking with his wife about me? He doesn't know me."

"I agree. So, make sure you're not alone with him. Okay?" He raises his eyebrows, waiting for my response.

I nod. "Okay."

The outer door opens, and cool air from outside blows in.

"Hi, Molly. I believe you're having some issues with the wiring upstairs."

"Uh, hi, Martin. Yeah, I am. I'll grab Max and we can head up."

"That's okay. You can show me." He smiles, showing divots in his cheeks, which are mostly hidden by his beard.

I stand and make my way to the door to the workshop. "Oh, that's okay. Max wants to be there since he's the landlord and all." I call out to Max to let him know Martin's arrived.

He stops what he's doing, and I lock the outer door for now since I won't be in the office. Max steps into the office to meet us. "Hey, Martin. Thanks for coming out quickly. We appreciate it." They shake hands.

"No problem." Martin looks across at me. "I didn't want to leave you without hot water."

His concern for me seems a bit much considering we don't know each other. I'm glad Max insisted on being present while Martin's looking at the wiring. The three of us head upstairs to my small apartment. Max and I point across the room to show Martin where the bathroom is. I make it to the bathroom, assuming the guys are following me, but when I turn to speak to Martin, he's nowhere to be found.

Poking my head through the doorway, I find Martin staring at the family photo I have displayed on the wall in the living room. He's standing so close to the image I'm surprised he can see anything at all. His face has gone as white as the paint on the wall.

Max is standing behind him, his arm crossed over his chest, his thumbnail running across his plump bottom lip as he watches Martin closely. I'm puzzled about what could be so interesting in the photo.

"Are you okay, Martin? You look … pale."

He turns toward me, then glances back at the photo. "Nicole." He looks back at me, then points at the photo. "That woman is my Nicole."

Max looks between the photo, Martin, and me. His confusion matches mine. "Who's Nicole?"

"Nicole is my mom," I answer Max, then walk toward Martin. "What do you mean, '*your* Nicole'?" Martin opens his mouth and closes it again. Looks at me and then back to the photo.

"What the fuck is going on, Martin? You're acting fucking weird," Max snaps.

He looks between Max and me. "I knew you reminded me of someone. You look a lot like her, but I convinced myself I had to be wrong."

Max comes to stand beside me, offering his silent support without touching me. My gut's churning and I'm afraid to hear what Martin's about to say.

He takes one step closer to me, his posture softening. "I dated your mother in high school." He covers his mouth and turns away from me. His hand moves up to cover his eyes and a shudder racks his body.

I step toward him, wrapping my arm around his shoulders. I'm guessing he just made the connection that his old high school flame has passed away. I rub my hand up and down his back, attempting to offer him some form of comfort. Tears well in my eyes and I blink to hold them back. He doesn't need me to fall apart as he works through his grief.

Even though it would have been a long time since he saw her, I guess it would be a shock to learn what he's discovered today.

His familiarity with me makes sense now. I *do* look a lot like Mom.

He takes in a deep breath and wipes away the tears from his eyes. "I was telling Beth how you reminded me of Nicole, but she didn't believe me until she met you on Saturday. Beth was one of your mom's friends in high school. We all used to hang out together. She's going to be devastated when I tell her this."

His body stiffens and he moves back to the photo. "So, uh, did Nicole have another child?" His hand shakily comes up to his mouth as he glances at me.

"Yeah." I move to stand next to Martin, pointing at Ethan. "My younger brother, Ethan." I point to Jack. "That's his dad, Jack."

Martin nods slowly. "Anyone older than you?"

I shake my head. "Nope. I'm the oldest. She had me when she was eighteen." I wonder if Martin knew my dad?

The little color that had returned to his face drains. He covers his mouth again as he staggers backward and drops onto my couch. His elbows rest on his knees and he drops his head, capturing it in his hands. He's clearly upset about something. He speaks without looking up. "I … uh … I was dating Nicole when she got pregnant." His head lifts and his steely-colored eyes lock onto mine. "She was seventeen, I was nineteen. We'd been together for nearly three years."

All the air is sucked out of the room and a haze forms around the edges of my vision. The rush of blood in my ears is deafening as my legs collapse out from under me. I don't hit the floor as I expect, instead strong arms scoop me up, but I can't make sense of what's happening around me. I'm under-water, moving through sludge, everything going in slow motion. My body connects with my soft mattress, and I can make out static mumbling, but can't decipher the words.

The mind is a tricky thing. It shuts down as a form of protection. It did it to me when the police officers knocked on my door to break the news about my family's accident. This is different, though. Instead of shutting down, it's like my mind is running on overdrive but is blank at the same time. It doesn't know what to process first. The whirling thoughts are moving faster and faster, and I can't make sense of anything.

Mom left here because she had no support when she found out she was pregnant.

Her father wanted her to have an abortion.

My father disappeared.

My grandmother didn't support Mom one way or the other.

She was alone, facing an unknown future.

Martin may not be my father. Maybe she was seeing someone else, and that's why he abandoned her.

I curl into a ball and pull the bedcovers over my head. I want to go to sleep and when I wake up; I want everything to make sense again because none of this is making sense to me at the moment. And I really need things to make sense.

—molly—

I WAKE IN THE DARK, A FAINT LIGHT STREAKING ACROSS MY room from the living room. I close my eyes again, remembering everything from this morning. I must have slept all day.

"You okay?" Max's deep rumble comes from the corner of the room.

Peeling the covers away from my face, I peer over at him sitting on the chair in the corner that I picked up from the second-hand market. I take stock for a few moments. "I think so. I'm sorry I let you down today."

He sits forward in the chair, his elbows resting on his knees. "Please don't apologize to me. You had a major bombshell dropped on you this morning." He moves across to sit on the edge of my bed. Carefully, he brushes what must be a rat's nest out of my face. "Martin's not doing much better than you. I had to call Beth to come and get him." Words won't come, so I nod. "Maybe give yourself some time to digest what you've learned today, then you probably need to have a chat." I lick my dry lips and nod again. "Do you want something to drink?"

I try to sit up, but with Max sitting on the bedcovers, I can't move properly. He lifts his butt and helps me to sit up, propping the pillow behind me. "Thank you. I could use a glass of water." I tuck my matted hair behind my ear. "What time is it?"

"Six."

"Shouldn't you be at your soccer game?" I can't believe I've screwed up Max's day so badly.

"Nope. This is where I needed to be." He leaves the room and returns quickly with a glass of cold water for me. I take a long drink, soothing my dry throat. When I've finished, Max takes the glass from my hand and places it on the nightstand for me. "You wanna talk about it?" I shrug. My mind is such a jumble. I'm not sure where to start. "Take your time. I'm not going anywhere."

Sounds from outside infiltrate my sleep and I slowly open my eyes. Something heavy across my middle makes it hard to move. I look down to see what it is and glance over my shoulder to confirm I'm not imagining what I'm seeing.

Nope!

Max is lying on top of the bedcovers curled around my body, his arm slung across me. I study his face. He looks different relaxed in sleep. The scruff on his cheeks is thick this morning, adding to his appeal. My stomach flips and I feel like a schoolgirl whose crush said 'hello' in the hall.

He stayed.

When I needed someone, he was there. Same as he's always been since we first met.

Maneuvering my body, I twist carefully in his hold. I don't want to wake him, but I want to study him more closely. He bands his arm around my body, pulling me in tight as I get comfortable.

"Stop moving, Dimples." My girly parts wake at the sound of his deep, raspy morning voice, and I freeze. His hand slides up my back, cupping the back of my head beneath the fall of my hair. "Your hair smells so fucking good." He kisses my forehead. I'm not sure if he's aware that he's being affectionate with me in his half-asleep state, but I'm not about to point out his behavior. I don't want him to stop. His fingers slip through the long strands, then he closes his fist around them. "So, goddamn silky." I doubt that. I'm certain it's a tangled mess at this point. He runs his lips down to the tip of my nose, landing another kiss. I smile to myself and snuggle in closer, wrapping one arm around his middle.

Lying like this, our bodies would touch at every available point if Max wasn't on top of the covers. I can't believe he isn't cold.

"How are you feeling this morning?"

Recalling yesterday, my mood drops. "Do you want my honest answer?"

He pulls away to study my face. "Always."

"I'm confused. I don't know what to think about any of it." Taking a deep breath, I take a few seconds to gather my thoughts. "At first, I felt bad for him finding out that his high school girlfriend had passed away. I imagine that would have been a shock. But then when he said he was dating Mom when she became pregnant … the world sort of fell away beneath my feet." My eyes sting and I have to glance away from Max's bright green gaze. I lose the battle and tears trickle down the side of my face, crawling over the bridge of my nose, and down into my hair. Max's deft fingers massage the base of my skull and I hide my face in his chest. I'm not sure why I'm crying again today. I should be happy that I may have found my father, but my thoughts won't stop spinning.

He abandoned Mom. Essentially, he abandoned me, too.

"I have too many thoughts running through my head at the

moment. I'm finding it difficult to make sense of everything if I'm honest."

"It's completely understandable, Mols." He squeezes the back of my neck gently. "And you can take as long as you need to work things out."

I nod into his chest, then peer into Max's eyes. They're full of compassion and understanding. His breath tickles my face and I drop my eyes to his lips. He moves forward slightly, and I take the cue to meet him in the middle. At first, it's a simple press of lips against lips. Max's whiskers tease the skin around my mouth, adding to the sensation. He sighs, then presses in firmer and I meet his pressure. My tongue slips out to taste the soft pillows of his lips. Max tightens his hold and he glides his fingers up to grasp my hair close to my scalp. He tightens his hand into a fist, tugging my head back, and I peel my eyes open to find Max's heated gaze on me. He plants the softest of kisses down the side of my face, swiping my tears with his tongue. My breaths speed up and I press my boobs into him, silently begging for him to kiss me. To really kiss me. I fear he's going to come to his senses and stop.

He surges forward and I open willingly, allowing him to invade my mouth with his tongue, exploring and tasting me. I match him with an exploration of my own, bringing my hand up to run my fingers through the short strands of his hair. Our teeth clash as our tongues rut against each other. This kiss is hungry. No, it's more than that. It's like we've been starved for too long and we need this to survive. My lungs burn, but I don't want to break away. I don't want to lose this.

Max slows the kiss and I panic that he's going to stop. Reaching up, I press his head toward mine. His lips spread wide against mine. "Don't worry, Dimples. I'm not stopping." My lips match his in relief and he moves forward, nipping my bottom lip before sucking away the sting.

Using his body, he rolls me onto my back and then situates

himself on top of me and I wish to all that's holy that we didn't have the bedcovers between us. What I would give to feel his naked skin against mine. My body heats at the thought and I lift my head from the pillow to steal another kiss. Our lips meld and move together as though we were always meant to kiss like this. It's a kiss that I'll remember forever as it sears an indelible mark on my soul.

He moans as I push my pelvis up to meet his. I need relief, but he presses his hips firmly against me, stopping my movements without losing an ounce of focus on what he's doing to me with his mouth.

I'm dizzy with lust.

My overloaded senses are begging for attention. My hands grasp his back, feeling the stretch and pull of his muscles. He pulls back, cupping my face in his large, calloused hands, and presses his forehead to mine. "This is wrong." His eyes drop to my nose ring as he toys with the blue ball.

My breath gushes out of me, replaced with disappointment. *Why is he fighting this so hard?*

His eyes move back up to mine. "But I don't want to stop. You need to be the strong one, Mols. Tell me to stop." He closes his eyes, blocking his forest gaze from me.

"I don't want you to stop. Don't ask me to be the strong one."

He tilts his head to the side and starts all over again. My breath whooshes out of my body in sheer relief. He pillages my mouth with rough strokes as he cups my face with a gentleness that doesn't match. My breaths are ragged and I don't care.

The buzz of my alarm steals the moment and we both pull away, panting. "Damn alarm," I mumble as I throw out my arm to mute the offending noise. Max rolls off me to allow me to twist further. Finally, my hand makes contact and I silence the stupid thing. It's five o'clock and I don't want to leave my bed to get my exercise today when I could have a perfectly good workout here.

With our moment gone, Max climbs out of bed and pulls me up. He tugs me forward and places a delicate kiss on my forehead, then spins me toward the bathroom. Smacking my ass, he laughs at my pout. "Go for your run. I'm gonna head home for a shower." He adjusts the obvious bulge in his jeans. "I'll see you back here for work."

"But I don't wanna run," I whine. "I wanna keep doing what we were doing." I'm close to stomping my foot on the ground to punctuate my sentence, but I fear that would remind him of our age difference. I'm certain it's one of the reasons he's been keeping himself in check around me.

"No arguments, Dimples. I have a busy day. I had to rearrange my schedule yesterday." He nudges me toward the door, but I stop and turn.

"I'm sorry, Max." I rest my hand over his heart. "My mess shouldn't impact you. I promise it won't happen again."

He reverently slides my hair behind my ear, his eyes locked on mine, as his fingers move to glide down along my jaw where he uses his knuckles to tilt my head back a little. "Yesterday was an anomaly, Molly. I would cancel everything all over again to be here with you when you needed me. I'll be here every step of the way as you navigate your way through this new informa-tion. That's if you want me to be here with you." His eyes dart back and forth between mine.

Raising my hand, I grasp the back of his neck and pull his face closer to mine. "Of course I want you here," I whisper against his lips before pressing a sweet kiss against them.

CHAPTER 21

—molly—

BENT OVER AT THE WAIST, I WORK TO CATCH MY BREATH AS I walk slowly around the parking lot in front of the workshop. Tires crunch over gravel and I turn to see who's driving into the lot this early. My heart races as I read the sign on the side of the truck: *DeLuca Electrics*. He parks and turns off the engine. For long moments, he remains seated inside his truck as we watch each other.

I don't know if I'm ready for this conversation.

I was hoping the run would help me sort through my scattered thoughts. But I'm still as confused as ever. I suck in a deep breath and take a couple of steps toward the man who may well be my father. He takes that as his cue to exit his truck. We stand a few feet apart, silently studying each other. Mom always said I had my father's eye color and dimples, but it's weird to stand across from this man and see eyes that match my own. Something I hadn't noticed before. Probably because I wasn't looking. I swallow my nerves and give him a timid smile. "Martin."

"Hey, Molly." He tucks his hands into his pockets and rocks back on his heels. "I ... uh ... hope you don't mind me coming over. Beth said I should give you more time, but I think we've already lost enough."

I gesture over my shoulder with my thumb. "I can't talk long, because I need to get ready for work, but would you like to come upstairs for a coffee?"

His shoulders drop and a legitimate smile slowly spreads. "Yeah. I'd like that." He reaches inside his truck, pulling out a box the size of a shoebox. He locks the doors and then follows me upstairs silently. To say I feel awkward would be a gross understatement. I'm not sure where we go from here.

Unlocking the door, I gesture for Martin to follow me inside. "Please, take a seat." I gesture toward my two-seater dining setting. "How do you like your coffee?"

He pulls out a chair and sits, placing the box he brought on the table. "Cream, no sugar. Thanks."

Well, that's easy to remember, since it's how I have *my* coffee. I make our drinks and then carry them to the table. I pull out a chair and sit opposite him, looking at the box positioned in the middle of the table between us as though it contains poisonous spiders. We sit in silent contemplation; me studying the box; him studying me.

"This is awkward." I chuckle mildly, trying to break the ice.

He chuckles, too. "It is a bit." We both take a sip of our coffee.

He lets out a long, drawn-out breath, his posture softening. "I'm sorry, Molly."

Those three little words unlock the flood. Tears stream unbidden down my face, and I hide behind my hands as my body shudders from the onslaught. Martin's chair scrapes across the floor and then I'm engulfed in his arms. If my body was racked with sobs before, it's worse now. He rubs his hand up and down my back.

"Shh, shh, shh. It's okay. We'll work through this. I promise it will be okay." He kisses the top of my head, reminding me of the way Jack would soothe me when I was upset. It's such a fatherly action. He pulls away, tucking the hair that's fallen out of my ponytail behind both of my ears at the same time. Gray eyes to gray eyes, he gives me a tentative smile. I return it the best I can, but it's shaky.

"I'm gonna go wash my face. Be back in a minute." I close the bathroom door and study myself in the mirror, sucking in as much air as I can. After rinsing my face with cool water, I pat it dry, then take a couple of deep breaths, reminding myself I can do this. I'm strong, just like Mom.

I walk back to the table with my shoulders back and a new resolve to work through this. "Do you think we should do like a … paternity test or something?" I stammer. "You know, to make sure."

He opens his mouth and closes it again. "I guess so. If that's what you would like to do." He reaches across, covering my hand with his. "But I don't need it to know you're mine, Molly. I can see it in your eyes and the timeline matches." I can too, but I wanted to give him the option. It must be tough to suddenly meet the daughter you've never laid eyes on before. He grips the box and draws it close. "I brought some photos to show you. I thought it might be a good place to start."

I nod. "You have photos of Mom in high school?" Excitement bubbles in my stomach at the prospect of seeing photos of her when she was young. For obvious reasons, she had nothing to show me from her life back here.

"Yeah. You wanna see?" He smiles and his dimples, which match mine, pop.

He opens the lid with a flourish, and I can't wait to see what he has to show me. He pulls out a handful of photos and shuffles through them, then slides one across the table to me. It shows Mom, sitting on a picnic blanket beneath a giant tree. She looks tiny compared to the trunk behind her. "She's about fifteen in that photo. I thought Nicole was the prettiest girl in school and even though my friends gave me a hard time about dating a junior, I didn't care one bit."

Martin spends the next fifteen minutes showing me photos of Mom when she was a teenager. She looked so carefree and happy—a regular teenage girl, spending time with her boyfriend and her friends.

The rumbling of an engine reminds me I should be getting ready for work. I look at Martin with apology. "I'm sorry. I need to get ready for work. Max already had to rearrange his schedule yesterday because of me. I don't want to let him down again today."

Martin collects the photographs quickly. "Sure. I understand. I'll get out of your hair." He digs into his pocket and pulls out a card, sliding it across the table toward me. "Uhm, here's my number. Maybe when you're ready, we could … uh … meet for a coffee and a chat. I'd like to get to know you if that's okay with you?"

"Of course. I'll call you and we can work out a time."

He slides the box closer to me. "You can keep that if you want. Look through the photos at your own pace. If you have questions you want to ask me, I'm an open book. Really, I am." He holds out his hands.

The vibe between us is weird. We're both nervous and unsure of what to do. Should I hug him goodbye? I decide to go for it. He accepts the gesture and pulls me in tight, swaying from side to side.

It feels weird to hug a relative stranger this intimately.

A knock at my internal door disrupts the moment and we pull apart.

CHAPTER 22

—*max*—

MARTIN'S TRUCK IS PARKED IN FRONT OF THE WORKSHOP AS I pull in, making my temper flare. I can't believe he showed up this morning. It would have been better to give Molly some time to get her head around their relationship, rather than bombard her the very next day. I draw in a deep breath because ultimately, it's between the two of them to work out. It's none of my business.

As I climb the stairs, I prepare to lay eyes on the woman who's quickly overtaken my life. Sleeping next to her and waking with her in my arms is something I could easily become addicted to. I run my hand through my hair and sigh. I probably shouldn't have kissed her. She has enough going on in her life at the moment. But could I stop myself from tasting her? *Hell no.* And if it weren't for her alarm, I'm not sure I would have stopped at all. I wanted to strip her bare and taste every inch of her body, paying special attention to the haven between her thighs.

I knock on the door when all I want to do is storm inside and demand Martin gives her some space. It opens, revealing Molly still wearing her running gear. He must have been waiting here when she came back from her run and because she's a sweetheart, she didn't turn him away. Her smile is instant and genuine; their time together must have been okay, because she looks relaxed, which means I can calm down.

"Hey." She waves her arm out for me to come in and looks across at Martin. "Martin was about to leave so I could shower and get ready for work. I don't want to let you down again."

I step through the doorway and place my hand on her hip as I lean in to touch my lips to hers. Now that I've kissed her, I want to do it all the time. She sucks in a sharp breath but doesn't pull away.

"Hey," I whisper against her lips. I tip my chin toward Martin. "Martin." Clearing the door, I close it behind me. "Take your time. If you need today off, that's okay too. Yesterday took a toll on you." I glare pointedly at Martin.

"Thank you, but I'll be okay. It's better if I stay busy, anyway." She thumbs over her shoulder toward the bathroom. "You two can catch up if you like while I get ready." She glances between the two of us, then heads into the bathroom. Martin and I stay put until she closes the door, and we hear the water turn on.

I step toward him, my eyes narrowed. "Do you think it's a good idea to show up here today?" I wave my arm out. "You could have given her a couple of days to come to terms with what the two of you figured out yesterday." I'm proud of how well I temper my tone when, in reality, I want to punch this guy in the face and I'm not a confrontational person.

He steps toward me. "I appreciate your concern for Molly, but this is a family matter between the two of us." Martin raises his brows.

"I get that. But you didn't see how upset and confused she is about this." I run my hand through my hair in frustration that he's not considering Molly's well-being.

His shoulders drop. "Beth said I should give her more time,

but when I think about everything," he shrugs, "I've already missed too much. I don't want to miss another second."

I blow out a heavy breath. There are no winners here. Both of them have a lot to work through. "I'm sorry. I didn't think about it from your point of view." A squeal sounds from the bathroom and the water shuts off.

"Shit. I never fixed the wiring yesterday. I'll go down and grab my tools and fix it now. The heating system's wiring is likely corroded. I'll take a look." He heads for the outer door.

"Thanks. I completely forgot about it yesterday." I move to the bathroom door to check on Molly. "You okay in there?"

"Yeah. The water turned freezing again." The door opens, exposing Molly wrapped in a threadbare towel. She peers around the apartment. "Has Martin left?"

"Not yet. He's gone downstairs to grab his tools. He'll fix the wiring today since we all forgot about it yesterday."

Molly blows out a breath. "Oh, thank goodness. Every time I have a shower, I cross my fingers that it won't go cold, but it doesn't work." She giggles. I'm not sure how she's still finding humor after everything she's been through. "I'll get dressed. Back in five."

Yeah right. I've never known a woman to be ready that fast. I openly admire her long legs until she closes her bedroom door. Sure enough, she comes out of her bedroom as Martin steps back inside to fix the hot water.

As Molly and I share lunch, I study her for any signs that she's still upset. But there's nothing. I shouldn't be surprised, because she gave no outward sign about her situation or how much she'd lost until the other night.

"Are you okay?" I'm not going to attempt to guess how

she's feeling. Having two sisters, I know how difficult it can be to gauge a woman's emotions.

She raises her head, her eyebrows scrunched. "Yeah?" Her voice is unsure, the single word coming out more like a question.

"Are you okay after Martin showed up unannounced this morning?" I'm still pissed about it, and it had nothing to do with me.

"Oh right. It was a surprise, and I definitely wasn't ready. But I didn't have the heart to turn him away." She scrunches up her nose. "It was pretty awkward. He left some photos of my mom for me to look at, though, which is pretty cool. I never saw what she was like when she was young. When she left, she didn't take any of that sort of stuff with her." She shrugs and stays silent for a few moments, and I think that's all she's going to say. "I'm a bit confused, though."

"Yeah. What about?"

"I dunno. He … he basically abandoned Mom when she told him she was pregnant. But he seems incredibly upset about missing out on being in my life. His reaction doesn't add up." She shrugs and picks at her sandwich.

I run my thumbnail across my bottom lip as I collect my thoughts. "Maybe he's always regretted his decision. I don't want to make excuses for the guy, but he was *only* nineteen when he knocked up your mom."

She drops her sandwich back onto the desk and straightens. "My mom was *only* seventeen. But she took full responsibility. Made important decisions and stuck with them." Her eyes scan around the office like she's looking for something. "Mom had to grow up fast and face the reality of her situation. She didn't walk away—she couldn't. Her life was hard. Damn hard raising a baby on her own. Living in a car. Barely getting by. Working minimal jobs that allowed her to keep a baby in the back office for short periods of time." Her voice cracks and her eyes become glassy.

Well, fuck.

I move my chair closer to hers and wrap my arm around her shoulder to drag her in close. I gently press her head against my chest. "Your mom sounds like she was an incredible woman. She made tough choices and followed through. You're an amazing person as a result of her parenting." I stroke my hand down her soft hair. "The only way you'll get answers is if you ask Martin directly. Maybe there was some sort of misunderstanding? I dunno. I wish I had the answers and I could take away this pain for you."

She nods. "I know."

Molly peels away from me and heads to the bathroom to wash her face and gather her composure while I clean up from lunch. She opens the door, looking marginally more put together. "Are you gonna be okay? You can take the afternoon off if you need."

She waves away my concern. "I'll be okay. It's better if I keep busy. I promise I'm alright."

I hug her, place a gentle kiss on her forehead and then head back out to the workshop to get on with the tire change and wheel alignment I need to finish.

"Uncle Maaaaax!" Kenny's sweet voice shouts from the opposite side of the workshop.

Shit. I lost track of time and I forgot to let Molly know Emma was bringing the kids by this afternoon. Apparently, she needed to drop something off, but I think it's an excuse to check out my new office manager so she can report back to the rest of the family.

I drop the torque wrench and hurry to the office door before Kenny decides to run across my workshop to get to me. The kids know the rules. They're not allowed on the workshop floor unless they're right beside me or Emma, but Kenny gets excited and makes her own rules.

As I close in on the door, Kenny leaps at me—I love how much she trusts me. I catch her easily, throwing her into the air with a flourish. She giggles as I catch her and kiss her forehead. "How's my Kenny?" I press my forehead to hers. She's one of the sweetest kids I've ever met, and I don't think I'm biased because she's my niece.

"I'm good. We came to visit you." Her face is alight with joy, her body is practically vibrating with excitement.

"I can see that." I tap the tip of her nose, then place her back on her feet.

"Hi, Uncle Max. What are you working on over there?" Austin points in the direction I just came.

I muss his hair. "Hey, Buddy. I'm doing a tire change and wheel alignment."

His eyes light up. "Can I help?"

I glance at Emma for guidance but she's too busy smiling at her son's enthusiasm. "Probably not today. I can't stop for too long. The owner will be here to collect his car soon." His little face drops and his body sags. "Maybe next time I do the tires on the Dodge, okay? I'll have more time and we can do it together."

His eyes light with happiness. "Really?"

"Yeah. Really."

He runs to Emma. "Did you hear that? I can help Uncle Max change his tires one day. How cool is that?" My eyes catch on Molly. She's smiling as she watches my niece and nephews.

I move closer to Lachlan. "Hey, Lachlan. How are you doing today, Buddy?"

"I'm good. Thank you for asking, Uncle Max." Emma steps next to Lachlan.

"Show Uncle Max what you brought over for him." She leans into me. "Hey, little brother." I roll my eyes and Molly giggles. It's comical that she insists on calling me little brother.

He nods and then walks toward the door, picking up a square timber box. It looks a little heavy, so I move to help him. Molly makes room on the desk, and we place it down carefully. The workmanship is incredible. "What's this?"

Lachlan focuses on making eye contact with me and I smile inside at how far he's come over the past twelve months or so. "Theo helped me make this sorting box for you. You can put the different-size nuts and washers in here." He points to several of the compartments. Molly's hand comes up to cover her mouth and Emma's face is full of pride.

I crouch down to Lachlan's level. "This is incredible. It looks exactly like the one I was looking at buying last month. I keep mixing up all of my nuts, washers, and bolts and need something to help me keep them organized." His little chest puffs out with pride. "Thank you, Buddy. It's amazing."

"You're welcome, Uncle Max."

I lift my eyes to Emma. "This is incredible. Thank Theo for me, won't you?"

"I will. I'm pretty sure Lachlan did most of the work, though." She grins at her son.

I realize I haven't introduced Molly to my family. "I'm sorry. You guys haven't met Molly."

Kenny butts in. "Yes, we have. We already said hello before we saw you. She looks like Elsa, from *Frozen*. She's so pretty, Uncle Max."

Emma, Molly, and I all burst into laughter. Kenny's always comparing pretty ladies to her Disney princesses.

"We already introduced ourselves." Emma angles her body

in such a way that she can raise her brows at me without Molly seeing. With wide eyes, she mouths, "She's beautiful."

I shake my head and huff out a laugh. Beautiful is an understatement, in my opinion.

"You should come to Lachlan's birthday party!" Kenny shouts as she spins around the room.

Molly's eyes snap to mine in confusion.

"Oh, you totally should. We'd love to have you come," Emma adds with glee. She knows exactly what she's doing. She's fucking stirring the pot. If she knew where I slept last night and what I was doing this morning, she'd be all over it and I'd never hear the end.

Molly's like a deer caught in headlights as her head swings between me and Em. "Oh, uhm, I wouldn't want to intrude on a family event."

"You wouldn't be intruding at all. The more, the merrier. Right, Lachlan?" Emma runs her fingers through Lachlan's hair.

He doesn't seem convinced. "Yes." He tilts his head up to Emma. "What does that mean? The more the merrier?"

I crouch down to Lachlan's level. "It means a party is more fun when there are lots of people."

His face scrunches up. "I don't like to be around a lot of people. It's too noisy."

"That's okay. I don't have to come, Lachlan," Molly offers. Sheer relief on her face that she has an excuse.

"Molly doesn't make all that much noise, Buddy." I smirk at Molly.

"Oh, okay then. But will she be mean like Mona?" he asks.

My grin drops and I shake my head. Mona was a fucking bitch to my family. I shouldn't have stayed with her as long as I did. I didn't realize the kids had noticed, but I shouldn't be surprised because Lachlan notices everything. "No, Lachlan. Molly wouldn't know how to be mean. She's incredibly kind."

He nods. "Okay then." He moves closer to Molly. "You can come." He turns to his mom. "Molly doesn't smell terrible like Mona did."

An embarrassed huff escapes from my sister and she mouths an apology to Molly, which she kindly waves off.

"Yay!" Kenny jumps up and down in excitement. "Can I braid your hair like Elsa?"

Molly's mouth opens and closes, her hand over her heart. "Thank you, Lachlan. I'd love to come to your party." Then she turns to Kenny. "I'd love to have you braid my hair like Elsa. I'm not sure it's as long as hers, though."

"That's okay. I'll make it work." Kenny nods to herself, then continues to spin.

"Okay. Well, that's settled. We really must be going." Em gathers the kids together. "It was nice meeting you, Molly." Then she turns toward me. "Do you mind helping me with the kids, Max?"

That's code for I need to speak with you about Molly. "Sure."

The door to the outside is barely closed when Emma nudges me. Hard. "Oh my gosh, Max. She's so gorgeous and incredibly sweet."

We walk toward her car, and I help buckle the kids into their seats. "Yeah, she's pretty great."

"Pretty great, huh?" Em raises her eyebrows. "She thought I was a single Mom, who had turned up on the wrong day to get my car repaired. She was so freaking apologetic."

Sounds like Molly. "She *is* an incredibly sweet girl. She's been through a lot."

Emma's face turns sad. "Oh, the poor thing. Well, make sure she comes to Lachlan's birthday. Everyone's gonna love her."

"Hang on a minute. You realize she's just my office assistant. The family doesn't need to 'love' her." As I say the words, I know I'm not fooling anyone, especially myself. She's already more than an office assistant to me.

"You keep telling yourself that, little brother." She presses up on her toes and kisses my cheek before climbing into her car. "Whatever makes it easier to work alongside her. But mark my words. She'll be part of our family soon enough." She winks, then closes her door, not allowing me to respond.

And I know. I know she's right. Damn it. This wasn't supposed to happen.

CHAPTER 23

—molly—

MAX LOCKS THE FRONT DOOR OF THE WORKSHOP, THEN TURNS to me. "I can come with you if you want?"

I think he's offered to come to dinner with Martin at least six times today. There hasn't been another kiss since Tuesday morning, but he's been checking on me at every opportunity. He's being incredibly sweet, even if he's not giving me what I really want.

It's comforting knowing he's concerned about me, and I don't have to deal with the fallout from Monday's revelation on my own. That he'll be available if I need him. I don't think he realizes the gift he's giving me.

I smile. "I promise I can do this. Thanks for offering your support, Max. It means a lot to me."

He searches for something in the top drawer of the desk, looking triumphant when he finds it. Placing the sticky note on the desk, he writes something and hands it to me. "My address." I look at him for clarification. "If you need someone to talk to after you finish with Martin, I'll be up late. Even if the lights are off, just knock. Okay?" He raises his eyebrows, waiting for my answer.

I take the paper from him as my heart expands to double its size at the gesture. "Okay. Thank you." I want to land a kiss on his cheek, but I'm not sure it'll be welcome since he hasn't kissed me since the other day.

He smiles. "Good girl." Flutters explode in my stomach with his praise. *Shit!* I had no idea I liked that so much. I can even feel my cheeks heating. "Where are you having dinner?"

"*Parable?*" I'm reasonably sure that's what it's called. "It has a heated outdoor patio area to sit."

He nods. "I know that place. It has great food. Do you know how to get there?"

"Yeah. I looked it up at lunchtime." He's being a mother hen and I love that he cares this much about me.

He steps closer, placing his hands on my hips. His touch sears through the fabric of my pants and sends my heart racing. *Will he finally kiss me?* I tilt my head up, locking eyes with his olive-green ones. "Good luck. I hope you get the answers you need and that the two of you work out a way to move forward from everything that's happened." He finishes with a lingering press of his lips to my forehead, which isn't exactly the type of kiss I want from him, but I feel it all the way to my soul, like a brand. "I'm only a phone call away if you need me."

I swallow my emotions. I don't want to burst into tears. "Thank you," I whisper. "I promise if I need you, I'll call."

He nods and drops his hands from my hips. Leaving me cold. "I'd better let you get ready." He lingers, making no move to leave. I think this may be harder for him than it is for me. His care and concern for my well-being fill the parts of my heart that have felt empty for the past couple of months.

"Okay. I'll see you later." Our goodbye is awkward.

I want us to be more than two colleagues saying bye.

I want hugs and lingering kisses.

I want him to tuck my hair behind my ear.

I want his hands on me.
I want to feel his arms around me.
But I get none of that.

My legs are shaky as I walk into the restaurant. I thought I was doing okay until it was time to climb out of my car and walk inside. As I step inside, I'm worried I haven't chosen the right outfit. Perhaps I should have worn something a little dressier. I opted for the capris I used to wear for work and paired them with a white shirt and denim jacket to help dress them down a little.

Worrying about things that can't be changed right now filters through my mind as I wait for the hostess—*What if I disappoint him in some way? What if I'm not the type of daughter he expects me to be? What if I'm not good enough?*

A middle-aged woman with jet-black hair and striking features greets me at the podium. "Welcome to *Parable*. Do you have a reservation?"

I nervously tuck my hair behind my ear, my hand shaking. "Uh, yeah. I'm with Martin …" Shit! I can't remember his family name. I saw it on the side of his truck, but I'm drawing a blank right now. "Uhm, I'm sorry. I don't remember his surname."

She smiles at me with warmth. "That's okay. I have a booking here under the name of Martin DeLuca. He's the only Martin we have, so I'll assume he's your companion for the evening."

I fidget with my bracelet and give her a grateful smile. "Thanks. I'm incredibly nervous and I couldn't remember, but that's his name." I chuckle nervously.

"He's already here. If you'll follow me, I'll show you to your table."

We weave through the tables, and my eyes don't know what to take in first. The garden is lush. When Martin said it had a heated outdoor patio area, I didn't expect the restaurant to be like something I'd expect to find in a city like Palm Springs. Glancing up, thick vines grow over beams and hundreds, if not thousands, of fairy lights are strung up to add to the atmosphere. This place is gorgeous. By the time we arrive at the table, I've been distracted enough that I'm a little calmer and my legs feel less shaky. Thank goodness.

Martin stands abruptly, knocking his chair over as we stop at the table. A grimace forms on his face as he corrects his chair, and the hostess leaves us to our evening.

"Sorry about that. I'm a little nervous." He pulls out my chair for me to sit, but I awkwardly turn to hug him. I feel slightly better knowing he's feeling nervous, too. He squeezes me tight and then pushes my chair in as I sit, then takes his seat. "Uhm, I didn't order any wine because I wasn't sure if you drink wine or what you like to have."

"Oh, that's okay. I'll have a beer if that's alright?" *Am I supposed to drink wine? Will he think less of me because I drink beer?*

His shoulders drop and he gives me a shaky smile, running his fingers through his thick salt and pepper hair. "That's perfectly fine." He catches the eye of the waiter and orders two beers.

We're both silent.

I fidget with my bracelet and peer around the restaurant awkwardly. Martin's tearing the paper napkin to shreds as the waiter returns with our beers.

"Thank you." He nods to the man, and I give him what I'm sure comes across as more of a grimace. Martin holds his beer up toward me, so I pick up mine. "To new beginnings."

I tap the neck of my bottle against his. "To new beginnings." We both take a sip. Mine is small while Martin seems to finish almost half of his bottle in one go. A small smile touches my lips. "I'm nervous, too."

My words seem to put him somewhat at ease. "Did you go through the photos I left?"

"Yeah. It's amazing to see Mom when she was that young. I mean, we had a few photos from when I was a baby, so she was young in those, but these … I don't know. They seem like they're from a different time. She looked so carefree."

"I'd love to see those photos of you as a baby some time … uh … if you want to show them to me, that is."

"Of course. There aren't many, but I can show you next time. I didn't think to bring them with me tonight." I chuckle lightly. "It didn't even cross my mind to return your photos. I'm sorry." I hope he's not angry with me for keeping them this long.

He waves me off. "Keep them as long as you like. I can probably print you a set."

"That'd be great. If you don't mind." There were quite a few photos in the box. It wouldn't be cheap to print copies.

"Not at all. Tell me about your childhood." I guess it's a fair question, but what will he think about the way I grew up? *Will he think Mom did a terrible job?*

The waiter interrupts us. "Are you ready to order?"

We glance at each other and chuckle. "My apologies. We haven't looked at the menu. If you wouldn't mind giving us a few more minutes? We'll do that now."

"No problem." He leaves and we both study our menu.

The waiter returns after a few minutes, and we place our orders. I order the double cheeseburger with house-cut Kennebec fries, the cheapest thing on the menu. While Martin orders the grilled NY steak with potato leek gratin, rainbow chard, and pan jus, the second most expensive item on the menu. I get paid once a month, so I need to be careful with how I spend my money. This meal will mean I have to be more careful for the rest of the month.

Once the waiter's gone, Martin turns his attention back to me. "Tell me everything." He raises his eyebrows and offers a smile.

I rack my brain. Where do I start? What do I include? What do I leave out? I don't want him to judge Mom harshly or think poorly of us. Glancing around me, I try to think of what to say. I don't know why I didn't think about this before I came tonight. Of course, he was going to ask me about my childhood and growing up.

I can't pick a spot to look at, my eyes darting everywhere as I work to gather my thoughts, but there are too many to sort through. Maybe this was a bad idea?

Martin reaches across the table, laying his weathered hand over mine. "Perhaps that was too much. I only want to get to know you. I'm devastated I've missed so much of your life." He blows out a heavy breath. His eyes, so much like my own, are full of regret.

Maybe I should ask a question of my own.

I fidget with the cardboard coaster on the table. "Do you mind if I ask you a question?"

"Of course not. As I said the other day, I'm an open book." He gestures with his hands at the same time.

"Uhm ... You ... uh ... seem really upset about not seeing me grow up." I swallow. "But after Mom told you she was pregnant. You disappeared and left her to deal with the aftermath on her own. Mom left because you abandoned her and then her dad wanted her to abort me. She didn't want to do that. She thought her only option was to run. I'm a little confused, to be honest." I lick my dry lips and take a shaky sip of my beer.

Martin's face falls and his shoulders slump. His eyes skate over the people around us and he runs his hands through his hair. It's become a mess with all of his nervous attention. "I was nineteen."

Not this. Anything but this. "She was seventeen," I toss back.

He nods slowly. "I know. When I say I was nineteen, I say it to point out that I was a dumb kid." He holds up his hand to stop me from interrupting. "Nicole was always too good for me. Even though she was two years younger than me, she was far more mature." He takes another drink of his beer, draining it. He draws in a deep breath and blows it out. "I did. I disappeared. I'm not proud of my behavior. She came to me crying that she'd missed her period, so she took a pregnancy test. When she showed me the white stick with two pink lines. Well … let's just say I didn't handle it well." He draws in a deep breath and rubs his hands down his face. "I blamed her. Shouted at her." He shakes his head. "I'm embarrassed to tell you I cussed her out. Told her she was ruining my life and walked away." He rests his elbow on the table and leans forward, rubbing his hand across his mouth. "It took me a few days to calm down and think through our situation. I loved Nicole. She was everything to me. Even though we were young, I couldn't see my future without her in it." I open my mouth to question his love, but he stops me with his palm facing me. "I know it doesn't sound like I did, but I did. And I'll circle back to the fact I was a dumb kid back then. Once I calmed down, I started thinking about what we could do. I was halfway through my apprenticeship to be an electrician, so I figured we could make it work. Things wouldn't be easy, but so long as we were together, we'd be okay."

The waiter interrupts with our meals. I'm not feeling all that hungry now. I want to leave. Hearing this is too difficult, and I don't like what he's told me so far. I don't like this man at all.

I'm supposed to like him, right?

He's my dad.

Neither of us touches our food. He draws in another deep breath. "I went back to see Nicole about a week after everything fell apart. She was gone. Her mother was devastated and her father beat the shit out of me. I ended up with fractured ribs and a broken collarbone, a smashed eye socket, and a broken nose." He points to the crooked bridge.

A gasp escapes and I cover my mouth in shock. Oh my God!

He shrugs. "I deserved it. And probably a lot worse. I left without any answers that day and staggered home. I gave it a few days and then went back when Mr. Lewis wasn't home. I hoped to have a better chance at getting information out of Nicole's mom. But she had no idea where Nicole had gone. She'd disappeared into thin air."

I nod. "I knew she'd left and not told anyone where she was going. She told me she didn't know herself. She didn't have a plan. She kept driving until she felt she was far enough away. Mom cleaned out the money she'd saved from birthdays over the years to get her to Portland."

Maybe if she'd held on a few more days, Martin and Mom would have sorted it all out.

Maybe things would have been different. But then I wouldn't have had Jack as my stepfather and there would never have been Ethan. I don't want to think about that. I loved Jack like a father and he loved me like a daughter. And Ethan. I loved my brother so much. It hurts thinking about them. About losing them.

I peer back up at Martin. His eyes appear glassy ... and sad. Worry lines his forehead and he blows out a harsh breath. "I ... I'm sorry. My immaturity back then has been my greatest regret. You probably hate me now, and I'm guessing I'll lose you all over again." He smiles, but it's sad and full of defeat.

His posture is that of a man who's lost something he thought was guaranteed.

I return his sad smile and shrug. "I think I'm going to need a little time." As much as I don't like to waste food, because I know how hard it is to come by, I've lost my appetite and I don't want to be here anymore. My skin is itchy and too tight. I need space away to work through everything I've learned tonight. "I'm sorry." I point toward my plate of uneaten food. "I'm not usually wasteful, but I can't eat this and I'd like to leave if you don't mind."

He nods as though he was expecting me to walk away. "I understand. I'm truly sorry, Molly. For my actions back then and for everything we've both lost. If you give me the chance, I'll make it up to you. I'll be the man I should have always been for you. I'll spend the rest of my days making it up to you. If you'll allow me."

"I … I think I need some time to think. Can you give me that?" A storm is swirling in my stomach and I'm fighting to contain everything this conversation has stirred up inside me. I need to get out of here.

"I can try. Only if I know there's some possibility I haven't truly lost you when I've only just found you."

I give him a sad smile. "I can't make promises, Martin. This. It's … it's been a lot." I stand. "Bye, Martin." I can't bring myself to hug him. I don't want to touch the man who caused Mom so much pain. I was young when she told me why I didn't have a daddy, but I felt her pain. It rolled off of her in waves even though she tried to hide it from me. I spin and walk away quickly, unsure how my shaky legs will carry me.

CHAPTER 24

—molly—

As soon as I close myself inside my car, the storm I was holding inside breaks free, streaming down my face and dripping from my chin. I drop my head to my steering wheel and let the tears come. I need to purge this hurt out of me.

A warm hand slides around my back, underneath the fall of my hair, and I scream. I didn't even hear the door open. The hold tightens on me and I turn my head. Only my hair blocks my view.

"Shhh, it's only me, Dimples." Max pushes my hair away from my face, and I'm embarrassed at how I must look.

"Wha– … what are you doing here?"

One side of his mouth tips up and he shrugs carelessly. "I couldn't sit at home waiting and not knowing if you'd be okay. I've been sitting in the parking lot for the last thirty minutes, watching and waiting." His eyebrows scrunch low. "Do I need to kick Martin's ass?" His tone is deadly serious. Max is not a confrontational man, so for him to offer to kick Martin's ass means the world to me.

I drop my head to his shoulder and wrap my arm around him, pulling him close to me. A relieved smile touches my lips as I shake my head in the negative. Having him here settles the storm and calms my soul. I know I don't have to deal with this alone. Max has quickly become my new anchor, whether or not he realizes it. A sob breaks free, but it's full of relief knowing someone has my back. I've been missing the support since I lost my world.

"C'mon. Let me take you home. We can come back tomorrow to collect your car. Grab your purse."

I nod into his shoulder, hiding the mess that must be my face. Max helps me out of my car and into his. I spend the drive staring out of the window, not seeing anything, my mind running over everything Martin said. It's not until we pull into the driveway of an unfamiliar house that I turn to Max.

"Where are we?"

"My place. I don't think you should be alone tonight. You can have my bed. I'll sleep on the couch." He climbs out of the car and comes around to my side to collect me. Helping me out of the car, he carries me to the front door, only putting me on my feet to unlock the latch. As soon as it's open, he picks me up again.

"I can walk, you know." I chuckle. Secretly, I don't want him to put me down. His care is soothing.

"I know, but I want to care for you. You need some TLC." He plants a gentle kiss against my temple, melting my heart. The man who says he's *only* my boss and that we can't be anything more than that carries me across the living room, placing me on the chaise portion of his heather-gray sectional couch. He lays my legs out gently and props a large, red cushion behind my back. I remove my shoes and drop them onto the carpet next to the couch. I don't like having shoes on the couch. "Did you eat? You didn't seem like you were inside long enough to eat."

I shake my head. "I lost my appetite. To be honest, I'm not hungry."

"How about a hot chocolate, then? Mom taught me how to make the best hot chocolate for times like these." He looks hopeful, his hands tucked into his back pockets, tugging the denim tight across his firm thighs.

I smile. "That'd be nice. Do you mind if I use your bathroom? I wouldn't mind cleaning up a bit." I circle my fingers around my face, not that I want to draw his attention to the mess.

"Uh, sure." He rushes forward to help me up from the couch. "I'll show you where it is."

As he guides me through to the bathroom, I take in my surroundings. His house is bare but tidy. It has the essential items, but nothing more than that. I wonder if it's because he likes it this way, or maybe he hasn't been here all that long. He said it took a while for him to afford a house of his own away from the workshop.

The light turns on in the bathroom with a flick of the switch and Max leaves me alone, closing the door quietly behind him. Studying myself in the mirror above the sink, I cringe at my ruined mascara, smudged around my eyes with light black streaks down my cheeks. Oh my gosh, it's every bit as bad as I thought it'd be. I set about doing what I need to do, go to the toilet, and wash my hands. Max meets me back in the living room with a steaming cup of hot chocolate.

"Sorry, I don't have any snacks to go with the drinks," he says apologetically and passes me a cup once I'm situated to his satisfaction back where I was before. He's placed a tray on the couch next to me, so I don't have to reach forward for my drink.

"It's okay. I don't think I can stomach much, anyway." I draw in a deep breath of the steaming liquid. "This smells amazing. Thank you."

"You're welcome. If you want to talk about what

happened, I'm here. If you would rather just watch a movie and forget for a while, we can do that too."

"Can we forget for a while?"

"Sure."

Max turns on the television and flicks through the channels. I catch a glimpse of a *Friends* episode. "Ooh, can we watch that episode? I think it's the one where Ross whitens his teeth."

He flicks back to the right channel, and we settle down, Max choosing the cushion next to mine. I rest my head on his shoulder and he takes my hand, placing it on his thigh, drawing circles on the back of my hand with his thumb. We both chuckle as Monica and Chandler lay eyes on Ross's teeth for the first time. The banter between them is so funny that Max and I chuckle. We giggle through episode after episode, my body sagging lower and lower until my head is resting in Max's lap and he's stroking my hair, lulling me into a sleepy state.

I wake slightly when Max's arms slide beneath my legs and shoulders. "Huh?"

He kisses my forehead. "You fell asleep so I'm putting you to bed."

"Mmm, 'kay." I snuggle into his warm body, too sleepy to offer to walk myself.

He lays me on the bed. "Uhm, do you want a T-shirt or something to sleep in so you're more comfortable?"

"Mmm, thank you." I give him a sleepy smile and begin unbuttoning my shirt, pulling it open to expose my cotton bra. Max's eyes widen and he rushes over to the drawers. Next thing I know, he's dragging a T-shirt over my head to cover me. He's already seen me naked, so I'm not sure why he's in such a hurry to cover me now. I undo my bra and pull it out through the sleeves, then take off my capris, leaving my clothes on the floor beside the bed. Lying down, I pull the bedcovers over my body. Max picks up my clothes and places them over the chair in the corner and then comes back to tuck me in.

Gently pushing my hair away from my face, he leans down and presses a soft kiss to my temple. "Good night, Dimples."

"Mmm, night." In my sleepy state, I realize he's not climbing into bed. I reach out my arm toward him. "Please stay." I open my eyes when he takes too long to respond. His face is full of indecision. "Please."

That seems to do the trick, and he undoes his jeans and removes his T-shirt. I wish I had my wits about me to appreciate my hot boss wearing only his jocks, but sleep is working hard to pull me under. He slides under the covers, keeping distance between our bodies, and turns out the lamp. I roll over and snuggle into his warm body, sighing at the feel of him beneath my hands and cheek. His steady heartbeat sends me into a deep sleep.

—max—

I *WAS* TRYING TO BE A FUCKING GENTLEMAN. I HONESTLY WAS. I don't trust myself to share a bed with the woman who's taking up so much space in my head and, if I'm being completely honest, in my heart, too. I haven't slept properly since Monday night when I spent the night in her bed. Even though I spent the night on top of the covers, her scent surrounded me, and holding her close, felt … right.

With her body curled into me and her leg thrown over mine, I lay awake for what seemed like hours with a raging hard-on.

We fit perfectly together.

When she rested her head over my heart and released a contented sigh, I knew I would do anything for her. Anything to make this transition she's about to go through with Martin as pain-free as possible.

When I saw her drop her head to her steering wheel and her body heave in the parking lot outside of the restaurant, I knew she'd taken an emotional hit over dinner with her dad. I couldn't stop myself from going to her and outing the fact that I was following her. I didn't care.

I only wanted to be there for her.

To take away her pain.

Sitting with her snuggled into me on my couch and listening to her giggle at the TV eased some of the rage I'd been feeling toward Martin for upsetting Molly. She's already been through enough. She doesn't need this shit dredging up stuff that's gotta be tough for her. I wanted to ask her what he'd said, but I respect that she needs time to digest what she learned tonight. I blow out a long breath and work to relax my body. I wrap my arms around the woman I'm falling for and kiss the top of her head as she sleeps. She sighs contentedly, and my body relaxes further.

Before I even open my eyes, I know she's looking at me. I can feel her stare burning into the side of my face. Her hand scorches my lower abdomen and my cock thinks it's an invitation to rise for attention. I kept my boxer briefs on last night, so he's somewhat contained, but he's doing his best to escape the confines of the fabric.

I groan as her fingers trace the trail of hair that leads from my navel downward. I grasp her hand to stop her from reaching the elastic band and discovering the issue I'm trying to control but am failing. Her tits are pressed into the side of my body and every single inch of me is aware of every single inch of her. Every breath. Every beat of her heart.

"Morning," her whispered raspy voice reaches my ears and my cock jolts. He likes that just awake timbre. Fuck, she's sexy.

I crack my eyes open and turn my head slightly. "Morning." She's gifting me those dimples, and the idea that I want to see those dimples first thing every single morning for the rest of my life hits me hard.

"I didn't think you were going to wake up."

I reach up and tuck her loose hair behind her ear, sliding my fingers along the strands, admiring its silkiness. I've never felt hair so soft and silky. She leans forward a little, putting our lips a mere inch apart. Her breath fans across my lips and the urge to taste her builds.

I'm trying to be a fucking gentleman. *Remember that, asshole.*

Her eyes drop to my mouth and I swipe my tongue to moisten my lips. Suddenly, they feel as dry as an empty radiator, but my mouth is watering for a simple taste. Just one little taste. I tell myself it's only a taste—one little kiss. But it's a lie. I know it's a lie.

We both close the distance, meeting in the middle. The first press sets fire licking down my body, the second has me rolling her to her back so I can climb on top. Using my knees, I push her thighs apart, creating a space to cradle my cock against my girl's pussy; the heat radiating from her scorches my dick. She wraps her gorgeous long legs around me, locking them at the base of my spine and pulling me in tight to her core.

It's my fantasy come to life. I've dreamed about her legs wrapped around me, trapping my body to hers. The only thing that would make it better is if we were both naked.

Moving my hips slowly, I rub my shaft against her mound, drawing moans from both of us. My body is on fire for this woman as her hips rise to meet mine in a rhythm that could get me in trouble. She glides her hands down my back and scrapes her short nails along my spine on the way back up, sending goosebumps radiating across my flesh. I don't want to cum in my boxers like a sixteen-year-old virgin dry-humping his girlfriend in the back seat of his car. I tear my lips from hers and kiss my way behind her ear, continuing down the tendon in her neck, and across her collarbone, nudging the fabric of my T-shirt out of the way as I go. She arches her back, pressing her glorious tits into my chest. I want the fabric that's keeping her flesh from me, gone.

Her hands tickle down my spine to the top of my boxer briefs, where she follows the waistband to each side of my hips. "Can I take these off, Max?" she pants against my ear as she tilts her head to the side to allow me better access to her neck.

I pull back to check she's completely in the moment, and that I'm not pressuring her. Her irises have almost disappeared with desire, her cheeks flushed prettily, her lips swollen from my kisses. I nod and pull away to drag them off.

Her hands cover mine. "Can I do it?" Her eyes have dropped to my heavy cock, working to escape its confines.

I remove my hands and climb from the bed to stand. She crawls over to the side of the bed on her hands and knees, her tits swinging back and forth beneath the fabric covering them. The neck droops enough that I can watch them sway. My eyes zone in on the action and I almost miss that her cotton-covered ass is exposed as my T-shirt gathers in the middle of her back.

She rises in front of me, landing a kiss on the underside of my jaw and I drop my head back, relishing the touch of her lips. Her fingers tuck into the waistband of my briefs and she slides them down, pulling them forward slightly to work around the crown of my dick. Her eyes drop to watch what she's doing, and they widen. She licks her lips, then drops forward, swiping her tongue across my glistening slit. My heart pounds with a heavy rhythm to match my breaths.

"Fuck." My body jolts at the first swipe. She looks up at me with a satisfied grin. "You're a little minx, aren't you, Dimples?" She raises one perfectly sculpted eyebrow before leaning back in. I hold her shoulders still. "Uh, uh, uh. I need you naked. Now."

Her eyes sparkle as she pushes my underwear down further. They slip down my legs and I step out of them. I glide my hand beneath the fall of her hair and grasp the strands at the base, using my grip to pull her back up to my mouth. Her lips part in surprise and I swipe my tongue inside without warning. She gasps and I take advantage to thrust my tongue forward against hers. She presses her body against mine and I move one hand down to her silky thigh and slide it beneath the fabric of the T-shirt. I repeat the action on the other side, gliding my hands over her hips, to the dip of her waist, and along the side of her breasts.

"Lift up," I whisper against her lips, tapping against the side of her body.

She raises her arms and I slide the offending fabric from her stunning body and throw it over my shoulder, not caring where it lands. My eyes start at the top of her head and trail slowly over her face, noting her lustful gaze on my dick. She licks her lips, making them glisten. I need to have a taste. I lean forward, swiping my tongue along the same path.

Pulling away, I continue my perusal. The pulse point at the base of her throat is beating out a rapid rhythm. I grip her lightly around her throat, my palm against the pulse point, studying her heavy-lidded gaze. Molly whimpers, her eyes locked on my mouth. She generously drops her head back, allowing me to kiss the base of her throat and I smile against the rapid pulse, then suck on the flesh, drawing it into my mouth and tasting it with my tongue. She tastes fucking delicious and I'm looking forward to tasting her pussy. My dick throbs and taps against my abdomen at the thought. Molly's hands slide up my arms, along my shoulders, and up the back of my head. Her fingers glide through the strands of my hair and my eyes close in pleasure.

"Max," my name is whispered on a hot breath, her fingers tightening on the strands as she pushes my head lower, toward her tit. I lick my way down under her guidance, then lave the pink areola, before drawing the nipple into my mouth. Her hand pushes my face into the mound, and I suck hard. She presses her breasts forward and I cup her other tit, rolling the nipple between my fingers; it puckers beautifully under my touch, so I switch my mouth across to it.

Licking, sucking, teasing.

I pull back enough to praise her. "You've got beautiful tits. Full and perfect and pink. Look at how they're showing off for me." I pluck them both as I watch them harden further. "Fucking beautiful."

My eyes trail down her flat stomach and freeze on the silver jewelry decorating her navel. I drop, so I can investigate it further, then glance back up at her from my lowered position. Fingering the jewelry, I lean in to lick it with my tongue and then kiss my way to the top of her underwear. "You're full of surprises, Dimples. First the nose ring, now the navel piercing. Fucking sexy as hell."

She giggles, which morphs into a moan as I continue my path downward. Her fingers sift through my hair as I run my nose down her mound, sucking in a deep breath the lower I go. Her excitement is evident from the wet spot staining the cotton. I swipe my tongue over her clit, then nip it gently through the fabric. Her hips buck and she sucks in a sharp breath. I smile against the fabric, then look up at her. The view is fucking sensational. "Mind if I take these off?" She shakes her head, and my disappointment is swift and strong. "Okay." I can't believe I misread the situation so badly, but I pull back. I'm not the guy to force the girl beyond where she's willing to go.

"Why are you stopping?" Her eyebrows scrunch together, causing a crease between them.

"I figured you wanted me to when you didn't want me to take these off." I twist the elastic band of her underwear with my finger.

She chuckles. "I meant I didn't mind. Please. Take them off." She slides them down her athletic thighs, but I stop her.

"I want to do that. Lie down for me." She lies down like a good girl, resting on her elbows, still watching me.

"Good girl," I whisper. She bites her bottom lip as she watches me slowly tug the flimsy fabric down her long, smooth legs. I throw them over my shoulder to join the rest of the discarded items on the floor. Starting at the top of her foot, I glide my hands up the inside of her legs, toward the junction of her thighs, pushing them apart as I go. Goosebumps form under my touch, and her muscles quiver. "You have the most incredible legs. So long and sleek." Following the path of my hands, I place the softest of kisses on the silky skin until I reach the apex and my goal. I run my nose from the base of her slit to the top and back again, drawing in a deep breath and filling my lungs with her musky scent. "Hmmm." Meeting her eyes, I give her a wink and part her pussy lips, flatten my tongue, and take my first taste.

She's fucking luscious.

"Mmmm, Max," she moans as she presses her feet to the bed, bringing her hips up to meet my mouth. I smile against her mound and shake my head slightly.

"Don't be in such a hurry, Dimples. I've got you." I use my finger to slide up each side of her slit, gathering her essence before slipping into her opening. "Fuck!" The heat of her channel sears my skin, and my dick jumps in excitement for what's to come. I drop my mouth to lick and suck her clit in time with the movements of my finger. I slide the sole digit out and replace it with two. "Fuck. I can't wait to get inside you."

"Can you hurry and do that now?" she whispers as she tugs on my hair, attempting to drag me up her body.

My eyes snap up to hers. "What's the rush? Somewhere you need to be?"

"Nope. I just need to be filled with you. I feel like I've been waiting forever." I drop my head back down and return my focus to her delicious pussy. As I feast, I keep my eyes on her. Her tits shiver with each breath and the jewelry on her belly quivers as her muscles tense. "Max, I'm so close." She drops her head back like it's too much to hold up right now.

"While I'm busy down here, play with your tits for me." She brings her hands up, sliding them over her plump globes, pushing them together, and cupping them. I wish I could clone myself and have my mouth on them as well as on her pussy right now.

"That's a good girl," I whisper against her mound, moving my fingers inside her in a come-hither motion.

"I'm so close. Don't stop."

I shake my head in the negative because there's no way on this earth I would stop now. I keep my movements consistent— I don't move harder or faster. She needs to come so I can get inside her.

I fucking need to be inside her.

My balls are heavy as fuck and I need some relief, but not until she comes the first time. Her channel tightens around my fingers and the flutter of her muscles presses against them. She's getting close. The combination of her natural lubrication and the thrusting of my fingers creates a squelching sound as she tightens her legs around my head. I'm getting harder by the second. "Fuck, yeah. Just like that!" It's so sexy how into this she is.

Her entire body tightens and shakes as she moans long and low, her internal muscles strangling my fingers. She's gonna suffocate my dick and I'm gonna love every single second of it. I slow my movements and gentle my kisses, lapping up her cum.

She really should taste herself. I slide my fingers back inside to collect her cum and then move up her body to paint her lips. "Taste how fucking luscious you are," I demand before I kiss the hard peaks of her breasts. Her nipples have darkened from a pale rose to a dusty rose, looking amazing against the pale color of her flesh. A sheen of perspiration coats her skin, giving her an ethereal glow.

She licks her lips and moans. "I want to taste me on you." She slides her fingers into my hair to tug me up to her.

I don't hesitate.

I slam my mouth down on hers, pushing my tongue inside as she opens for me. Her eagerness to taste herself heats my blood and builds my excitement. Rolling on top of her, I notch my dick between her pussy lips and grind down. Long, slender legs wrap around my waist as the heels of her feet dig into my ass, urging me to keep moving. She tries to wedge her hips up as I slide downward, connecting with her entrance.

I tear my mouth from hers. "I need to grab a condom."

I hope I still have some here that haven't expired. Pushing up from Molly, I roll over to check the drawer. I have one left. I check the expiration date. My shoulders drop and disappointment fills my belly. I glance back at Molly, whose heavily lidded eyes are following me.

"What's wrong?"

"It's two months past its expiration. It would still be better than using nothing, but it's up to you." I smooth my hand up her leg. "I'll understand if you want to stop. I can grab some from the store and maybe we can pick this up again some other time."

She pushes herself upright and presses a gentle kiss against my mouth. Her eyes flick between mine. "I get the shot every three months. I have two weeks until I need my next one." She tucks a messy lock of hair behind her ear. "I'm clean."

"I'm clean too." I point over my shoulder toward the doorway. "I can show you if you like?"

She smiles, putting her dimples on full show. "I trust you."

I don't need any further encouragement. I dive straight back in, sucking on her nipple, cupping her breasts together, and massaging them. Her head drops back as she thrusts them forward into my face and hands.

Without wasting any more time, I shuffle her up the bed and spread her silky legs open wide, cradling my rock-hard shaft at their apex. Sliding down, I notch my head at her entrance, then hold my breath as I push inside, inch by inch, for the very first time. "Ah, fuck!" I pause, pulling back to peer into my girl's eyes. The light gray of her irises has turned into molten mercury. They're begging me to move, but I want to enjoy the feel of her heat around me before I take us where we both want to go—heaven. Her lips part and I fill her mouth with my tongue.

Skin to skin, breath to breath, heartbeat to heartbeat. I can't be any closer without climbing inside her.

Sucking in a deep breath, I pull out, so the head of my dick sits just inside her entrance and then push in and up, making her tits jiggle. "I love your tits."

I don't know where to look. My eyes skate between her breasts and my cock sliding in and out of her body, her flushed pink pussy lips spread wide to accommodate me. Sliding one arm beneath her leg, I position it over my shoulder to open her wider to me.

"Ohhh, Max." Molly pushes her hips up, meeting each and every one of my strokes into her body, taking me deeper. My body's on fire and her moans make me hotter by the second. I'm going to self-combust at the rate I'm going. The flush climbing over Molly's body suggests she's feeling the same. It's incredible how in sync we are for our first time together.

She fits around me like a silken glove and when I lift her other leg over my opposite shoulder, my balls tighten up.

Tingles race down my spine, collecting at the base. Urgency takes over and I can't maintain the steady rhythm I had before.

She needs to come.

"I need you to get there," I breathe heavily against her ear, between harsh pants. Her short fingernails dig into my back as she raises her hips. Her walls tighten around my shaft, making my eyes roll back in my head. "Be a good girl and come for me," I grit out between clenched teeth.

"I." Thrust. "I'm." Thrust. "Close." Thrust.

"Fuck. You feel incredible." I slide my hand between our bodies and press gently against her clit. It's gotta be sensitive after coming a short while ago. Massaging small circles around the bundle of nerves, her walls begin to flutter, tightening further. My shaft grows and the cum in my balls is close to the surface, but I've got to hold on ... *fuuuck!*

I couldn't do it. Streams of cum flood out of me and into my girl, my shaft pulsing as I coat her internal walls, filling her with my essence. Her channel contracts and we both moan; freezing in place as my orgasm sets off hers.

I suck in as much air as I can and drop my mouth back down to hers. This time, I kiss her slowly, reverently, carefully. I want to show her how much it meant to me that she allowed me the privilege of sharing her body. It's never something I take for granted, but for Molly to give this to me, it's special and meaningful. This isn't a quick fuck for either of us. It's not about just feeling good in the moment. It's about sharing a deep connection with another person, and we want to express that physically.

My eyes skate around her face as I pull back. Her eyelids have dropped closed, and she has a serene smile on her gorgeous face. She raises one eyebrow without opening her eyes. "You're staring at me." She giggles.

I press my hips forward, pushing my softening cock inside so she can't push me out. "Yes, I am. You're so fucking beautiful and you look stunning lying there all flushed and mussed up. I don't want to take my eyes off of you."

Her dimples deepen and I lean forward to lay a kiss on each one. "I probably look a mess."

"You definitely don't. Maybe I need to work harder to mess you up?" We both chuckle.

CHAPTER 26

—molly—

MAX INSISTED ON DRAGGING ME OUT OF BED, SO HE COULD clean me up, only to mess me up again as he was drying my body. I chuckle to myself at the expression he wore when he realized we'd need to have another shower.

"What's that chuckle about?" he asks as he slices fresh fruit for our breakfast. My favorite.

"Nothing." I pop a strawberry into my mouth and give him a wink.

I can't believe I had sex with my hot boss!

Awesome, life-altering sex.

With the man who's been diligently keeping everything professional between us, no less. The one who didn't see me as a woman and thought it was okay to invite me for drinks with the boys after soccer. I want to squeal with excitement, but I don't want to remind him I'm younger than him or that he's my boss—the sticking points that have been holding him back. I'm not sure what changed, but I'm glad it did.

Max carries the fruit to the small dining table, while I carry the juice. He grabs the yogurt, while I grab the bowls and spoons. We work silently to get breakfast set up as efficiently as we can. Max scoops fruit into both of our bowls and then I top them both with a healthy serving of yogurt.

"Damn. I forgot the honey," Max mumbles as he moves back to the kitchen. When he comes back, he holds up the container. "Would you like some?"

Honey's freaking expensive, and not something I've eaten very often. "Not normally. But I'll try some. Thanks." He dollops a small amount in each of our bowls, then sits. We both eat quietly for a few minutes, stealing glances at each other with satisfied smiles on our faces. I rub my toe up Max's leg over the top of his gray sweats. "I love these sweats." I wink at him. He brings out a cheeky side to me I'm enjoying.

His spoon stops halfway to his mouth, and he raises his eyebrows. "Yeah?" I nod and go back to eating. "I'll keep that in mind." After a few minutes, when we're both finished, Max rises and takes our dishes to the kitchen. "Would you like a coffee?"

"Thanks, I'd love one." I step beside him to wash the dishes as he makes us both a coffee. He glances at me with the strangest expression. "What's wrong?"

He shrugs. "Nothing."

Once the coffee's ready, we step out on the back deck to enjoy it. His backyard is low fuss. No garden, only grass with a decent-sized workshop I'm guessing he uses for car stuff. I take my first sip and close my eyes in appreciation, humming my delight.

"Did you want to talk about what happened with your …" He runs his hands through his hair. "Uhm, your … Martin?" I'm guessing he was going to call him my dad. Which is what he is, I guess. "You don't have to if you don't want to. I just want you to know I'm here."

I reach across the space between us and grasp his hand. "Thank you. He, uh, he told me his version of what happened when Mom told him she was pregnant. He didn't respond well. Cursed her out and told her she was ruining his life."

My stomach rolls as Max's eyebrows shoot up and if fire could shoot from his eyes, I'm certain it would. "He what?"

I shrug and give Max a pointed look. "He blamed it on being nineteen." I raise a brow.

"Sorry. Men … no, boys are fucking dumb at that age. We have a toddler brain which is all about food and sex. Anything else doesn't compute."

I can't hold back my chuckle at his explanation, though it doesn't change how things unfolded all those years ago. "It sounded like he treated her terribly. I couldn't sit across from him any longer listening to his story. I get that he's regretful. But his actions had an enormous impact on our lives. I can't pretend it doesn't matter." Max laces his fingers with mine, squeezing them in silent support. "I told him I need time. I'm not sure how long, but it was a lot to digest." Max's gaze follows my tongue as I lick my dry lips. "I walked away, not liking the man who says he's my father. In fact, I'm not sure I have any respect for him."

Max tugs my hand, pulling me across to him. He situates me on his lap, stroking his hand along my spine. "I'm sorry, Mols." I sink into his warm body. "You were right to walk away if that's what you needed to do. You don't owe him anything at this point."

Silence surrounds us as I work my mind back to the night before. Then further back to when Mom explained to me why I didn't have a daddy who lived with us. I think she still loved him. Even after the way he hurt her.

"Do you want to come to lunch with my family?" Max breaks the silence. I turn my face to study his. Even though he seems surprised that he's invited me, his offer is genuine.

"Thanks for the invite, but I'm not in an emotional space today to meet the rest of your family." I kiss the scruff on his jaw. "I'll come to Lachlan's birthday, though." I hope he understands I feel too raw to be around people.

He returns my kiss, rubbing circles on my back. "Of course. I get it."

"I guess I should get out of your hair so you can get ready. Do you mind dropping me back at my car?"

"No problem. I'll put on a load of laundry and then we can head out."

The salty breeze off the ocean tickles the strands of hair across my face as the sun sets on another day of my new life. Resting my arms on my knees, I drop my chin down to rest on top. A smile touches my lips as I remember this morning. Was it only this morning? It certainly 'feels' like it happened this morning.

He's a generous lover who definitely knows his way around the female body. I guess that decade between us has given him the opportunity to gain extra experience. My stomach squeezes at the thought of Max with another woman, though I have no right to be jealous. We both have our pasts, which include previous lovers. A shiver runs down my spine as I remember how my body responded when he pushed inside me for the first time. The way he praised me and called me, 'good girl'. I chuckle quietly. *Who knew I'd like that so much?*

I focus on the waves lapping on the shore as the sun drops even lower on the horizon. I think this is my favorite thing to do. My chest tightens as I recall dinner last night with Martin. I'm unsure how to move forward. Blaming him won't change what happened or the path it led Mom down. He seemed genuinely remorseful and worried about the impact telling me his side of the story would have on our relationship now. It was confronting to hear his side of the story and the way he behaved to the news of Mom's pregnancy. I get it was probably a shock, and he was young, but shit, Mom was young too and I would imagine equally shocked. The situation would have been scary for her. Perhaps when it's not so raw, I'll be able to move past how I'm feeling at the moment.

Arriving home, my headlights land on a figure sitting on the bottom step leading up to my apartment in the dark. The closer I get, I recognize Martin's wife, Beth. My stomach sinks like a rock to the bottom of the ocean and dread fills me. I just need some freaking time.

Is that so hard?

I park around the back in my designated space, draw in a deep breath and remind myself that I'm a reasonable person and that my response to Martin last night was understandable. I was well within my rights to feel the way I felt as he shared his side of the story.

Beth rises from the bottom step, dusting off her pants as she stands to face me. Her face is drawn tight, and she gives me a smile that comes across as more of a grimace. "Uh, hi, Molly. I'm sorry to intrude, but I wanted to check on you and make sure you're alright after last night."

Well, that wasn't what I was expecting. I figured she was here to put Martin's case forward. "Hi, Beth. Thanks for stopping by. I guess Martin told you dinner didn't go so well."

She shakes her head. "Something like that. If I know Martin, I'm sure he blurted everything out without considering how it would be received or how distressing it may be for you to hear."

I huff out a breath. "Do you want to come upstairs?"

"Sure. Thanks." She runs back to her car, grabs her purse, and then follows me upstairs.

I unlock the door, turn on the light, and disarm the alarm before hanging my keys on the hook by the door and dropping my purse on the floor. I probably should buy an entry table, but money is still a little tight. "Make yourself at home. Would you like a glass of water? I don't have much else, sorry."

She waves me off. "A glass of water would be great. Thank you." Beth takes a seat on the small sofa and when I walk in with two glasses of water, I find her staring at the box of photographs Martin left behind. "There are some great memories in that box."

I nod. "I'm sure. It was nice to see some photos of Mom before she had to deal with the stresses of parenthood."

Beth nods. "We were all friends, you know." I got that impression when I looked through the photos and Martin said the same thing. There were several of Mom and a much younger Beth, as well as photos of the three of them. "I was devastated when Nicole disappeared. She was my best friend." She takes a sip of cold water, her hand shaking slightly. "It took months before Martin told me how he'd behaved toward her when she told him she was pregnant … and only after I'd got fed up with him being overly reckless. He turned to drink. One night, while he was drunk, he confessed everything. I didn't even know Nicole was pregnant until he blurted it out. She never said a thing. Just vanished." Tears are tracking down Beth's cheeks, so I grab the tissues and hand them to her. "Thanks." She takes a couple and wipes her eyes, then blows her nose. "Sorry. Whenever I reflect on that time, I get very emotional." This must be hard for her if they were as close as she says. Not only did she lose Mom back then, but she's also found out that Mom has passed away.

I nod. "I figured you were all friends from the photographs Martin left for me. How did it come about that you and Martin got together?" Oh, that was probably a little forward. "If you don't mind me asking."

"It was some time after. Martin and I remained friends and then I went through a terrible breakup. The guy I was with liked to communicate with his fists." She waves off the last part like it's inconsequential. "Martin stepped up and helped me get back on my feet physically and emotionally. One thing led to another ..." she shrugs, "and here we are." Her eyes rise from studying her glass to meet mine. "I know I've always been his second choice. If Nicole had ever come back, I think he would have left me in a heartbeat."

I'm certain my head snaps back as though she's slapped me. "But you have kids together."

"I'm not sure that would have mattered. I don't know, and I guess I never will now." She reaches across, laying her hand over mine. "I'm truly sorry about your mom, Molly. When I picked Martin up from here last week and Max filled me in on what the two of you had discovered, I was devastated to learn that Nicole was gone. Even though I hadn't seen or heard from her in all these years, I still thought of her often and I missed our friendship."

Her pain is radiating from her in waves. But I have to wonder how she's lived in Mom's shadow all these years. Wondering if her husband would stay or leave if Mom ever returned. I don't think I could live that way.

"If I'm being completely honest, the more I'm learning about Martin, the less I want to get to know him. The way he reacted to Mom when she told him she was pregnant, to the way you're not even sure if he would have stayed with you had Mom returned. What I'm hearing is that he's a man who only thinks about himself. Not a quality I like."

Beth draws in a long breath. "Don't get me wrong. The man has his flaws, just as anyone does, but he is a *good* man. He's great with his kids; loves and adores them. He would do anything for them and for you … if you'll let him. He's been a fantastic husband. Attentive, supportive, and loving. What I mentioned before is my self-doubt." She brings her hand over her heart. "If I were to dig deep, I know he wouldn't walk away from me and the kids. He's too good a man for that." She pauses and nods her head slightly. "He would have done the right thing by you and Nicole if she hadn't left before he got himself together. I have no doubt about that."

We're both quiet for long moments. I'm not sure where we go from this point.

"Did he show you photos of our children?" Her voice is timid, as though she's unsure she should bring them up.

I shake my head. "No, he didn't. We mainly talked about Mom, and I needed to get ready for work. Then last night, I asked him to share his side of the events and, well … that didn't go down so well."

She digs out her phone, navigating to the photo album. "I think you may be surprised. You look a lot like Nicole but take a look."

She holds out her phone and I take it, preparing to see my half-siblings for the first time. Because out of all of this, I've learned I have a sister and a brother. I gasp as my eyes connect with my sister. Her hair is darker than mine, almost black like her mom's, but we are definitely sisters. I glance up at Beth with wide eyes. "How?"

"I don't know. I'm guessing that even though you have a lot of Nicole in you, you also have enough of Martin that you maybe didn't recognize because you weren't looking for it."

I guess so, but this is unreal. I flick to the next photo, which is of my brother. He looks like the male version of his sister, which means our resemblance is also strong.

"Noah doesn't have dimples," I comment and Beth shakes her head. I glance back at my brother. He looks about the same age as Ethan. "How old are they?"

"Holly is seventeen, while Noah is fourteen." The pride that fills Beth's face is unmistakable.

I raise my brows. "What are the chances that my name's Molly and your daughter's name is Holly?" I chuckle a little, because, well, that's just weird.

She lifts one shoulder and allows it to drop, shaking her head from side to side with a half-grin. "I dunno."

"I had a brother, Ethan. He was thirteen." My throat tightens as a lump forms, my heart beating double time like it has to beat for him too. I work hard to keep my tears at bay. Beth must sense my battle and moves closer, wrapping her arm around my shoulder and I can't fight the sadness any longer. "I miss them so much," I sob.

"Oh, sweet girl. I can't imagine what it's been like for you." She wraps her other arm around me and squeezes me in close.

I let go.

In this stranger's arms. I break down.

All the pent-up tears and emotions.

The heartache and the loss.

It all comes pouring out of me like a tsunami. She comforts me like a mother would as her hand cups the back of my head while the other one rubs up and down my back.

I burrow into her, deep into her shoulder, and release my misery.

My utter devastation.

When I eventually regain my control, I pull my head away from Beth, noting the large wet patch on her shirt. I want to hide away, embarrassment swamping me.

She cups my face, tucking the loose strands of sweaty hair behind my ears. Her face is full of compassion. "You know, I've been thinking about you coming back here. How you and Martin found each other. It feels as though you were brought to us, Molly." She smiles sadly. "Perhaps Nicole guided you home so you could be with us."

I nod. I've thought the same thing. Perhaps I was supposed to come here and find my family. Everything fell apart so spectacularly after the accident that I had no choice but to make a major life-changing decision. Maybe Mom wanted me here. Wiping my tears, I try to give Beth a smile of reassurance. "Perhaps."

She scrunches her eyebrows together and glances down at her lap, then draws in a deep breath before raising her eyes back to mine. "I know I'm not your mom and I could never fill her shoes. But I want you to know that I'm here for you. Whenever or whatever you need."

I lick my lips as a couple more tears escape. "Thank you, Beth."

"Maybe one day, we could be friends," she hedges.

I nod slowly. "Maybe."

The silence in the room has become stifling. "I'd better get home. The troops are probably wondering where I am."

We both stand and Beth collects her purse. "Thanks for stopping by." And I mean it. When I first saw her sitting on my steps, I didn't want to speak with her, and I was close to brushing her off. I'm glad I didn't.

She gives me a gentle smile. "Thanks for not sending me away. I hope we can chat again soon."

"I'd like that."

CHAPTER 27

—max—

I PULL THE TOW TRUCK IN BEHIND THE WORKSHOP, A SMILE OF satisfaction touching my lips. I can't wait to start work on this baby. It's going to be a huge project but I'm up to the task. I've been wanting to get my hands on one of these for a while now. Molly steps out through the back door of the workshop, her hand shielding her eyes from the early morning sun, the other resting on her hip. Her almost-white hair appears to be glowing in the morning light, and I can't wait to press my lips to hers. I would have been climbing into her bed last night if I didn't get the call yesterday afternoon to collect the truck I've had my eye on.

She's waiting at the open door for me when I drop down from the truck. I wrap my arms around her and drag her into me, loving how we fit together. I rub my nose alongside hers and then press my lips to hers. She opens for me without delay, and I sweep my tongue inside. My hands drop to grab her perfect ass and I press her closer, rubbing my cock against her lower belly. Remembering the jewelry she has dangling above her navel makes me even harder. She's so fucking sexy in the most unassuming ways. She wraps her arms around my neck, pulling me closer as she climbs my body like a fucking tree.

And isn't that the hottest thing?

This girl is as far gone for me as I am for her, and she's not shy about letting me know. Using one hand to hold her up, I use my other to guide her head the way I want, tilting my head so I can deepen the kiss. Our tongues move against each other as though we've been doing this for years, not days. Molly's heart pounds out a rapid beat to match my own as we reconnect.

We slow the kiss and shift back far enough to catch our breath and study each other. We're both breathing heavily as our matching smiles grow. I move in and lay a quick peck against her swollen lips, satisfaction filling me at the sight. "Morning, Dimples," I whisper against her lips.

She drops her forehead to mine. "Morning. I missed you last night."

I've never been with anyone before who hasn't played games with me. Molly's open heart and honesty are possibly one of her most attractive qualities.

"Me too." We've been spending most nights in her bed or mine. Once we crossed that line last Sunday morning, we haven't been able to stop. Taking every opportunity to spend time together—naked!

"How was the drive? I was worried about you driving so far, so late." She moves to drop her feet to the ground, and I reluctantly let her go.

"It was okay. I got to the guy's place around ten, bought it, and got back on the road. I ended up pulling over for a couple of hours of sleep." I tuck her silky hair behind her ear. "I have no idea how you slept in your car for all of those weeks." My admiration for her skyrocketed last night as I tried to get comfortable in the tow's cab, which has a ton more space than her compact car. "I'm tired, but a coffee, shower, and breakfast should get me going for the day."

"Show me this truck and I'll make you a coffee while you shower."

I take her hand and guide her toward my next project. I love that she's interested and understands the beauty I see when I look at the rust bucket. "The engine's frozen, and she has a lot of rust, but she's going to come up a treat." I drop my hands to her hips, rubbing my shaft against her. "Why don't you come in the shower with me?" I ask with my eyebrows raised in hope.

She laughs as she pushes me toward the bathroom. "Nope. We need to open soon, and you need to have breakfast. I'm going to run across the road and grab something for you. Get in the shower and I'll have everything ready when you come out." She briefly presses her lips to mine. As if that would ever be enough for me. I cup the back of her head and hold her in place while I take my time giving her a proper kiss. Since she won't join me in the shower, I'm going to have to rub one out—damn it.

I have one car on the books for today, which works out well unless someone brings their car in without a booking, which happens occasionally. Once I'm finished, I'll move the new project off the tow truck and clean her up a bit before I park her in my usual bay. Satisfied with my plan, I step out of the bathroom to be greeted by the delicious aroma of coffee and a breakfast sandwich.

"Thanks, Molly. How's Lawrence? I don't see him all that much now that you pick up our lunch."

"He's great. His daughter's coming home for a visit on the weekend, so he's excited about that."

"I don't think he sees her very often."

The bell at the front door rings. "I'll get that. You eat." She points to the desk as she lands a swift kiss on the top of my head on her way past and returns a few minutes later with a set of keys and her trusty clipboard. Molly's idea of asking clients to complete a simple questionnaire saves me a lot of time. I don't get caught up with the clients discussing basic information, which inevitably leads to talking about what's going on in the community or about whatever sporting team is at the top or bottom of their game this week.

After a hectic day, which included two callouts and an unexpected wheel alignment, I'm sliding the heavy front door closed when a young girl near the front gate catches my attention. Her hair's almost black and she's staring at the building. Something about her is familiar, but from this distance, I can't quite make out her features.

"Can I help you?" I call out to her. She's on foot, so I'm assuming she's not looking for a mechanic unless her car broke down and she walked here.

The girl steps forward, one slow step at a time. As she gets closer, I suck in a sharp breath. She looks a lot like Molly. A brunette version of my girl. The similarities are uncanny. I'm guessing this is one of Martin's kids.

"I'm looking for Molly." The girl seems a little nervous, a little unsure as she brushes her bangs out of her eyes.

"Yeah? Why are you looking for her?" I don't want this girl upsetting *my* girl.

She twists her fingers in front of her as she steps closer to me. "She ... uh ...she's my sister."

"Max, I'm about to clo—" Molly freezes in place as her eyes land on the girl. "Holly?"

Holly swallows hard, her eyes wide. The two women stand, locked in place, their eyes scanning and cataloging each other.

Seeing Holly next to my girl gives me an insight into how Molly must have looked during high school. Holly isn't as tall or willowy as her older sister. She's more petite, like her mother, but they definitely look like sisters. I bet the boys used to drool all over Molly. I rub the back of my neck. I don't like the thought of anyone drooling over Molly. *She's mine.*

"Did you. Uh, did you want to come inside?" Molly offers as she gestures over her shoulder.

The grace she's shown since finding out that Martin is her father is astounding. She told me all about Beth turning up unannounced and that she invited her in. Now she's doing the same with her sibling. She could have easily turned them away, and I would have completely understood.

"Yeah. Come inside." I wave my arm out to welcome her.

She steps forward, and the two women move toward the office. I wonder if I should give them their privacy. Perhaps I'll hang around for a little while until I know Molly's going to be okay. I need to get to soccer, but the guys will understand if I'm a little late.

—molly—

HOW BRAVE IS THIS GIRL? TURNING UP HERE, NOT KNOWING IF I would welcome or reject her. I show her into the office, but I think it might be better if I take her upstairs to my little apartment. "Do you mind waiting here for a sec?"

She nods. "Sure."

I don't need to search far to find Max. Realizing he can eavesdrop from here, I smile to myself as he sorts his workbench, which is adjacent to the office. He's been my greatest support as I navigate my new reality and come to terms with finding my father and his family, *my* family.

"Hey, you." Reaching up, I land a kiss on his cheek. "I'm going to take Holly upstairs to talk, and I'm not sure how long we'll be. I'll probably be late to your game, so I wanted to wish you good luck!"

He cups my cheek, his eyes studying me closely. "Are you gonna be okay? I can hang around down here in case you need me."

His offer eases my nerves and I realize that as much as I love having his support, I can do this on my own. Later, I know I can lean on him if I need to.

"Thank you." I turn my head and land a kiss on the palm of his hand. "Would it be okay if we catch up later?"

"Of course. Whatever you need, Dimples. If I don't see you at the game, I'll come straight back here after." I blow out a long breath. He didn't hesitate for one single second. God, I'm lucky.

"You don't need to do that. Have your drinks with the guys. I'll still be here." He pulls my face forward with care and kisses me. Stealing my breath and my heart. Now that I know how he can work my body, I react instantly to his kisses. My clit pulses and I squeeze my thighs together to temper my response.

We say our goodbyes and Max finally leaves for his weekly soccer game. I'm pretty sure the guys don't care if they win or lose. It's all a bit of fun and an excuse to catch up each week.

Holly and I head upstairs. "Can I get you anything? I have juice or I have water." I wave my arm out toward my tiny couch. That couch has been privy to some interesting conversations over the past couple of weeks.

"Juice, please." She sits and I prepare our drinks.

I hand her glass over and she takes a sip. "Do your parents know you're here?"

"Mom does. She dropped me off. She said I could text her and she'll come straight back to pick me up." I nod. "Is it weird for you how much we look alike? Because it's freaking weird sitting here, looking at you." She chuckles.

"Definitely weird. When your mom showed me photos of you and Noah, our similarities surprised me because I'm a lot like my mom." I point toward the photo I have on my wall. "Even though we all look similar, it seems Noah missed out on the dimples."

She nods as she gets up and moves closer to study the photo. "Yeah. He's happy about that, though. Says they're girly, which pisses Dad off something fierce. Wow! You really look like your mom." She comes back to sit on the couch beside me, not making eye contact with me. "It was pretty shocking to learn I had a big sister." She looks at me. "Not gonna lie. I was worried."

I tilt my head to the side, frowning. "Why would you be worried?"

She shrugs. "I've always been Daddy's girl."

We're both quiet for a long time as we contemplate how me being on the scene changes things. Whether or not we want it to, both of our lives have changed.

"Can I tell you a secret?" Holly nods, uncertainty written all over her face. "This has all been a huge shock for me and I'm still coming to terms with what it all means. I'm scared." Her eyes widen. "I'm twenty-six and I've only now met my father for the first time. What if I'm not a good enough daughter? I know I can be a great big sister to a brother, but I've never been a big sister to a sister before. What if I'm shit at it?" She laughs and the ice between us is shattered.

"Well, I've never been a little sister, so we can work it out together." My shoulders drop and I know that we'll be able to muddle our way through this new relationship. Holly seems like a sweet girl, much like her mom.

"Your mom told me you're seventeen. How's your senior year going?"

She shrugs. "Okay, I guess. I don't like school. The kids are freaking annoying, and the boys are so immature." She rolls her eyes.

"I'm sorry to tell you they don't improve until their late twenties." I chuckle at the look of exasperation on her face.

"Thanks. That's something to look forward to. Not."

"What do you want to do when school's done?"

She flicks her hand down her body. "I want to be a fashion designer." She stands up. "I designed and made this."

Wow. I stand and make my way around her. "This is gorgeous. It looks like something I'd see in a fancy boutique."

Holly puffs up at my compliment. "You think?"

"I do."

"Mom and Dad always say stuff like that, but I figured they have to say that. You know?"

We talk for a while about her plans, and she tells me a little about Noah before her expression grows serious. "Dad is a genuinely great person, you know." I'm a little taken aback at her sudden declaration. "I overheard my parents talking about how you walked out on him when you guys met for dinner. He was crying and telling Mom that he was worried that he'd blown his chance to get to know you."

My heart sinks. I don't want her to hate me because I upset her dad. *My* dad. God, that's weird to get used to. "I'm sorry, Holly."

She shakes her head. "I didn't tell you to make you feel bad. I'm trying to put myself in your shoes. It must be weird to meet your dad for the first time. I don't exactly know the story or what happened between Dad and your mom, but I get the impression she was his first love. It grosses me out. Mom was … like … friends with them when they were dating." She grimaces and shivers. "I know my dad and I know it's important to him to have a relationship with you now he's found you." She shrugs. "I just want you to give him a chance. He's been the best dad a girl could ask for." She smiles and turns her head around, showing me her fancy braid. "He did this. Mom can't braid my hair if her life depended on it. Dad's always been the one to make my hair all fancy. I haven't bothered learning how to do this stuff, because I know he'll do it for me." She chuckles as she shrugs. "But it's more than fancy braids. I know if I need him for anything, he'll be there. He won't judge me or make me feel bad for making a mistake. He'll help me work things out so I can get back on track. Dad's never let me down. Like ever!"

I lay my hand over hers to settle her. She likes to fidget with her fingers like I fidget with my bracelet. "I'm thrilled to hear that. It's important for girls to have a great role model in their dad. I had a fabulous stepdad who always showed me exactly what I was worth. He taught me a lot about myself, and I only have happy, fond memories of him now." I shrug. "I think things with your dad, *our* dad, will settle down eventually. We just have to find our way."

Her eyes widen. "Does that mean you'll give him a chance?"

"Of course. I was always going to give him a chance. I just … I need some time, Holly."

Her smile reveals deep dimples to match mine, and her eyes light up. "I'm so happy to hear that. I'd better message Mom to come get me. It's getting close to dinner, and I still have homework to do." She drops her head back on her shoulders and groans. "I hate homework."

"We all do. Trust me, you're not alone. I can drop you home if you're not too far from here. I don't know my way around the city very well yet."

"I don't live that far from here. I could have walked, but Mom wanted to make sure I got here safely."

A few minutes later, I stop in front of a stunning three-story home. The lights are already on inside, giving it a welcoming feel. "You have a lovely home."

Holly looks up at it from her position in my car. "It's okay." She shrugs. "It's just a house." She has no idea how lucky she is to have a home, let alone one so beautiful. I'm glad that she takes it for granted because it means she's never gone without. Holly opens her door. "Thanks for the ride. Will I see you again?" she asks timidly.

"Of course. I have years of teasing to catch up on." I wink at her.

"Cool. Bye." She slams the door and takes the steps up to

the front door, two at a time. Beth's waiting at the door for her. She waves at me, and I return it, then turn my car around so I can watch Max's soccer game.

CHAPTER 29

—molly—

WE STUMBLE THROUGH MY DOORWAY, MAX ALL SWEATY FROM his soccer game, his lips locked with mine as he disarms the alarm. He grabs my ass, hoisting me up, and I automatically wrap my legs around his hips as he kicks the door closed. He twists around and I lock the door. We work in tandem as though we've been together for years. I've never been with someone that I'm in sync with on so many levels.

He drags his mouth away from mine, kissing along my jawline to my ear. "I should have a shower."

"I don't want to let you go." I tilt my head to the side, giving him better access to my neck.

Tightening his muscular arms around me, he walks straight into the bathroom. Without hesitation, I drop to my feet and drag his shirt up his body, then toss it to the floor once it clears his head. I lean forward, placing kisses on his heart tattoo, and run my hands down his flanks until I reach the top of his shorts. His mossy eyes are quickly being overtaken by his dilating pupils and I give him a wink as I tuck my thumbs into the waistband, ensuring I have his boxer briefs and tug them down his legs in one swift action. I giggle. "I should have taken your shoes and socks off first."

His hand goes to my hair, and he pushes me down to my knees. Oh, I like this side of him. I drop willingly, unlacing his sneakers and removing each one along with his socks.

"You look so fucking good down there on your knees."

I tilt my head up; the tension across his shoulders and the intensity on his face steals my breath for a moment. His cock is only an inch from my mouth; without taking my eyes off my man, I lean forward to swipe the head with my tongue. He drops his head back on his shoulders with a groan and then drops his gaze back down to me. His stomach quivers as I take the next swipe from the root to the tip, then take the crown into my mouth. I bite down softly at the base of his crown and his hand tightens in my hair. The power that grows inside me while I do this to him is incredible. I feel like I could do anything right now.

"Good girl. Now take it deep."

I do my best to take him as far as I can and swallow around the head. I struggle to go as deep as I'd like because my gag reflex is a bitch. His stomach muscles tense and he uses his hold on my hair to move my head the way he wants.

"Mmmm," I hum around his shaft, stroking the underside with my tongue as he moves my mouth up and down his length. The base of his cock is exposed, so I wrap my hand around it firmly, stroking to match the movement of my mouth, and use my other hand to massage his balls, which are drawing up tight to his body. My pussy clenches around nothing as I press my thighs together. My blood thrums through my body as my heart pounds.

"I'm gonna spill my cum down that sexy throat of yours and you're gonna take it all like the good girl you are."

I can only nod as I struggle to draw in enough oxygen into my lungs. They're on fire and saliva's dribbling down my chin.

My eyes are watering and I'm certain I'm a mess, but when Max looks down at me, I feel beautiful. The heat and adoration in his eyes as his dick throbs and grows inside my mouth is clear to see.

"You ready?"

I nod again and moan around his shaft. It's all he needs to let loose. His cum coats the back of my throat and it seems like a lot of fluid as he pauses his movements. He groans long and low, creating a throb in my clit. I work hard to swallow all of his essence down because I don't want to disappoint him. He loosens his grip on my hair as he gradually pulls his dick from my mouth like it's the most painful thing to do. He swipes the head of his cock back and forth across my puffy lips, spreading what I'm sure is excess cum and saliva across them.

He releases my hair, massaging my scalp with tender strokes. "Such a good girl." He smiles at me, sliding his hands around to cup my face. He leans down, taking my lips in an uncontrolled kiss. It's messy with teeth and tongue, but it's full of gratitude and it's perfect. Using his hold on my face, he urges me to my feet and my hands find their place on his flanks, which are still trembling from his orgasm. He pulls back and uses his thumbs to rub the mess from around my mouth.

Resting his forehead against mine, his breath touches my lips as he whispers, "How did I get so fucking lucky?"

I press a kiss to his lips. "I'm the lucky one here."

His hands glide down each side of my neck, across my collarbones, and down my arms until he reaches my hands. He steps back toward the shower, taking me with him. He leans in, stretching and flexing his firm body as he turns on the water. "Let's get you naked, Dimples. I have plans for you."

The deep timbre of his voice and the dark promise sends shivers down my body, straight to my needy clit. We soap each other up, caressing the other with sensual strokes. We share plenty of steamy kisses, the shower space filled with pants and moans. I'm incredibly turned on at this point; I'm unsure how I'm still standing.

Max turns off the water and drags me out of the shower, drying my body with purpose. Whatever he has planned didn't involve the shower.

"I hope you're fucking ready, Dimples."

My stomach flips at the promise in his voice as he dips down, situating his shoulder into my middle before standing and striding to my bedroom. He drops me onto the bed without ceremony and I bounce slightly before settling in the middle of the mattress, resting on my elbows so I can watch him. He prowls toward me.

"Be a good girl and open your legs for me." His voice is commanding and I eagerly comply with his direction. He positions my feet flat on the bed to his liking, raising my knees. "Let them drop to the bed." Even though I'm incredibly exposed like this, I do as I'm told. He folds his arm across his chest, then rubs the thumbnail of his other hand across his bottom lip as he studies me. It's an action I've seen him do a thousand times, but it's goddamn sexy in this moment. I'm so exposed like this, but I'm panting in anticipation. His eyes rise to my breasts, which quiver with each rapid breath. "Fucking beautiful," he rasps on a heavy exhale.

He crawls onto the bed and drops his head between my legs, swiping his tongue from the bottom of my pussy to the top, sending a shiver through my body. A sigh escapes, and I drop my head back on my shoulders enjoying the sensations. Everything he does to my body makes me hotter and sends me higher.

Once he's teased me close to release, he stops and moves behind me, leaving me feeling empty. He rests his back against the headboard and pulls me into the cradle of his thighs, his erection pressing into my lower back. Taking each of my legs, he positions them on the outside of his, keeping me open wide. I wriggle against him.

"Stop it. It's my turn to play."

With one hand, he collects my hair and lays it over one shoulder, exposing my neck to his roughened cheek. He kisses behind my ear, dragging his lips in lazy kisses down my neck and across my collarbone. My blood vibrates through my body with arousal. He moves back and sucks on my neck as his hands move around to my quivering stomach. One work-roughened hand glides up to cup my breast, rolling and pinching my nipple as he continues to suck on my neck.

The sensations are overloading my senses and he hasn't done much yet. I don't know what I'm seeking, but I need something, so I push my hips forward. His other hand caresses down my stomach, flicking my navel piercing as he nips my neck. My pussy clenches the closer he gets to the tiny patch of hair right above my pubic bone.

"I fucking love this." He pinches the hair between his fingers and pulls firmly, making me gasp.

With a firm hand, he tilts my head and takes my mouth. Invading with his tongue, he strokes and tangles with mine as his fingers keep working over my breasts and then slide down through my soaked folds. I reach back to wrap my hand around his head, keeping his lips locked to mine as his deft fingers circle my clit before driving into my opening. My pussy clenches at the welcome intrusion. He moves two fingers in and out of me before returning to my clit to circle the bundle of sensitive nerves. Teasing me and sending my body higher. His other hand leaves my head and moves downward, teasing my breast before continuing down to my pussy. His fingers slide down my pussy lips, stretching me open wide.

"Good girl. You're so wet for me." He lands a kiss on my shoulder, dragging his roughened cheek along my neck. The feel of his bristles against my smooth skin adds to the overload of sensations, taking me closer to the edge.

I moan and push my pelvis up, hoping he'll breach my opening again. Instead, he taps my clit and glides his hands down and back up the inside of my thighs, leading back to my pussy lips, making my thighs tremble under his roughened touch. He drags his fingers through my folds; one hand tending my clit while he finger fucks me roughly. His long fingers find that special place inside which can send me flying. "Please, Max."

He withdraws his fingers, circling my clit, then caresses his way back up toward my breasts, leaving my pussy empty and throbbing. Frustration builds strong and swift, but he has plans and no amount of begging on my part will interfere. I've learned that he likes to be in charge and I trust him to give me the pleasure I need. He squeezes the mounds of my breasts together and plucks at my nipples until they're hard peaks.

"Look at your sexy body."

I glance down at my body and am surprised by how erotic it looks. My nipples are erect, and their soft pink color has become a ruddy rouge, my stomach's trembling, and my hips are moving without any guidance from me, my legs open wide and shaking. My skin's covered in a sheen of sweat and is flushed a pretty pink. I can't see my pussy, but I know it's throbbing.

"You're so fucking beautiful like this. Look at this greedy pussy, waiting for me to fill her up." I can only moan in response, words evading my brain.

His hand slides down my trembling body and I suck in a sharp breath as he thrust three fingers inside me. I'm so wet and ready to come. I raise my hips and turn my head to look up at him. "Max, stop teasing me. I need to come." I sound like a whiny brat.

"I want to play with you first. Now be a good girl and stop

moving." He pushes my hips back onto the bed and continues his ministrations. Every time I get close to coming, he moves away and tends to another part of my body. Holding my throat, he kisses me deeply, tasting my desperation.

I've never been left on edge like this, especially not for this long. I'm terrified I'm going to rip in half when he finally lets me come. His tongue thrusts in and out of my mouth as his fingers mirror the action in my pussy, as his palm presses down on my clit. My internal muscles clench and I finally explode.

Blackness swamps my vision and the breath in my lungs seizes as my entire body convulses. My toes curl under, cramping at the extreme release of tension. I trap his hand between my thighs to prevent him from leaving me.

"That was fucking beautiful. You're gorgeous when you come," he rasps in my ear. His breaths heavy, his heart pounding against my back. I think I may have blacked out for a second or two.

He kisses me tenderly. Slowly. Reverently.

My body's a quivering, boneless mess of limbs and flesh. I'm mildly aware of him sliding down the bed and situating me over his cock, which is standing straight up from his body. He lowers me slowly, lining up my still throbbing pussy and easily sliding inside. I drop forward, resting my hands on his firm thighs, the hairs tickling my palms. Trying to catch my breath and regain my senses, Max lifts my hips, sliding me up and down his steely shaft. He's using me for his own pleasure now and it's so damn hot.

He groans and I answer him with a moan. "You feel so damn good," I whisper.

He thrusts in deeper, and I circle my hips on the downward stroke. "*We* feel so damn good, Dimples. You and me together."

I sigh internally. This man always seems to say the right

things. But they're not empty words, he always follows up with actions.

Max and I work in tandem to build a solid rhythm. He thrusts up as I drop down, swiveling my hips each time to make sure he hits that special place inside of me. Dragging his cock out of my body, he swivels me around until I'm laying on my back. He rises over the top of me, sweat dripping down the side of his face, his muscles taut as he holds himself over me. I grip his shaft and guide it back into my body, sighing as he strokes in deep. The V leading down to his pelvis is stark and guides my eyes to where we're joined intimately.

"Be a good girl and watch me destroy your pussy."

I glance up at him, nodding that I heard his command, then drop my eyes back to where his penis draws out of me inch by glorious inch. The glistening shaft gradually revealed before he lunges back inside with a forceful thrust.

"Wrap those gorgeous legs around me," he grunts.

I do his bidding, locking my feet at the small of his back and bringing my pelvis up off the bed. We move together in time, working toward our mutual release. Every time he thrusts inside me, he releases a sexy grunt, his breath blowing across my face and I glance up at him. His veins are pulsing along his neck and sweat drips from his temples as he grits his teeth. The concentration and focus on me and his task are sexy as hell. This man is all about getting the best out of both of us, and he's doing a damn fine job.

"I ... I'm so close. I ... I nee—" I pant as my muscles draw tight, ready for release.

"I know what you need," he grunts, his voice rough, as he moves one hand down to pinch my clit.

And I'm gone.

I'm floating in the stratosphere. Untethered to the earth. It's beautiful in this place in between, as my body falls apart. Max's cock swells and pulses as he grunts out his orgasm. He throws his head back and I rise to lick the sweat from his Adam's Apple. His hot cum coats my walls as my muscles tighten and squeeze his pulsing shaft.

"Oh my God! I think I had an out-of-body experience."

"I *know* I had one. Fuck! That was incredible." He kisses me tenderly. "You're incredible," he whispers.

I drop my legs from around his hips as he pushes in and out slowly, gently. The aftershocks rattling through my body. Max rolls to the side, taking me with him, trapping me to him by throwing one leg over mine and pulling me close to his body, not leaving any space between us. He kisses my forehead and strokes my sweaty hair away from my face so I glance up at him. "That was amazing." Three little words want to escape, but I hold them in. I think it may be too soon, but I know I'm falling in love with him.

He hums in response, and I drop my head to rest over his heart, which is beating a furious rhythm to match mine. As my body cools, I shiver, and goosebumps cover my skin.

"Are you cold?"

"A little."

He taps my ass and releases me to climb out of bed, then he pulls the bedcovers out from beneath me and covers my body. "Back in a sec." I hear the faucet turn on and off in the bathroom and he returns with a washcloth. "Here, let me clean up my mess." He uncovers me and opens my thighs, wiping my entrance and paying special attention to the surrounding flesh and upper thighs. A smile slowly forms as he studies my pussy, dragging his fingers through the slit from bottom to top, causing me to wince slightly. His eyes glance up to mine before dropping back down, a furrow forming between his brows. "Did I hurt you?"

I shake my head. "No. It's a little tender, but it's a good tender." I smile at the relief that takes over his face. He steps out of the bedroom and returns a few moments later with a glass of water and some Tylenol. "I'll take the water, but I don't need the pain relief. I promise I'm okay." I wink at him. "You said you were going to destroy me. I think we can both agree that you succeeded."

He huffs out a laugh and shakes his head at me. "Only you, Molly. The fact you don't need the pain relief suggests I didn't destroy you at all." He turns off the bedroom light and climbs into bed, rearranging me to his liking as he curls his body around mine. Planting a kiss on my temple. I swoon internally at his gentle care. "Go to sleep, Dimples. You need your rest."

"Okay. Night, Max." I blow out a heavy breath of content-ment. Lying in his arms and falling asleep here, with him wrapped around my body, I know I'm safe.

"Night, Dimples."

CHAPTER 30

—max—

I PULL MOLLY'S HAND INTO MY LAP TO STOP HER FROM fidgeting with her bracelet. "I don't know why you're nervous. My family's not that scary."

Her head snaps around to me. "Oh, I'm sure they're not. Your sister's lovely, as are her kids. It's that I'm not used to extended family get-togethers." I squeeze her hand. "It was only Mom and me for so long and then Jack came along. Then, a few years later, they had Ethan. It was only ever the four of us for birthdays and special holidays."

I glance at her, then back to the road. My heart breaks for this woman and the things she's missed out on. "It's noisy, but it's always fun. If it gets too much, give me the signal and I'll get you out of there." I wink at her before settling my eyes back on the road.

She chuckles. "What sort of signal?"

"How about you tug on your left ear and give me a wink with your right eye?" We both burst out laughing and I think it was exactly what she needed to calm herself down.

"Thanks. I needed that." She shuffles the gift bag sitting between her feet on the floor, a crease forming between her sculpted eyebrows. "Do you think Lachlan will like his present?"

"He's going to love it. But I have to warn you. He won't be overly demonstrative about how much he likes the gift. It's just the way he is." I glance across at her. "He's on the Spectrum, which means he responds differently to things."

She waves away my warning. "That's okay. All kids are different. Ethan never liked people making a fuss over him. When he was little, he would cry whenever we sang happy birthday." She chuckles a little at the memory. "I think we all have our idiosyncrasies; not everything has a label."

I love that view. Mona always had awful things to say about Lachlan whenever she spent time with my family and I would have to remind her to keep her opinions to herself. I can't, for the life of me, work out why in the hell I stayed with that woman.

"Tell me. What was it like having a younger brother that much younger than you?" She doesn't open up and talk that much about her family so I hope I haven't overstepped.

She takes a deep breath. "It was wonderful. I was old enough to appreciate him and his different stages. Though I remember it didn't impress me when he'd wake up during the night for a feed, I soon learned to sleep through the noise. I used to love it when Mom would let me sit on the couch and cuddle with him when he was a newborn. Even though he was tiny, he was a chubby baby. He'd look up at me with his big inquisitive eyes and wrap his fingers tight around my finger. When he was a little bigger, he would suck on my nose." Her eyes are full of love and her smile confirms it's a happy memory for her. "I remember when he first started eating solids. The stinky smell of his diaper." She scrunches up her nose as she giggles and my heart soars to hear her laughing as she remembers her brother. "Jack used to pretend to faint." Her dimples are deep, and her eyes are sparkling with joy. Jack sounds like he was a terrific stepdad to Molly. I only hope her biological dad can be equally terrific.

"Oh yeah, I remember Em's boys used to stink when they first switched over to solid food. It's not pleasant. I was never too keen to change their diapers once that happened." I take the turn into Emma and Theo's driveway and turn off the engine.

She turns to me with wide eyes. "We're here already?"

"C'mon. It'll be fine. I promise." Leaning across the console, I give her a chaste kiss, then climb out of my car. I know the second Mom lays eyes on me with Molly, she's going to know that I'm head over heels in love with this woman. My only hope is that she doesn't embarrass me too much.

With Molly's hand secure in mine, we make our way up to the porch. Sarah's standing inside the door when we enter and, knowing her, she saw my car pull up and made sure she would be the first one to greet us. She's probably annoyed that Emma has already met Molly.

"Max. It's great to see you." She wraps her arms around me, pulling me in close. I refuse to release Molly's hand, so I return her hug with my free arm, whacking her in the back with the gift bag I'm carrying for Lachlan. "Oh my gosh, she's so freaking pretty … and tall," Sarah whispers in my ear before pulling back to greet Molly. "Hi, I'm Sarah. I'm Max's favorite sister." She leans forward to embrace Molly. "It's nice to meet you, finally." Molly gives Sarah her full smile, dimples and all. Sarah's eyes widen as she chuckles. "I can see why Kenny thinks you're a Disney princess."

Molly laughs. "Hi, Sarah. It's lovely to meet you."

"Uncle Maaaaax! Aunty Mollyyyyyy!" Kenny comes running from the back of the house, leaping at my body. "You came!" She squeezes my cheeks in her tiny hands and lands a kiss on my nose. "And you brought me a princess to play with."

Molly, Sarah, and I chuckle at our niece, who stole our hearts from the minute we first met her.

Molly tickles Kenny under her arm. "Hi, Kenny. I washed my hair, especially this morning, so you could do a special braid for me."

Kenny reaches across, smoothing her hand down Molly's long hair. "It's so silky." Her eyes go wide. "I collected all of my best hair ties and ribbons together and I have my special brush and comb. It's gonna be so much fun." She wriggles her body, so I place her on her feet. Molly chuckles as Kenny runs back to where she came, shouting. "Mommy. Daddy. Uncle Max's princess is here!"

Molly's eyes widen and her cheeks flush prettily. "Oh my gosh. I'm so far from being a princess."

Sarah turns to her. "Are you sure about that? With your pretty eyes, gorgeous platinum hair, and dimples. Not to mention," she waves her hand up and down Molly's form, "your stunning figure. You're like a real-life Disney princess." She moves closer to Molly and motions for her to lean down. "Is my big bro being good to you?"

Molly smiles widely as she nods. She looks at me as she answers Sarah, "He absolutely is. He's the best."

My hand tightens around hers and my chest puffs out a little, knowing that I'm giving her what she needs. "Uh, Sis, do you think you can let us into the house?"

We're still standing inside the front door, for fuck's sake. She pokes her tongue out at me and spins on her heel, leading the way to the back of the house. I lean down slightly and steal a quick kiss from my girl.

"Ewwww, Uncle Max is kissing Aunty Molly." Austin's voice rings out, breaking the moment. I drop my forehead to Molly's and we share a laugh. When I pull back to study Molly's face, she's flushed, and her eyes are sparkling with happiness. I love this look on her. It's one I hope to keep on her face for a very long time. I love that the kids are already calling Molly, aunty. It's like they've been inside my mind.

It's all I can think about.

How I can make her mine forever.

We step into the kitchen, and I place my gift for Lachlan on the counter and drag Molly forward to meet Mom. I wrap my free arm around the woman who made me the man I am today and pull her in close, kissing the top of her head. "Hey, Mom." I pull Molly in beside me. "This is my girlfriend, Molly."

Molly freezes momentarily, her mouth partway open as she glances up at me. "Hi, Mrs. Stanfield. It's lovely to meet you." She holds out her hand for Mom, but Mom pushes through, wrapping her arms around Molly and drawing her in tight. Molly awkwardly returns the hug one-armed, Lachlan's gift bag dangling from her forearm, because I refuse to let go of her hand.

"Oh, my dear girl. Thank you for joining us today. It's all Kenny could talk about." She rolls her eyes light-heartedly. "But please, call me Sally. Or Mom." She smiles at Molly, then her face goes ashen, and her smile drops. Her hand rises to her necklace, and she fidgets with the chain. "Oh my, I'm so sorry. I didn't mean that … I mean … oh dear." Mom's flustered as she tries to recover, looking to me for guidance.

I wrap my arm around her shoulder. "It's okay, Mom."

Molly grins and waves her off. "Please don't feel you have to watch what you say with me, Mrs. … I mean, Sally. I promise I won't break down."

Mom nods and I can tell she's holding back what she would like to say. Knowing Mom, she wants to wrap Molly up in a warm hug and tell her everything will be okay. That she has us now and that we'll take care of her. It's exactly what I want to do, but I know Molly's extremely independent and likes to stand on her own feet.

Dad comes in from the back deck, which Theo extended when Em and the boys moved in. It was already big, but now it's huge, with doors that open onto it, giving the impression that the kitchen and deck are one space.

"Son!" Dad walks straight toward me with a slight limp, and we embrace.

"Dad. How's your knee?" He was jumping on the trampoline with the kids last weekend and fell as he was climbing out, twisting his knee.

"Oh, it's fine. I'll be back to trampolining in no time." He pats my arm and finishes with a squeeze. "And who do we have here?" He turns to Molly.

"Hi, Mr. Stanfield. I'm Molly." She holds her hand out to shake and Dad treats her to the same fierce hug that Mom gave her. I've told my family a minimal amount about Molly, which included why she moved here. You can imagine how that went down with Mom and Dad. Mom was a sobbing mess and Dad wasn't too far behind her.

"Call me John. Mr. Stanfield is my father." He chuckles at his own joke.

Molly chuckles too, as she looks at me with a raised brow. "Sounds familiar."

"Can I do your hair now?" Kenny tugs on Molly's dress to gain her attention.

Emma steps inside. "Kenny. You need to wait until a little later. We're all gonna eat and have some cake, and maybe then you can braid Molly's beautiful hair." She looks at Molly for confirmation.

Molly crouches down to Kenny's height. "Oh yes. I'm too hungry to be able to sit still long enough for you to make my hair pretty. Do you mind waiting until after we've had the birthday cake?"

Kenny places her hands on her hips and tilts her head to the side. "Actually, come to think of it, I'm pretty hungry, too."

She nods at Molly, then glances up at Em. "Are we gonna eat soon? I'm starving."

Em giggles. "Of course. I've come inside to grab what we need to set the table." She wraps an arm around Molly, squeezing her close. "Hey, Molly. I'm delighted you came today." Then she pats my arm on the way to the kitchen drawers and whispers, "You've done good, little brother."

Molly places Lachlan's gift on the counter alongside my gift and extricates her hand from mine, pressing up to land a chaste kiss on my cheek. "Can I help with anything? I'm happy to set the table." Everyone in the kitchen freezes, eyes on Molly. She flushes that pretty pink and her eyes widen. She looks across at me for guidance. "Did I say something wrong?"

I laugh and pull her into me, landing a kiss on her lips. "No, Dimples. You've said and done everything right." I turn to my family. "Stop making my girl feel uncomfortable."

Everyone returns to their chatter and whatever they were doing before and Molly fits in seamlessly, helping wherever she can. It's like she's always been part of this family and pride fills me that she's mine. We all carry the plates, dishes, silverware, and glasses out to the deck and work together to set everything ready for lunch.

I introduce Molly to Theo and his dad, Cristo, who takes both of Molly's hands in his. "You must come into my restaurant. I'll make an enormous feast for you both."

Theo chuckles. "Not everyone wants to be stuffed so full they can't move, Dad."

Cristo looks affronted. "What do you mean?"

They argue over the merits of eating until you can no longer breathe, and Molly and I collect our gifts to give them to Lachlan. I let Molly go first since she's been nervous about her gift for him.

"Happy birthday, Lachlan. I brought you a gift." She hands it to him.

He briefly glances at her, then his eyes settle over her shoulder. "Thank you." He's getting better at making eye contact with people, but it's still a work in progress with new people. He digs into the bag and pulls out a tool belt that should fit him perfectly. His eyes snap up to Molly's and one side of his mouth tips up. Dropping the gift bag, he tries to wrap it around his waist but isn't quite coordinated enough to pull it off.

"Would you like me to help you?" Molly asks. Lachlan nods, and Molly moves closer to assist him, settling the belt on his hips. I told her not to worry about the tools because he has that part covered with Theo's tools. "I wasn't sure if you already had one. Your Uncle Max told me how much you like to work with timber, and I hoped this would be a good idea."

His eyes snap up to hers and a full smile touches his lips. "I don't have one. Thank you very much." He steps away and heads straight for Theo. He runs his hands over the leather as he shows his stepdad his new belt. "This is the most useful gift I've been given today. I'll be like you now." He's standing tall, pride filling his little body.

Theo squeezes his shoulder and crouches down to inspect the belt more closely. "This is exceptional quality. I need a new one. I'll have to ask Molly where she got this one from."

I have to admit; I wasn't sure about Theo at first. He seemed like a total dick the day we all went to the beach, but the way he loves my sister and her boys, as well as how he stepped up for his niece, settled my concerns quickly. He's a genuinely good guy and I'm thrilled that he and Emma found their way to each other, even though the road was a little rocky for the two of them.

"Hey. I brought you a present too," I remind the birthday boy.

"Oh. Sorry, Uncle Max. I didn't mean to leave you out." He holds out his hand for the gift, which is probably lame compared to the tool belt. I hand him the gift bag and he dips his hand in, pulling out the Lego box. "Woah! You got me the Spider-Man Molten Man Battle set. This has two hundred and ninety-four pieces and shows the epic battle between Spider-Man and Molten Man from the movie, Far From Home." He looks down at the box with awe and I'm pretty happy that I chose a gift he'll enjoy. "Thanks, Uncle Max. I won't open it now because I don't want to lose any of the pieces."

"Fair enough. I'm glad you like it." He gives me a rare hug and runs inside to put his gift away for safekeeping.

Theo claps his hands together. "Okay, everyone. Let's eat. Kids first, then adults can sort themselves out."

The kids are served and set up to eat at the large table Theo built, quickly followed by the adults. At first, everyone's quiet as they enjoy the delicious barbecue Theo and his dad cooked, as well as the salads that Mom and Emma put together.

Gradually, everyone shares about their week. Theo puts down his knife and fork and asks me, "Did you get the truck you were after?"

I swallow the bite of food in my mouth. "Oh, yeah." I can't contain my smile. "She's fucking beautiful."

"Max!" Mom chastises. Molly elbows me at the same time, looking mortified.

I grimace at the kids. Inevitably, a fuck or two slips out at family gatherings. The kids mostly ignore it. I don't know why Mom still feels the need to pull me up on it. "Sorry."

Kenny giggles. "You're so funny, Uncle Max."

"Thanks, Munchkin."

Emma directs her focus to Molly. "The kids know Uncle Max has a potty mouth and they're not allowed to repeat the grown-up words he says."

"I don't know where you learned to talk like that." Mom shakes her head, pretending to be more upset than she actually is.

I sort of like that I'm the inappropriate uncle; it solidifies my place in the family. Molly leans in close and presses a kiss to my shoulder. Turning my head, I'm able to return the kiss on her cheek. When I glance back at the table, everyone's eyes are on us. Sarah and Emma have matching smirks, and I don't even care that they're going to give me shit later. I'm finally happy.

We all finish eating and Molly's the first to stand to collect everyone's dishes. Once again, my family is stunned into silence. I'll have to explain their reactions to her later. I get up to help, but Emma and Sarah tell me to sit back down. Mom jumps up too, and the three of them collect the dishes and silverware from the table and follow Molly inside. My gut tells me she's safe with them, but I don't trust them not to inadvertently drop me in the shit.

I prepare to stand, but Dad puts his hand on my shoulder, pushing me back into my seat. "Let them have their girl time. I'm sure Molly can handle it."

"I know she can handle it and I trust Mom and the girls implicitly to be kind to her. I don't trust that they won't tell Molly about stupid shit I did as a kid, though."

The guys laugh. "May as well find out if she'll stick around sooner rather than later." Theo offers with a shrug.

I huff. "I wanted to ask if you'd be interested in helping me redo the timber for the flatbed of the truck I picked up."

He scratches his fingers through his short beard. "Yeah. That'd be a great little project." He leans forward, resting his elbows on the table. "What sort of timber are you planning to use?"

"What would you recommend?"

He thinks for a moment. "Perhaps Asian Keruing or Apitong. It's commercially harvested and has the best strength-to-weight ratio." I nod. "It's reasonably dent and scratch resistant too, which would be an important feature.

And it doesn't bend and flex easily, which helps to support heavier loads."

I'm impressed by his knowledge as he shares the pros for the timber. "Sounds good. I'll let you know when I get to that point."

He nods as the girls step onto the deck with fresh plates and Lachlan's birthday cake. Molly catches my eye and winks at me with a cheeky smile and a raised eyebrow. At least she didn't run away. That has to be a positive sign. Right?

The kids follow behind the girls and everyone takes their seat, with Lachlan at the head of the table. Sarah places the Spider-Man cake she made on the table directly in front of the birthday boy and he looks up at her with a smile. "Thank you, Aunty Sarah."

She ruffles his hair and leans down to press a kiss to his cheek. "You're welcome, Lachlan. I hope you like it."

"I love it. I don't want to cut into it and ruin it."

"That's okay. That's what cake is for, and I took heaps of photos." She winks at him.

Austin climbs into my lap as Emma lights the ten candles on the cake and we all sing happy birthday to my eldest nephew. I'm not sure where the time's gone. It seemed like yesterday I was holding him as a newborn. I miss those days.

I'm pretty sure I'm not supposed to feel my biological clock ticking, but I do. I want to be a dad. Like my dad, I want to be a great father. I study Molly and wonder if she'd think I was a psycho if I wanted to get her pregnant this soon into our relationship. I mean, I only referred to her as my girlfriend when I introduced her to Mom, otherwise, we haven't talked about our relationship or where we're heading.

We have amazing sex. Fuck me. The sex. She blows my fucking mind. But it's not only the sex. She blows my mind out of the bedroom, too. She's been through so much in her life, and nothing drags her down. I have an incredible amount of respect for the woman sitting beside me, something I've not felt for the women I've dated in the past. Our connection is deep on a fundamental level. I know she said her birth control shot was due, but I can't remember when that was. Maybe I could convince her to skip it.

The cake is cut and handed out and we all go silent except for the occasional moan. I hate that I notice Emma putting on a show for Theo as she moans around her fork and then slides the cake off in a long stroke. She glances up, noticing me watching her. I raise one eyebrow in a 'what the fuck are you doing?' look. My fucking sister smirks at me and shrugs. Typical.

As soon as Molly swallows her last bite of cake, Kenny cheers. "Yay! I can do your hair now." She hops down from her seat. "C'mon. Let's go inside. I have everything already set up."

"Ah, Munchkin. I think you'd better wash your hands first. I don't think Molly would like chocolate cake smeared through her hair." Theo rises ready to clean up his daughter. Well, niece, but that's neither here nor there since he adopted her.

Molly stands as Theo takes Kenny inside. "You don't have to let her braid your hair. You know." Emma clarifies.

"Oh no. I'm looking forward to it. Honestly." She gives my sisters the full dimple experience and I can tell my sisters think she's pretty great.

The girls move inside while I help Dad and Cristo clean up from dessert. Kenny runs into the living room excitedly. "I need *Frozen* on while I do Aunty Molly's hair."

Of course she does because the million times she's already watched it will never be enough. Lachlan and Austin groan. "Noooo. Not again." Austin drops his head back on his shoulders, looking up at the ceiling, adding to his dramatic response.

Molly chuckles. "She needs to make sure she's doing the braid correctly. Which means Kenny needs the movie on as a reference."

Lachlan latches onto Molly's explanation. "Yes. It's like when I build my Legos. I need the picture as a reference to know I'm building it correctly."

Molly smiles at my nephew. "That's right. We won't mind if she has the movie playing, right?"

"No. I guess that will be okay. But I'm gonna go play outside with Poppa and Pappoús," he responds.

"Me too," adds Austin.

The boys head out the back with Cristo and Dad, and Molly sits on the designated cushion on the floor, crossing her legs. I know she was worried about being around this many people, but she's coped like a champion. The opening scene of *Frozen* plays and Kenny attacks Molly's hair with a brush, dragging Molly's head back sharply.

Emma steps in, placing her hand over Kenny's, stopping her. "Kenny." She waits until Kenny looks at her. "You need to be gentle. You don't want to hurt Aunty Molly."

Kenny's bottom lip quivers. "I'm sorry. I didn't mean to hurt you, Aunty Molly."

Molly twists around and drags Kenny into her lap, snuggling her close. "You didn't hurt me, lovely girl. I wasn't quite ready. Long, smooth strokes work best with my hair." She winks at my niece, putting her at ease.

See, she's gonna be a great mom. I need her to have my babies.

Kenny brushes, combs, twists, and miraculously braids Molly's hair as she patiently sits for almost an hour. She has fancy hair clips sticking in and out of everywhere and it looks a total mess, but when Kenny asks Emma to take a photo to show Molly, she gushes over how fabulous her new hair-do looks.

Mom, Emma, and Sarah all look at me with *that* look on their face. The one that says they know I've found the one. The one that's perfect for me *and* perfect for our family.

Trust me. I know.

As the party winds down, we say our goodbyes. Each member of my family hugs Molly for long minutes, almost to the point it's a little uncomfortable. Even Lachlan gives her a brief hug, which is unheard of until he's known someone for a while. I remember he latched onto Theo quickly, too. Perhaps he has a sixth sense about whether someone is a decent person.

Mom hugs me extra tight as she whispers in my ear. "Molly's wonderful. She's definitely a keeper." When she pulls back, she pats my cheek. "I'm so proud of you."

I'm not sure what I've done to make her proud, but I'll take it. I'd rather she be proud of me than disappointed.

Molly and I climb into my car and as we pull out of the driveway, she releases a long breath, then giggles. "I don't know what I was worried about. Your family is amazing." She looks across at me. "I felt especially welcomed from the minute I walked in the door. You are incredibly lucky to be surrounded by such great people." She leans across, laying a chaste kiss on my bristly cheek. "Thank you for bringing me."

"You're welcome. I'm pretty sure my family's in love with you and will expect you at every Sunday lunch from this point forward."

Her head snaps toward me and her eyes widen. "Really? I'm glad I made a good impression. It meant a lot to me to be invited. I didn't want to mess it up."

I reach across and squeeze her thigh. "I don't think you could ever mess up after my last girlfriend." I tense my jaw and look out the passenger window before looking forward. "She, uh, she wasn't very nice to my family. You're the complete opposite."

"I wondered what those funny looks were about. I was worried I'd done something wrong." She fidgets with her bracelet.

"Nah. They were in shock that I brought home someone so

sweet." She chuckles and I'm relieved that she's not going to dig any further about my previous girlfriends. I haven't had the best track record with the women I've brought home in the past. "Are you gonna tell me what you girls were talking about in the kitchen after lunch?"

"Are you nervous?" She raises one eyebrow and gives me a cheeky smile.

I shrug like I don't care one way or the other.

She pushes my shoulder playfully. "Sarah was fascinated with my nose ring. Then I showed them my navel piercing, and she started asking all sorts of questions about how the jewelry will go when I'm pregnant."

And doesn't that put the perfect visual in my head. "Oh yeah? How does it go when you're pregnant?"

"Once my stomach expands, I'll have to remove it. It's easy enough to do." I look across at her midsection, imagining it swollen with our baby. Maybe now would be the time to bring it up with her?

"Hang on. You're wearing a dress. How did you show them your stomach?"

Her cheeks flush pink. "Oh, uhm, it was only the ladies, so I lifted my dress. I have underwear on, so there was nothing to see."

I groan and readjust my position at the image of her innocently lifting her dress, and exposing her underwear. "Do you think you'll want to have kids?" I glance across at her.

She smiles. "Absolutely. I love kids." She pauses. "What about you?"

"I'd have kids tomorrow if I had my way."

Her smile widens. "Really?"

"Did you end up going back for your birth control shot last week?" I'm hoping she forgot, but I don't think Molly would do something like that.

"Yeah, I did. Why?" Creases have formed between her

eyebrows and I want to smooth them away with my thumb. "I would never take the chance of getting pregnant unexpectedly. I saw what happened to Mom."

Of course. Fuck, I'm a stupid ass sometimes. I take her hand in mine and squeeze. "How about I take you to my favorite spot to watch the sunset and we can talk a bit more?"

"Okay." She pulls her hand from mine and fidgets with her bracelet. I've noticed she does that when she's uncomfortable or nervous.

I turn up the radio to combat the silence that's descended over us. I want to say something to put her mind at ease, but I don't know what to say. I figure it's best to keep my mouth shut for now.

—molly—

I HOPE HE DOESN'T THINK I'M THE TYPE OF WOMAN WHO would trap their boyfriend with a pregnancy or that I'm irresponsible with my birth control. I had hoped he knew me better than that. Now he wants to talk. About what? Have I done something wrong? Maybe he didn't like me showing my piercing to his family. I figured it would be okay. There weren't any men in the room. It's not like I have anything different compared to his mom and sisters. I didn't show them anything they wouldn't see down at the beach, but maybe he's weird about that stuff?

Actually, that reminds me. "Did you realize you introduced me to your family as your girlfriend?" I twist in my seat to face him fully. "Is that what I am?" I mean, we haven't given this thing between us a label.

He glances across at me with creases between his eyebrows. "Aren't you?" I watch his Adam's Apple bob up and down. "Did I misstep?"

"We haven't really spoken about our relationship." I hitch my shoulder. I'm not even sure if I should use the term 'relationship'.

He doesn't answer, which fills me with dread as he pulls the car into a quiet parking lot. There's only one other vehicle, which probably belongs to whoever's working in the food truck.

"Do you want something to eat before the guy closes up for the night?"

"I'm still full from lunch and cake, so I'm okay, thanks."

He gestures over his shoulder. "I'm gonna grab some wedges or something."

"Okay." We climb out of his car, and he takes my hand as we wander over to the food truck. Max orders a basket of sweet potato wedges and a couple of bottles of water, while I step closer to the beach and look out across the ocean, tugging my sweater around my body as the temperature drops with the sun.

I always find it peaceful watching the waves break on the shore. They never stop. No matter what. They remind me that you have to keep going. The salty breeze is cool, and I pull my sweater even tighter around my body. Warm arms wrap around me from behind and Max's body presses against mine, reducing the chill. He leans down, resting his chin on my shoulder.

"I love watching the sunset. I don't get down here nearly as often as I'd like," he quietly contemplates.

I turn my head and press a kiss to his temple; he turns, returning my kiss. Our lips touching sets fire licking through my body and my underwear quickly grows wet. It's difficult to keep it chaste, and neither of us tries to.

"Order's up!"

Max groans and pulls away, returning to the truck window to grab his food and our drinks.

"Come on. We can sit in the car and watch the sun sink below the horizon without you feeling cold." He places the wedges on the console between us and they smell so damn good I'm wishing

I'd ordered some for myself. I glance across at the food truck, but he's closing everything down for the night. I don't blame him. It's not like anybody's here. Max nudges the basket closer. "Have some. I got the large serve in case you changed your mind."

Of course he did because he's always making sure I eat when I'm in his company. He still buys my lunch every day. We eat in silence for a few moments and I'm waiting for 'the talk' to start. He twists his body to face me directly and I mirror him.

"I'm not sure where to start or how to say what I want to say, so I'll just say it." I nod for him to continue and try to swallow down the food in my mouth, but my throat feels too constricted. "I don't know about you, but I'm in pretty deep with you already."

I breathe a sigh of relief and reach across for Max's hand. "I'm in the deep end with you."

He blows out a long breath and gifts me his gorgeous smile, which I return. "Fuck, that's a relief." We both chuckle. "I can't see a time when I won't feel this way about you. The more time I spend with you, the deeper I get, and I'm not even trying to swim for the shore."

"Me too," I whisper.

"It's happened really fast, but I know how I feel. I've fallen in love with you, Molly." A tear escapes, followed by another one and another one. "Dimples. Please don't cry. I never want to be the one to make you cry."

I swallow and smile at Max, shaking my head slightly. "They're not sad tears. They're happy tears." He rubs them away with his thumbs as he cups my face, pulling me forward for a kiss. After a moment, I pull away because I need to share my confession with him. "I think I fell a little in love with you the very first Thursday I started working for you. The kindness and care you showed the single parents that day. You've shown me the type of man you are time and again. I fell hard and fast for you. I love you, Max."

His smile is bright as he pulls me forward, taking my mouth in a searing kiss that marks me all the way to my soul. There's nothing teasing or delicate about our joining. It's all tongues and teeth, hot breaths, moans, and sighs. It's an epic confirmation of our mutual connection. He grips a handful of my hair and tugs my head back slightly; his eyes locking onto mine. "I need to be inside you."

I glance across, finding we're alone in the parking lot. There isn't a soul around. "I want that too."

We move the food to the dash, climb out, and adjust the front seats forward so we can climb into the back of his car like a couple of high schoolers. There's no preamble or foreplay. We're both ready to get to the main event. Max undoes his jeans and pulls them and his briefs out of the way, exposing his thick shaft. He's already weeping for me, as I am for him. He reaches for me, positioning me over his dick. His face is in shadow, but from experience, I know his pupils will have overtaken the mossy green I love. Hot puffs from his breaths hit the side of my neck as I balance on my knees and hold on to his shoulders, ducking my head to avoid the roof.

"Are you ready for me?" He swipes his knuckles over the panel of my panties, keeping my modesty for the moment. "Oh yeah. Your panties are fucking soaked already." He smirks up at me, then pulls the panel to the side and notches his head at my opening. I slide down easily, taking him all the way. We both groan at the sensation of being joined.

"I love having you inside me, Max," I whisper, then lean forward to swipe my tongue along his bottom lip. He opens for me, and I slide inside, tangling my tongue with his, enjoying the rasp of his five o'clock shadow on my skin.

He pulls back. "Be my good girl and show me your tits."

I raise my eyebrow at him. "Take your shirt off first." He smirks at me, then grabs his shirt from the back of the collar, pulling it off awkwardly in the confined space. As he tosses it to the side, I take off my sweater, undo the side zipper of my dress, and slide my arms out. Next to go is my bra as the cotton fabric pools at my waist. Max pushes the fabric down until he exposes my silver jewelry.

He flicks it with his finger and looks up at me. "I fucking love this." He pushes up into me. "Hold on, Dimples."

I comply, and he rewards me with a hard thrust and grind. His mouth drops to my breast, and he sucks as much of the globe into his mouth as he can. "Oh God. You're not messing around." I drop my heavy head back on my shoulders.

"I'm never just messing around with you. I hope you know that." Thrust. He uses his grip on my hips to guide me up and down his shaft as he repeatedly pushes up into me. I add a swivel to my hips, making sure to rub my clit against his pelvis.

Our bodies are slick. Our breaths come out in harsh pants and I'm sure if someone were to pull into the parking lot, they'd know exactly what's going on in here. The windows are fogging up with each labored breath and the car is rocking in time with our bodies. I can't find it in me to care. I want my release. My muscles are tensing and it's getting harder to keep up with Max's rhythm. My focus narrows to where we're joined and making sure I don't falter. I squeeze Max's dick.

"Fuck. Do that again and I'll come." I take the challenge and squeeze him again on the next stroke. He pinches my nipple with a frown marring his forehead, making me giggle.

He finds his way to my clit beneath the pooling fabric of my dress and circles it with deft fingers, returning his lips to my mouth. Hunching down, I use my legs to push myself up and down, bouncing over his cock as he takes me ever closer to my release.

Every thrust up pushes the air from my lungs and stars dance around the edge of my vision. His penis swells. He's as close as I am. Tingles spread all the way from my toes, up my legs, and down my spine. I drop one final time and break apart all over him. "Yeeees!" I gasp for air and lean down to kiss him. My kiss is sloppy as he comes undone, groaning into my mouth.

"Fuuck! You feel so damn good, Dimples." He returns my sloppy kiss. "I'm gonna fill you with my babies one day soon," he moans and my already racing heart picks up speed, thumping against my rib cage, trying to burst free. I pull back to study him. Guys say all sorts of stuff in the heat of the moment, and I wonder if he realizes what he's said. He opens his eyes to find me studying his face as if I can find the answer somehow. "I mean it. I want you to have my babies. I don't want you to get your next shot."

I blink at him. "You want to have a baby with me?"

"I sure as fuck do." His eyes move back and forth between mine. "Do you?" His Adam's Apple bobs. "Do you want to have a baby with me?"

"You don't think it's too soon to be talking about babies?"

His body stiffens and I place my hands on his shoulders, rubbing my thumbs along his collarbones. "You think it's too soon?"

I shrug. "We've only known each other for just over two months."

"I know it's fast, but I don't see the point of waiting when I know you're the one for me." He reaches up and tucks a lock of hair that's fallen across my face behind my ear. "I'm all in, Molly."

I nod, slowly at first, increasing in enthusiasm. "I'm all in too. I think you'd be the best daddy."

He smiles and moves in, taking my mouth. Our tongues

entangle, and I feel him grow inside of me. Obviously, the idea of knocking me up has him excited. We move together, slower this time, languidly joined with our kisses as well as our sex. The interior of the car is filled with the scent of our coupling as Max takes over my body, my heart, and my soul. A sheen of sweat coats both of us as we climb higher and higher before we break apart. It's not as explosive as the first time, but it feels deeper, more meaningful somehow. We separate to draw in lungfuls of much-needed oxygen. Our eyes connect and I'm positive mine reflects his happiness.

"When can we start?" he asks with a cheeky grin. I giggle at his eagerness. "Fuck, don't do that. You nearly pushed me out." He pouts playfully and thrusts his hips up to push his half-soft dick back inside, making me giggle again. "Damn it, woman."

He slides out of me and the sensation of his cum trickling from my body moves me into action. Using the fabric of my dress, I rise higher and clean myself up as best I can in the limited light. I dread to think about the mess we've made on his leather seat. I shuffle slightly, pulling my underwear back into place, then rest my backside on his knees.

Resting my hands on his pecs, I lean forward and press my lips to his. Pulling back slightly, I break the news. "I definitely can't get pregnant within the next three months and it can take up to one year for my periods to regulate. But I could possibly get pregnant in as little as three months once the shot wears off."

Even in the limited light, I can see his face light up with his smile. "Well, that gives us time to practice our technique." He wriggles his eyebrows up and down.

I giggle. "That sounds good to me."

His hands squeeze my hips, and he drags me back in close to his body, my exposed breasts pressing against his chest. I sigh, deeply content to sit here like this all night. He rubs his hands up and down my spine in a soothing motion. With two orgasms under my belt, I close my eyes and enjoy the sensation, my breathing slowing down.

A rap on the window and a bright light shining inside startles both of us. We must have dozed off. "Everything okay in there?" Comes a muffled voice through the glass.

I look around, instantly alert. My eyes land on the police cruiser parked right next to us. I'm sure he can see my state of undress. *Shit!*

"Everything's fine, officer. Thanks. We were getting ready to leave," Max speaks for both of us.

"Okay. Just to remind you that public indecency is a fineable offense, and we'll leave it at that."

"Thank you, officer." I finally find my voice. The bright light disappears and the officer steps away from Max's car. "Shit!" I whisper-giggle.

"Damn. I felt like a kid again." He searches around on the seat for my bra but comes up empty. It's too dark to see anything. I pull the straps of my dress up and shiver as I do up the zipper. "You're cold. C'mon, let's go."

Max drags his underwear and jeans back up and we both climb out of the back seat and readjust the front seats. I grab my sweater and put it on as I situate myself. The officers give us a tilt of their heads as Max starts the engine and pulls out. Once we're on the road, we both break out into laughter.

When we settle down, Max takes my hand in his, resting it on his firm thigh, and rubs his thumb back and forth. "I think you should move in with me." He glances across at me.

"You're full of ideas tonight," I chuckle.

He shrugs. "It makes sense. I don't see the point of wasting time. As I said, I'm all in."

I bring his hand up to my mouth and kiss the palm. "I'd love to move in with you."

His smile is big and bright, and I know I've made the right decision.

CHAPTER 32

—*max*—

COULD LIFE GET ANY BETTER?

Nope. I don't think it can.

Molly's all moved in. Having her toothbrush in the holder with mine gave me a sense of satisfaction this morning that can't be explained.

Mona constantly hinted that we should move in together, but I didn't want her in my space. I needed time and space away from her and didn't want her in my home for more than the night. She'd always linger on a Sunday morning and I'd hate it. But with Molly, I wish we didn't have to leave the house to come to work. If I could stay home with her all day, it wouldn't be long enough. I huff out a chuckle to myself as I disconnect the muffler bracket from the worn rubber hanger.

My, how things have changed. I never thought I'd feel this way, but here I am. *And I fucking love it.*

I slide out from under the car I'm working on to be greeted by a pair of work boots. My eyes follow the path upward to identify the owner of the boots. Martin. I quickly glance across to the door that leads into the office.

Martin follows my path. "Hey, Max. Molly's not in the

office." I push up from the trolley and stand. "I came to see her. I … uh … I've tried to give her some time, but I think we need to talk." He tucks his hands in his pockets, shuffling on his feet.

I nod. "Hey, Martin. She's probably grabbing our lunch." I wipe my hands with a rag. "You don't think it'd be better to wait for her to contact you when she's ready? She was pretty upset after your last chat." *That's an understatement.*

He glances down at the floor and shrugs. "It's been a month. I've already lost too much time. I want to get to know my daughter. I *need* to get to know my daughter." He runs his hand through his salt and pepper hair. "Beth and Holly have spoken with her and they said she was open and friendly. I'm hoping I can repair some of the damage I've caused with my carelessness."

"Maaax! Lunch is—" Molly freezes in the doorway of the office. I can tell from here that she's trying to decide what to do. She takes a tentative step forward—*so fucking brave.* "Hi, Martin." She stops a couple of feet away, then looks at me. "I didn't realize Martin had his car booked in today."

Martin steps closer to her. "Hey, Molly. I didn't. I … uh … I hope you don't mind me stopping by unannounced, but I wanted to see you." His shoulders drop. "I'm sorry. I probably should have called first. I keep messing this up." He takes a step back and spins on his heel to leave. "I'll leave you two to enjoy your lunch."

Molly glances at me, her eyes wide. "What should I do?" she whispers.

"It's up to you, Dimples. He just wants to talk." She blows out a breath and studies the floor as if the answer lies there somewhere. She spins around and runs after him. I follow along at a slower pace. Molly catches up to Martin as he's about to climb into his truck.

I can't hear what's being said from here, but Molly points

toward me. He nods and she comes to me. She stops close and I use the loops of her jeans to pull her closer. I study her eyes carefully and she smiles at me. "I'm okay." I nod and kiss the tip of her nose. "Do you mind if I spend my lunch break with Martin?"

"Of course not. You don't need to ask my permission." I glance up at Martin. He's watching us closely and I want him to be aware that I'm watching out for Molly. I lean down and take her mouth in a heated kiss. It takes a beat for Molly to respond, but when her tongue strokes against mine, I wrap my arms around her and hold her tight. We pull apart slowly and I touch my forehead to hers. "I'll be here if you need me."

"Thank you." I don't understand how she fills two simple words with so much gratitude, but she does. "We're going to the park down the road." She thumbs over her shoulder.

"Take your lunch with you." I dash into the office to grab it for her.

She climbs into the cab of Martin's truck. With narrowed eyes, he lifts his chin at me, and I return the action. I watch the truck until they disappear, then return to the office to eat lunch on my own. I hope this chat goes well. Family's important to Molly and I want her to have family surrounding and supporting her. She deserves to have the world.

My phone lights up with Theo's number. "Hey, Brother. What's up?"

"Hiya, Max. I wanted to let you know I've sourced the timber you'll need for the truck. I'll keep it in my workshop to allow it time to dry out properly."

"Thanks, man. Appreciate it."

"No problem. How're things?"

"Damn good. Molly's moved in with me. Life's feeling pretty great."

He huffs out a laugh. "She's a keeper. Kenny hasn't

stopped talking about her since Lachlan's party. Emma loves her, too."

"Don't worry. I'm never letting her go."

"Good to hear, man. I gotta go. See ya on Sunday."

"Sure. And thanks for sourcing the timber."

CHAPTER 33

—molly—

As we turn onto the street, my fingers instantly find comfort in twisting my bracelet.

"So, you and Max, huh?"

I snap my head toward Martin and narrow my eyes. "What do you mean?"

He fidgets in his seat. "Are you together? More than boss and employee? More than friends?" He glances across at me. "I mean, it's none of my business, but I'm happier knowing you have someone and you're not completely alone." He clears his throat. "Not that you're alone. You *do* have us, we just need to find our feet."

"Uh yeah. It's pretty new. We started as boss and employee, then developed a friendship. It grew into more." I shrug. "I moved in with him on Sunday. It's pretty serious." Once I agreed to move in, Max drove straight to the apartment and we packed my stuff. He was a man on a mission.

Martin pulls into the parking lot and we climb out of his truck to stroll toward a vacant picnic table. "You don't think it's too fast?" Hmmm. My muscles tense. I'm not sure where he's going with this line of questioning, but I'm old enough to make my own decisions. It's not like he's been part of my life. He gives me a tight smile. "I'm sorry. I crossed a line, it's none of my business. It's hard to take off the dad hat sometimes. Max is a good guy. I'm sure he'll be good to you."

I shrug. "He's been nothing but fantastic to me so far. I can't see that changing. Ever." I take a bite of my sandwich as Martin opens a home-packed lunch box filled with vegetables, crackers, cheese, meat, and hummus. "I should make lunch for me and Max rather than him buying it for us every day."

"Beth insists on packing me a healthy lunch every day. She allows me to buy my lunch on Fridays." He smirks at me. "It's her love language to care for and feed her family." He dips a carrot into some hummus and chews thoughtfully. "She fell in love with you. Couldn't stop talking about you when she got home. That's why Holly wanted to meet you, too. She's stead-fastly in the Molly fan club as well."

I blush. "They're both incredibly sweet. I thought it was coincidental that your daughter's name is Holly and mine is Molly." I chuckle.

"Yeah, it is, and it isn't. Nicole and I liked a lot of the same things. We often had the same thoughts at the same time. We were unquestionably in sync in that way." His body's still here, but his mind is somewhere else. He slowly comes back to the moment. "Look, Molly. I can apologize to you for the rest of my life, and I'll happily do so, but nothing is going to change how things happened all those years ago. I need you to know that I have regretted my response to Nicole's pregnancy every single day of my life. It wasn't my finest moment and it's not something I'm proud of. I lost so much because of my youthful stupidity. I only hope that one day you can forgive me and we can develop some sort of relationship."

I reach across the table and place my hand over his. "Thank you. I'm sorry I responded so badly at dinner."

He covers my hand with his. "You don't owe me an apology, Molly. I should have been more thoughtful in the way I shared the events of that time with you." He smiles sadly. "I would like the opportunity to get to know you, though."

"Me too." We both release a heavy breath. There's no point in holding a grudge. He genuinely wants to build a relationship with me, and I'd be stupid to turn down the opportunity to get to know my family. I think Mom would want me to put the past behind me and open my heart to Martin and his family. *My* family.

"So, uh, I can't believe I have to ask you this question, but when's your birthday?" He drops his eyes to his food.

"August thirty. I'll be—"

"Twenty-seven this year."

I smile. "Yeah."

"I figured you were born around there somewhere."

We study each other for long moments. It's comforting seeing my eyes staring back at me. "It surprised me how similar I am to Holly and Noah. I always thought I looked so much like Mom."

"Yeah. It's uncanny. The first time I laid eyes on you, I couldn't stop staring. The resemblance was remarkable to Nicole and your sister and brother. I went home and told Beth about you. She didn't believe me until she laid eyes on you the day we bought the car from Max." He glances away, then his eyes lock back on me. "When she had to come and pick me up from your place that day we worked out that you are my daughter. Beth wanted to pack you up and bring you home. We lost Nicole all of those years ago and then we lost her all over again that day."

The breath in my lungs seizes. I was so overwhelmed that day and I've been caught up in my own grief and loss as well as coming to terms with meeting my father, that I hadn't taken the time to consider his and Beth's loss. I've been so selfish.

"I'm sorry you had to find out about Mom like that. It would have been tough."

He shrugs. "Is there anything you can share with me about yourself? What's your favorite thing to do?"

A genuine smile spreads. "I love to sketch. My stepdad, Jack, taught me and my brother, Ethan, how to draw. Ethan mostly drew cars, but I'll draw pretty much anything."

"Really? Holly's always sketching new designs for her clothes." The tension disappears between us as we find some common ground. Conversation flows more easily as we chat about Holly's passion for design.

I glance at the time. "Oh, my gosh. I need to get back. I only get thirty minutes for lunch."

"Sure." We quickly clean up our mess and head back to the workshop. Martin parks out front and then turns in his seat toward me. "Uh, would you like to come over for dinner one Saturday night?" I freeze. I'm not sure I'm ready to face his whole family at once. "You can bring Max with you."

"Do you mind if I think about it and let you know?"

He shakes his head. "Of course. No pressure."

"Thanks. And, uh, thanks for today. This was … nice." I open the door and climb down.

"Thank you for agreeing to have lunch with me. I hope we can move forward, Molly." I nod.

"Bye, Martin."

"Bye, Molly."

I close the door and head inside the workshop. A squeal escapes as I'm lifted off my feet from behind. Muscular arms wrapped around my waist tightening to keep me in place. Max's familiar scent swamps my senses. "You scared me." He places me back on my feet and I spin around. Immediately, I'm engulfed in his warm embrace as he studies my face closely, his brows scrunched together. I smile at him. "I'm okay. Lunch went well."

He blows out a breath and glances between my eyes and mouth, then leans in to kiss me. It's not a kiss to welcome me back, it's a kiss that fills me down to my toes. It makes me feel cherished and cared for. He's reminding me he's here for me and I don't have to deal with my new reality on my own. I return his kiss. Pouring my appreciation for his support into it. We separate slowly, gradually opening our eyes. "You're sure?"

I nod. "I'm positive. We even got invited to dinner one Saturday." His eyebrows shoot up. "I wanted to check that you would be able to come with me before I accepted."

"If you're there and you want me to be with you. Then that's where I'll be, Dimples." He presses his lips to my fore-head, pulling me in tighter to his body, and I sigh. "Even if I had something on, I would cancel to be with you."

Luckily, he's holding me tight; I think my knees would have given out on me if he weren't. "Thank you. I'll let Martin know later. Now, what'd I miss?" With our arms wrapped around each other, we make our way into the office.

CHAPTER 34

—molly—

MAX STROLLS INTO THE KITCHEN AS I'M OPENING AND CLOSING every cupboard. "What are you looking for? Maybe I can help."

"Do you have any lunch boxes?" I wave my hand in the general direction of the cupboards.

He glances around, then shakes his head. "I don't think so. Why?"

I fidget with my bracelet. "Today, at lunch, Martin had a lunch box that Beth had prepared for him. I wanted to start making our lunches. It's expensive to buy it every day. I can pack them the night before, and it'll be easy enough to keep them in the fridge at work." I hope he doesn't think it's a stupid idea.

He moves into my space, hooking his fingers through the belt loops of my jeans. He pulls me forward and smirks at me. "You wanna make lunch for me, for us?"

"Yeah. You don't think it's stupid, do you?"

He shakes his head. "Nah. Dad always made our lunches for us when we were living at home. But I buy our lunch every day to support Lawrence's business. I could have been taking lunch to work, but I'd rather help him out. He gives us a discount because we buy from him every day. But if it would make you fee—"

Of course, he does it to help his friend; that's Max all over. "Oh, I didn't realize that's why you did it. Forget I said anything." I press into him and lick his bottom lip. He opens and I slide my tongue inside to share a heated kiss. I love this man. "I love you."

Max's eyes widen and his lips spread wide to match. "Say that again, Dimples."

"I love you, Max. You're such a good man." I press a chaste kiss against his mouth.

"I'll never get tired of you saying those words. I love you, Molly. You're the sweetest, kindest woman I've ever met." His eyes are full of emotion, and I know the words are completely true. He's not saying them because I said them. He means them as much as I do.

He hoists me onto the kitchen counter, pressing his body into the space between my open legs. Our lips meet as his hands slide beneath my shirt, setting my skin on fire. I shuffle forward, making contact with his erection confined within the denim.

Suddenly, there's an urgency between us. Clothes go flying left and right until we're both naked, neither of us caring where they land.

His fingers slide through my slit as he kisses my breath from me. I'm already soaking and I want him inside me. Now! "I need you." I press my pelvis forward and reach for him, wrapping my hand around his long, hard shaft. "Please don't make me wait," I pant. My heart's hammering, swollen with love for the man who's about to fill my body, just as he's filled my life since I arrived.

"I need you. I promise we'll go slow later."

"Don't care. Just get inside me." I pant.

He thrusts in. Hard. Forcing all the air out of my lungs. My mouth drops open in bliss. "Fuck. You look so good with my dick in your pussy." I moan. God, I love his filthy mouth. "Look down, Dimples. I want you to see how beautiful your pussy looks stretched around my cock."

I tilt my head down. The sight is erotic as he slides out; his shaft glistening from my arousal. He slides back in with a groan and I press forward, meeting his push with my own. His lips drop to my breast, and he sucks the nipple into his mouth, sending shockwaves to my clit. I run my hands across his shoulders and down his back, feeling his muscles tense and move with his thrusts. I kiss the top of his head and he tips his face up to meet my mouth. His hands grasp my hips tight as he holds me in place to take his punishing pounding. My heart thumps hard against my ribcage as my breaths become choppy.

"Oh my God. That feels so good. I … I'm getting close. I … I need …" I whisper with harsh breaths.

One hand leaves my hip and he brings his fingers to my clit. He pinches the bundle of nerves, then rubs tight circles, building me higher. My toes curl as I run my hands through his sweaty hair, pulling his head in tighter to me. My breaths are short and sharp, matching the warm puffs of his against my neck. He pulls back, our eyes locking as I break apart and I feel his gaze drilling into me, all the way to my soul. My muscles clench around his shaft and Max grits his teeth. The veins in his neck are pronounced as he slows his thrusts through my orgasm, my cum coating his cock. His head drops and his mouth envelopes my other breast. I moan as my muscles continue to pulse.

Max looks up at me, one side of his mouth tilted up. "I fucking love making you come. The way your body flushes and your pussy strangles my cock. I'm never gonna get enough of this. Enough of you." We both lean forward, our tongues reaching for the other, sealing his words with a savage kiss.

He pulls out of my pussy partway and surges forward. He pounds into me, hammering my pussy. His shaft grows inside me, setting off a second, smaller orgasm I wasn't expecting. His dick pulses. "Fuuuuck! Your pussy is heaven." He throws his head back. "Fuck!" His cum streams out of him and into me and I wish this was the time we were making a baby.

Dropping his head back down, he roughly takes my mouth and I wrap my legs around him, keeping him locked inside me as long as possible as we share a prolonged kiss. Running my fingers through his hair, I grasp the strands at the base and keep him exactly where I want him. We're messy in this moment as our tongues twist around each other, our teeth clash, and I'm completely and utterly his.

No question about it.

We separate, dropping our foreheads together. Our eyes locked, our breaths combining. Gray eyes to mossy green. "I fucking love you, Molly."

I smile. And it's full and happy. "I fucking love you, Max." I chuckle.

We hold each other as our bodies cool, staring into each other's eyes. I can see right to his core, and I know what we have is rare and special. Not everyone is lucky enough to find this and I'm never going to let it go. And I know with certainty Max feels the same.

—max—

"Do you mind if we get some fresh fruit?" Molly fidgets with her bracelet. I noticed how much she enjoyed the fresh fruit we had for breakfast the morning after the first night we slept together, and she always had some in her apartment.

I stop, pulling the cart to the side of the aisle, and turn Molly to face me. "Of course we can buy fresh fruit and vegetables and whatever else you need, Dimples. Why are you worried about asking?"

Her eyes skate around me, glancing everywhere but at me. "Fresh fruit was … still is a luxury for me. When I have money, it's one of the first things I buy. I wasn't sure if fruit was something you have on the regular and I didn't want to impose my preferences on you. I notice you don't seem to eat a lot of fruit and you don't have any in your fridge."

Such a simple thing. I've always eaten fruit. Mom always made sure we had fresh fruit every day with breakfast and Dad always packed fruit in our lunch box. As an adult, though, I can't remember the last time I took fruit to work that wasn't in a pie or muffin. I usually have a small amount of fresh fruit in the fridge at home for snacks or breakfast, but if I skip eating it for a day, I don't really think about it. Shit! It's not something I've thought about, which means I take it for granted. Here's Molly, who's always lived on the poverty line or close to it and she would never take something as simple as having fresh fruit every day for granted. She considers it a damn luxury.

I pull her in close and kiss her forehead. "If it will make you happy, we can have fresh fruit and vegetables for every single meal. I never want you to think you can't ask for what you want, for what you need. Being on my own, I didn't bother keeping much in the house. I'd make simple meals for dinner, and I was slack with breakfast. We can do better with two of us."

We make our way to the fruit and vegetables, and I watch as Molly carefully handpicks fruits and vegetables with glee written all over her face. Glancing at the prices, I note she's choosing the basic options that aren't too expensive.

I'm not having it. "Do you like berries?"

Her head snaps up to mine, then she glances across to the berry display. "I love raspberries, but they're a little expensive."

"I love raspberries too. Let's get some." I push the cart across and grab two containers of raspberries, two of strawberries, and one of blackberries. My girl will never go without the necessities of life again. Shit that we all take for granted.

Molly steps closer to the cart, studying the contents. Her gray eyes slowly creep up to mine and she tucks a lock of her silky hair behind her ear. "Oh, that's a lot. I don't know if we'll get through all of it before it goes bad."

I shrug. "I'm pretty sure I can eat a whole container in one sitting. I doubt it'll be a problem." I peck her forehead. "C'mon, we need to keep moving." I need to make sure my girl has everything she needs at her fingertips. We move down the aisles, filling the cart with groceries. More than I've ever bought before, but I'm not stopping until the cart is full. We have one more section to go. Ice cream. "What's your favorite ice cream flavor?"

She licks her lips and studies the freezer for long moments, then she glances at the cart. "I don't think we need anything else." She huffs out a laugh. "We already have more than we need."

"We need to have ice cream. C'mon, what's your favorite?"

She looks back at the freezer. "I am partial to vanilla caramel fudge. What's your favorite?" I grab a carton of her favorite and a tub of pistachio for me, holding it up so she can see. "I'll have pistachio. You don't need to grab two different cartons of ice cream. It's too much."

"Nah. As much as I love you, I don't share my ice cream." I press a kiss to the tip of her nose and dump the ice cream in the cart as Molly giggles.

We head to the front of the store to pay as Molly grumbles about how much food we bought. A couple of ladies have stopped in the aisle to have a chat and as we get closer, I realize one of them is Beth. She's speaking to an older woman. Neither of them has any groceries, so they must have just arrived. Molly hasn't noticed because she's still studying our cart with a frown. Beth's eyes catch on us and her mouth drops open slightly. She glances at the older lady and back to us several times. For some reason, she looks uncomfortable. Almost like we've caught her doing something she shouldn't.

Molly's feet lock in place as she notices Beth. "Hi, Beth," she greets, smiling.

"Molly. Max." I've only met Beth a couple of times and I don't know her all that well, but her usual friendliness is missing. Molly's smile drops and creases form between her brows; I'm not the only one who noticed the frosty greeting. Beth glances back at the older lady she's with as we all stand awkwardly. The lady turns around and her eyes widen, her mouth dropping open. Her hand rises to her chest as she grips her blouse. Beth gestures to the woman. "Uh, uhm. This is Joanna. Joanna *Lewis*." She raises her eyebrows at Molly.

Lewis. That's Molly's surname. My eyebrows shoot up. *Fuck!*

I move closer to Molly and wrap my arm around her. Her eyes skip between Beth and Joanna and I can see her putting one and one together. "Joanna Lewis?" Molly asks Beth.

Beth nods. "Joanna. This is Molly. She recently moved here from Portland."

Joanna steps into Molly's space, studying her closely. "Molly? That was my mother's name." She raises her hand, almost touching Molly's face before she realizes what she's doing and pulls back sharply. "I'm sorry. You look so much like …" She shakes her head as though she's trying to shift a memory.

Beth steps forward. "Joanna."

"How about we pay for our groceries and you can follow us home for a chat?" I cut her off. The ladies shouldn't have this conversation in the middle of the store. I'm not sure if Molly's come to the same conclusion I have, but if she's who I think she is, this conversation should happen in private.

Everyone agrees, and we pay for our groceries and load them into my car. Molly's been silent the entire time, fidgeting with her bracelet. Once we're on the road, I pull her hand across to rest on my thigh. "You okay?"

She tears her eyes away from her window and glances at me. "Do you think she's … do you think she's my grand-mother? I mean, her name is Lewis and the way she was looking at me and she said that her mom's name was Molly. Mom told me she named me after her grandmother." The words tumble out of Molly's mouth, each one coming faster than the last.

"I think she might be. How do you feel about that?" *What a fucking stupid question.* God, I'm an idiot sometimes.

"I don't know. I never even thought about finding Mom's

parents. They didn't support her and her dad wanted the pregnancy aborted. Wanted *me* aborted. That's why she left." The despair in her voice is thick and I glance across to check on her. Storm clouds filled with rain look back at me. "Will she even care that Mom's gone?" She brings her hand up to wipe away the tears that have escaped. "I don't know if I'm ready for this."

"I can pull over right now and tell them we've changed our mind. We don't have to do this until you're ready, Molly." I squeeze her hand.

She's quiet for a long moment. "No, it's okay. I don't want to upset anyone." She straightens her shoulders as if she's preparing for battle.

"You're my priority. I don't give a fuck about upsetting anyone else. I don't want *you* upset. You've already had to deal with too much. I didn't think when we were in the grocery store. Before I invited them home, I should have checked with you. I was trying to keep the conversation that was about to happen private."

She flips her hand over, twining her fingers with mine. "Thank you. You're right, the grocery store wasn't the place for a family reunion." She draws in a deep breath. "May as well get it over and done with."

Fuck, she's brave.

"I want you to know that I have an incredible amount of respect for you. The way you deal with everything thrown at you with your head held high. You are a fucking queen." I lift her hand to my mouth to press a kiss to it.

We pull into our driveway and she draws in a deep breath. "Here we go!"

The ladies pull in behind us in two separate cars. Molly and I grab a couple of bags of groceries each and take them inside. Beth and Joanna grab some bags and help us, making quick work of unloading my trunk.

"My. How many people are you two feeding? This seems like a lot of food." Beth chuckles.

"Just the two of us. I didn't have much in the house and now that Molly's living here, we needed to stock the pantry."

Molly offers coffee and makes it while I put away the food that needs to be refrigerated or frozen. The rest can wait until later. Beth and Joanna stand awkwardly by the counter as Molly and I seamlessly work around each other in the kitchen. An uncomfortable silence filling the space.

Even though it's a nice day, I can feel a chill in the air as the sun drops lower. "How about we move into the living room?"

I show the ladies through and then head back to help Molly. "Do you want me with you or I can stay in here? Whatever you need."

She smiles at me, cupping my cheek. Her eyes are full of love and appreciation. "Do you mind sticking close by? I'm not sure how this is going to go."

Turning, I kiss the palm of her hand. "Of course." We grab the cups and head into the living room.

Beth and Joanna are standing in front of the same photo Martin saw in Molly's apartment. As we place the cups on the coffee table, Joanna turns around with tears in her eyes. "You– … you're my granddaughter."

Molly stands up straight and sucks in a sharp breath, nodding slowly. I hate seeing her so unsure of herself. She's done absolutely nothing wrong in this whole fucked up situation. I don't care if the woman is elderly, if she fucking upsets my girl, I'm throwing her ass out on the street.

Joanna walks straight to Molly and engulfs her in a tight hug, sobbing loudly. Her whole body's shaking. Molly's hands slowly rise to comfort the woman, but she's holding her body stiff. Beth and I watch as the older woman breaks down, her body shuddering with her sobs. I glance at Beth and she looks lost. I go in search of some tissues and drop the box on the coffee table.

Joanna pulls back, holding Molly's upper arms. "You're so beautiful. And tall!" She looks Molly up and down. "You're so much like your mother." Joanna looks around suddenly as if she's looking for something. "Is Nicole back home, too?"

I look at Beth. "You haven't told her?"

Beth's bottom lip shakes. "I … I didn't want to tell her in the grocery store. I was about to invite her to my home so I could tell her there. We lost touch and I haven't seen Joanna since I saw Molly. I didn't even think about it, to be honest. Now I feel terrible. It was sheer coincidence that I bumped into Joanna today."

"Tell me what?" Joanna asks as her eyes skate between the three of us.

I can read the dread on Molly's face, in her entire body. "Joanna, maybe you should sit down. I … I need to tell you something."

Joanna nods and sits. "I can't believe I'm sitting with my granddaughter. I never thought this would happen." She pats Molly's knee and leaves her hand resting in place. "Where's Nicole? Has she forgiven me? Can I see her?"

Molly glances at me, then at Beth before settling her eyes on Joanna. "Uhm. Mom's not here." She swallows and I know this is killing her. I can't let her do this on her own, so I take the cushion next to her and brush my hand in a soothing path up and down her delicate spine.

Molly takes Joanna's hand from her knee and holds it between both of hers. "Mom can't come home. She … uh … was in a …" She turns and looks at me over her shoulder and I reach up to tuck a lock of her silky hair behind her ear and kiss her temple.

"You've got this, Dimples. I'm here." I press a kiss on her temple.

She turns back to Joanna and draws in a deep breath. "She was out with my stepdad and my brother, Ethan." Joanna's eyes widen at learning she has another grandchild. "They were looking at the Christmas lights. It was something we did every year. Last Christmas I was volunteering, which meant I couldn't go with them. On the way home, Jack, Mom's husband, had a heart attack at the wheel. They ... uh ... got into an accident with a truck."

Joanna raises her free hand to her mouth. Her wide eyes are locked on Molly as she breaks this devastating news to a stranger who happens to be her grandmother. "No!"

"No one is more sorry than I am to tell you she didn't ... she didn't survive. None of them did." Molly's voice cracks and I pull her back into my arms. This woman who looks so delicate on the outside is made of fucking steel.

Joanna folds in on herself, a loud wail escaping her. Beth moves over, wrapping her arms around Joanna in comfort, while I comfort my girl. I wish I could make all of this pain stop.

When will it fucking stop for her?

How much more is she supposed to endure?

Her body shakes in my arms with her silent tears and my heart splinters into a million pieces that I can't protect her from this pain.

The light in the room is fading with the sun. Our coffee sits cold on the coffee table and everyone's hearts are broken. This is not how I saw our day going.

CHAPTER 36

—molly—

GOD. I CAN'T BREATHE.

Everything feels like it's closing in on me.

I have to tell this woman that her daughter will never come home. I absorb Max's comforting touch as I recount the events that stole my family from me, sending Joanna's world crashing to the ground and mine spiraling downward as well.

The sadness in the room is stifling and if it weren't for Max holding me, I would do what I always do when everything gets too much. Curl up in my bed and hide under the covers. Try to block out the world with sleep and hope that when I wake, things are back to the way they should be. Mom would always let me have my time to wallow, then she would insist that I make a plan and move forward. It's what she always did.

"M– Molly." I turn toward Joanna. "I … I'm so sorry. Do you think you can find it in your heart to ever … forgive me?" Her eyes are swollen and red and I know that if I could see inside her chest, her heart would be in tiny pieces like mine. Her heartbreak is oozing from every pore. "I've missed Nicole and you every single day since she left us. I only hope you've had a good life."

"My life's been good. It's been hard at times, but I've had a great life." Max huffs behind me, mumbling something.

"Hard would be an understatement, Molly." He looks at me with disbelief in his eyes. He glances up at Joanna and Beth. "They lived out of Nicole's car until Molly was eleven." Joanna and Beth gasp and I stare at him in disbelief, trying to block them out.

Hurt fills me swiftly and I pull away from him to stand on shaky legs. "Max. I shared that with you in confidence. It wasn't your place to tell anyone. You had no right." I scan the room, seeing faces full of pity. I spin on my heel, grab my bag, and take off out the front door before anyone can stop me.

Run.

I need to run.

Even though I don't have my running gear on, I take off sprinting down the street, the sun sits heavy on the horizon as the streetlights turn on. I'm not sure where I'm going to go, but I can't be in that house with Beth and Joanna looking at me with eyes full of pity and guilt. I'm not sure why I'm hurt that Max told them about my living arrangements growing up, but I am.

My lungs burn and my feet hurt from pounding the concrete in the wrong shoes, but my mind won't switch off. What are they going to think of me? Will they think I'm less than because of the way I grew up? Will they blame Mom? I don't want them to. She did the best she could with what she had. She could have taken better-paying jobs, but she always put me first. She never wanted to leave me in care, and we had no family to look after me, to allow her to work longer hours.

I don't want them to judge her.

I don't want them to judge *me*.

Max's workshop comes into view, and I slow down. At the bottom of the steps, I kick out my feet with my hands resting on my hips to catch my breath. I'm tempted to go upstairs and curl up on the bed, but Max might come here looking for me and I can't face him right now.

Walking around to the back of the workshop, my car comes into view. I've been leaving it here most nights. It's easier for Max and me to share a ride to work now that I'm living with him. I climb in and drive.

It's not like I have anywhere to go. I drive aimlessly through the streets until I find myself at the beach. I'm not surprised I ended up here. There's something about the beach that calms and settles me. Reaching into the backseat, I grab the jacket that I left there and climb out of my car. I lock it and head down to the shoreline, my shoes sinking into the soft sand as I trek closer to the water's edge. Crossing my legs, I drop to my butt and watch the waves kiss the shore beneath the moonlight. I pull my jacket tighter around my body and drop my chin to my knees. I get lost in watching the waves roll in and out.

Max never gave me the impression he felt sorry for me, but maybe he does. I never want anyone's pity. I think that's part of the reason I enjoy volunteering at the women's shelter. I know the women don't want pity, and I'm able to interact with them on a level that doesn't include pity or shame or judgment. It's not something Mom or I ever wanted and I know it's not something they want.

I draw in deep breaths and release each one slowly, trying to untangle my thoughts.

CHAPTER 37

—max—

FUCK!

I fucked up badly.

She's right. I had no right to share that information with anyone and until then I hadn't told a soul. Even though none of it happened to me, I have a sense of protectiveness over Molly and I'm angry at Martin, Joanna, and her husband on her behalf. But I should have kept my fucking mouth shut.

Beth, Joanna, and I stand in my living room in stunned silence. Slowly, Beth turns to me. "I had no idea. I don't think she told Martin because he would have said something to me."

"Why didn't Nicole come home? I don't understand." Joanna mumbles in disbelief. "That poor girl. Living in a car for her childhood. We could have helped her," she sobs.

"Look. I've already said too much, obviously. But I need you to leave. I need to find her and make sure she's okay. I need to apologize to Molly."

"Of course. Please let us know she's okay." Beth reaches into her purse and hands me a business card. "You can reach me on this number." She turns toward Joanna. "If you give me your number, I'll call you once Max calls me."

"Sure." I shuffle them toward the front door, stepping out with them and locking the house.

"Do you think she'll be okay?" Joanna asks.

I stop and study the two women. Creases across their foreheads display their worry. "Molly's been through a lot and she's as tough as steel beneath her delicate features. She'll be fine. She needs some time and space to deal with everything. It's been a lot for her. Losing her family," I raise my eyebrows at them, "finding her father, half-siblings, and now her grandmother. She's gone from having nobody to having a whole new family she never knew. She packed up her life over east and made her way here on her own. In my opinion, she's fucking amazing and she'll find her way through anything life throws at her. What I've learned about Molly is that she's proud and extremely independent. She won't want your pity and she doesn't want handouts." I stride toward my car. "I need to go."

I climb into my car and gun the engine, not allowing them to respond. They're not my priority right now. I need to find my girl. It's almost completely dark, and I don't want her out here on her own.

Where would she have gone? I know she's fit and can run for miles, but she didn't have her running shoes on. I have to assume that would limit her somewhat.

Think. Where would she go?

I drive to the park a couple of miles from home. Maybe she's there. It looks empty. Most families would be eating dinner now, leaving the park empty. I climb out to check the park on foot. The darkness makes it hard to see too far into the distance. I'll have a better chance of seeing her if I walk through the area.

"Molly!" My steps pick up speed when I don't get a response. "Molly!" I check in the tunnel kids often use to hide in. Empty. "Molly!" I call out as I wander around the entire space, becoming frantic.

Nothing. I don't think she's here.

I head back to my car. Maybe she went to the apartment at the workshop. She still has a key. As I pull in, I note the apartment is dark. If she's inside, she's sitting in the dark. I pull up around the back. Dammit, her car's gone. She could be anywhere. My mind races, trying to think of places she'd go.

Frustration bubbles up inside me and I slam my hands on the steering wheel. *Fuck!* I pull out my phone and press her number. The phone rings and rings. She doesn't have voicemail set up, so I can't even leave her a fucking message. I try again and again. Each time the phone rings out, my frustration builds. She has to know I'd worry about her. Why isn't she answering me?

Because she's pissed at me. That's why, asshole.

I drive for hours through the streets and along the riverfront. It's not until I'm driving along the coast that I finally spot her car in a parking lot at the beach. Relief fills me, then anger floods my system. I've been so fucking worried about her. She could have let me know she was okay. I park next to her car and jump out, glancing inside, but it's empty. Following the path down to the shore that I assume Molly would have taken, I use the flashlight on my phone to guide the way. As I get closer to the water, I see the lone silhouette of someone sitting close to the shore.

I take deep breaths to calm myself as I approach, then drop to the sand beside her. She doesn't even flinch, she simply draws in a deep breath.

I want to pull her into my body.

I want to wrap her up and never let anything hurt her ever again.

I want to protect her from all the awful shit.

"I've been worried about you," I whisper, "and with good reason. I could have been anyone coming up behind you, Molly."

Without lifting her head from her knees, she turns her head toward me, her eyes glistening in the moonlight. "I knew it was you. I heard your car pull in." She turns back toward the water. "I'm sorry I worried you." Her voice is small, sad. I put aside my frustration and move closer to wrap my arm around her. Pulling her in tight, I kiss the top of her head and she melts into me, heaving out a heavy sigh. "I shouldn't have run like that. I'm sorry, Max."

I blow out a heavy breath. "I'm sorry, too, Dimples. I shouldn't have said anything. It came out before I could think about it." I turn her chin with my fingers, making her look at me. "I can't help feeling protective of you and when you told me your story, I became pissed on your behalf. I know I have no right to be pissed at the people who let your mom down, but I do. When they were looking at you and your grand-mother said she hoped you had a good life, I couldn't keep my frustration inside." I sigh. "I promise I haven't told anyone else. I know it's your story to tell." I lean forward and press my lips to hers; the taste of salty tears coating my lips. "Please forgive my stupidity."

Her shoulders relax and she offers me a sad smile, her dimples barely making an appearance. "Only if you can forgive me for worrying you."

"Now that I know you're safe, you're forgiven. But please don't run like that again. Go to another room in the house or something, but don't take off."

She nods and we both move forward to seal our apology with a kiss. Beyond the taste of tears is Molly.

My beautiful, sweet Molly.

My future. My world.

Cupping the back of her head, her silky hair fills my palm and I guide her mouth where I want it. Tilting it to suit and applying pressure to keep her lips locked with mine. Our tongues press forward, tangling with the other, apologizing with their own embrace. Without breaking our kiss, Molly climbs into my lap and straddles me. I drop back, taking her with me and we share scorching kisses which promise so much more. Stroking, licking, and sucking, our kiss goes on and on.

We separate to catch our breath. Molly presses her forehead to mine, our eyes locked on the other as our chests rise and fall with each new intake of oxygen. Her silken hair curtains us from the world, creating our own cocoon.

"Can I ask you something?" her whispered words blend with the breeze coming from the sea.

I scan her face, glancing between her eyes. "Of course. You can ask me anything."

"You promise to be completely honest with me?" I nod. "Knowing what you know about my life, do you pity me?"

She holds her body stiff as she waits for my answer, and I take a second or two to understand what she's asking me. I shake my head.

"There are many things I feel about you, Molly. Pity definitely isn't one of them." I reach up and tuck her hair behind her ears and give her a lazy smile. "Out of everything I feel for you, the biggest one is admiration. I fucking admire your strength of character so much. You are an incredible human being who handles life with courage and grace." She smiles at me, but it doesn't expose her dimples that I love. "The way you grew up doesn't factor into my feelings for you. It has no bearing on how I see you or how much I fucking love you. But it *does* factor into how much respect I have for you and your mom. Your life could have turned out so differently. *You* could have turned out so differently, but look at you. You are smart and determined. Strong and fiercely independent. I think you're one of the kindest, sweetest people I've ever met. You give your time to help others because you genuinely want to make their life better." I lower my head to rub my nose along hers.

"Wow. I wasn't expecting all of that."

"I'm not fucking finished," I snap and she giggles. "You inspire me to be a better man because I want to be worthy of you and your love. I want to be your equal in all ways, Molly." I rise to take her mouth. Licking my tongue across her lips, I beg for entrance. She doesn't deny me, opening up and allowing me to swipe inside. She moans into my mouth and grinds her hot pussy down on my hard cock. I lift my hips to meet her and increase the pressure.

"I need you, Max. Please."

Fuck. How can I deny her?

I slide my hands beneath the stretchy fabric of her leggings and grasp her glorious ass, pulling the cheeks apart and squeezing the globes. Our breaths become pants as I rub her pussy along my engorged shaft, trapped behind the zipper of my jeans. I push the fabric of her panties and leggings down below her cheeks, exposing her pussy to the cool night air. My fingers are so close to her slit, and she tilts her hips up in need. "You want me to finger fuck your pussy?"

"Ye– yes, please. Please, Max." She moans against my ear, her hot breath burning my flesh.

I slide one hand between our bodies, seeking her clit, and circle it with firm strokes as I press my fingers inside her dripping heat. My body shivers at the sensation of her walls tight around my fingers. Pushing them in and sliding them out, I add another digit to open her up to me.

Fuck, I need to get my dick in here. "You're such a good girl, taking my fingers. Lift your shirt and let me suck on those beautiful tits of yours."

She moans and lifts her shirt and bra enough for me to capture her pretty nipple when she drops her body forward over my face. As she grinds down on my hand, her walls tighten around my fingers, creating a vacuum. My cock throbs and weeps in my jeans, fighting the constraints of the denim.

Fucking her like this in the moonlight, sweat making her glisten under the stars, is perfect. I groan as she shatters on my fingers, her mouth dropping open in a silent scream.

Fucking beautiful.

I want to fuck her like this every single day for the rest of my life. Her limp body drops to press against mine and she takes my mouth in a messy kiss. She bites my bottom lip, then soothes it with her tongue, and I can taste the copper when she pushes her tongue inside my mouth. I slowly slide my fingers out of her channel and tap her thigh to lift up.

We wrangle one leg out of her leggings and release my cock from his confinement. Molly wraps her smooth hand around my shaft and gives it a firm stroke before notching it at her hot entrance. She teases her swollen opening with the crown, then pulls away.

"Don't fucking tease me," I grumble.

She giggles. "You tease me all the time. Turnabout is fair play. Don't you think?"

"No. I don't fucking think. Let me inside." I raise up and steal her mouth, kissing her until her breaths are labored. I take my cock in hand and notch it against her opening and press my hips up as she drops. Our joint moans are swallowed by the night air as our eyes lock together. I can't see her properly, but I know her skin is flushed, and her eyes will be mercury. I sit up and use my hold on her hips to guide her up and down my dick.

Heaven.

Fucking heaven.

Warm and tight and welcoming every single time I've been inside her.

"Be a good girl and ride my cock." She nods and with our eyes locked, she bounces up and down on my dick. Swiveling her hips, she creates a powerful rhythm. We sigh into each other's open mouths, exchanging breaths. "You fucking own me, Dimples."

She drops, throws her head back, and cries out, breaking apart beautifully over my cock. "So fucking beautiful."

Her elongated neck begs for my tongue and kisses so I lick up the side of her throat and nip her earlobe, then suck it into my mouth. She cries out again. Her long hair tickles my hands as I lock her hips in place and follow her into oblivion. I grit my teeth and my shaft grows inside her; my cum pouring out of me and into her. The same as my love for her. Our mouths join and our tongues dance slowly as our heartbeats gradually return to normal.

Fuck! She owns me.

Pulling away, I press my forehead to hers. "I know this isn't romantic and I should probably shut up and plan some way to ask you in a way you deserve. But I'm a selfish asshole and I wanna ask you now." She shivers, so I pull her top down to cover her and draw her in close to me. "Will you marry me?" Her eyes widen and her mouth drops open, but her head automatically nods. "Is that a 'yes', Dimples?"

She smiles, gifting me her dimples as she nods more vigorously. "Yes. I'll marry you, Max."

We move forward at the same time, sealing our commitment with another kiss. My heart beats wildly against Molly's and I tighten my arms around her body, holding her to me.

I'm never letting this woman go.

Tilting my head slightly, I deepen our connection, and my cock, which is still semi-hard inside her, grows. We both moan with the heat building between us again and move together in a slow, sensual dance under the moonlight, with the waves kissing the shore, and the salty breeze cooling our skin. This time, our joining is slow and measured. Our tongues match our hips, and we moan into each other as we surrender to our orgasm.

I bring my hands up to the side of Molly's face. Her heated skin sears the palms of my hands. I brush her sweaty hair away from her face. "I'm going to get down on one knee and ask you properly. I promise."

She giggles. "You don't need to do that. This was perfect." She leans forward and presses a gentle kiss to my lips. "Take me home?"

We peel apart and dress, cursing the sand. Holding hands, we run up the sand to our cars in the parking lot. After a lingering kiss, we make our way home.

I intend to make love to my fiancée all night long.

CHAPTER 38

—molly—

I'm still floating when I walk into *Shelter*. I can't believe Max proposed to me. It's all happened fabulously fast.

"Afternoon!" I wave and call out to Simone, who's at the desk assisting a young woman. The young woman turns around, her duo-colored gaze locking onto me. "Hey, Ronnie. It's nice to see you." I walk toward the young woman, noticing bruising up her arms. My eyes slide up to Simone and she subtly shakes her head. I take the hint and keep my mouth shut. "Once you've signed in, we can catch up. Do you wanna meet in the dining hall and we can have a juice or something?"

She smiles at me and gives me a wordless nod. I thumb over my shoulder. "I'll check the coffee buffet is stocked. Chat later?"

"Sure." She returns her attention to Simone. The door opens and a woman, balancing a baby on her hip while trying to wrangle a toddler, as well as struggling to carry what looks like their worldly possessions enters. I head straight for the woman and reach for her possessions. She twists her body away from me, blocking my help.

"Hey. I'm Molly. I volunteer here a couple of nights a

week. Would you like me to help you with your things?" I give her my brightest smile and glance down at the little girl who's making life difficult for her mom. I drop to my haunches. "If we help your mom, we have some great toys and crafts you can play with." I drop my best smile on her, too, but she's not buying it at all.

The woman turns back to me, her posture relaxing. "Thanks." She gestures for me to take her belongings, a grateful smile on her tired and battered face.

Simone comes around to greet her. "Hi, I'm Simone. Welcome to *Shelter*. We're glad you found us." She gestures over to the same set of chairs we first chatted in and the woman sighs as she sits, her daughter climbing onto her lap. Simone glances up at me. "Would you mind taking those to room six? I think that will suit nicely."

"No problem." I wave at the little girl, and she gives me a pout in return. I get it. I truly do. Life is miserable when you're torn from your one safe place and everything's different. Ronnie notices my struggle to balance everything and rushes forward to help. She slings her backpack over her shoulder, then takes one of the ladies' bags, and we head through the building to room six. "How have you been, Ronnie? I haven't seen you around for a while."

She shrugs. "I only come in now and then when I want a proper shower and a decent night's sleep without worrying about perverts." She looks over her shoulder back at the new woman with her two small children. "Other people usually need the bed more than I do." She says it like it's no big deal.

But I know it *is* a big deal. Awful stuff happens to the homeless who live on the streets and have nowhere to go. We were fortunate to have our car. Mom kept me away from a lot of the stuff that happens on the street as a kid. She was always selective about where she parked, choosing locations that were in the nicer areas that she felt would be safer.

We stow the family's belongings in room six and close the door. "Do you want to come and chat with me while I stock the coffee buffet?"

Ronnie shrugs again. "I'd rather have a shower first. Is that okay?"

"Of course. I'll see you in a little while, then." We separate, her heading for the showers, and me to the dining room.

"Hey, Rhonda!" I call out as I step into the kitchen.

"Hey, gorgeous. You look particularly happy today." She studies me closely.

I'm bursting to tell someone my news. We told the guys after soccer last night, but they're Max's friends. I step closer to Rhonda, ready to burst. "I got engaged." My smile must be stupidly big.

She squeals and pulls my left hand up to her face. "Where's the ring?"

I pull my hand back. "I don't have one yet. It was an impromptu thing on Saturday night."

"Well, whoever he is, he's one lucky man. Congratulations, Molly. I'm so happy for you, girl!" She leans in, wrapping me in a hug. Her hair smells like roast beef and her hug feels like a warm blanket.

"Thank you." I shake my head and smile at her. "I can't believe it, but I'm over the moon. He's a great guy, and he's been amazing to me since I moved here."

"Well, I'm glad. I'd love to stop and chat in-depth, but this dinner won't cook itself and it looks like we have a full house tonight."

I blow out a heavy breath and nod. "I'll quickly make sure the buffet's stocked, then I'll come and help in the kitchen." I'm not sure how I ended up in the kitchen every time I come here, because I'm pretty useless. But Rhonda's been teaching me some of her tips and tricks, and I've been enjoying her lessons. I'm finishing up when Ronnie steps through the doorway to the dining room. She glances around the room and when her magical eyes lock on me, she heads my way.

"Hey. Do you need any help?"

"Thanks for asking, but I'm almost finished. How was the shower?" Her chocolate-colored hair looks even darker now that it's wet.

She sighs and a slight smile touches her lips. "It was heavenly. It's the one thing I miss. Regular showers."

I nod. "I know, right? It gets tiresome doing the rough wipe down in public toilets." Her eyes widen. "I was homeless until I turned eleven when Mom met this fantastic guy." Her nose crinkles in disgust, but I ignore it. I gathered from our previous chat that she hasn't had the best experiences with men. "Then when I lost my family late last year, followed by my job and my home, I moved here. I didn't know anyone and had little money, so I was living in my car."

"Shit. You come across all sunshine and smiles. I figured you'd had it easy and were volunteering here out of some sense of duty because you're better off than the rest of us."

I'm not offended by her judgment call. I worked hard to portray that everything in my life was perfect. Too prideful to ask for help. "Yeah, well. You can't judge a book by its cover and all that." I shrug.

"I'm sorry."

"You don't need to be. How would you know what my life was like? Just like I don't know what your life is like." I turn my body to face her fully. "But I'm here because I want to give back. Mom and I would stay in shelters when it became too cold to sleep in the car. Especially when I was a baby. She was like you. She didn't want to take a bed away from someone who needed it more. She always said we had our car, which was more than other people had." I nod at her arm. "Do you need anything for that?"

She looks down at it as though she'd forgotten it's bruised.

"Nah, I'm okay. A guy got a little handsy last night. I kicked him in the balls and made a run for it. Pretty sure he won't be adding to the population anytime soon." She snickers and I join her.

"Good for you."

"Molly! Could you help me in here for a minute?"

I look over my shoulder at Rhonda. "Sure." I turn back to Ronnie. "Sorry, gotta go." I touch her arm gently. "If you need anything, just shout."

She gives me a lopsided smile. "Thanks."

CHAPTER 39

—max—

WHILE MOLLY'S AT *SHELTER*, I THOUGHT IT WOULD BE THE perfect opportunity to visit the jewelry store. I step inside and wander around the store, studying the displays carefully. The cabinets are full of ostentatious rings, which I can't see Molly wearing. When I step up to the last cabinet, the perfect wedding set catches my eye. It must be white gold because I don't think they make wedding rings in silver. It has one medium-sized diamond in the middle which looks a little like a snowflake, with two diamonds on either side, becoming smaller. Small gaps between the diamonds are filled with some fancy design on the band. It reminds me of the delicate jewelry Molly wears and I think she'd really like this.

"Can I help you, Sir?" I startle at the woman's voice. She glances at the cabinet, her eyes catching on the ring I was admiring. She smiles at me. "That's a pretty ring. Would you like to see it properly?"

I nod. "Yes, please."

As she unlocks the cabinet, I step back to give the woman space. "I'm Stephanie. Did you want to look at the matching wedding ring, too?"

"Thanks." I lift my chin. "I'm Max."

She nods as she collects both rings and places them on a cushion on top of the counter. "These rings are eighteen-karat white gold. The largest diamond in the engagement ring is zero point five zero carats, the next two are zero point two five carats each, and the smallest ones are zero point one zero carats each. Giving the ring a total of one point two zero carats." She uses a pointer to indicate each diamond as she speaks. Then she picks up the wedding band. "The two outer bands are linked with alternating diamonds of zero point two zero and zero point one zero. There are seven of the larger diamonds and six of the smaller ones." She turns the ring over to show the underside is solid. "The diamonds total two carats." She places them on the cushion and slides it forward, along with a magnifying lens. "Take a look. It's a beautifully delicate piece."

I study both of the rings carefully and can imagine them on Molly's finger. Before I blurted out my proposal, I probably should have bought the ring. "I think my fiancée will love these. They're delicate like the jewelry she already wears."

Stephanie's eyes sparkle as her eyebrows shoot up. "You've already proposed?"

"Yeah. I blurted it out without being prepared."

She chuckles. "You'd be surprised how often that happens." Well, that makes me feel marginally better. "Do you know her size?"

I pull the string out of my pocket. When she was sleeping last night, I tied a piece of string around her finger to make sure I bought the correct size. "Will this work?"

Stephanie picks it up. "I think so. Let's see what we have." She grabs a cylindrical measuring tool and slides the string carefully down the shaft until it can't go any further. "I'd say we're looking at a five-point five." She searches through a set of bands until she comes to the one she's looking for. "Does this feel about right?"

I slide it on my pinkie. "Yeah, I'd say so. She's slender and has long, slim fingers." She smiles and nods at me. "Do you have her size in stock?"

"Let me check." She locks the display set back inside the cabinet. "I'll be back in a moment." Then she disappears through a doorway.

I tuck my hands in my pockets and rock back on my heels. Molly didn't hesitate to say yes when I asked her to marry me. And yes, it's quick, but it feels right. She's perfect for me and fits in seamlessly with my family. Even though the proposal slipped out, I had no thoughts about rescinding it.

Stephanie returns with a bright smile and two small ring boxes. "You're in luck! We only have a couple of sets in stock and her size was one of them." She places them on the counter and opens each box. "I think it was meant to be."

"I think so, too. Can I take them with me today?" I dig my wallet out of my back pocket, ready to pay.

"Certainly, Max. If you would like to come over to the register, we can get that sorted."

I pay for the rings and Stephanie tucks them into a small gift bag, wishing me congratulations. Choosing the ring didn't take long. I check my watch. I may still have time to grab some flowers.

When I arrive at *Blooms and Balloons*, the best florist in the city, the woman is locking up. "Damn," I mutter, then spin on my heel.

"Excuse me. Were you wanting some flowers?" the woman calls.

I spin back around to face her. "Yeah. But that's okay, I'm too late."

"You're not actually. I was sneaking out a little early because we were quiet. If you're happy to select a pre-made arrangement, I'd be happy to unlock the store for you." She turns back toward the door with her key in hand.

I quickly step closer. "I'd certainly appreciate it. I hope to propose properly to my fiancée tonight."

"Oh. How sweet. Well, I'm happy to unlock the store and help you out. I'll even make a fresh arrangement for you." She opens the door and ushers me inside, turning on the light as she goes. The fragrance as I enter the store is beautiful.

"My name's Cassia." She wraps an apron around her waist. "What type of arrangement were you thinking of?"

I'm blank. "Hi, Cassia. I'm Max. I hadn't thought about it. I was just gonna grab a bunch of flowers." I shrug.

She chuckles. "Fair enough. Do you know her favorite flower?"

I grimace and shake my head. Then it dawns on me. "She uses rose-scented body wash. I guess she probably likes roses." *See, I'm working this out.*

"Red roses would be the go then. I have these stunning black velvet roses." She holds up a finger and disappears through a side door and returns a few moments later with a stunning, deep red rose. The petals look like velvet.

My eyes snap up to her. "This is beautiful."

"I know, right?" She smiles at me and raises her brows. "Would you like the traditional dozen?"

"Yes, please." She disappears out the back again, returning with an arm full of roses.

"Because these roses are so stunning, I would recommend a simple arrangement containing only the roses. I'll remove all the thorns and excess leaves, wrapping some of this gorgeous gold ribbon around the stems." She holds up the ribbon. "How does that sound?"

I have no idea. I guess she knows what's best. "Sure. That sounds great."

She smiles at me and gets to work. "What's your fiancée's name?"

I smile. "Molly. We haven't been together very long, but it feels right. I don't want to let her go and I can't see a future without her in it."

"I don't think the time frame matters all that much. It's more about the connection you feel with that person. I get people in here who have been together for all different lengths of time before they get engaged." She shrugs and keeps working, tidying up the stems. Carefully, she bundles them together and wraps the gold ribbon around the stems several times, leaving the bottom open. She holds them up for my approval. "What do you think?"

"It looks stunning." I move my eyes back up to hers. "Thank you for opening up for me. I appreciate it."

"No problem. I'm always happy to help with matters of the heart."

I pay for the roses and I'm on my way. I can't wait for Molly to get home.

Smooth fingers glide down the side of my face and my lips tip up in a smile as I slowly slide into consciousness.

Shit. I must have fallen asleep.

The softest lips press against my forehead and the glide of a finger dances across my forehead, brushing my hair away. I reach up and grip the back of her neck and guide her mouth to mine. We open, our tongues dancing with each other in welcome. Using my other hand, I pull her down on top of me and she giggles as we kiss.

"Hey, handsome," she whispers against my lips.

"Hey. How were the ladies at *Shelter*?" I open my eyes, locking onto her silvery ones.

She pulls back slightly, her breath coating my cheek as she releases a heavy sigh. "I nearly offered my car to one of the semi-regular ladies tonight. She came in with bruises up her arms." She shakes her head. "Mom always kept us safe from that sort of stuff because we had our car. She would park in neighborhoods that were a little nicer. Not the fancy neighborhoods, because it would be hard to go unnoticed, but the sort of middle-class ones. You know? If Ronnie had a car, she wouldn't have to be on the streets."

That's my girl. She doesn't have much, but she would willingly give a stranger her car. "If you think that would help her, you should do it. We can manage with one car. I mean, we work and live together. I can drop you off and pick you up on the nights you go to *Shelter*, and you've been coming to my soccer games every week. Or, if you want to, you could offer her the apartment." I shrug.

Her eyes widen. "Really? You'd do that?" She grasps my face in both hands and kisses me with gratitude and heat. "You're truly a good man, Max." Her eyes slip away from mine and then return. "She doesn't strike me as someone who would accept a handout. She barely comes into the shelter because she doesn't want to take up precious space from other women who may need it more."

I press up and kiss the tip of Molly's nose. "Sounds like someone I know."

"I'll think about it. If I can work out a way to offer it to her without impinging on her pride, I'll do it. I'm not sure when I'll see her next, but I'll be ready with a plan."

"Good. Now speaking of plans. I have a plan of my own." I smirk at her as I sit up. Grabbing Molly's ass, I encourage her to wrap her legs around me and I stand. She wraps her arms around my neck with a chuckle, and I kiss her soft lips.

"Oh yeah?" She has that sexy, seductive quality to her voice that drives me wild. It always comes out when she's horny.

"Yep." We move through the house, locking the doors and turning off the lights. I place her on her feet outside our bedroom door. "I'm gonna need you to wait out here for a second."

I kiss the tip of her nose and slip inside the bedroom before she gets the chance to respond. Quickly, I turn on the fairy lights I strung up around the room and turn the overhead light off. I check the ring is in place and grab the roses I bought. Holding them behind my back, I swing open the door with a flourish and then bring the roses out to present to Molly.

Her mouth forms an O shape as her eyes widen. Her eyes flit between me and the roses and then around our bedroom. "Oh, Max. This is gorgeous." She takes the bouquet from me, bringing them up to her nose and then stroking a petal. "These are the most beautiful roses I've ever seen." Her eyes have become glassy as they make their way back up to mine. She reaches her hand around my neck and drags me in for a kiss. "Thank you so much. I love them."

My hands slide to her hips, and I use my hold on her to pull her further into the room, exactly where I want her positioned. Then I deepen our kiss. She holds on tighter with one arm banded around my neck and both of my arms banded around her middle, holding her tight to me. The heat between our bodies matches the fire building inside of me and I remember I want to get down on one knee, so I pull away slowly and drop down in front of the woman who has stolen my heart. Her gaze follows me as her lust switches to surprise. She brings her hand up to cover her mouth, and a tear falls from her bottom lash to land on her cheek.

"Molly, I know I've already asked you to marry me, but I wanted to do it properly." I draw in a deep breath. "The morning I arrived at work to find you asleep in your car has led to this moment." She giggles and I raise my brows and tip up one side of my mouth. "I had no idea that day that I would fall irrevocably in love with you. You were completely unexpected and such a beautiful surprise." I take her hand in mine. "And while you are one of the most beautiful women I've ever had the pleasure of laying eyes on, it's what's inside your beautiful heart and your character that brought me to my knees. Your kindness to others blows me away and your warmth and genuine desire to help anyone in need are like nothing I've come across before. The icing on the cake is the way you deal with whatever life throws at you with quiet strength, grace, and a steely determination to come out the other side stronger than you were before." I kiss her hand gently, smoothing my finger along her bare ring finger. I glance down at that finger, then flick my eyes back up to hers. "I can't imagine anyone else I would want to spend the rest of my life with. Raise a family with. Grow old with. Molly, will you do the honor of becoming my wife?"

She drops to her knees, her dimples on display as tears streak down her cheeks. "Of course I will, Max. I can't imagine a better man to spend the rest of my life with. You're the man I want my children to call Daddy and you're the only man I want to grow old with."

I breathe a sigh of relief and meet her in the middle for a kiss that's full of the promise of a long and happy future together. I pull back and grab the ring box. Opening it, I take her left hand and slide the delicate band onto her finger. Her eyes drop to watch. "Oh, Max. This is gorgeous." She holds it up in front of her face, twisting her hand this way and that. The twinkling of the lights strung around our room creates a sparkle.

"I thought it suited you. It's simply beautiful without being flashy. Just like you."

"You didn't need to go to this much trouble for me. I already said yes."

"Nothing was too much trouble for you, Dimples. You deserve the best. Always."

She wraps her arms around my neck and pulls me in for another kiss, which leads to clothes being discarded every which way and me sliding into heaven. I want to climb inside her and live there. She's my home, the one who holds my heart and soul in a way that feels eternal.

Drawing back, I lock my eyes with hers, dirty green to mercury. Her hold around my neck tightens as I move in and out of her heat, our mouths open and barely touching. Me breathing in her essence, taking her breaths as my own.

Resting my elbows on the floor, I cup her head, stroking her hair away from her beautifully flushed face. "I love you, Molly," I whisper breathlessly against the soft pillows of her lips. Our bodies move in sync as I enter and withdraw repeatedly from Molly's hot pussy. I make love to her mouth and her body, building us both to our mutual orgasm until we're both a mess of boneless limbs and sweaty flesh.

She smiles against my lips as we catch our breath. "I love you, Max. So much," she says with panting breaths. I rub my nose along hers and collect her to me, burrowing my face in the crook of her neck. I lick and suck the hammering pulse point, then move onto my knees and pull her up with me. With her arms and legs wrapped snugly around my body, I stand and walk us into the shower, where I tenderly wash her and then defile her all over again.

CHAPTER 40

—*max*—

I'M LOCKING THE FRONT DOOR TO THE OFFICE WHEN I SEE
Martin pull in. He pulls to a stop and jumps out, heading
straight for the door like a man on a mission, so I open it.
"Hey, Martin."

"Hi, Max. I was hoping to see Molly." What is it with this
family turning up unannounced all the time? I mean, my
family does it, but this is a completely different situation.

"Molly's not here."

He looks around my body into the office as if to check for
himself. "Where is she? Will she be back soon?"

"She's volunteering at *Shelter* tonight. It usually runs pretty
late."

His shoulders drop, disappointment dripping from his
features. "Beth told me about Molly's childhood."

I blow out a heavy breath. Me and my big mouth.

"Look, I shouldn't have said anything because it wasn't my
place. Molly didn't want you guys to know. She's embarrassed
that you know how she lived as she was growing up and she
doesn't want any pity."

He huffs out a harsh breath, running his hands through his

hair. His expression reminds me of Dad when he was pissed at Preston after he told Em he wanted a divorce. "I have a right to know how my daughter grew up," he snaps. His posture stiff, his attitude demanding.

Hang on a minute. "Uh, pretty sure you gave up that right when you turned your back on Molly's mom." Not that it's my business, but I don't like that he thinks he can waltz into my girl's life and be privy to things she would rather not share.

His eyes snap up to mine and narrow. "Look, Max. I know you're together and all that, but this is family business."

I shake my head. "See, that's where you're wrong, Martin. She's my family now. This *is* my business. I won't have you storming your way into her life when she's not fucking ready. Have some damn respect for what she's been through and dealt with on her own. She'll come to you when she's damn well good and ready." I step into his space, towering over him. "This shit." I point to the floor between us. "You turning up whenever you please, expecting to talk to her, is gonna stop. She needs time."

"What do you mean, she's your family now? You've only started dating recently." He steps back slightly, putting more space between us.

"I mean, she's wearing my ring and agreed to marry me. Which means I'm gonna watch out for her."

"But you don't need to protect her from me. I'm her father. I'm not here to hurt her or cause her harm." His posture's softened and his voice is full of sincerity.

I soften my voice and my posture to match. "Look. I know you won't intentionally hurt her, and I know you want to get to know her. I get it. I do. This is an impossible situation. But what you need to understand is that Molly and her mom only had each other for a long time, surviving through dire circumstances. Apparently, it took Nicole a long time to trust Jack. Can you imagine the bond between Nicole and Molly? Can you even fathom what she's lost? Her mom. Her brother. Her stepfather. All gone." I raise my eyebrows at him. "That sort of loss would be unimaginable. On top of that, she then lost her apartment *and* her job. Everything. Gone. Just like that. But she dealt with it all on her own." I huff out a harsh breath. "Storming in here, demanding to see her is unacceptable. You need to give her time."

He sighs and his eyes grow glassy. He drops his head, studying his boots and for long moments, we stand, silent. Blowing out a long breath, he raises his head. "I hear what you're saying, Max, and I appreciate you laying that all out for me. I've been caught up in my agenda to reconnect with my daughter and I hadn't considered any of that. Maybe I've been coming on a little too strong." He glances away, then back to me, his expression pained. "I don't want to lose her again. I only just found her."

I lift my hand and squeeze his shoulder. "Family's important to Molly. If you can give her some space, I know you won't lose her."

"I don't want her to think I've given up if I stop coming around. What if she thinks I don't want her anymore because we know how she grew up?"

"I'm not saying to stop contact with her. I would never say that because I want Molly to have as much family around her as possible. What I'm saying is you need to check with her before you turn up. Shoot her a text. Ask her if she's available for a coffee or chat. Invite her to dinner. But don't just turn up; you're not at that stage yet. She needs to feel like it's her decision. That you're not taking the choice out of her hands. It will give her time to mentally and emotionally prepare. When you turn up unannounced the way you do, you put her on the back foot and that makes her uncomfortable." I hope he listens to what I'm saying.

He nods, seeming to accept my advice. "Thanks, Max.

Beth and I would like to have you both over for dinner sometime. I'll be in touch."

He climbs back into his truck and pulls out of the parking
lot. I drop my head, studying the pavement. I hope he takes my
advice.

—molly—

A VIBRATING SOUND BREAKS MY CONCENTRATION ON THE order form I'm filling out. I peer around the office, trying to work out where the sound is coming from. It happens again and I remember I put my cell in the top drawer. I barely use the thing. It's not like I have anyone contacting me on the regular. I pull it out and read the screen to find a message from Martin. My heart beats faster and my hands become clammy. I haven't spoken to him since Max blurted out my history to Beth and Joanna.

> MARTIN
>
> Hi Molly. Beth and I were wondering if you would be free to come over for dinner on Saturday night?

I place the cell on the surface of the desk. Shit! I don't know if I'm ready to spend time with everyone at the same time. It's sort of been manageable one on one, not that it's always been easy, and after the last time I saw Beth and Joanna, I'm a little embarrassed.

MARTIN

Sorry, I forgot. You can bring Max along too

Max told me Martin stopped by last week while I was at *Shelter*. I don't want to use Max as a crutch, but he's been my rock through all of this. Does it make me weak that the offer is more appealing, knowing I can take Max with me? I'm normally independent and have no problem facing things head-on, but for some reason, I'm struggling with coming to terms with my new family.

MARTIN

Beth reminded me to mention that the kids won't be here. Holly is staying at a friend's house for the weekend and Noah is going to camp. It'll just be the four of us

Warm lips meet the crook of my neck and I automatically tip my head to the side to give Max the freedom to kiss me however he wants. He nuzzles his roughened cheek against my sensitive skin, sending electricity shooting through my body. "Hey, Dimples. I missed you."

I chuckle. "I've been, like, fifty feet away from you."

"It's too fucking far," he argues.

My phone lights up with another message.

MARTIN

Please say yes

Max moves around to face me. "Why does Martin want you to say yes?"

I unlock the phone and show Max the string of messages. He reads through them, then moves his eyes back up to me. "Do you wanna go?"

I drop my shoulders and blow out a breath. "I do and I don't."

"You want to talk it through? I can be a good sounding board."

I prop my elbow on the desk and drop my chin into my hand. "You're busy. Maybe after work."

"I've finished and it's almost closing time. How about I clean up and bring the car out ready for collection, then we can grab a bite to eat and talk this through?"

"Didn't you want to work on the truck this afternoon?" Why am I trying to find excuses to put off this discussion?

"It'll still be waiting for me tomorrow. This is important, Molly."

"Okay. Thank you, that sounds good." I force my lips to tilt up, but my attempt at a smile is half-hearted at best.

Max leans forward, pressing a kiss to my forehead, careful to not touch me with any other part of him because he's filthy. My smile grows at his care for me. The longer I spend with him, the more I come to realize what a good man he is. He has a golden heart hidden beneath that mechanical tattoo.

"Max! Molly! It's so good to see you. Come. Come. Let me find you a table." Cristo greets us enthusiastically, coming out from behind the podium to hug us both.

"Hi, Cristo," I say as he kisses my cheeks.

"We were walking by, deciding what to have for dinner, and thought we'd stop in to see if you had a table," Max explains. "We hope you don't mind."

"Of course. I'll always have a table for family. Follow me." He weaves his way through the tables toward the back corner of the restaurant to a private space, with us following diligently behind. "Here. This is my special table." He winks at us. "Allow me to select your meals, I have something special."

"Thank you, Cristo. You don't need to go to any trouble for us."

"It's no trouble at all, Molly. I'll bring some wine." He pulls out my chair and I sit. Max positions his chair closer to mine and sits next to me instead of opposite, as I expected. His thigh presses against mine and he rests his arm on the back of my chair, his warmth soaking through my clothes and searing my skin.

"Thanks, Cristo."

Max kisses my temple as Cristo makes his way toward the bar. "You don't think we're imposing, do you?"

Max looks across to the bar. "Nah. You saw how happy he was to see us."

Max's thumb creates patterns on my shoulder, sending goosebumps scattering across my body and heating me from the inside out.

Maybe we should have stayed in?

Cristo returns with our drinks, then bustles off to the kitchen. Max holds up his glass, gesturing for us to toast. "To the future. To loving together, living together, and working together. I can't wait to see what our future holds. Thank you for agreeing to be my wife."

My body heats further with his words, and my smile is wide. We clink our glasses together and take a sip. "I have a toast too. To the man who brought me back to life, has shown me nothing but kindness, and showers me with his love and support every single day. Thank you for asking me to be your wife, Max. I can't wait for our future." I'm dizzy thinking about what our life will be like. We lean forward, our lips meeting halfway in a soft kiss. His hand tightens on my shoulder, and he deepens our connection.

Pulling back slightly, he presses his forehead to mine. One of my favorite gestures. "I love you, Dimples."

I gift him with my dimples. "I love you, too, Max."

A plate slides onto the table in front of me, followed by another one in front of Max. Cristo stands like a proud father. "One of our most popular dishes. Pasticcio. This is the ultimate Greek comfort food. I'll go get the salad." He disappears and Max and I study the deliciously rich-smelling dish in front of us. With layers of pasta noodles, minced beef, and a thick, thick layer of béchamel sauce, I can't wait to dig in. Cristo returns with a mixed green salad which will complement the rich dish. "Enjoy."

"This looks and smells divine. Thank you, Cristo."

He bows slightly, his smile broad, and I can tell he gets a real kick out of feeding people good food. "You are most welcome. If you need anything else, please let me know." He bows again, then spins on his heel and heads back toward the front door.

Max and I glance at each other before digging in. The first mouthful is divine. Pure and simple. The food is more than something to fill your belly, it's soul food. "Mmmm, this is so good." I turn to Max with wide eyes.

He nods as he takes another forkful of food. "I came here once before when Theo proposed to Em. Cristo knows how to feed people."

We're both quiet, enjoying our meals for a few moments, the hum of other guests in the restaurant buzzing, wait staff weaving between the tables with delicious-looking meals. The surrounding aromas tantalize our senses. Max's leg presses against mine.

"Do you wanna work through how you're feeling about that invitation to dinner tomorrow night?"

I place my fork down and try to gather my thoughts. "When I saw the first message, my instant reaction was hell no, I'm not ready. The thought of joining them all for dinner was too much. Then the second message came through and I thought, well it will be more bearable if I have Max with me.

But I don't want to use you as a crutch. That's not fair and it's not a partnership if one person always has to prop up the other. I also don't want to lose my independence. I used to deal with everything on my own, you know?"

Max nods thoughtfully, taking his time to respond. "But you realize we will have times where I support you through something and the roles will reverse at other times, where you'll need to support me when I'm having trouble. Leaning on someone when you need help doesn't mean you're going to lose your independence. It takes strength to recognize you need help and to ask for it when you need it."

"I know. But it's early in our relationship and I don't want to start out that way. I already feel as though you've done too much for me, that I've been too needy. I'm used to being inde-pendent and working my way through stuff on my own; only having Mom and then Jack to help me." I'm certain his stead-fast support has been the one thing that's kept me going since I moved here.

He nods and tucks a loose lock of hair behind my ear. I love how he does that. It's such a tender gesture. "I know."

"But … if it's only going to be the four of us, that might work. I mean, it might be a good idea to get all the heavy stuff out of the way, so we can move forward." I take a sip of my wine. "What do you think?"

"I think it doesn't matter what I think. It matters what you need. What do you need to become comfortable with Martin? What will help you build a relationship with him? Because he's not going to let you go. You realize this?"

"Yeah, I know. And honestly … I don't want him to let me go. I want to get to know him and his family … *my* family. I guess … I guess I feel like I'm betraying Mom in a way. I can't explain it. He turned his back on her, on us, and now that the tough part's over, he wants in. I don't know what Mom would think of that." I drop my eyes to my plate. As I say this next part, I can't look at Max. I don't want him to think less of me. "He really hurt her, Max. I feel as though I shouldn't let him off the hook so easily," I whisper.

He takes my hand in his and uses his fingers to turn my head, ensuring I look at him. "Molly. Your loyalty to your mom is understandable. I get it. Even *I* feel a certain level of protectiveness over your mom where Martin's concerned. He made his choices, as stupid as they were, but … Molly … he's also deeply sorry for what he did all those years ago when he was young and dumb. You can't keep punishing the guy. That's not who you are. And, without knowing your mom, I don't think she'd want you to do that."

I nod because I agree with every word. "Thank you for understanding and for gently reminding me of the person I am." My throat is tight, and the back of my eyes are stinging with tears that want to burst free.

"I think your mom would want you to connect with him. I don't think she would want you to be without family. And I know how important family is to you." He kisses my temple and the tears I've been choking back escape, dropping over my lashes. Max wraps his arms around me and pulls me into his warm body, which now feels like home. I bury my head in his chest and quietly release my pain.

I catch my breath and wipe my tears as I pull away. "Thank you. Would you mind coming with me tomorrow night?"

"Anywhere you are is exactly where I want to be. Of course, I'll come with you." He kisses my temple with tenderness.

"Thank you." I give him a watery smile.

"Why don't you message him now? I bet he's stressing out that you're gonna say no."

I nod and pull out my phone.

ME

Hi Martin, Thank you for your invitation. Max and I would love to come to dinner tomorrow night

Within seconds, my phone lights up. It's like he had it in his hand and I suspect Max may have been right.

MARTIN

Thank you

ME

What time would you like us to come?

MARTIN

Seven?

ME

Okay. Can we bring anything?

MARTIN

Just yourselves. Thank you so much. You don't know how much this means to me

"Well, there ya go. I bet he's been pacing, waiting for your reply." Max glides his hand along my spine.

I blow out a breath and turn to him. "He *does* seem to want to build a relationship with me."

"Of course he does. Anyone who meets you falls in love with you." He presses his lips to mine and butterflies erupt in my stomach.

CHAPTER 42

—molly—

STANDING ON MARTIN'S FRONT PORCH, MY HAND SHAKES AS I reach for the doorbell. Max grasps my hand and turns me to face him. With his hands gently cupping my cheeks, he peers into my eyes, mossy green to steel. "You have nothing to be nervous about."

"What if I'm not the daughter he was expecting to have? I mean, look at Holly. She's doing really well in school and wants to be a fashion designer. I did okay in school, but I'm not super smart or talented like she is. I don't even know what Noah's like. What if I'm not up to—"

He presses forward, stealing my words with his kiss. "Stop it. He should count himself lucky that he can call you his daughter. You *are* fucking talented, and you *are* smart. You picked up my system at the workshop without any guidance. Your sketches are incredible. You're a kind and generous person. He'll be proud of you. I promise."

The front door flies open, breaking the moment and both of our heads swivel toward the intrusion. Martin's standing in the doorway, glancing between the two of us. "Would you like to come in?"

Max chuckles. "That's why we're here."

I smooth down my dress and take the first step over the threshold into my father's home. "Uhm, hi." The three of us stand in silence, peering at each other.

Beth steps out from a room down the hallway, her face lighting up when she sees us in the entry. "Hi. I'm so happy you could join us for dinner." She comes toward us. "Martin, let them inside." She swipes at his arm, and he finally makes the move to guide us further into their home.

Their beautiful home.

The only other homes I've been to as nice as this were Emma and Theo's home and his parents' house. Max's house has the potential to be lovely, but it's still a bit of a bachelor pad.

"You have a beautiful home."

They glance around the space as if they don't realize they live in a gorgeous house. "Thank you. It wasn't much when we bought it, but we've renovated it over the years. Made it our own." Martin holds out his hand. "Come through. Would you like a drink?"

Martin prepares drinks while Beth collects a tray of pre-dinner snacks and guides us out to a covered deck with an outdoor heater for the cooler evening. Everything is immaculate, nothing is out of place, and nothing looks worn or misused. It's like one of the homes you see on TV.

My clothes feel cheap and uncomfortable and I suddenly feel itchy. Like I don't belong here. Max senses my discomfort and reaches across to lay his hand on my thigh, settling my nerves.

Beth leans forward in her chair. "I believe congratulations are in order." My eyebrows draw down low in confusion. Her eyes flick down to my left hand, then back up to me. "Your engagement." She holds her hand out, asking with her eyes to look at my ring. I lift my hand, allowing her to admire the gorgeous seal of our promise. "It's beautiful, Molly. Max made the perfect selection because it suits you."

"Oh, thank you." I look at Max. "It was a surprise. A really great surprise." Max lifts my hand and kisses my palm, easing some of my nerves.

"Any idea when you'll get married?" Beth asks.

I hadn't even thought about the actual wedding. Somehow, I skipped over that part and went straight to being married.

"As soon as possible." Max blurts and I stare at him in surprise. I'm certain I appear completely startled.

Beth giggles. "Well, if you need any help, I'm a wedding planner so it's kinda my thing."

Martin turns his head toward his wife, his face full of pride. "She's always booked out well in advance because she's one of the best in the city."

She waves him off. "It doesn't matter how busy I am, I can help you any way you need. Just shout out." She takes a sip of her wine and offers us a wink.

I tuck a loose lock of hair behind my ear. "Thank you. That's very kind of you to offer."

She stands from the table. "If you'll excuse me, I need to put the finishing touches to dinner. I hope you're hungry."

I stand to help, but she tells me to stay where I am, leaving Max and me with Martin, who has barely spoken since we arrived.

He clears his throat, now that it's only the three of us. "Uhm, Molly. I wanted to start with an apology." This is unexpected. He already apologized to me at lunch and I accepted it. "Actually, I have several apologies to make." He draws in a deep breath and releases it slowly. "I'm sorry for abandoning you and Nicole back when she told me she was pregnant. It's something I've always regretted and it's something I have no excuse for. I was young and stupid and selfish and I will go to my grave regretting my choice back then."

A boulder has formed in my throat and I'm having a tough time swallowing around it. Max reaches across and takes my hand, squeezing it in reassurance.

Martin glances at Max and then returns his apologetic gaze to me. "I'm also sorry for being pushy in my eagerness to insert myself into your life. I had no business bulldozing my way into your life and expecting that I could be your father, purely based on the fact that biology makes you mine. It takes more than sperm to make a man a father and I need to give you time to get to know me and for us to find our way forward in this new reality. I only hope you can open your heart to the possibility of a relationship with me. And with Holly, Noah, and Beth."

Saliva fills my mouth and that familiar stinging at the back of my eyes is becoming too much. I blink rapidly, doing my best to maintain my composure.

"The last thing I want to apologize for is how my choices impacted on your life." He gives me a sad smile and I glance up at his eyes, looking for his pity, but it's not there. All I see is hurt and sorrow. "Molly. I was devastated all over again when Beth told me about your childhood living arrangements. I can't help but feel responsible for all of it. If I'd been more mature … a better man … anything, your life would have turned out differently."

I lose the battle and the tears burst forth on a sob. It's like my heart's been split down the middle with an ax and I can't get enough oxygen into my lungs. Max's arms come around me, pulling me into his warm body. I rest my ear against his heart, listening to the steady rhythm as I work to calm myself. Thank God he's here.

"I … I'm sorry, Molly. I didn't mean to upset you," Martin whispers.

"It's okay, Martin." The vibration of Max's voice touches my ear as he calmly strokes my hair and reassures Martin.

How do I explain these tears aren't because I'm angry or

hurt, it's because I needed him to acknowledge his mistakes so I could move forward? These tears are full of relief that he's owned up to his choices, and he's taken responsibility for them, even though some of them were technically out of his control.

"Oh, dear. What's going on out here?" Beth's voice breaks the silence.

I pull away from Max and wipe my eyes. "I promise I'm okay. Sorry about that. Do you have a bathroom where I can clean myself up?"

"Of course, follow me."

I clean up and when I come back out, Martin, Beth, and Max have moved to the table where dinner has been served. Roast chicken with all the trimmings. I love roast chicken. It was something we rarely had because it's so expensive, but Mom always made sure to have it for my birthday after we started living with Jack. As I sit, I promise myself that I'm going to enjoy this meal and I won't become swamped with memories—it's not fair to everyone else if I'm always breaking down into tears.

Martin and Beth serve us and the first few moments are quiet as we all dig into the delicious meal. The chicken tastes different from the way Mom cooked it. It has more of a smokey flavor to it. "This is delicious. Thank you for going to so much trouble."

Beth waves off my compliment. "It was no trouble. It's a family staple in this house. One of Holly's favorite meals."

I smile at her and it's genuine and full of hope. "It's my favorite, too." Beth smiles, appearing pleased at her choice of meal. These small connections are giving me hope that I'll be able to forge strong relationships with my new family.

As we eat dinner, Martin and Beth glance at each other, then their eyes land on me. "I have a funny story to share about Nicole, Beth, and me if you'd like to hear it?"

My eyes slide to Max and I swallow. Maybe hearing about

some of their fun times will help. "I'd love you to share it with me." Max reaches across under the table and lays his hand on my thigh, squeezing it in support.

"Oh, no. Which story are you going to share?" Beth chuckles.

Martin looks at her with a sparkle in his eye. "Remember Mr. Fitzroy?"

Beth's eyes snap to mine, then back to her husband. "Oh. Do you think that's the best story to share?"

"Hell yeah. It was hilarious. Not that we thought it was funny at the time, but looking back." He sighs and glances away. "Good times." He nods to himself as he becomes lost in the memory.

Beth's eyes come back to me. "They were fun times. I think we were about sixteen. Well, you were eighteen." She swipes Martin's arm in jest. "Old enough to know better." She winks at me.

"Mr. Fitzroy was Nicole's neighbor. He had a swimming pool." I feel like I already know where this story might be heading.

"He was the only person with a swimming pool in the neighborhood," Beth adds.

"He was away on vacation and it was the hottest, muggiest night. We couldn't escape the heat. It had been days and days of the same stinking, hot, unbearable temperatures. The girls and I deci–"

Beth shoves her hands on her hips. "Hang on there. If I remember correctly, you coaxed Nicole and me to do it. We weren't so sure it was a good idea."

Martin tilts his hand from side to side as if Beth's recount isn't quite accurate. "Maybe, maybe not. Anyway, we took the opportunity of Mr. Fitzroy being away and decided to go for a swim late one night after we'd been at a party. The guy used to keep his gate locked, which meant we had to climb his fence to sneak around the back. The girls and I stripped down to our underwear and jumped in. It was heaven."

Beth nods. "I remember the sheer relief to finally have a reprieve from the heat. It was so good."

"Yeah. I'm not sure how long we swam, but we were having a great time. Suddenly, all the lights inside the house came on and before we could react, all the lights across the back of the house switched on and Mr. Fitzroy came storming out of the back door, yelling at us and threatening to call the police to report us for trespassing on his property." Beth and Martin chuckle.

"I don't think I've ever moved so fast. I jumped out of that pool, scooped up my clothes, and ran to the corner near the fence where it was still dark." Beth giggles. "Nicole, though …" she shakes her head, "she wasn't so keen on climbing out with Mr. Fitzroy watching because she had white underwear on."

A gasp escapes as I imagine Mom's embarrassment. "Oh, no."

Martin grimaces. "Yeah, I climbed out quickly, too, not realizing I left Nicole in the pool all on her own. Mr. Fitzroy was cursing up a storm something fierce. Lights came on next door and Mr. and Mrs. Lewis came out to investigate what was going on. Nicole was still in the pool, clinging to the edge, trying to hide her body while Mr. Fitzroy was shouting across the yard to her parents about what a terrible job they had done and that their daughter was a miscreant." Martin chuckles and Max joins in.

"Her parents were yelling at her to get out of the pool and she was yelling that she couldn't because her underwear was see-through. I was trying to put my clothes back on over my wet skin. Martin was hopping on one leg, trying to get his jeans back on and Nicole stayed in the pool, defiant."

"Oh my gosh, that sounds just like Mom," I add with a chuckle.

Martin nods. "Yeah. She was stubborn." I nod in agreement. "Anyway, eventually Nicole's mom came over with a towel and Nicole climbed out of the pool with most of her dignity intact."

"After that, Nicole was always careful to avoid Mr. Fitzroy," Beth finishes.

"I'm not surprised. Did she get into trouble with her parents?"

"Not really. They thought she'd learned her lesson. She was mad at me for days after that. Didn't speak to me because she blamed me." He shakes his head, but he has a twinkle in his eye. "Beth got her to come 'round, eventually." He smiles at her and she returns it. I wonder how difficult it is for Beth to remember those times when Martin's heart belonged to someone else. He kisses her temple and Beth's eyes flutter closed for a moment. "They were good times."

Beth nods. "Yes, they were."

"That sounds like something me and my sisters would have done when we were younger," Max adds.

Beth and Martin continue to share stories of the three of them throughout the meal, giving me an insight into Mom as a teenager. Before her life got heavy and complicated. She sounds like she was fun to be around, not that she wasn't fun. She would find ways for us to have fun at the park or the beach. Simple things that didn't cost money.

I help Beth clear the table and set up for dessert. As she rinses the dishes to stack in the dishwasher, I use the time while it's only the two of us. "Thank you for inviting us to dinner. This evening's been lovely."

"You are more than welcome. We hope this is just the beginning, Molly." I swallow down the lump that forms at her kindness and blink away the sting in my eyes. I refuse to cry again tonight.

CHAPTER 43

—max—

BETH AND MOLLY CARRY OUT SOME TYPE OF CREAMY-LOOKING dessert. "I hope you like Tiramisu." Beth proudly places the dessert in the middle of the table while Molly distributes the bowls.

"It looks great, Beth. Luckily, I have a bottomless pit for a stomach." I pat my stomach.

Martin and Beth chuckle. "Beth makes the best Tiramisu." His eyes are full of pride as he looks at his wife.

Beth dishes up and we're all quiet as we take our first spoonfuls. Molly moans in delight and it reminds me of the sounds she makes when I'm balls deep inside her. My cock swells in my jeans and I discreetly adjust my position and will him to behave. Molly glances across at me, then down at my lap. Her eyes widen and a half-smile touches her lips when she sees my predicament. She licks a smudge of cream from her bottom lip and raises a sculpted brow at me. Minx. She knows exactly what she does to me and I'll be sure to collect retribution when we get home.

Molly clears her throat, glances at me, then locks her sights on Martin. "Uh, Martin. I hope you don't mind, but I need to say something I think is important."

"Sure." He braces himself and Beth places her hand over the top of Martin's in a show of support. "Go ahead."

Molly tucks a lock of hair behind her ear and fidgets with her bracelet for a moment. Her eyes rise slowly, and she draws in a deep breath, then releases it. "I appreciate your apology. It meant a lot to me to know that you took responsibility for what happened all those years ago. But I think we all know Mom didn't necessarily need to run away to the other side of the country and leave everyone behind. I know she was doing what she thought was right and I don't pretend to know what she was going through or thinking at the time. In her mind, she wanted to protect me, and I'll be forever grateful for that. I'm not going to wish my life was different, because my life has been good. Great even. I had a loving stepfather who was the best dad a girl could ask for. He loved me as though I was his biological daughter."

Martin nods and his posture deflates a little.

"If Jack hadn't come into our lives, I would never have had Ethan. He was an awesome kid. I loved him with all of my heart." Her eyes are glassy, so I wrap my arm around Molly's shoulder and draw her in close. "And while I appreciate you feeling responsible for the way I grew up, none of that falls on your shoulders." She reaches across, taking Martin's hand, and a tear drops over her bottom lashes to coast down her cheek. "I don't blame you or hold you responsible. I'm happy, mostly, with how my life was as I grew up. I was loved and cared for. I knew I was the most important person in Mom's life and Jack's life when he came along. Mom always made sure I had nutritious food whenever she could, and she always made sure I was safe. I went to school and did all the things that I was supposed to do. So please, please let that go."

I'm fucking proud of my girl. I glance across at Martin as

he stands, his eyes red, tears streaming down his cheeks. He moves around the table and drags Molly up into his arms, embracing her. They hold each other close. They hold each other in acceptance of a past that can't be changed, and for a future spread out in front of them. My eyes flick across at Beth. She's crying too, but her lips are tipped up slightly at the edges, her hand clutched in front of her heart.

She glances at me and nods. And I know we're thinking the same thing. Everything's going to be okay.

As soon as we get through the front door, I press Molly up against the wall and cup her face in my rough hands. "You are so fucking strong." I press the palm of my hand to her heart. "Your heart is pure and giving and kind. I feel privileged that I have even a small place in it."

I rub my nose along the side of hers, drawing her scent into my lungs. She smells like springtime; like a garden in bloom. I skate my lips across hers, swallowing her sigh. Dragging my hand down her body, I slide my fingers between hers and raise her arm above her head, trapping it against the wall. Repeating the process, I trap both of her hands above her head in one of mine.

Her breasts heave in time with her harsh pants as I leisurely drag my eyes down her lush body. "I love you, Molly." I lunge forward, taking her mouth in a harsh kiss. A kiss full of lust, love, and fucking gratitude.

Gratitude that this strong, sexy woman is mine.

She whimpers into the kiss, and I thrust my tongue inside to tangle with hers. I hold both her hands with one of mine and slide my other hand down her arm until I get to the side of her breast. She trembles beneath my touch and my internal caveman beats on his chest.

Me.

I get her this hot.

She presses her pelvis forward as our teeth gnash, our breaths coming in hard pants as we battle for oxygen. "Max. I need you to fuck me. Please."

I draw back, admiring the glazed look in her steely eyes. "Well, that's convenient, because I need to fuck you."

She gifts me her dimples and raises her eyebrows. "That sounds like a win-win situation."

"Absolutely," I whisper as I kiss my way down the side of her neck, nibbling the space where it meets her shoulder. I trace down her body, kissing over the top of the fabric of her dress. Dropping to my knees, I fulfill a fantasy and lift the skirt, dropping it over my head until I'm completely shrouded by the black material. I press my nose against her black cotton panties, inhaling her scent and nuzzling her clit. She presses her hips forward, creating more friction, and my tongue slips out to stroke the fabric, which is soaked with her arousal. "So fucking hot," I murmur.

"Mmm, Max," she mumbles.

I grasp her underwear and slide it down her legs to give me uninhibited access to her hot pussy. Without hesitation, I swipe my tongue through her lips. Her heat sears me and I moan. "Fucking delicious."

Actually, I decide I don't like being covered by her dress. I can't see her face as I taste her, and that won't fucking do. Standing, I make quick work of removing her sweater and dress, exposing her sublime body to me. I reach around behind her and flick the release on her bra. As it loosens, Molly slides each strap down her arms and throws it to the floor. She's completely naked for my perusal. "You are goddamn beautiful." I reach forward to cup her breasts. "Perfect." Leaning forward, I take a rosy nipple into my mouth while I roll and pinch the other to a hard peak. I swap over, paying the other globe the same attention, then kiss and lick my way down her body. Her stomach trembles, making the jewelry there catch the moonlight streaming in through the entry window.

She moans as she grasps my hair, pushing me to where she wants me most and I chuckle, huffing a hot breath across her pretty pink clit which is swollen and begging for attention. I position one leg over my shoulder and lean forward to draw it into my mouth with a firm suck, then glide my tongue around the bundle of nerves. Molly's hips shoot forward with a gasp.

My eyes scrape up her body, flushed with arousal, a light sheen of perspiration coating her skin. Her head is tipped back in pleasure and her breasts tremble with anticipation. I glide my fingers through her lips and then thrust inside without warning, my eyes locked on the beauty of Molly's lust. Her mouth drops open and a mewl escapes. Her walls flutter around my fingers as her clit pulses on my tongue.

I pull out and away from her body.

She drops her head, opening her eyes. "Why ... why'd you stop?"

I raise an eyebrow. "Remember what you did to me during dessert?"

Her eyes widen. "I ... what?"

"You made me fucking hard with your little moans, and then you thought it would be funny to fucking lick your lips and tease me even more."

Her eyes narrow. "And ... what does that have to do with this?"

"It's time for payback." I remove her leg from my shoulder and stand to my full height—I have roughly five inches on her —and I move in close. Our chests touch, her soft breasts pressing into my shirt. This is taking all of my willpower because I want to drop back to my knees and finish what I started, have her cum all over my fingers and tongue, but I have a dire situation in my jeans that needs attention. I press my cock against her pelvis. "Feel that?" She nods. "It needs your attention. Be a good girl and drop to your knees."

Without a word, she presses her hands against my body, putting space between us. She drops to her knees, keeping her eyes locked with mine. "Such a beautiful sight." I slide my fingers through her silky hair as her hands lift to my belt to release it and my jeans. I'm sure I hear my cock sigh. It pulses as she slides the denim from my hips, taking my boxers with them. They drop to my feet and Molly wastes no time, wrapping her hand around my heavy shaft and swiping it with her tongue, from base to tip, causing a shiver to climb up my spine.

I clench my hands at my sides, to allow her the freedom to do whatever she wants to me. Her mouth is what I imagine heaven to be like. Warm and inviting. She takes my cock to the back of her throat and hums around my shaft. My hips thrust forward without instruction. "Fuck." Her molten eyes snap up to mine and hold as she licks, sucks, and draws my orgasm forward like it's her goddamn job.

Fuck, that's hot. I slide my hand into her silky mane and clutch the strands at the base of her skull, dragging her mouth along my rock-hard length. She gently scrapes her teeth along my flesh, and it's almost my undoing. "You're such a fucking good girl."

She moans and draws her mouth from my shaft. "Only for you, Max." Her lips curl up and she winks before dropping back toward my dick. Using my grip on her hair, I hold her back because I never come first. It's one of the few rules I hold fast to. I bend down and pull my girl up, pressing her back against the wall. "Why'd you stop me?"

I run my nose along the side of hers. "Because that's not how I do things, Dimples." I roughly push my fingers back into her dripping center. Eliciting a long, beautiful moan. Dropping my head, I suck her nipple into my mouth and continue to thrust, ensuring I massage the spongy front wall as my thumb lightly circles her needy clit. I take her mouth in a hard kiss as her walls tighten around my intrusion, strangling me. Her short fingernails dig into my shoulders and I hope she leaves her fucking mark on me. Pushing my tongue inside her mouth to match the cadence of my fingers in her pussy, she rides out her orgasm through whimpers and gasps. Her arms wrap around my neck, her fingers sliding up into my hair to grasp it.

Removing my fingers, I line my cock up with her opening and slide slowly inside as her walls continue to pulse. My hands find Molly's ass and I lift her, pushing my cock in deeper as her long legs wind around my hips, and she tugs at my shirt to pull it off.

I press her harder into the wall and drag my shirt off by my collar, discarding the offending fabric to the floor. She wraps her arms around my neck, tightening her hold as my hands return to her gorgeous ass. Slipping my fingers down, I collect her cum and use it to ease a finger into her back entrance. Her eyes open wide and lock on mine as her mouth drops open with a silent moan.

Bracing my feet, I lift her as I slide out, then drop her down as I thrust up. She takes over the action, using her hold on me to bounce up and down on my cock while I drive into her over and over again. Molly and I have no problem creating a rhythm that builds us quickly.

"Ohh. I'm gonna come," she cries out as my dick thickens and pulses. Her walls tighten around me, strangling me, tightening on my finger and my cock. Our slick bodies slide against each other as we both chase our high.

Electricity races down my spine and my balls draw up close to my body. Molly's breaths are hot against my ear, and she leans forward to bite the lobe. Cum shoots out as my cock throbs and pulses, setting off Molly's orgasm.

We both moan as our bodies spiral into bliss.

Our chests heaving for air.

Eyes locked, mossy green to mercury.

I take her mouth in a searing kiss and then slow it down. Gently, I caress her mouth. Showing how much I adore her and appreciate her trust. How much I value her. I tenderly draw away, pressing light kisses to her lips. I drop my forehead to hers and our breaths mingle.

She scrapes her nails through my hair, then drags her hands around to cup my face. Her eyes flit between mine and my mouth. A smile grows, and she gifts me those gorgeous dimples. "Thank you," she whispers.

She fucking undoes me. "You never need to thank me for fucking you, Molly. It's a goddamn privilege that you share your heart and body with me."

Her eyes go soft. "I *do* need to thank you. Thank you for always taking care of me. Whether it's giving me your support as I navigate my new family or making sure that I have record-breaking orgasms every single time we come together. You've made my new life here truly remarkable."

She's the fucking remarkable one. Molly uses her hold on my face to draw me forward and presses her lips to mine. She swipes her tongue across the seam, and I open willingly. My semi-hard cock wakes up and I start slow, languid strokes in and out of heaven. I toe off my shoes and step out of my jeans, and carry my girl to bed, so I can take my time to love her the way she deserves.

—molly—

My phone buzzes with a text from Martin. I'm not sure if I'll ever call him dad, but he doesn't seem to mind. We've been messaging regularly over the last two weeks, and he's even stopped in and had lunch with me a couple of times. He hasn't pressured me to share any more details about my life, but I've shown him my sketches and shared with him how much I enjoy running.

MARTIN

Would it be okay if I bring Noah around this afternoon? He's eager to meet you

ME

Sure. We close at 2. Come then

MARTIN

Great. See you then

I send him a thumbs up and then make my way out to Max. His body's twisted as he works on something underneath the dash of the car he has in the bay. "Hey."

He maneuvers his body out of the cramped space, a smile

instantly brightening his face, which has a streak of grease down the side. He's so freaking handsome I can't stand it. I lean forward and swipe my lips against his and then lean on the open door.

"Hey. I'm gonna need your lips back here, Dimples. I wasn't finished." He gestures, flicking two fingers at me in a come here motion.

I chuckle. "Maybe later." I raise an eyebrow at him. "Martin messaged me. He asked if it was okay to bring Noah over. I hope you don't mind. I said they could come at two when we close."

"You know I don't mind." His eyebrows draw together, causing creases in between. "Are you gonna be okay? I know you've been anxious about meeting him." He stands, his eyes full of concern for me.

"I can't avoid him forever and I really do want to meet him." I shrug. Max wipes his hands with the rag he always seems to have handy and then glides his thumb down the side of my face in a barely there touch. His eyes bury themselves deep in mine as though he's searching all the way to the depths of my soul for my truth. "I promise I'll be okay. I'm going to do my best not to compare him to Ethan. Ethan was his own person, just as Noah is. I want to get to know him. By all accounts, he sounds like a sweet boy. There's no pressure if we meet here." I chuckle lightly. "He'll probably be more interested in your truck than he will be in me. He's crazy about cars."

"Yeah, I remember Martin telling me about that when we took the Sprint out for a test drive." Max glances across at the truck that he's started dismantling.

I follow his eyes. "I'm up-to-date in the office. Mind if I sketch the truck for a while?"

He turns back to me. "Go for it. I'm looking forward to seeing your sketches evolve as I restore the old girl."

I press a chaste kiss to his lips and skip back to the office to grab my sketch pad and pencils. Max gets back to work, and I get comfortable and start outlining.

"Woah!" The sudden intrusion breaks my focus and I peer up at the boy standing next to me. His eyes are wide as he studies my sketch. "Did you draw that?" He points at the page I'm working on.

I smile at him. "Sure did. You must be Noah."

Without hesitation, he drops to his butt beside me, crossing his legs to get comfortable on the cement floor. "Sure am. I wish I could draw. The best I can do is stick figures. My grade one teacher taught us how to look for shapes in things to help us draw, but I could never figure it out." His eyes drop back to my sketch.

"I could teach you if you like. It's not that hard."

His head starts nodding and his wide eyes rise to mine. "Really? You wouldn't mind?"

I chuckle. "Not at all."

"Holly can draw too, though she draws boring clothes. Your drawing is way cooler."

"I dunno about that. I saw the clothes Holly designed and they were pretty cool. I bet her sketches are amazing."

He scrunches his nose. "Yeah, I guess so. I'm not into clothes." His eyes widen. "But I *am* into cars. I want to be a race car driver one day."

"Really?" He nods like a bobble doll, and I glance over my shoulder, spotting Max and Martin talking several feet away from us. I wave over my shoulder. "Hi, Martin."

He smiles at me and moves closer. "Hey, Molly. Great to see you." He bends down and kisses the top of my head in a fatherly way. It's strange how our dynamic has changed in such a brief space of time. "Is this what you're working on at the moment?" He gestures toward my sketch pad.

"Yeah. I'm going to sketch the truck at different stages during the restoration as a record for Max." I smile up at Max.

"You should see the one of the Sprint in the office." Max gestures over his shoulder toward the office.

Noah stands. "Where is it? I wanna see."

I stand, too, and we all head into the office where Max proudly shows off my work.

"This is fantastic, Molly," Martin states without taking his eyes off my work.

Noah turns to me. "You know. I wasn't sure about having another big sister, because one is enough already. But I think I'm gonna like having you around, Molly."

We all chuckle lightheartedly, but my heart swells. I was worried about meeting Noah and how we'd get along, but I needn't have. He's a great kid. Even though I promised myself I wouldn't compare Noah and Ethan, they seem very similar in disposition.

As I walk Martin and Noah out to say goodbye, I decide to throw caution to the wind and invite them to Max's birthday barbecue tomorrow. Emma phoned me last week to ask if I had any plans for Max's birthday, which came as a surprise since I wasn't aware his birthday was coming up. I agreed to marry the man and I didn't even know when his birthday was. I felt like a terrible fiancée.

I've carried on the ruse that I don't know it's his birthday tomorrow, but I've planned a barbecue at a park down by the lake to celebrate with his family. Martin and Noah readily agree to come, promising that Beth and Holly will come along too. I can't wait to see the surprise on Max's face.

I spin on my heel and head back into the workshop, locking

the door behind me, feeling lighter than I have in a long time. Max cleaned up and took off his overalls while I was outside.

He draws me in close, wrapping his arms around my lower back, resting his hands on my butt, locking us together. "How are you feeling, Dimples?"

I pause for a moment to assess how I'm feeling. Peering up into Max's caring eyes, which are almost brown today, I answer honestly. "I'm not gonna lie. I was nervous. He's the age that Ethan never got to be, and I wasn't sure if I'd be okay … emotionally. You know?" I draw in a sharp breath as Max nods. "I didn't want to be a sobbing mess in front of him and make things awkward."

Max presses his forehead to mine, kissing the tip of my nose. "You've lost so much and yet you're still thinking about everyone else. You're incredible. You know that, right?"

The heat that rises to my cheeks is embarrassing. "Not really. I didn't want to start with grief between us. He's just a kid and I'm a stranger. I'm glad we could connect with my drawings, though. I think having something we can do together will make it easier for us to get to know each other."

"He was impressed with your talent. But I feel sorry for the kid. He now has to deal with two sisters. I might have to give him some tips." I swat playfully at Max's arm, which he attempts to dodge, but I'm too quick and make contact with his muscular bicep. "C'mon, Dimples. Let's get outta here."

CHAPTER 45

—max—

I WAKE TO MOLLY'S MOUTH WRAPPED AROUND MY COCK, HER silky hair tickling my thighs. A moan escapes and I raise my head to look down my body at the gorgeous sight of my dick disappearing into her warm mouth. The sensations are incredible, and I prop one hand behind my head to watch. I sift my fingers through her silky strands to push them away from her face, to give me an unobstructed view.

Her eyes lift to find mine and she smiles around my cock at me. I gently massage her scalp, watching her saliva coat my cock as it slides out of her mouth. Her hand follows the movement while her other hand cups my balls. She squeezes gently and I moan, pressing my hips up.

"Take it deep," I grunt, as I push my pelvis up again. She swallows around the shaft, then uses her teeth to lightly graze my dick as she slides her mouth up. My body trembles, anticipating the downward stroke and hitting the back of her gorgeous throat.

Tight and hot.

She moans as she sinks back down, and I'm gone. "Good girl," I groan as my fingers clench in her hair, my balls draw up tight, and darkness flickers around the edge of my vision. I shatter, my heart tearing apart and gluing back together in one swift action. Cum streams down her throat and the eager lover that she is, she swallows it all down. I drop my head back, panting for breath as she cleans my shaft with her delicate tongue, and I finally release my harsh grip on her silky hair.

I peel my lids back open as I feel her sliding up beside me; her swollen lips caressing my torso on the way. Her slender fingers flick and pinch my nipples as she makes her way up my body.

"Happy birthday, Max."

I raise my eyebrow. I didn't think she knew. "How did you know?"

Her dimples make an appearance. "Emma." One word.

"Well, thank you for my birthday gift. I loved it. Feel free to give me gifts like that whenever the mood strikes." I gently brush her hair away from her face, raising my head to take her mouth in a grateful kiss, but she pulls back slightly.

"Why didn't you tell me it was your birthday today?" I'm not sure if she's hurt or not, her eyes glimmer with something, but I don't think it's hurt feelings. It feels more like … curiosity.

I glide my hand down her hair in a long stroke, moving down her slender back to rest on the cheek of her ass. "I didn't tell you because you've already given me so much. I didn't want you to feel obligated to buy me a gift or to make a fuss. You're enough. Until the end of my days. You're all I need. All I want." Her eyes go soft and she presses forward, touching her lips to mine in a slow exploration. "I fucking love kissing you," I whisper, my lips touching hers as I roll over.

As I line up my needy cock with her slick heat, I thrust my tongue inside to mirror the action of my hips. We both moan, closing our eyes momentarily as we're lost in the bliss. Every time I'm inside this woman, our bond grows, the tether between us tightening.

"I want us to get married soon. I don't want to wait." The words roll off my tongue. I don't know what it is, but when I'm inside her, it's like a truth serum explodes through my veins and I can't keep my thoughts inside.

Molly's eyes spring open. "Like how soon?"

"Like next month soon. Say you will."

She smiles, big and bright. "Of course. Can we get married on the beach, where you proposed to me?"

"Sounds perfect." I lean forward and press my lips against hers. "This is the best birthday ever."

I slide my hand down her slender thigh and pull her leg up high, opening her to me and return my mouth to hers as I slide my hips back. With lips barely touching, eyes locked tight, I drive into my girl over and over again. Our breaths blend and meld. The scent of sex fills the air, adding to the headiness of our lovemaking. Molly meets me thrust for thrust, building our pleasure.

She whimpers as I slide my hand under her ass and tilt her hips, changing the angle. Her short nails are sure to leave scratches on my shoulders as she grips me tight. The thought of seeing her marks on me makes my cock throb and pulse, my balls getting ready to shoot my load. One of these days, that cum is going to knock her up and I can't wait for that day. Until then, I'm happy to take us to completion as many times as possible until we get it just right.

Molly's walls spasm and I grunt as I work to hold back my release. I move closer to her ear. "Be a good girl and choke my cock." I suck and nip the lobe and she cries out as her walls squeeze around my shaft. Her body stiffens, and her breaths turn choppy. I grit my teeth to hold on to my release. "Don't fight it. Come," I demand, harshly.

Her release washes through her body like a wave as her pussy clamps down around my cock, choking it to oblivion, and I shatter. "Fuuuuck!" I press my hips in tight to Molly's. If

I could fucking climb inside her right now, I would. I smooth her sweaty hair away from her face and smile at the serene look. I want to beat my chest in pride that I'm the man to put that look on her face. Her leg drops away from my hip to the bed and she squeezes her internal muscles. "Fuck. Stop." Shit. She chuckles. That almost hurt.

I drop my forehead to hers. "Happy fucking birthday to me," I whisper against her lips. Then I capture her mouth in a kiss that I hope she feels all the way to her toes.

Molly wanted to drive today. She said she wanted to give me the full treatment. After the spectacular way she woke me up, she cooked a full breakfast of bacon, eggs, hash browns, sausage, and roasted tomatoes. Now she's taking me somewhere before we head to Mom and Dad's for lunch.

"Where are you taking me?" I thought I had an idea where we were going, but she's turned down this long, winding, unpaved road and I'm not sure I know what's down this way.

She glances across at me with a half-smile. "You'll have to wait and see."

We drive around a wide bend and the road opens up to a parking lot alongside a wide grassed area with barbecues, picnic tables, and a wicked nature play area for kids, which overlooks a medium-sized lake with a small island in the middle. I'll have to bring Kenny and the boys here. They'll love it. "I can't believe I've lived in this city all my life and I didn't know about this place. How did you find it?"

"When I first moved here, I had nothing else to do on the weekends, so I would drive around to familiarize myself with the city. There's still a lot of the city I'm unfamiliar with, but I stumbled across this place and fell in love."

The parking lot is busy, but Molly finds a space and we climb out. Hand in hand, we make our way to the edge of the lake. I peer around at the people enjoying this sunny spring day and my eyes freeze on a group at a picnic bench by the edge of the water before the grass becomes a forest. I glance at Molly to find her dimples on full display. "Happy birthday, Max."

I pull her to a stop. "You did this for me?"

She nods. "With Emma's help." I drag her around to face me properly, then cup her gorgeous face in my hands. Her hands come up to hold onto my wrists, her eyes locked on mine. "I hope you don't mind."

"How did I get so lucky?" I touch her lips with mine. "Thank you, Dimples."

"You're welcome. Emma helped, though. I can't take all the credit." She presses her lips firmly to mine, then pulls away too quickly. "Come on. Everyone's waiting." Dragging me forward, we reach my family quickly.

Mom and Dad are the first to greet me. "Happy birthday, Max."

Mom reaches up to cup my bristly cheeks. Her eyes are full of love as she scans my face. "I can't believe my baby boy's thirty-seven." She glances at Dad. "When did that happen?"

I bend down and kiss her forehead. "It's been a long time since I've been a baby, Mom."

Emma interrupts, wrapping her arms around me. "Happy birthday, little brother." She smirks at me, knowing I hate to be called little.

I wrap my arm around her, pulling her in close. "Thanks, Em. And thanks for helping Molly with this today."

"I really like her. I'm so glad we get to keep her," she says with a softness in her eyes.

Mom and Dad nod in agreement. "Us too."

"You did good, brother." Em kisses my cheek.

Molly joins us with Kenny holding onto her back like a

koala. "I'm gonna take the kids to the playground." She glances across at Emma. "Sorry, I probably should have asked first. Is it okay if I take the kids to the playground?"

Em waves her off. "Of course. Cristo will probably tag along." She points toward her father-in-law, who's busy setting up trays of food on the picnic table.

"I'll go too," I offer. I love that Molly's bonded so well with Em's kids. Every Sunday, she's become closer and closer to my sisters. She's well and truly one of the family.

Sarah joins us, wrapping her arms around me and squeezing tight. "Happy birthday, big brother."

I squeeze her back. "Thanks, Sare." Molly's smiling at our interaction and I raise my chin to her. "Do you wanna tell the girls the good news, or shall I?"

Everyone's eyes snap to Molly's stomach and she flushes pink. "Not that." She fidgets with her bracelet. "Max and I have decided to get married next month on the beach where he proposed to me."

The girls jump up and down, squealing in delight as Martin and his family approach our group. "Oh my God, next month. That doesn't give us a heap of time." Sarah's slightly panicked.

"It's only going to be family and probably some guys from soccer, maybe Molly's friends from *Shelter*, if they can make it. Don't get carried away."

Beth doesn't wait to be invited into the conversation. "Are you talking about your wedding?" Her eyes are wide, shimmering with excitement.

"Yeah." Molly steps forward, welcoming her family and introducing them to mine. I'm surprised they're here, but she must be feeling more comfortable with them. I know she speaks regularly with her sister, who occasionally drops by after school since the first time she turned up out of the blue. And dinner last month cleared the air between Molly and Martin. They still have awkward moments as they get to know each other, but they've come a long way.

"Come on, Molly. I wanna go play." Kenny reminds my girl.

Molly jiggles her. "Sure. Come on, Munchkin." She turns back to everyone. "Maybe we can talk about it later. I promised the kids I'd play with them and I always try to keep my promises."

"We can come too," the women offer. "The guys can organize the food."

Molly presses up to kiss my cheek. "See you in a while, Fiancé." She winks as she turns away with Kenny on her back and Lachlan, Austin, and Noah trailing behind, followed by five women all itching to help plan a wedding. She reminds me of the Pied Piper.

I chuckle to myself as I head over to Dad to see if I can help him with the barbecue. "Need any help?"

"You don't fancy talking about wedding planning?" He chuckles and Theo joins in.

"It's not that I don't want to." I glance across to the nature play area where the girls are chatting while the kids play. "I wanted to give Molly the opportunity to bond with the girls. I don't expect she's ever really had that because it was only her and her mom for such a long time."

Theo nods, but Dad's the one who responds, "Good thinking, Son."

"I know Em and Sarah will help wherever they can. Sarah was a great help to Em. Em probably still has her wedding folder somewhere. She was incredibly organized, she had little pockets for everything." Theo's eyes seek Emma out across the park.

Dad hands Martin, Cristo, Theo, and me a beer each and I take a drink, then respond. "Beth's a wedding planner. I'm assuming the girls will probably have everything sorted out quickly."

"Beth has all the contacts you two need. She loves planning a wedding, but I think this one will be special to her. She already thinks of Molly as her daughter," Martin adds, then takes a long drink.

"Family is incredibly important to Molly." I give Martin a meaningful look. I hope he doesn't hurt her.

Martin returns my look. "I know what you're thinking. I don't plan on hurting her. Ever. She's my daughter, whether or not I was with her while she grew up. I have a lot of time to makeup and I intend to do so." He steps closer to me. "I'll be talking to Molly about the wedding when I get the chance, but I'd like to give you a heads-up. I'd like to pay for everything, including your honeymoon. If the two of you will let me."

"That's a mighty generous offer, Martin. If you're doing it to win Molly over, you're going about it the wrong way. She's not about material stuff. She's about time, care, and commitment." I study him closely. "But that'll be between you and her. I'll go along with whatever she decides. It won't be an expensive event. We've already discussed keeping it small with little fuss."

He nods. "Fair enough. I'm not doing it to get in her good graces. I want to do it because I missed out on so much of her life."

The afternoon is great fun, and we all agree to come back in the summer to allow the kids to enjoy the lake.

—molly—

DRIVING HOME FROM THE LAKE, I FILL MAX IN ON EVERYTHING the girls told me. "Beth's going to work on getting the permits we need to have our wedding ceremony on the beach. We would normally need longer than five weeks, but because she deals with that sort of stuff all the time, she's pretty sure she can get it approved more quickly for us. She also has a celebrant that she uses regularly, so she's going to check if she's available." I draw a breath.

"Sounds good, Dimples."

"Yeah. And Emma told me about the florist she and Theo used." I rack my brain, trying to remember the name. *"Blooms and Balloons*, I think." I glance across at my groom-to-be. "I think we'll have everything organized quickly with everyone's help."

"That's where I bought your roses from. Cassia, the owner, is incredibly helpful." He lays his hand on my thigh. "Don't forget I can help too. Give me a list of tasks and I'll get them done." And there I go, falling in love a little more. "It's my wedding too. I don't expect you to do everything, especially since I'm the one who wants to get married quickly."

"I want to get married quickly, too. There's no point in waiting." I flick my eyes across to Max, then look back at the road. "Did Martin talk to you about paying for everything? He wants to cover the whole thing, including our honeymoon if we want one."

"He spoke to me about it and I said the decision would be yours. It's an incredibly generous offer."

"I know. He said it's the least he could do since he hadn't contributed financially while I was growing up." Max's hand lands on my thigh and he squeezes it. "I didn't accept his offer because I wanted to speak about it with you. I hadn't realized the two of you had already spoken."

We pull into our driveway and head inside. Max pulls me into his arms. "It's up to you. It might help Martin with some of the guilt he's carrying about letting Nicole and you down." He shrugs and leans forward, pressing his lips tenderly against my forehead.

"I'll think about it, but not right now. I have a gift for you." His eyes widen as I pull away to collect his present. "Go sit in the living room. I'll bring it to you."

He's sitting on the couch when I return. I'm hoping he likes his gift because I struggled to figure out something at short notice. "Happy birthday, Max." I hand him the gift bag.

He accepts it with a curious smile. "You didn't need to get me anything. Organizing the barbecue at the lake with our families was more than I ever expected." He takes my hand, kissing the palm. "My favorite part was the way you woke me up this morning," he says as he wriggles his eyebrows.

Leaning forward, I chuckle as I taste his lips. "Open it."

He pulls out the large square gift to open first. I'm hoping he doesn't think it's a stupid idea. He peels away the paper, revealing the custom map I had made. He reads the inscription. "When Max asked and Molly said yes." He looks at me. "What is this exactly?"

"It's what the night sky at the beach looked like the night you proposed to me." I hold my breath, waiting for his response.

His eyes widen as he studies the map. "Fuck. This is incredible. We need to get one done for when we get married and every time one of our kids is born. We can make a wall of these babies." He leans forward, cupping the back of my head, and pulls me into him and we meet halfway. I open immediately, welcoming him eagerly.

I love kissing this man.

"I'm relieved you like it. I was worried you'd think it was pointless." I point my chin toward the bag. "You have something else in the bag."

He dips his hand in, pulling out the small box. He glances up at me and then tugs at the paper to open the box. He studies the contents for a long time, then glances up at me. Holding up the keyring I had specially made, he asks, "Are you serious? This is my car. How did you do this?"

"It's from a little store on Etsy. I managed to get a rush order at short notice."

He's wobbling his head from side to side as though he can't believe I bought him something for his birthday. "These gifts are really thoughtful. Thank you so much." He wiggles his eyebrows up and down and stands, holding his hand out to me. "Allow me to show you how much I love these gifts."

My lady parts flutter in delight. I'm about to get very lucky.

I wipe my sweaty hands down my jeans. My heart feels like it's going to beat right through my rib cage. Max wanted to come with me, but I needed to do this on my own. I needed to prove that I can still deal with things that may be difficult by myself.

That I haven't become completely dependent on Max. I knock on the door and hear little claws scratching on the floor before tiny barks greet me through the door. Footsteps sound and then I hear, "Shhh, shhh, Christian."

The lock disengages as the dog continues to bark. Surprised blue eyes so much like Mom's greet me above a wiggling gray ball of fur. "Oh, Molly. This is a wonderful surprise." She steps away, then returns with a key to unlock the screen door. "Please come in. I'm thrilled to see you."

She steps to the side, allowing me inside her home. When Beth gave me Joanna's address and phone number, she also gave me some information which made my decision to visit easier. I want to get to know *all* of my family. Life's too short to miss out on opportunities. "I hope you don't mind me dropping by unannounced."

"Not at all. I'm just so happy that you have." She leads me through to a sitting room that overlooks a common area in the middle of the unit complex. My eyes catch on a large photo of Mom hanging in a prominent position on the wall. She notices me gawking and gives me a small smile. "Nicole was such a beautiful girl. So spirited and full of life." Her smile turns sad.

She offers me a drink and then sets about making it while the little gray fur ball acquaints himself with me. He's adorable. His name seems very formal, though. Joanna returns with cups of coffee on a tray and what appears to be home-made shortbread. "Would you like some?"

"Thank you." I point down at her little dog, which has finally settled on his bed, huffing out a sigh and dropping his head to his little paws, his ears still twitching. "Your dog is cute."

Her eyes drop to him, and she smiles. "I always wanted to have a dog, but my husband would never agree. The place I lived in when I first left him didn't allow pets. I finally saved up enough to buy this place fifteen years ago and one of the first things I did was get a rescue. Unfortunately, that dog passed away and then I got Christian. I named him after one of my favorite book characters." The connection dawns on me, and I'm certain my eyes are as wide as saucers. Does that mean my grandmother has read *Fifty Shades of Grey*? "Have you read the books?" she asks with eyes full of mischief, reminding me of Mom when she was sharing exciting news with me.

I shake my head, my voice mute for a moment. "Uh, no. Can't say I have." The awkwardness I felt earlier has increased tenfold, knowing my grandmother reads soft porn. I don't know whether to feel mortified or proud. I mean good on her, I guess. Perhaps I should introduce her to Rhonda. They could compare book boyfriends. I giggle internally at the idea of Rhonda with her bright pink hair swooning over book boyfriends with my grandmother, who appears to be as proper as a minister's wife.

I came here to apologize for my behavior when we first met. Once I calmed down, I was mortified at how I had run out of the house and left Max to deal with the aftermath. It was unfair and probably not the best first impression to give my grandmother. I take a sip of my coffee to soothe my dry throat and draw in a deep breath for fortitude. "Uh, I … I, uh, owe you an apology."

Her posture softens. "Oh, Molly. You don't owe me anything at all. It's *I* who owe *you* an apology. I should have fought harder and stood up to my husband. I never should have allowed him to speak to Nicole the way he did. I believe she ran away because of what he said to her. Because of his threats." A loud sob escapes. "I'm so sorry, Molly. I let my daughter down, and I let you down." She covers her face with both hands and the urge to comfort this stranger is strong.

I move to the cushion next to her, wrapping my arm around her shoulder. Beth told me that Joanna left her husband, my grandfather, not long after Mom ran away. She blamed him and his demand for an abortion for losing Mom. I'm not sure I'd be sitting here if she were still with him, because I don't think I could get past the way he spoke to Mom.

He didn't want me.

How could I possibly forge a relationship with the man?

The idea is impossible.

I'm not sure what I can say to make things better for Joanna. Do I accept her apology? But to me, that would mean I blame her. And deep down, I don't. I've been thinking about the whole situation a lot since I moved here. And I mean a lot!

I love Mom and I'll forever be on her side no matter what because ultimately, she thought she was doing the right thing. The choices she made were to protect me because she wanted me. But … now I've heard the other side of the story and I've learned that maybe if Mom had taken a few days to let things settle instead of reacting so quickly, things probably would have turned out very differently. Which means some of the responsibility has to fall on her shoulders and it makes me wonder if she ever doubted the choices she made. Did she ever consider going home? Is it possible she realized her mistake but was too proud to return to her family and friends?

I understand being prideful. After all, I get that trait from her.

"Joanna." She removes her trembling hands from her face, revealing tear-stained cheeks and puffy red eyes. "The entire situation was unexpected and messy. Things were said and choices were made. Were they the best choices?" I shrug. "Maybe, maybe not. But they were the choices made at the time in the heat of the moment. We can't go back and change anything and, to be honest, I wouldn't want to. Was life difficult as a result? Yes, it was. I'm not gonna lie or sugarcoat things." I give my grandmother a small smile of reassurance. "But life was also great. Mom and I had a bond that not all mothers and daughters share." A boulder forms in my throat as I think about Mom and I have to swallow it down so I can continue.

"We were close, and our love for each other was unbreakable. Not once did I ever question how important I was to her or how much she loved me. She always, always put me and my needs first. Even though we couldn't afford a traditional home, she always made sure I had nutritious food, even if it meant going without herself. Then Mom met Jack." I smile as I remember meeting him for the first time.

"He was the best man you could hope your daughter and granddaughter to have in our lives. He was kind and generous to both of us. From the beginning, he treated me as if I were his flesh and blood. And then Ethan came along." And my heart cracks a little, as it does whenever I think of him, and a life cut too short. "I wouldn't wish for a life where I'd never had him. So, maybe things didn't turn out the way you maybe hoped they would, but we had a good life."

She takes my free hand in both of hers. "I hope you can forgive me, though."

I give her a small smile. "There's nothing to forgive."

She squeezes my hand. "Thank you, Molly. You're being very gracious. Perhaps someday you'll share stories about growing up and tell me all about my grandson."

I nod. "I'd be happy to." I fidget with my bracelet. "I don't know all that much about Mom's childhood or teenage years, so perhaps you can tell me more about her?"

She smiles at me. "Of course. I still have all of her photo albums. I think I even have some videos." She chuckles. "Though I may need to get them transferred into another format since I don't have a video player anymore." She pats my hand and climbs to her feet. "I'll grab the photo albums. We can look at them now."

Joanna comes back carrying several albums. When she

opens to the first page of the first album, a gasp escapes me. "Oh my gosh. She was so cute. I'll have to bring the few baby photos I have so we can compare how much I looked like her."

She studies me. "You hold a remarkable resemblance to Nicole, even though you have some of Martin's prominent features. I'm sure you looked just like Nicole when you were a baby."

Joanna spends the afternoon showing me photos of Mom until the age of seventeen when the album abruptly remains starkly blank. We're both silent for long moments at the reminder of the years she's missed. Christian breaks the moment when he suddenly wakes and starts barking at nothing.

I remember I have some more recent photos on my phone, so I show them to her. Tears fill her eyes as she sees her daughter as a grown woman with the family she made for herself.

After long quiet moments, I decide now is the time to invite my grandmother to my wedding. "Uhm, Joanna. I have something I would like to ask you. Max asked me to marry him and I said yes." My stomach still flips when I think back to his proposal on the beach.

Her face lights up. "Oh, he seemed like such a lovely young man. He cares very much for you. I'm thrilled you've met such a wonderful man."

"Me too." My lips spread across my face, thinking about Max. "I was wondering if you'd like to come to our wedding? We don't have a date or time just yet, but it will be next month."

"Oh, I'd love to. Thank you for the invitation." She jumps up from her seat. "I'll be back in a moment."

I'm puzzled by her abrupt departure, but I stand to look out of the window at the shared gardens while I wait for her.

My grandmother has a peaceful view out of this window. Perhaps I should call her grandma or something?

Joanna returns with a small box. She hands it to me with a timid smile. "This is something my mother gave me to wear at my wedding and I had hoped Nicole would wear it for hers." Her smile becomes somber. "I would be thrilled if you would consider wearing this on your special day."

I open the box and my mouth drops open. Inside is a beautiful sparkling pendant. I tip my eyes back up to Joanna. "This is beautiful. I would love to wear this, though I don't know what the design of my dress will be yet."

She raises her hands to her chest. "Oh, you've made me so happy. It's meant to represent the stars in the night sky."

"Max proposed to me under a moonlit sky, so we're planning to get married at sunset. This would be amazing. Thank you."

CHAPTER 47

—molly—

MAX HAS HIS NEPHEW, AUSTIN, OVER FOR THE AFTERNOON TO 'help' him change the tires on his Dodge. Austin was almost exploding with excitement when he arrived to spend the afternoon working on his uncle's car. The day Max offered Austin the opportunity to help him in the future with his tire change, I figured it was lip service because Austin's so young. But I should have known better. Max is a man of his word and he didn't hesitate to include his nephew in his afternoon plans. It was so cute how Austin turned up in overalls, much like the ones Max wears. He's going to be such a great daddy one day.

I thought I'd leave them to their male bonding afternoon and spend the time getting to know my siblings. When I phoned to organize this afternoon, I half expected Noah and Holly to make up some excuse to avoid me. After all, I'm a complete stranger who happens to share their dad. I wouldn't blame them, but they were as keen as I am for us to get to know each other.

I've set up our afternoon snacks on the picnic blanket at the park near the workshop. I wasn't sure what type of snacks to bring, so I brought a little of everything. Whatever's left over,

I'm sure Max will eat, but if I remember correctly, there won't be anything left with a teenage boy around. If Noah's anything like Ethan was, he'll have a bottomless pit for a stomach.

My breath catches in my lungs when I realize I thought about my brother without my heart splintering into a million pieces. Sure, the memory of him has pain attached, but I'm starting to feel less bogged down by it. I know my sense of loss associated with my family will never go away, but I hope that when I think about them, it won't always result in me breaking down in a sobbing fit. I need to remember there were a lot of good times, happy times. The only truly sad memory of my family is that they're no longer here.

I make a promise to myself to focus on the happy times as much as possible.

Dragging my backpack across to me, I check that I have what I need inside and pull out the sketch pads and pencils I brought. I promised Noah I would start teaching him how to sketch today. I figured Holly and I could show him some simple techniques to get him started. There are loads of sketching opportunities for Noah at this park.

When I glance up, I spot Noah and Holly walking toward me, matching smiles on their faces, one with dimples, one without.

I stand as they close the distance. "Hi, guys." I'm not sure if I should hug them in greeting or not. I always hugged my family and I hug Max's family too. I decide to do what I've always done. They can let me know if they don't like it. Stepping forward, I hug Holly. "Hey, Holly." Then Noah. "Hey, Noah. I'm glad you guys could make it today."

They each return my embrace. "We've been looking forward to spending some time with you. We were bummed we missed out on dinner with you and Max." Holly smiles at me, then glances at her brother. *Our* brother. Geez, that's hard to get used to. "Right, Noah?"

Noah nods. "Right. I can't wait for you to teach me how to draw as good as you."

Holly's brows tighten. "I could have taught you how to draw, you know. All you had to do was ask."

He huffs out a breath and toes the ground with his shoe. "You draw girly stuff." He flings his arm out in my direction. "Molly draws cool stuff like cars."

Oh shit! My eyes widen. I don't want to compete with my newly found sister. "I love Holly's clothing designs. The stuff she draws comes from her imagination. I just draw what I can see."

Holly's eyes snap up to mine and I gesture toward the picnic blanket for us to take a seat. Noah eyes off the array of snacks as he sits as close as possible to the food and I quickly open the containers for him. "Help yourself. I didn't know what you guys liked, so I packed a few different options."

"Thanks," Noah replies as he reaches for a chocolate cupcake.

"Holly, what would you like?"

She scans the food and then takes a carrot stick, dipping it into the hummus. "Thanks."

"You're welcome." I grab a couple of strawberries and enjoy their sweet juice on my tongue. Max always insists on having berries in the house because they're my favorite.

We enjoy the snacks in silence for a while, then Noah points toward the scrapbook and sketch pads I brought along. "Is that your book? The one with the car sketch I saw."

I chuckle at his enthusiasm. "Yeah." I glance between my new siblings. "I, uh, I also brought my brother's scrapbook to show you. I figured you'd like it because he only drew cars."

My heart pounds as I share something that's deeply precious to me.

Holly's eyes go soft and she glances over at her brother. Creases form between her brows and then she reaches across to smooth down Noah's unruly hair. He pulls away, giving her a puzzled look. Her gaze comes back to me and it's full of sorrow and I know she's thinking about what I've lost.

Noah breaks the moment with his excitement, completely oblivious to his sister's sadness. "Really. Can I see his drawings?"

"Of course." I select Ethan's book and shuffle closer to Noah, then open to the first page. "This book shows his progression clearly. You can see this first drawing is quite basic. But wait until you see his sketches at the end of the book." Holly balances on her knees behind us, studying E's drawings closely as I turn each page.

Her hand creeps between Noah and me, stopping me from turning to the next page. "This is where his skill leveled up." She traces her finger over the line of the roof of the car. "You can see the confidence in his lines." She snatches her finger from the page. "Sorry. I probably shouldn't have touched it."

"That's okay. And yes, you're right. This was the turning point." I flick to the next page.

"They all look really cool to me." Noah glances at me with wide eyes. "Do you think I could draw like Ethan?"

"I don't see why not. Shall we get started?"

"I'm ready." He reaches into his backpack and pulls out a sketch pad and some pencils. Holly and I chuckle at his excitement.

Holly and I spend the next couple of hours showing Noah some basic techniques, reminding him to draw what he sees, not what he *thinks* he sees. "That's the trick. Our mind wants to fill in the spaces, but we mustn't let it, or our drawing won't be accurate." He nods, his face full of concentration.

When I glance at Holly's sketch pad, I notice she's drawing a new outfit. I tip my head toward it. "That looks beautiful. You're incredibly talented." She glances up at me with a smile.

"She designed and made that outfit she has on," Noah states proudly.

"Yeah?" She flushes a pretty pink and tucks her dark hair behind her ear. "It's gorgeous. Did you apply for Art College?"

"Yeah. I got accepted and I'm excited to start!" Her eyes sparkle with delight. "At least I'll finally be doing something I enjoy."

I wrap my arm around her, pulling her in close for a hug. "Congratulations. I'm honestly not surprised you got accepted. They'd be crazy to reject your application." I lean back, releasing her.

I swallow down my nerves because I think now would be a good time to ask her to be part of my bridal party. "You know how Max asked me to marry him, and we're getting married soon?"

Noah and Holly nod. "Yeah. I really like Max. Well, I mostly like that he works with cars because I don't know him all that well, but he seems like a cool guy."

I chuckle at Noah. "He *is* pretty cool." Then turn my attention to Holly. "Well, Holly, I was … uh … wondering if you would be my bridesmaid?"

She squeals and leans forward, wrapping her slim arms around me. "I'd freaking love to. This is amazing. Thank you so much." We sway awkwardly from side to side, giggling with happiness. It feels fabulous to have a sister.

"God, you girls are weird!" Noah huffs out as he steals yet another cupcake.

Holly and I giggle. "Would you mind if I designed my bridesmaid dress?" Her eyes are filled with excitement.

Oh my gosh, I hadn't even thought of that, but what a fabulous idea. I nod, my eyes wide with joy that she wants to do something so amazing for someone she barely knows. "On one condition."

She freezes, looking unsure. "Uhm, okay?"

"You'll need to make a complementary dress for Kenny. She's going to be my flower girl, and I'd love for you two to match!"

Holly squeals. "Oh my God, yes. She's so freaking adorable. Thank you for trusting me with something so important."

I chuckle as she draws me back in to embrace me tight. "Of course. I love your work. If it wasn't such a short time frame, I'd ask you to design and make my wedding dress, but it would be too much. It's less than three weeks away." My heart stalls when I realize how soon I'll become Mrs. Stanfield. "Will that be enough time for you to make two dresses? I don't want to put any pressure on you."

She waves off my concern. "I can definitely do them in three weeks. But I'll need to measure Kenny within the next few days."

I message Emma and we make plans to meet up with Kenny. I feel like I'm going to burst with happiness and excitement as I say goodbye to Noah and Holly. This afternoon worked out better than I could have hoped, and spending time with Noah wasn't anywhere near as difficult as I thought it was going to be.

I blow out a breath in relief and glance up at the cloudless sky. "I miss you," I whisper to the heavens. "But I think I'm gonna be okay."

A gentle, warm breeze rises, blowing my bangs out of my eyes, and I blink to keep the tears at bay because it reminds me so much of when Mom used to slide them out of my eyes. I don't want to cry today. It's been too perfect and I don't want to ruin it. I pack up my stuff and head home to my soon-to-be husband. *Eeek!*

CHAPTER 48

—max—

TODAY'S THE DAY I TIE MOLLY TO ME FOREVER.

Thank fuck!

I never want to lose this woman. I've missed her. After her volunteer shift at *Shelter* last night, she stayed with Martin and Beth, saying she wanted to follow tradition. I feel like I haven't been able to take a proper breath since she kissed me goodbye. Any minute now, I'll be able to lay eyes on her and I can't wait.

The late afternoon is perfect, the temperature is ideal, with a light warm breeze coming off the ocean, and the simple setup looks incredible. The circular timber ladder, which will frame the sun as it drops below the horizon, is decorated with Molly's favorite flowers—blush pink roses. It will act as a dais for Molly and me to exchange our promises. Simple wooden chairs for the small number of guests have been set up facing the wheel. Molly, Beth, and the girls have done an incredible job of pulling this together as quickly as they have.

Aaron stands beside me as I scan the small group of people gathered to witness our commitment to each other under a cloudless sky. Three chairs sit empty in the front row and my heart clenches as my eyes pause on each photograph of her family.

Today will be bittersweet for Molly.

In the second row on Molly's side, sits Beth, Joanna, and Noah, as well as her friends, Simone and Rhonda from *Shelter*. Molly was thrilled they could take a couple of hours out of their evening to share this special moment with us. On the opposite side of the aisle sits my family, and I spot Mom already wiping tears before we've even started the ceremony. Emma, Theo, and the boys sit with Sarah and Cristo, chatting quietly among themselves. The soccer boys are behind them, looking casual in shorts and T-shirts.

"Are you ready to lock yourself to one woman forever?" Aaron asks softly.

When I asked him to be my best man, he agreed without hesitation. We've been friends since elementary school, which means he's been witness to my failed relationships over the years. He saw the same thing in Molly as I did and that's why he gave me the nudge I needed to pursue her.

"Absolutely. I know it's been quick; just over five months. But when you know, *you know*. I'm not letting Molly get away." My heart's never been as full as it has since Molly came into my life. Knowing she feels the same for me is incredible.

"I would do exactly the same thing, man. She's an exceptional woman and I'm rapt that you came to your senses and pursued her." He sighs. "I have to admit, I'm a little envious."

I tear my eyes away from the direction Molly will come from to study my long-time friend. "It'll happen, man. When it does, it knocks you on your ass. So be ready."

He huffs out a laugh. "Oh, I will be."

The music changes to *I Get to Love You* by Ruelle and I snap my focus back to the crest of the pathway leading to me. Holly and Kenny are standing at the top of the sandy dune. They walk toward us, hand in hand, with bright smiles, wearing gorgeous blush pink dresses designed by Holly. When Holly asked Molly if it would be okay to design her dress, Molly jumped at the opportunity to support her creativity so long as she followed one request. To make Kenny a dress to match. Holly was rapt that Molly trusted her and dived straight into the project, designing and making both of their dresses in record time.

Kenny breaks away from Holly and runs straight for me with the widest of smiles. She leaps at me, and I catch her easily. "Uncle Max!" She squeezes my cheeks with her little hands. "Aunty Molly is a princess. Like a really real princess. She's so pretty."

I rub her nose with mine. "Is she as pretty as you?"

She chuckles. "You're funny, Uncle Max." I glance up, noticing movement on the dune. I kiss Kenny and place her on her feet next to Holly, all of my attention focused on my future wife.

Molly's revealed to me slowly as she crests the dune until she stands unobstructed at the top. I draw in a breath as my eyes devour her. With her platinum hair tied away from her face, her joyful smile is obvious, even from this distance.

I'm barely aware of Aaron patting me on the back and telling me how gorgeous she is. Her hand is carefully tucked into the crook of Martin's arm as he leads her to me; a proud expression on his face. My heart pounds the closer he brings her, and I can't believe I get to call this woman mine for the rest of our lives. Her top half is sheathed in lace, which fits her like a glove, accentuating her beautiful breasts until it meets a satin skirt that drags along the sand, making Molly appear to be floating across the surface. Occasionally, her toes peek out as she steps forward, giving me a glimpse of sexy jewelry on her feet instead of shoes.

Molly and Martin stop where the chairs for our guests begin, and I can't peel my eyes away from her. Martin whispers something in her ear, making her smile, and kisses her cheek, then takes the empty seat next to Beth. He's beaming broadly, showing the dimples that match his daughters'.

Molly moves forward on her own and I can't stand it. I want her to know that she's no longer on her own. I will walk any pathway with her from here on out, so I take long strides to meet her in the aisle between the small number of guests we invited today.

I reach forward, taking her smooth hand in my calloused one. "Hey," I whisper. I know I'm not supposed to kiss her yet, but she looks too divine to not lay my lips on hers.

She smiles at me, and I take my first full breath in the last twenty-five and a half hours. "Hey," she whispers back.

We stand with our eyes locked, silver to hazel, the warm salty breeze blowing the loose strands of Molly's hair around her gorgeous face. "You are stunning."

Her eyes skim down my body and then return to mine. "You're incredibly handsome, yourself, Max." She left it up to me to choose what I wanted to wear today. I chose a sandy-colored linen suit with a white shirt, leaving my feet bare. Aaron's wearing the same getup.

"Are you ready to become Mrs. Stanfield?"

Her smile widens further, deepening those dimples I love so much. Beneath the early evening sun, her eyes twinkle and she nods. "Absolutely, Mr. Stanfield."

I hold out my arm and Molly nestles her hand in the crook, holding her bouquet of blush pink roses in her other hand. We take the final few steps toward the celebrant together. Exactly how we're going to tackle everything from now on.

The celebrant, an older woman who is a friend of Beth's, smiles at both of us. "Are you two ready to make your lifelong promises to each other?"

I nod. "Yes, I am." Let's get this show on the road. The

sooner she says those magical words and signs the formal paperwork, the sooner she's mine in every sense of the word.

Molly smiles. "Me too." She glances at me and then turns back to the celebrant, squeezing my hand in hers.

The celebrant raises her voice slightly. "Before we begin, I would like to thank you all for attending today's ceremony to bear witness to the joining of Molly Lewis and Max Stanfield. I am duly authorized by law to solemnize marriages according to the law. So, everything that happens here today will be legal and binding." She gives everyone a bright smile, her kind eyes glittering in the early evening sun. "We are here today because Max and Molly want to be bound together in the eyes of the law. A marriage is a joining of two souls who are complete and fulfilled in their own right but choose to tie themselves to a partner for life because they want to share their life's journey with that person. I've had the pleasure of spending time with Max and Molly, and I've gotten to know two highly capable, kind, and caring individuals who, on their own, could navigate their life's journey just fine. However, together, I believe they will lead a beautiful life rich in love, family, and togetherness. Marriage is about compromise and compassion, understanding and unity. I see all of that between Max and Molly." She looks at me. "Max, would you like to share your promises with Molly?"

I turn toward Molly as I nod and lock my eyes on my future, taking her soft hands in mine. "Molly. When I first laid eyes on you, I was struck by your beauty. However, based on how you looked, I developed a preconceived notion of what you would be like as a person. You have spent the last few months destroying my incorrect assumptions and have surprised me at every turn, showing me that the beauty inside of you surpasses that which we can see. Which is spectacular." I wriggle my eyebrows at Molly, making her and our guests chuckle. "Since I first met you, you've shown me you're a compassionate, forgiving, resilient, and strong woman. You've shown courage and grace in situations that would break most people and my respect for you is only surpassed by my love.

"In you, I see the qualities I've always wanted in my life partner and the mother of my children. Because of this, I promise to spend my days working alongside you, building our business, raising our family, creating a home, and enjoying family time and vacations. I promise to spend my nights cuddled up on the couch with you, loving you, and lying beside you. I promise to care for you, support you, and love you through good times and bad, until the very end of time.

"Molly, I prayed for someone exactly like you and here you are. I am incredibly proud to have you as the woman who will be standing by my side for the rest of our days. I promise to be the best man I can be, the man you deserve. Because, Molly, I never want to let you down or disappoint you. I never want to make you sad. I want to give you the world and I look forward to building this life together." I lean in, swiping my lips against hers, and whisper, "And even though we're going to create our own family, I also give you mine." Her eyes become a little glassy as I touch my forehead to hers.

"Every day, I want to swim in the deepest part of the ocean with you. I love you, Molly. Today and every single day to come until my last breath." There's no way I can resist the temptation of her lips so close to mine as our breaths join in the shared space. I touch my lips to hers in a way I hope shows everything she means to me.

"That was lovely, Max. Molly, would you like to share your promises with Max?"

She nods and turns her gaze on me, making my heart pound. "Max. From our first interaction to now, you've always kept me safe and ensured that I have everything I need, whether it was making sure my car was running perfectly, or that I ate, or that I had a safe place to stay. You gave me sunshine during some of my darkest days and I will be forever thankful that you were brought into my life.

"As much as I love the way you look, it's what's inside that made me fall in love with you." She raises her hand, placing it over my heart. The heat from her touch burns through the fabric of my clothes into mine. "It was your kind and tender heart, your generous soul, and the way you care for your family and the people in the community, expecting nothing in return that made me fall for you. You're a good man. The very best, Max. And you're the man I want by my side as I navigate this life. Your patience, compassion, care, and understanding are the qualities I've always looked for in my partner because they are the qualities I consider most important for my children's happiness. You are the man I want to father my children, to nurture them, and to help them grow into the best possible people.

"I promise to always put you and our family first above all others and the busyness that life can become. I promise to always support you, encourage you, and cheer for you, as well as congratulate you and commiserate with you. I plan to be by your side through everything life throws our way, whether it be good, bad, or in between. I promise to give my all, every single day, to you and the family we create." She wriggles her eyebrows, making me chuckle. "Max, I look forward to falling in love with you every single day until I'm no longer here to fall." She presses her lips to mine. "I love you, Max. And I can't wait to swim in the deepest part of the ocean with you, unequivocally yours."

She leans forward, and I cup her face in my hands and meld our mouths together. This woman, who's had so little, gone through so much, gives so freely of herself to me and others. I pull back the smallest amount and whisper, "You slay me, Molly."

The celebrant clears her throat, reminding me we still have

shit to get through before I can ravage my wife's mouth. "That was beautiful and very meaningful, Molly."

We complete our vows with the traditional promises to care for each other through sickness and health until death do us part. The muscles in my body seem to breathe a sigh of relief that Molly is now officially mine.

Finally, we exchange rings. As I slide Molly's diamond-studded band onto her delicate finger to join the engagement ring, I feel something settle deep inside. Seeing the physical token of her bound to me on her finger gives me a sense of peace I never anticipated. And when she slides my heavy-duty black tungsten band down my finger on my left hand, I see the same feeling of peace in Molly's eyes.

We both tilt our heads up, our eyes locking on the other as the sun sinks below the horizon. The golden glow on Molly's skin makes her appear to be an angel, reminding me of the first impression I ever had of her.

When the celebrant finally pronounces us husband and wife, our families and friends cheer as I seal my mouth to my wife's. My world narrows to this moment, to the sensation of her lips beneath mine, my tongue tasting her. Our shared breaths bind us together in a moment that transcends all others that have come before this.

She is my heart, the reason I'm here. She is my future, my life, my forever. Our bodies press against each other, molding together perfectly, our hearts beating in sync against each other's.

Aaron clears his throat, tearing us apart and stealing our moment so we can sign the formal papers. If he weren't my best friend, I would fucking lay him out for interrupting the best kiss I've ever had. We step forward, officially husband and wife, to be congratulated by each of our guests. I keep Molly's hand in mine because I'm never letting this woman go.

CHAPTER 49

—molly—

I CAN'T WAIT TO GET MY HUSBAND NAKED. IT'S BEEN wonderful celebrating our marriage with our family and friends, but this is the part I've been looking forward to. I missed him terribly last night; I almost gave in and went home.

He hasn't let me go from the second he met me at the beginning of the aisle, and I haven't wanted him to. "I can't wait to see what you've got beneath this gorgeous dress, Dimples." My blood thrums through my veins and my body heats at his words. His hand tightens in mine and the hand at my waist pulls me in close to his body as we share a dance, his hard shaft pressing against my abdomen. I pull my hand out of his to wrap both arms around his neck and his hand drops to my waist, locking around me; making me feel secure, as though he's never going to let me go.

"Not long now, Husband."

He runs his nose along mine. "Say it again."

"Husband." I raise one eyebrow. He's been requesting the title since I said 'I do' as the sun settled on the horizon and subsequently set.

He pulls away, swiftly taking my hand in his. "That's it. I'm done. We're outta here." I giggle as he pulls me along. I'm glad I'm not the only one that's been feeling this way. He waves over his shoulder, calling out to our small number of guests. "Thank you for coming. We're heading out now."

I try to pull him to a stop because really, we need to thank everyone properly. Cheers rise, filling the intimate space. I guess they don't care if we skip out, but I still tug on his hand. "I'd like to say thank you properly before we leave."

Max sighs and we spin around to face our friends and family. He wraps his arm around my back, the heat from his hand searing my hip, and our guests quieten down.

"Thank you, everyone, for celebrating with us tonight. I especially want to thank all of my girls who helped put this beautiful day together with very short notice." I glance at Max and then back to the people who love and support us. "We didn't want to waste time. Life's far too short to wait and we appreciate that you could all make yourselves available to bear witness to our special promises with minimal notice." I swallow down the lump that's forming in my throat.

"To Max's family and friends. Thank you for openly welcoming me into your lives. I love you guys." Max's mom looks close to tears, and I don't want to cry, so I glance away, toward my family. My *new* family. "I know we haven't known each other long, but thank you for your patience with me as we navigated our new relationship."

Simone and Rhonda had to get back to *Shelter*, which meant they couldn't stay for the reception, but I was overjoyed they made it today. Everyone lines up to wish us goodbye, patiently waiting to hug us both.

Martin holds on extra tight as he whispers, "I'm so proud to have you as my daughter, Molly. I wish I could take credit for how you've grown into such an incredible young woman, but that's all you and Nicole. Thank you for allowing me to play a role today."

My throat clogs and I blink to keep the tears his words brought forth at bay. I return his squeeze, then pull back with a shaky smile. "Thanks, Dad." His eyes widen. "For everything. We appreciate it." He returns my shaky smile with one of his own.

"It's been my pleasure." He tips his chin over my shoulder. "I think your husband's growing impatient. You'd better go."

Twisting to glance over my shoulder, my husband's watching our exchange. "I'd better. See you soon." I give his hand one last squeeze and then turn toward my husband, my everything. "Ready, Husband?"

His grin is swift and full. "Absolutely, Wife."

We step out into the cool night air to make the short walk along the wooden boardwalk to our room for the weekend. We opted to spend tonight and the weekend in the hotel overlooking the ocean instead of going on a honeymoon. I didn't want to miss my volunteer evenings at *Shelter* and this way, Max only had to close his workshop for this afternoon and tomorrow. It seemed like an unnecessary expense to spend money on a lavish holiday when all we need is each other.

Max draws me to a stop halfway along the boardwalk, bringing me around to face him. Here, beneath the moonlight, he cups my face gently in his large hands and lays the gentlest kiss on my lips. "I love you so much, Molly. Today's been the second-best day of my life," he whispers, his lips brushing mine with each word. I pull back slightly, confused why today is the second-best day of his life. It's the best day of mine. He must read the question in my eyes because he explains, "The very best day of my life was the day I arrived at work to find you sleeping in your car. If not for *that* day, I wouldn't have *this* day."

My heart expands, sending warmth through my entire body. My smile is possibly the biggest it's ever been. "Well, that makes today the second-best day of my life, too."

Our lips meet in a heady kiss as our tongues explore and taste each other. I'm certain he can taste the champagne I enjoyed tonight, just as I can taste the whiskey he's been drinking. His hand slides beneath the fall of my hair to cup my head, using his hold to direct my mouth exactly where he wants it. I sigh into the kiss as he deepens it, pressing his thick cock against my pelvis. We draw back slightly, sucking in much-needed oxygen.

"As much as I could happily take you here, sex in the sand dunes doesn't appeal after spending days eradicating sand from my ass and jeans after our last time." He drops his forehead to mine as we chuckle.

"Well, we can't have that. Let's go." I collect his hand in mine and we hurry, side by side, to our room.

Max collected our keycard and dropped off our bags before the ceremony, meaning we don't need to check in and can head straight to our room without interruption. He opens the door, then lifts me into his arms to carry me across the threshold. As we enter the room, his kiss is passionate, just as it always is, but there's something more. A deeper connection and sense of belonging that wasn't there before today. "I need to make love to my wife," he whispers against my lips, his eyes especially dark and inviting.

Stepping further inside, the door latches closed behind him, and he flicks the lock, then carries me into the center of the stunning room. My gaze wanders around the space in amazement. Tiny candles cover every surface, shedding their flickering light across the walls, while rose petals cover the large rug centered over the teak wooden floor beneath the enormous bed. I'm pretty sure we won't need all that space because I won't want any space between my husband and me. "This looks beautiful." I glance back at Max. "Thank you for making this truly special."

"You're most welcome, Dimples." He brushes his nose

along the side of mine, finishing with a lingering kiss. I tighten my hold around his neck, keeping his lips locked with mine until the need to take a breath becomes too much.

Max releases my legs and slowly slides me down his firm body and I enjoy the feel of every hard inch of his body against mine. He cups my face reverently and continues our kiss from before, licking into my mouth, sending fire to my belly, and making my beautiful lace panties soaked. His hands slowly trace down my neck, across my collarbones, and down over my puckered nipples, sending goosebumps skittering across my heated skin.

He draws back slightly and our eyes lock together. "You stole my breath when I saw you crest the dune. You are stunning on an ordinary day. Today … today you are beyond spectacular." He takes a half-step back and his eyes lazily skate down my body. "This dress is incredible on you." His eyes slide up to my hair. "Your hair is gorgeous, your makeup … everything is perfect." He glides his hands from my shoulders, down my arms, over the lace cuffs around my biceps, and threads his fingers through mine. He lifts my hands away from my body, holding them out as his eyes peruse me. "I've gotta be the luckiest man alive to have you by my side."

Can a heart actually melt?

Because I fear mine is going to end up in a puddle on the floor with his beautiful words and his genuine compliments. I move back into his space, pressing my body to his. "I'm the lucky one, Max. You're the best man a girl could ever ask for."

He looks completely different in his linen suit. I reach up, sliding my hands beneath the lapels of his jacket to slip it from his shoulders. The feel of his hard, defined pecs under my hands is heady.

This man is mine.

All mine.

Nobody else will ever get to touch him like this. I toss his jacket over the back of a nearby chair as I kiss his scruffy jaw, the bristles of his short beard tickling my lips. He sends my heart thumping against my ribs with the way he's studying me, the heat in his eyes, and the obvious bulge in his pants he hasn't bothered to hide.

"Dimples, tell me how to get you out of this beautiful dress."

I turn my back toward my husband and peer at him over my shoulder. "See these tiny pearl buttons?"

He glances down at the buttons, then back up to me with an incredulous look on his face. "Are you fucking with me? I thought these were for decoration and there would be a zipper magically hidden behind them. This has been designed to torture a man." He groans.

I chuckle. "It's designed to build the moment."

He's quiet for a long moment. "There are thirty-five buttons here. I don't have the patience for this. I just want my wife naked." He huffs out but raises his hands to carefully and methodically undo the tiny fasteners, kissing my shoulder as he works, sending goosebumps racing across my body. I step out of my slip-on sandals, leaving me with the simple silver and pearl strands decorating my feet.

The fabric of the bodice gradually loosens, and he slides it away, undoing the hidden zipper in the silk skirt. The gorgeous dress drops to the floor, pooling like snowflakes at my feet. Max steps carefully until he's in front of me, offering his hand to help me step out of the puddle of silk and lace. His heated gaze skims up and down my body, presented only in white lace panties, like a lover's caress, sending sparks shooting to my core.

"No bra." He drops his head back on his shoulders with a groan. I'm lucky my boobs aren't that big and are still perky enough that I could get away without a bra today, relying on the built-in cups in the bodice to keep the girls in place. His heated gaze returns to me. "You're so goddamn beautiful."

My body heats at his words, moisture pooling at the apex of my thighs. "I feel disadvantaged, Husband." Stepping forward, I undo the buttons of his shirt to expose his firm torso to my hungry eyes and slip it from his shoulders, tossing it aside carelessly. "I love these tattoos on you." As I stare into his eyes, I run my fingers across his abs and the muscles quiver in response to my delicate touch.

Dropping my eyes down, I work to open his belt and linen pants; his penis makes a notable bulge and I'm eager to get my hands on the steely shaft. His pants and boxer briefs drop to the floor, and he toes off his shoes to step out of the loose fabric. He removes his socks and then returns to stand at his full height in front of me. I admire his body; his muscular legs, his veiny forearms, his trim, firm body up to his scruff-covered jaw, and those incredible hazel eyes that change color depending on his mood. "Your body is perfection to me, but," I press my hand against his heart, feeling it beat steadily. "I meant what I said today. It's what's inside that made me fall in love with you."

Neither of us wastes another moment as we both step forward simultaneously, crashing our bodies and mouths together. Everywhere he touches me, he leaves a trail of heat and want, building my body to the point where I think I could explode before he even gets close to touching my pussy. His thumbs tuck into each side of my panties and he slides them down my legs and I step out of the flimsy lace. Max fingers the jewelry I wore in place of shoes for the ceremony.

"These are fucking sexy. They're staying on." His hands glide up the inside of my thighs, reaching their apex, his fingers sliding through my pussy lips and then pushing inside me hard and without warning, forcing the air from my lungs. I drop my head back on my shoulders as my mouth drops open in a silent moan. Spreading my legs open, I grasp his hair as he moves in to tease my clit with his talented tongue.

"Such a good girl," he whispers against the bundle of nerves. I love having his mouth on me. He nudges my clit with his nose, drawing in a deep breath. "I love your scent. Whether you're fresh from the shower, after your run, and most definitely when you're horny." His voice is gruff with need to match mine.

"You make me horny, Husband. Whenever I'm around you, I need you inside me," I whisper, gripping onto his hair as a shiver racks my body.

CHAPTER 50

—max—

I *NEED* TO BE INSIDE MY WIFE.

It's a desperation to consummate our marriage in the most primal way. As I fuck my fingers into her tight, hot pussy, my dick throbs to get inside her silky heat. "Be a good girl and come for me, Molly." I grit out roughly and then suck the bundle of nerves, hard. Her hands grip my hair tighter, and I'll be surprised if she hasn't pulled out half of the strands. Her legs tremble and I know I need to give my girl support, or she'll collapse. Wrapping my free arm around her tight ass, I maintain the speed and pressure of my fingers and tongue, feeling her walls flutter. Peering up her willowy frame, her stomach muscles quiver and her breasts heave with every panting breath she takes.

Fucking beautiful.

I grasp her ass cheek tightly in my hand and bite her clit and am rewarded with a long throaty groan and her muscles strangling my fingers as they tighten with her orgasm. Her cum coats my digits beautifully, dripping down my hand. Holding my fingers inside her, I lap at her orgasm and then slowly slide out of her pussy as her shudders lessen and climb to my feet.

"Oh my God. That was outstanding, Husband of mine," she sighs. Her dazed eyes slide to mine and a sex-drunk smile touches her lips. I love her like this and if I can keep her this way for the rest of my days, I'll consider myself a fortunate man.

Reaching for her ass, I lift her, positioning my cock at her entrance as she wraps her arms around my neck and her legs around my waist. Her tits press against my chest, our hearts both beating a heavy staccato. Locking my gaze on hers, I notch my cock at her center and slide into her welcoming heat. Her moan mingles with my groan as we join in the way nature intended a man and woman to join.

"I fucking love being inside you," my lips touch hers as I whisper. I lick inside her mouth as I lift her and thrust back inside, seating myself deep. Her mouth drops open on a mewl and her pussy tightens around my shaft. I drop my mouth to her neck and bite the tendon there, which rewards me with another squeeze around my cock. "Bounce on my cock, Dimples."

Gripping her fine ass, I help her rise and fall on my dick, our heavy breaths filling each other's mouths as the sound of skin slapping against skin fills the quiet of the room. "Max, I'm gonna come again," Molly whispers against my lips, pressing closer to take my mouth in a fierce kiss. I match her need with my own as our tongues tangle and taste, teeth clash and bite, and lips suck and soothe. She breaks apart in my arms, shattering into oblivion, while I grit my teeth to hold back my release. I don't want to come yet. I don't want this to be over so soon. For our first time as husband and wife, I need to stay inside her for as long as possible.

Holding still inside her as the aftershocks rack her body, I trace my hand up her delicate spine and grasp her gorgeous hair, dragging her head back to expose her throat to me. "Such a good girl. The way you come all over my cock," I whisper against her burning skin, followed by nips and sucks of her sweet flesh as her pussy tightens around me.

She fucking loves it when I praise her. This woman was made for me. "Hold on." I swivel and walk the few steps to the California King bed. Holding the back of her head, I carefully lower us both, keeping my cock buried deep inside my wife.

Cradled between Molly's thighs, my dick snugly wrapped in her heat, I rest on my elbows and peer down into her lust-filled gaze. She smiles at me full of love and sifts her fingers through the short strands of my hair.

"I love how you love me, Max." She presses up, landing a chaste kiss on my mouth. "I love you."

Goosebumps spread out across my burning flesh as my cock swells with her words. Words that are full of heart and honesty. Smoothing her hair away from her face, my eyes track her delicate features, eventually locking on her pewter-colored eyes. "I plan on loving you exactly like this until I take my last breath. You are everything to me, Molly. I love you, Dimples." Dropping my head, we kiss.

Tenderly, slowly. Caressing inside each other's mouth with loving strokes.

Her body arches into mine and I slowly slide out of heaven and then glide back in, pressing to the base of my shaft. My heavy balls slap against Molly's ass and she tightens her legs around my middle, her feet pressing into my ass. Her hands slide from around my neck, taking up their place wrapped around my back, her fingers tickling up my spine to rest on my shoulder blades. My muscles shift and flex with each measured thrust of my hips. Perspiration coats our skin and the scent of sex saturates the air.

In. Out. I grind, I push, I thrust.

Building us both higher, closer to our release.

Skin against skin, Molly matches me stroke for stroke, her moans and pants building with my own. My heart hammers against my rib cage as though it's trying to break free and live inside her. She figuratively has my heart; she may as well literally have it, too. If I could reach inside my chest and give it to her, I would; knowing she would keep it safe and take tender care of it. Our tongues dance in time with our hips, our bodies moving in natural sync as we both build. "C'mon, Molly, choke my cock like a good girl."

She cries out, her pussy gripping my shaft like a vise. Her hands move up to pull on my hair. "Your filthy words make me so hot."

I reach between us, finding her needy clit and rubbing tight circles around it to push her over the edge. Her legs tighten around my hips as her body presses further into mine and she shatters beautifully. Her head pressed back into the mattress; her mouth dropped open seductively on a silent moan.

I grit my teeth through a couple more strokes. My balls draw up, my cock pulses, and my cum finally empties from my body to hers. I throw my head back with a long groan, the muscles in my neck tensing and straining as she shifts with me to kiss and lick my burning skin.

Sucking in lungfuls of necessary oxygen, I drop my head down to hers and kiss her. I give her everything I have from the deepest part of my soul, from the core of my very being. I desperately need to show her exactly what she means to me.

What her promises today mean to me.

Drawing back, my gaze searches her angelic face, finally stopping on her eyes. I bring her left hand to my mouth and kiss the rings that show everyone she's mine.

"Today's been incredible. The words we shared and the papers we signed locking us together in the eyes of our family and friends and the law. But this. What we shared just now. This is our true bond." Her eyes go soft as a tender smile touches her lips. "You generously taking me inside not only your body, but your mind, your heart, and your soul is what solidifies our connection today and for our future." I lay her hand on my heart and press the palm of mine to hers. "The love we share only grows stronger and more powerful, just as our bond does." I press my lips to hers and then whisper against the puffy pillows, "I love you with everything I have. Everything I am. Today and forevermore."

epilogue

CHAPTER 51

—molly—

I DON'T KNOW WHAT'S WRONG WITH ME. I HAD A GREAT SLEEP and yet I'm exhausted down to my bones. My boobs are sore, and my stomach feels bloated. Everything smells disgusting, except for Max. I flop back onto the bed. Maybe I'm finally getting my period; it's been such a long time since I had one, I think I've forgotten what they're like. Excitement bubbles at the idea of getting my period, the first one since my birth control ran out just before our wedding because that will mean we can get pregnant.

With the way I'm feeling, there's no way I can peel myself away from this cocoon today. I roll over with a huff and snuggle into Max's warm body. He automatically welcomes me into his space, wrapping his arm around me and tugging me in close.

"You okay, Dimples?" Tears spring to my eyes. He's always asking if I'm okay. He cares deeply for me and reminds me every single day with every little thing he does for me. Moisture drips down the side of my face, landing on Max's bare chest. He pulls away slightly and tilts my chin up with his fingers so he can study me closely. "What's wrong?"

My bottom lip quivers. "Nothing. It's just really sweet how you love and care for me."

He chuckles. "Always, Molly. You know that. Why are you crying about it?" He looks thoroughly perplexed.

I shrug, awkwardly. "I'm just not feeling myself, I guess. It's coming up to the anniversary of the accident and I think I'm finally getting my period. So maybe that's why I'm feeling blah."

His eyes go soft, and he pulls me in tight, kissing the top of my head. I rest my ear over his beautiful heart, listening to its strong and steady beat. The heart he says beats only for me. I smooth my hand over his taut stomach and sigh.

"I'm here, Dimples. Whatever you need." He kisses the top of my head, tightening his hold.

My lips spread in a genuine smile, and I tilt my head back to look up at the man who is everything to me. "I know. Thank you. Have I told you lately how much I love you?"

He grins at me, raising his eyebrows. "Not today."

"I feel like my heart's going to explode with the amount of love I have for you. Like it's too big to fit inside my body." I push up to lay a kiss on my husband's tempting lips.

"That's a lot of love." He returns my kiss with interest, stroking his tongue into my mouth.

I lay my head back on his chest. "Can we just lie like this for a little while?"

"We can lie like this for however long you need." His hand comes up to stroke my hair slowly. He caresses me down my back, then starts back at the top of my head and repeats the process over and over. Long, gentle strokes.

I slowly come into wakefulness. I must have fallen back to sleep, which isn't a surprise. Max is gone, leaving me alone in bed.

He steps through the door from the bathroom, a towel wrapped around his slim hips, water droplets running down his smooth skin as he uses a second towel to dry his hair. He beams at me, then kneels on the edge of the bed, dropping to his hands to crawl toward me. Skimming his finger across my forehead, he pushes my bangs away from my eyes. "How are you feeling?"

I smile softly. "Better, thank you. Sorry about my mini-meltdown."

"You can have a mega meltdown if you need to. I'm here for all of it. You need to allow yourself some grace as you come up to the first anniversary. Take some time for yourself. Do what you need for your emotional health." He leans forward and presses a soft kiss to my temple. "Anything you need from me, just let me know."

I nod as I soak up his warmth and affection. "Thank you." I stretch out. "What time is it?"

"Almost twelve."

I fly into a panic, scooting out of bed quickly. "Oh my God. We're going to be late." I quickly grab some clothes. "I'll be quick, I promise."

Max chuckles at me as I run around our bedroom naked. "No need to rush, Dimples," he calls out as I jump into the shower.

I quickly wash my body, avoiding getting my hair wet, then climb out to dry off and get dressed. Max leans against the doorjamb with his arms crossed, watching me dress. His eyes singeing my flesh. Once I'm dressed, I step into his body and wrap my arms around him. "Come on. I'm ready." I land a kiss on his lips, planning to pull away quickly so we can get moving, but he wraps his arms around me and deepens the kiss.

I sigh.

My entire body sags against his and sighs. I don't know how I ever survived without Max's kisses. He gentles the kiss and pulls away slightly. I slowly open my eyes to find his affectionate smile.

"C'mon, let's go." He grasps my hand, and we make our way out of our bedroom.

Yesterday, I used my grandmother's recipe to make shortbread, so I collect it from the kitchen and meet Max at his car. It doesn't take long and we're arriving at Mom and Dad's house. "We're the last ones here."

"It's okay, Dimples. Stop worrying."

"I hate to be late. It's rude."

Max presses a tender kiss against my temple and rests his hand on the small of my back. "Mom sets a loose time for lunch. Any time around this time is fine." He slides his hand across to my opposite hip and drags me in close. "Come on."

We make our way inside. The front of the house is quiet, meaning everyone's already in the dining room at the back of the house, probably wondering where we are. Holding my hand, Max leads me through the neat home to the back room which overlooks the deck. It only takes a moment for his family to realize we're here. They've been incredible to me, and I love having pedicure afternoons with Sarah and Emma. They've taken me into the fold as if I've always been part of their tight-knit family. I even call Mr. and Mrs. Stanfield, Mom and Dad, which I know delights Max's mom to no end.

"I'm sorry we're late. It was completely my fault," I say to everyone as I place the shortbread on the sideboard.

"Oh, don't be silly. When you get here, you get here." Mom cups my face, studying me closely, then places the back of her hand against my forehead. "Are you feeling okay? You look a little peaked."

I hold on to her wrist and smile. "I'm feeling better than I was this morning." I glance at my husband. "Max let me sleep in a little, which helped."

"Come and take a seat," Emma calls out, patting the seat next to her. I move around the table, kissing everyone hello. Emma's boys must be with their father and Cristo must have Kenny this weekend because they're not here today. I miss them terribly on the weekends they're not with us, but today I'm in tears at their absence. *What the hell is wrong with me?* "Are you okay?" Emma asks as she tucks a lock of loose hair behind my ear, her worried eyes studying my face.

"Yeah, I just really miss the kids when they're not here and today, for some reason, I want to cry because I miss them so much." A small smile graces Emma's face as her eyes go soft.

Max sits next to me, and his hand smooths up and down my back in a soothing caress. He leans across and kisses my temple, then turns toward the table. "It's coming up to the anniversary of the accident and Molly's feeling emotional. I told her she needs to be gentle with herself." His family knows my story now. Everything. And all of my worry that people would pity me if they knew how I grew up and everything I lost was a waste of time. Not once did anyone in this family show me pity. They showed compassion and understanding. They showed kindness and care, just like Max did when he found out. Not once did I ever feel judged or pitied; not even for one single second.

"Well, then." Sarah breaks the silence. "I think we need a pedi afternoon. What do you think, Em?"

"Sounds perfect. How about Wednesday afternoon? Can you get off early?" she asks Sarah.

"Definitely. I'll start early and then we can take our girl here out for pedis, followed by coffee and cake."

Em turns to Theo. "Do you mind watching the kids on Wednesday afternoon?"

He leans forward, kissing her tenderly on the lips. "Of course not. I'll collect them from school so you can go straight there."

And plans are made without a second thought. Max's sisters knew I needed support, and they were more than happy to provide it, as usual. I love this incredible family, their warmth, their love, and their support for one another.

When I arrive at *R&R Nail Salon*, Sarah and Emma are waiting out front for me. I almost canceled at the last minute, because I feel so damn tired. The girls take one look at me as I drag my ass toward them and frown. "You look worse today. Maybe you should see a doctor," Sarah suggests.

My shoulders slump. "Thanks. I feel terrible."

Emma slides her arm through mine, and we stroll inside the salon for our appointment. "I only came because I knew I'd only have to sit. I don't think I can manage anything more than that."

Sarah opens the door, and we step inside, finding Phillipa waiting for us with a smile. "Hi, ladies. Come through. We're ready for you."

We follow her to our designated chairs, and she offers us our usual Mimosa. "Do you mind if I only have juice today? I don't think I can stomach any alcohol." Em and Sarah glance at each other.

Phillipa nods. "Of course." She turns on her heel to get our drinks and I settle into the comfortable chair.

Emma reaches across, laying her hand on my arm, her eyebrows drawn tight. "Tell me how else you're feeling, Molly."

I blow out a long breath. "I'm so freaking tired. Like I'm dragging myself through the day. Smells make me feel nauseous and my boobs are so goddamn tender, Max only has to brush against me, and I feel like crying. Talk about crying. I'm teary all the damn time." I gesture toward my stomach. "And see this. I've never been bloated like this. It's so freaking uncomfortable." I swallow back the tears that are welling in my eyes. I don't want to come across like a total nut job. "Today's the anniversary of the accident, and on top of that, I think I'm getting my period." The tears I was trying so hard to keep at bay drop over my bottom lashes.

"Oh, Molly." Sarah wraps her arms around me, stroking down my hair. "You poor thing."

"Uh … Mols." Sarah pulls away and we look across at Emma, who's watching us with a smile. "I don't think you'll be getting your period anytime soon."

"Why not?"

She glances at Sarah, raising her eyebrows. "I think you might be pregnant."

My heart races with her words. Could that be why I've been feeling this way? "Really? What makes you think that?"

"Everything you just said. I think we need to stop at the drugstore after we've finished here and get you a pregnancy test."

My lips stretch into a smile for the first time today and my wide eyes slide from Sarah to Emma and back again. "Shit. I didn't even think of that. The doctor said it could take a while to get pregnant after stopping the shot. I didn't expect it to happen this fast because I haven't had a period yet." My mind's racing a million miles a minute as thoughts rush in and out of my head. "Oh my God. What if I'm pregnant? Max will be over the moon."

The three of us squeal a little in excitement. I'm not sure I can sit here for the time we need for our pampering session; I want to race across to the drugstore immediately. It would certainly turn what's been an emotionally draining day into a happy one if I found out I was pregnant. And help balance out such a terrible memory with a great one.

With fresh polish on our toes, the three of us exit the salon and make our way across the street to the drugstore. Emma takes us straight to the aisle with the pregnancy tests. I shake my head at the logic of their placement. Fancy having them right next to the condoms.

"There's so many to choose from." The selection is overwhelming. The array of boxes with various calls to action. I look at Emma and Sarah. "Any you guys recommend?"

Emma deftly collects one from the shelf. "Here. This one is effective and straightforward. Pee on the stick and a minute later, voilà, you'll have an answer." She collects a couple more boxes from the shelf, handing them to me. "Here, it's a good idea to have extra, just in case."

We head to the counter so I can pay for my purchases, and I say my goodbyes to Max's sisters. "Thank you for listening to me and for this." I hold up my paper bag filled with pregnancy tests.

"You're welcome." Emma leans forward, hugging me tight.

"Make sure you let us know." Sarah also hugs me goodbye.

"I promise you ladies will be the first to know." I chuckle. "Well, after Max, of course."

CHAPTER 52

—max—

I have a stunning arrangement of pink roses, wine, and her favorite ice cream ready for when my girl gets home. Cristo made Molly's favorite dish, Pasticcio, and dropped it over for our dinner tonight. I check my phone; I still have time. The girls' pedicures and coffee and cake always take a while.

I head through to our bedroom to shower and change before Molly gets home, then I'll put the dinner in the oven to reheat as per Cristo's instructions—he was very particular, which means I need to be careful not to mess it up. I hear the front door open and close as I'm pulling out a change of clothes, so I head toward the front of the house to investigate. Molly shouldn't be home yet.

"Hey, you're home early. Are you feeling okay?" She's been feeling like shit for a couple of weeks now, only admitting it to me on Sunday, but I've been watching her, and it's been going on for a while. I lean forward to kiss her.

She wraps her arms around my neck, pulling me into her, and deepens the kiss, something hitting me at the top of my back. "Hey. I ... I needed to come home to do something." Her eyes are brighter than they were when she left the workshop to meet the girls, which is a good sign. Today, especially, has been tough for her.

I wrap my arm around her and lead her deeper into our home. "What do you need to do, Dimples? Can I help?"

Her shoulders drop and she smiles at me. God, I love this woman's smiles and they've been missing for the last week, which has been completely understandable, but I have missed them.

"You know I love you, right?" She presses her hand against my stomach and lays a chaste kiss on my jaw. Holding the paper bag up, she grins. "While I was out, I was telling your sisters how I've been feeling." I nod. I'm glad she has them to talk to. "Emma suggested that I'm probably not getting my period because I may already be pregnant." Her voice rises at the end of the sentence in excitement, her sculpted eyebrows rising.

My eyebrows must be almost touching my hairline as my heart picks up speed. I crouch down slightly, ensuring my eyes are at the same level as Molly's. "Do you think you could be pregnant?"

She holds up the paper bag. "Only one way to find out."

I run my hands through my hair. "Fuck. Wouldn't that be something?"

"Wouldn't it?" She shakes the bag. "I'm gonna go pee on a stick." She spins on her heel toward the bathroom and I follow directly behind her. She steps into the bathroom and closes the door, jamming it into my body and she chuckles. "What are you doing? I have to pee."

I take a step back. "Yeah, right. Sorry." I quickly kiss her. "Will you be able to pee on demand? Like, do you need to run the water or something?"

Molly giggles, pushing against my chest until I clear the doorway. "I'll work it out."

I quickly give her one more kiss, then step out of the bathroom so she can get down to business. I press my ear up against the bathroom door; I don't want to miss anything, just in case she calls out for help. It seems to take forever before I hear the toilet flush, then the water run as she washes her hands. I don't wait to be invited, I open the door and step inside. A small white stick rests on the vanity. My eyes snap up to Molly and we share a smile. I turn her around until she's facing me properly and clutch her hips to pull her in close.

"I want you to know I love you. No matter the result on that stick; whether it's positive or negative, my love for you isn't based on the lines that show or don't show." I press my forehead to hers, keeping my eyes locked with my wife's.

She wraps her arms around my neck. "I know, Max. I hadn't even considered that I might be pregnant until Emma suggested the possibility. I'm excited at the prospect of being pregnant already. Of changing today from one of my saddest to one of my happiest."

Her body's vibrating with the possibility of a positive result. I hope for her sake it's positive. She deserves to have every happiness. I swipe my lips against hers. Every time I do it, my entire body revels in the feel of her lips beneath mine. She opens for me with a sigh, and I slide inside, moving my hands to cup her gorgeous ass and drag her into my body. I pour my love for her into the kiss and give her yet another piece of my soul.

We pull apart slowly and catch each other's gaze. Without speaking, we agree it's time to check the result. Molly picks it up, holding it between us, and we both look down at the same time. Our eyes snap up, finding each other, matching smiles on our faces. I lift my girl off her feet and take off running through the house, cheering and hollering like we've won the World Cup. Molly giggles like crazy, holding on for dear life, as I run around our house like a maniac.

Then it dawns on me: I need to be fucking gentle with her.

I shouldn't be manhandling her like a fucking Neanderthal. I carefully put her on her feet and cup her face in my rough hands, feeling her silky skin. "We're gonna have a baby!" I exclaim against her lips, our noses touching.

Molly nods with a smile on her face. "We're gonna have a baby."

I press my mouth to hers, fierceness in my kiss. She meets my fierceness, and we kiss with teeth clashing and tongues tangling for long moments, our bodies pressed together as tight as they can be. This woman is my whole fucking world, and she's already given me so much. Now she's going to give me the ultimate gift of a child. "Thank you, Dimples. I don't know how I'll ever thank you for everything you've given to me."

I kiss her again. My wife, my forever, the mother of my child.

Would you like a sneak peek into the future?
Sign up for my newsletter to visit Max and Molly to see what they're up to.
https://tinyurl.com/moonlitkisses-bonus

Have you met Max's eldest sister, Emma? Find out what happens when she meets her new neighbor in **Stolen Kisses.**

A neighbors to lovers romance

A steamy, emotional, stand-alone contemporary romance about a single mom giving her all for her kids and a single uncle learning how to be a dad while coming to terms with devastating losses.

https://books2read.com/dsj-stolenkisses

Are you ready to meet Max's baby sister, Sarah? She has a plan to have a baby, but sometimes the best-laid plans don't work out as we expect. Sometimes they turn into … **Unexpected Kisses**.

A strangers to lovers planned pregnancy romance

A steamy, stand-alone contemporary romance about a single woman with a plan to have a baby on her own and the sexy computer nerd who offers to help her fulfill her dream.

https://books2read.com/dsj-unexpectedkisses

Max's soccer friend and the owner of Brady's Pub, Finn Brady, meets his match in **Enemy Kisses***.*
An enemies to lovers romance novella

A steam-filled, angsty, stand-alone contemporary romance about a misunderstood pub owner who has no problem working for the affections of his brand-new neighbor and the baker who tries her best to guard her heart but isn't able to fight the tempting pull of her enemy.

https://books2read.com/dsj-enemykisses

pinterest

I put together a Pinterest board for Max and Molly's story. If you're interested, you can check it out here:
https://tinyurl.com/moonlitkisses-pinterest

debra's books

The Summer Twins

Loving Summer | *Kate Summer & Oliver Stone*

Second Chance Summer | *Toby Summer & Cassia Phillips*

The Summer Twins | Complete Series

Spin-off Novella

Loving Roman | *Roman Armstrong & Alice Reed*

Kisses

Stolen Kisses | *Emma Miller & Theo Drivas*

Moonlit Kisses | *Max Stanfield & Molly Lewis*

Unexpected Kisses | *Sarah Stanfield & AJ*

Kisses | Complete Series

Monday Knights | *novellas*

Enemy Kisses | *Finn Brady & Harriet Dubois*

Wicked Kisses | *Lincoln Kingsley & Sophie Chalmers*

Everlasting

Everlasting Love | *Shane Sutton & Violet Jamison*

Everlasting Promises | *Hope Sullivan & Benjamin Taylor*

Everlasting Vows | *Nixon Steele & Abigail Steele*

Debra has a list of her books available on her website.

You can find them here:

https://debrastjamesbooks.com

connect with debra

stalk me

You can stalk me pretty much everywhere!
https://debrastjamesbooks.com/connect/

How about joining my Facebook group?
https://www.facebook.com/groups/DebsBibliomaniacs

newsletter

Join Debra's newsletter to receive important updates before anyone else. Newsletters will be sent once a month unless something exciting is happening.
https://debrastjamesbooks.com/newsletter/

thank you

This wasn't the story I was supposed to write. Shane's story was supposed to be next, but after discovering a hidden truth about my paternity, I wasn't in the right mindset for his story. Last August, I learned the man I grew up believing to be my biological father, is, in fact, not my biological father at all. It turns out I've never met my biological father and I'll probably never know who he is. As you can imagine, my mind was muddled, so I decided to write Max's story, thinking it would be a little lighter than what I anticipate Shane's story to be. Perhaps this is why I wanted Molly to meet her father.

As always, I would like to thank Mr. St James and our two sons for their support and patience with me when dinner was late, or I didn't listen as attentively as I should have, or I didn't want to leave my cave because I was working on this baby.

To my beta readers, Kelly, Rita, and Wendy thank you for your invaluable feedback. Kelly and Rita, your regular comments as I was writing often had me in stitches! Thanks for helping me to keep going.

To my online support network, you were there for me on the days when I doubted myself. Ladies, you know who you are.

To you, the reader. Thank you for taking a chance on me; for reading my book. I truly do appreciate your time. If you've enjoyed reading about Max and Molly I'd love to hear from you.

about the author

Debra St James is an author of spicy, slow-burn contemporary romance that features cinnamon roll heroes who listen to their women's hearts and their words. She takes her time to weave a detailed tapestry of genuine characters, real-life struggles, love, and romance to create engaging stories that will have you so immersed in the story that you'll never want to leave. Her stories are always guaranteed to take you on an emotional journey that ultimately ends with a HEA!

Debra loves to read romance. Her family often finds her with her nose stuck in her iPad, swooning over her latest book boyfriend. She writes part-time from her Perth home, which she shares with Mr St James and their two sons, whose antics often make her roll her eyes and laugh in equal measure.

Writing a novel had never been on her radar. One morning, she was enjoying a coffee by the river and a story sprouted, seemingly from nowhere. At 51, she pulled up the Pages app on her phone and began to type, giving life to her debut, *Loving Summer*.

The rest, as they say, is history!

Debra xo

amazon.com/author/debrastjames

facebook.com/debra.stjames.books

instagram.com/debrastjames_books

bookbub.com/authors/debra-st-james

goodreads.com/debrastjames

pinterest.com/debrastjamesbooks